The story of *NIGHT WATCH* was conceived by Alistair MacLean—author of the world-famous bestsellers *The Guns of Navarone*, *Where Eagles Dare*, and *Santorini*—and, along with the immensely popular *Death Train*, was completed as a novel after his death. During his lifetime, two of his other story outlines, *Hostage Tower* and *Air Force One Is Down*, were written as thrillers and published to great acclaim.

His millions of loyal readers will be happy to know that with *NIGHT WATCH* the Alistair MacLean tradition of fast-paced action and pulse-pounding suspense continues.

Also by Alastair MacNeill
Published by Fawcett Books:

ALISTAIR MACLEAN'S DEATH TRAIN

ALISTAIR MACLEAN'S NIGHT WATCH

Alastair MacNeill

FAWCETT CREST • NEW YORK

PROLOGUE

On an undisclosed date in September 1979 the Secretary-General of the United Nations chaired an extraordinary meeting attended by forty-six envoys who, between them, represented virtually every country in the world. There was only one point on the agenda: the escalating tide of international crime. Criminals and terrorists were able to strike in one country then flee to another but national police forces were prevented from crossing international boundaries without breaching the protocol and sovereignty of other countries. Furthermore, the red tape involved in drafting extradition warrants (for those countries that at least had them) was both costly and time-consuming and many an unscrupulous lawyer had found loopholes in them, resulting in their clients being released unconditionally. A solution had to be found. It was agreed to set up an international strike force to operate under the aegis of the United Nations' Security Council. It would be known as the United Nations Anti-Crime Organization (UNACO). Its objective was to "avert, neutralize and/or apprehend individuals, or groups

1

engaged in international criminal activities.''* Each of the
forty-six envoys was then requested to submit one detailed
curriculum vitae of a candidate its government considered to
be suitable for the position of UNACO Director, with the
Secretary-General making the final choice.

UNACO's clandestine existence came into being on 1
March 1980.

*UNACO Charter, Article 1, Paragraph 1C

ONE

Messler & Goldstein, the firm of chartered accountants on the third floor of a converted warehouse on West 27th Street overlooking the Hudson River, was, in reality, a front for the Central Intelligence Agency's Section II, the department responsible for the recruitment, deployment and running of double agents abroad.

Brad Holden had been head of its computer section for seven years and a KGB agent for the past eighteen months. His deception had nothing to do with ideological principles or a disillusionment with the Great American Dream, it was all to do with money. Money he had desperately needed to square his gambling debts. He had paid off his markers in six months but, despite his meticulous attempts to cover his tracks at every turn, his duplicity had come to light and the CIA had decided to use him, albeit unwillingly, to spread disinformation back to his KGB masters in Russia. It worked perfectly for the next year, until a brown envelope had arrived on his desk containing half a dozen photographs of him meeting with his KGB handler in Tompkins Square Park. The cover note told him that he had exactly one calendar month to break into the top secret Alpha program and get the names of those agents involved in "Operation Quaternary," otherwise the negatives would be forwarded to the *New York Times* for publication. The incentive was the return of the negatives and twenty-five thousand dollars in cash. The unsigned note ended by saying that further instructions would follow. He decided to play along, for the money. Knowing the complexity of the Alpha program at the CIA's Langley headquarters in Virginia, he put in for immediate leave and spent the next sixteen days poring over his sophisticated array of home computers before he finally broke into the program and located the information on one of the CIA's most clandestine operations ever mounted. The instructions which followed exactly three weeks after he received the initial envelope included a sum of money for him to buy a return ticket to Schiphol Airport and a key to a locker at the Central Station in downtown Amsterdam. The money would be there. And a train service ran every fifteen minutes from Schiphol Airport to the Central Station. . . .

"*Dames en heren, Centraal Station.* Ladies and Gentlemen, Central Station."

The announcer's voice brought Holden out of his reverie and he instinctively touched the envelope in the inside pocket of his plaid jacket. He sat up and rubbed his eyes wearily, allowing himself to sway with the momentum of the train as it swung into the nineteenth-century neo-Gothic building and came to a halt at the platform. The doors hissed then parted and the first of the passengers began to disembark. He picked up his straw hat from the empty seat beside him and tugged it over his thatch of blond hair before getting to his feet, retrieving his canvas suitcase and joining the queue in the aisle. Whistling unevenly to himself he disembarked from the train, handed his ticket to the inspector at the barrier and entered the concourse, where he crossed to the lockers and unlocked the one corresponding to the number on his key. He carefully removed the black attaché case and, in its place, put an unmarked white envelope, then locked the door again and pocketed the key. He picked up the attaché case and walked towards the exit.

"Hey, just a minute!"

The voice rooted him to the spot. For a split second he had an insane idea to run but with his body weight he knew he wouldn't get very far before they caught up with him. If they didn't shoot him first. He knew the CIA's methods only too well. Slowly, fearfully, he turned around.

The man was in his mid-twenties with curly black hair and a friendly, lopsided grin. He was studying Holden intently. "You're as white as a ghost."

"Who are you?" Holden stammered.

"I'm a taxi-driver. I thought you might want a lift." The man chuckled. "Why, who did you think I was?"

"I don't know." Holden wiped the sweat from his forehead with the back of his hand. "You startled me, that's all."

"Sorry. So, you need a taxi or not?"

"Damn right I do."

The man took Holden's suitcase from him and led the way to the taxi rank. "Where do you want to go, mister?"

"You got a Holiday Inn in this town?"

"Sure," the man replied and put the suitcase into the boot of the taxi. "You want to put that attaché case in here as well?"

"No, it stays with me," Holden retorted brusquely then climbed into the back of the taxi and closed the door, the attaché case resting on his legs.

As the taxi pulled away from the Central Station, Holden picked up a copy of the *Times* which had been left on the seat beside him. The front page was dominated by a black and white photograph of Rembrandt's "Night Watch" with a headline which read: ART TREASURE BEGINS HISTORIC TOUR. Although he had no interest in art he still scanned the first couple of paragraphs to get the gist of the story. The Rijksmuseum was to be cordoned off the following morning while the priceless "Night Watch" painting was removed from the building, under the tightest security ever mounted in Amsterdam's history, on the first leg of a five nations tour. He noticed that New York's Metropolitan Museum of Art was scheduled to be a part of the itinerary—not that he would be queuing up to gawp at some old painting. He discarded the newspaper and turned his attention to the attaché case. Whoever sent him the money certainly had a sense of humour. The combination had been made up of the digits in his birth date. He smiled to himself as he lined up the coordinates; it *was* like a birthday to him. And his present was twenty-five thousand dollars in cash. Tax free. He savoured the moment then slowly raised the lid. He had only a split second to see the plastic explosives laid out neatly in the case before they detonated.

The taxi, having passed the Royal Palace moments earlier, was ripped apart by the explosion. Searing hot fragments of twisted metal were scattered across a wide radius, lethal projectiles which sliced through anything, and anyone, in their way.

Pandemonium set in.

The bomb killed five people, including a seven-month-old baby.

The majority of the country's newspapers speculated about a possible terrorist link but all were united in calling on the government to leave no stone unturned in their search for those responsible for the explosion.

There was still a heavy security presence at the Rijksmuseum that morning, even though there were fewer onlookers than expected to watch as the painting was loaded into the armoured van for the short journey to Schiphol Airport. From there it was to be flown out to Vienna for the start of its historic tour, culminating four months later in its arrival at the last of the five participating galleries, New York's Metropolitan Museum of Art.

TWO

Louis Armand was a small, dapper man in his early fifties with wavy black hair and a thin moustache which looked as though it had been drawn on with an eyebrow pencil. He was the Metropolitan Museum's resident expert on seventeenth-century Dutch art, having been poached from the Louvre seven years before.

He adjusted the carnation in the lapel of his pin-striped jacket, brushed an imaginary fleck of dust from his sleeve, then walked across the Grand Hall and out on to the museum's front steps. The heavy rains of the previous night had subsided into a steady, irritating drizzle and the throng of expectant onlookers lining Fifth Avenue had sought sanctuary under a sea of multicolored umbrellas. What were they hoping to see? He was hardly going to have the painting held up like some sporting trophy once it arrived from the airport.

"You'd think the President was coming, judging by that crowd out there," one gallery attendant said to another within earshot of Armand.

The Frenchman looked round and scowled at them. "Hardly. Presidents can always be replaced."

8

"Ah, Louis. Morning. I'm glad I could get here in time."

You should have been the first person here, Armand thought irritably to himself, then turned to Dr. Gerald Stanholme, the museum's gregarious director, and smiled fleetingly before glancing at his watch. "The painting should be here any minute now."

"You must be excited."

"Yes, sir, I am. It's a great day for the Met."

"And hopefully a great week as well. Financially, there won't be another exhibition this year to touch it."

Financially? Armand had always thought Stanholme a philistine. This proved it. How could he equate the presence of the "Night Watch" to the door takings? If Armand had his way, nobody would pay to see it. Any entrance fee was going to be derisory compared to the beauty and grandeur of such a priceless work of art.

A cheer went up from a section of the crowd to the south of the museum and the rest joined in as a patrol car appeared with the armoured van following closely behind it. The patrol car didn't stop and the driver gave the occupants of the armoured van a friendly wave before it disappeared up East 83rd Street. Photographers jostled for positions as the armoured van drew to a halt in front of the museum. The security guard in the passenger seat climbed from the van and scanned his surroundings cautiously. He was dressed in black with a nightstick and a .357 Smith & Wesson in holsters attached to his belt. He waited until the museum's own security guards had formed a human chain in front of the crowd on either side of the steps before pushing the visor up from his face and, taking a set of keys from his pocket, moving round to the back of the van to unlock the doors. Two more uniformed guards jumped out and took up positions on either side of the doors, M16 automatic rifles held tightly across their chests.

Stanholme descended the steps, revelling in the attention the photographers were giving him. He looked back and beckoned Armand to follow him. Armand could barely hide his contempt and reluctantly joined Stanholme in front of the armoured van. It was fast turning into a circus and Stanholme was the perfect ringmaster.

"Louis, give the cameramen a smile," Stanholme said jovially.

Armand complied, hoping it didn't look too much like a grimace.

A man in his early forties with a ruddy complexion and fine blond hair climbed from the back of the van, dusted off his pale-blue three-piece suit, then approached the two men, his eyes wavering from one face to another. "Dr. Stanholme?" he asked uncertainly in an unmistakable Dutch accent.

"I'm Gerald Stanholme. You must be Van Dehn."

"Van Dehn, Mils van Dehn, assistant curator at the Rijksmuseum," the man replied shaking Stanholme's hand.

Stanholme introduced him to Armand and the two men shook hands briefly.

"Tinus de Jongh asked me to pass on his good wishes to you."

"Tinus? *Mon dieu*. I haven't heard from him in years. Is he still the seventeenth-century expert at the Rijksmuseum?"

"He retires next year," Van Dehn replied.

"You'll have lots of time to talk later. Let's get the painting inside." Stanholme walked round to the back of the van.

Van Dehn looked about him in bewilderment. "I never thought one painting could generate such excitement. It's like a carnival atmosphere."

"This is America, what do you expect?" Armand replied with obvious distaste.

Armand and Van Dehn joined Stanholme to watch as the four hand-picked members of the museum's removal team unfastened the straps holding the painting against the inside wall of the van and, after two layers of plastic were wrapped around the waterproof case and secured with masking tape as an added precaution against the rain, it was finally removed from the back of the van. The photographers shouted a barrage of instructions at the four men, wanting them to pose with the case beside the van, and the cameras flashed furiously as the men glanced at each other, momentarily stunned by all the shouting voices.

"Get it inside," Stanholme hissed under his breath then turned to the row of kneeling photographers and gave them an appeasing smile. "Come on, boys, give us a break. Look, once it's hanging inside I'll give you ten minutes of exclusive photographs along with a statement before I open the doors to the public. I can't say fairer than that."

There were the normal mutters but, in the main, there was a consensus of agreement. The reporters from CBS and NBC, both with outside broadcast units on hand to film the painting's arrival for the evening bulletins, turned their attention to the crowd, hoping to pick up a couple of usable quotes to incorporate into the feature. They knew it was wishful thinking.

Van Dehn watched anxiously as the four removal men began to ascend the steps, his hands opening and closing nervously, his walk unsteady, ready to leap to the painting's rescue should any of the men's rubber-soled shoes fail to grip on the wet concrete.

Armand put his hand lightly on Van Dehn's arm. "They're the best we've got. They've never dropped anything since I arrived, and that's saying something. After all, the Met *is* the largest repository of its kind in the western hemisphere. We have a million items in stock at any given time.''

Van Dehn gave Armand a sheepish smile. ''I'm sorry. It's not that I don't trust your staff, it's just that I'm in charge of the painting and if anything were to happen . . .''

''If something was going to happen it would have already happened at one of the other galleries. You're at the Met now.''

They followed the removal men into the Grand Hall and up a flight of stairs to the second floor, where Armand took a set of keys from his jacket pocket and approached a wooden door in the corridor which separated the galleries specializing in European and twentieth-century art. It was marked: L. ARMAND—PRIVATE. He unlocked the door then stood to the side to allow the painting to be taken in.

Van Dehn entered and looked around. The room was immaculately furnished with a deep pile wall-to-wall carpet, a teak desk and a matching set of brown leather armchairs. The wall behind the desk had been converted into rows of shelves which were neatly stacked with hundreds of books relating to every aspect of the art world. An impressive collection by any standards.

''Tea? Coffee?'' Armand asked Van Dehn.

''Coffee, please,'' Van Dehn answered then sank into one of the armchairs.

Armand ordered two coffees then sat down in the chair behind the desk. ''I get the impression you'll be glad to get back to Amsterdam.''

''It's been a constant strain these past four months but even so, I don't regret a moment of it.''

''I can believe that. After all, it isn't every day one gets the chance to babysit 'The Company of Captain Frans Banning Cocq and Lieutenant Willem van Ruytenburch.' ''

Like many of his contemporaries, Armand never referred to the painting by its popular, but incorrect, title of ''Night Watch.'' The misunderstanding dated back to the early nineteenth century, when the tone varnish had darkened to such an extent that historians and art connoisseurs of the time genuinely believed the scene to be taking place at night. It was only when it was cleaned in 1947 that Rembrandt's original intention was revealed. It was a daylight scene. Despite this revelation, the name ''Night Watch'' stuck, much to the chagrin of experts like Armand.

An easel was brought into the room and one of the men asked Armand whether he wanted them to put the painting on it.

Armand got to his feet. ''Yes, put it on the easel. The sooner I examine it, the sooner it can be put on exhibition.''

''I don't understand, why must you examine it first?'' Van Dehn asked once the men had left the room. ''Are you questioning its authenticity?''

''It's standard procedure here at the Met for all exhibits to be checked before they go on public display.'' Armand crossed to the painting then glanced at Van Dehn. ''That's the official explanation. Unofficially, I've waited forty years for this moment. In my opinion, this is Rembrandt's greatest work, and now it's here in my office. Right now I feel very humble indeed. Of course I'm not questioning its authenticity, but surely you don't begrudge me a few minutes to admire it here in the privacy of my own office? Let's face it, I'll never have this chance again.''

''No, of course not,'' Van Dehn replied with a smile. ''Please, take your time.''

''The Company of Captain Frans Banning Cocq and Lieutenant Willem van Ruytenburch'' was commissioned in December 1640 by the opulent, ambitious Cocq on behalf of the Kloveniersdoelen, a company of musketeers who lived in the same street as Rembrandt. It took Rembrandt until June 1642 to complete the painting, the same month as his beloved Saskia, his wife of eight years, died. He was thirty-seven years old. The painting depicted Cocq and Van Ruytenburch in the foreground illuminated by the rays of some unseen fulgent light, surrounded by the rest of the company who were armed with an assortment of pikes and muskets, preparing to march out through the massive archway in the shadows behind them.

As far as Armand was concerned, Rembrandt's skilful use of light and shade to create the atmosphere of movement made the painting one of the finest examples of Baroque chiaroscuro he had ever seen. If it did have a weakness, and he was loath to admit it, it was the girl in white to the left of Cocq. Apart from the symbolism of the Kloveniers' claw emblem hanging from her waist, she seemed out of place amongst the armed musketeers. Even so, she detracted little from the painting's overall grandeur. He had seen it at least a dozen times at the Rijksmuseum and each time he had been struck by the apparent pride and dignity of the company; from the tall, handsome standard-bearer holding the green and gold flag proudly in front of him to the short, craggy-faced drummer partially visible on the right of the picture. They all seemed to have a definite determination about their actions.

His eyes lingered on the drummer. Something was nagging in the back of his mind but he was damned if he knew what it was. He looked at the brown mongrel by the drummer's feet, then at the gesticulating figure behind the drummer, but each time his eyes were drawn back to the drummer himself. Then it came to him. It wasn't the drummer, it was the drum. As far as he knew, the dot in the center of the drum was black. The dot in the painting was red.

Van Dehn noticed the consternation on Armand's face but when he tried to speak Armand held up a hand to silence him. Armand stared at the dot. A rare self-doubt crept into his thoughts. Had he been wrong all these years? Had he always imagined it to be black?

"What's wrong?" Van Dehn asked, exasperated by the prolonged silence.

"Turn around," Armand said brusquely.

"What?"

"Turn around, so that you're standing with your back to the painting."

Van Dehn shrugged but did as he was told.

"Now, what colour is the dot on the drum?" Armand asked.

"Look, this is—"

"I said, what colour is it?" Armand cut in sharply.

"Black, I think," Van Dehn replied, his hesitancy not lost on Armand.

"Isn't it strange how we take things for granted? I, for instance, grew up by the sea. By the time I was ten I just took it for granted it was there. You work amongst some of the greatest art masterpieces in the world and you naturally take them for granted. Some would call that sacrilege." Armand selected a book from one of the shelves, consulted the index, then turned to the relevant page. "I also thought it was black. We're both right." He tapped the plate in the book. "But the dot on the drum in your painting isn't black, it's red."

"That's not red," Van Dehn announced after studying the dot from several different angles.

"Call it crimson. Magenta even. But it's not black."

Apprehension showed on Van Dehn's face for the first time and he picked the book up off the table and studied the plate before comparing it to the painting. Armand, meanwhile, had found three more colour plates of the painting. In each case, the dot in the center of the drum was unmistakably black.

"There has to be some logical explanation," Van Dehn said, the desperation now evident in his voice. "The light perhaps?"

There was a knock at the door and one of the canteen staff entered with two coffees which she deposited on the table before leaving.

"If it were the light then it would also affect the rest of the painting. Take Cocq's clothes, for example. They're black in the plates and they're black in the picture. No, it's not the light."

Van Dehn put the book back on the table then sat down on the edge of the nearest armchair and stared at the carpet. He was shattered. When he looked up his forehead was glistening with sweat. He glanced at the two coffees on the table. "Have you got anything . . . stronger?"

Armand nodded then took a bottle of bourbon and a tumbler from the bottom drawer of his desk and poured out a measure for Van Dehn. He was about to recap the bottle when he decided that he, too, needed a drink. After drinking it down in one gulp he set about measuring the painting: 141 by 172 inches, the exact measurements of the original. A section had been cut off the left hand side of the original when it had been transferred to the Amsterdam Town Hall's War Council Chamber in 1715. Not surprisingly, the forgery had been cut in exactly the same place.

"What are we going to do, Armand? What the hell are we going to do?"

"For a start we're not going to panic. I'll call Stanholme. He'll have to take it from here."

Armand first tried Stanholme's office but, receiving no reply, he then rang the switchboard and asked the operator to bleep him.

A breathless Stanholme arrived a minute later. "The switchboard said you wanted to see me urgently. Nothing's happened to . . ." he trailed off and looked across at the painting.

"It's a fake!" Van Dehn blurted out.

Stanholme looked to Armand for confirmation of Van Dehn's words.

Armand pointed at the painting. "What colour is the dot in the centre of the drum?"

Stanholme studied it before answering. "A dark red. Call it crimson."

"Black?"

"Louis, for God's sake, stop playing games. Is Van Dehn right? Is it a fake?"

"Is it black, Dr. Stanholme?" Armand asked.

"No, definitely not," Stanholme replied without hesitation.

Armand indicated the four books on his desk. "Have a look at the dot on those plates. Is it crimson or black?"

Stanholme examined each plate carefully then rubbed his hands slowly over his face. "Jesus H. Christ. How could it have happened?"

Van Dehn shifted uneasily in his chair and both men looked to him as if waiting for an explanation. "You don't think I had anything to do with it, do you?"

"You had the opportunity—"

"Opportunity?" Van Dehn cut angrily across Armand's words. "Have you got any proof to back up that accusation? Or are you just looking for a scapegoat to shift the spotlight away from your precious museum?"

"Gentlemen, please," Stanholme said firmly, his hands raised in an attempt to placate them. "This isn't getting us anywhere. Louis, you aren't a detective. None of us are. Let's leave that side of things to the proper authorities. Our main concern right now is those journalists out there."

"What are you going to tell them?" Van Dehn asked anxiously.

Stanholme looked across the table at Armand. "How good a forgery is it?"

"Van Meegeren couldn't have done better."

"So you think it would be safe to put it out on display as planned?"

"Perfectly safe."

"But you realized it was a forgery."

"That's what I'm paid for, Dr. Stanholme."

"What I'm getting at, Louis, is that if you noticed the forger's mistake, then who's to say others won't as well?"

"I can think of three reasons off-hand. Firstly, because I did a thesis on the painting at university and I've come to know it like the back of my hand. Secondly, if there are five people in this country who know more than I do about European art then it's a lot. And thirdly, ninety per cent of the people who come to see it wouldn't know a Hals from a De Keyser or a Vermeer from a Rembrandt. To them it's just a gimmick. The remaining ten per cent who consider themselves art lovers aren't coming here to find fault with it, they're coming here to admire one of the great artistic masterpieces of the world. That dot could be any colour, I guarantee you nobody would think of questioning it."

Stanholme stared at the painting. "I still can't believe it. A forgery. Isn't anything sacred any more?"

"We'll have it moved to the gallery while you contact the authorities," Armand said, breaking the sudden silence.

Stanholme gave a resigned nod then got to his feet and left the room.

Armand gave Van Dehn a contemptuous look then reached for the telephone to summon the four removal men back to his office.

THREE

Sabrina Carver's friends dined at the Four Seasons, Lutèce and Parioli Romanissimo; drank Bollinger RD, Roederer Cristal and Tattinger; shopped for clothes at Boutique Valentino, Halston and Sym's; and wore the latest designs by Cartier, Fiorucci and Klein. In short, they read like a who's who of New York's élite jetset fraternity.

Yet none of them knew about her double life. They all thought she was a translator at the United Nations. It was the perfect cover story. They knew her father was a former US ambassador and that her childhood had been spent in Washington, Montreal and London before she went on to Wellesley College where she took a degree in the Romance languages. They also knew that she had completed her postgraduate work at the Sorbonne before becoming one of Europe's most popular and sought-after débutantes. What they didn't know was that on her return to the United States, and mainly through her father's influence, she had been recruited by the FBI, where she had proved herself to be an exceptionally talented shot. A growing feeling of resentment amongst some of her peers, who felt she was riding on her father's name, had finally forced her to resign from the department. She had joined UNACO a fortnight later and now, at twenty-eight and still the youngest of the field operatives, she was in her second year with them.

She parked her champagne-coloured Mercedes-Benz 500 SEC at the end of the wooden jetty then, taking her Beretta 92 from the glove compartment, climbed out and looked up at the sky. The dark, sombre rainclouds which had been threatening the city when she left her apartment thirty minutes earlier were now drifting out over the Atlantic Ocean leaving much of Brooklyn swathed in bright sunlight. She was dressed in a grey sweatshirt, baggy jeans and running shoes and was already beginning to feel the heat. The unflattering clothes did little justice to her sylphlike figure but her sparing use of make-up only seemed to enhance her classically beautiful features. Her golden-blonde shoulder-length hair, which she had tinted with auburn highlights at Christine Valmy's on Fifth Avenue, was piled up on her head and hidden underneath an LA Dodgers baseball cap. She slipped on a pair of sunglasses and took in her surroundings.

Thirty yards ahead, to her left, was a graffiti-scrawled warehouse, its windows long since shattered and its unpainted corrugated-iron roof a vast expanse of discoloured rust. A forty-five-foot trawler was moored directly opposite the warehouse. It, too, was corroded from years of neglect. Her assignment was to retrieve a black leather document case from the trawler which, she knew, was being guarded by three armed men. Their instructions were simple: to stop her from getting the case. And they could be hiding anywhere.

She plotted her first move. At least one gun would be trained on the trawler, probably from the top window in the warehouse, which made the jetty useless as a means of getting to the trawler. She contemplated the idea of swimming to the trawler but she would be a perfect target were she spotted in the water. The only way in was through the back of the warehouse. But would they have it covered? She knew there was only one way of finding out.

She darted out from behind the Mercedes and sprinted to the warehouse, pressing herself up against the unpainted brick wall. That had been the easy bit. It was the only windowless wall, so she was effectively on their blind side. She peered cautiously around the side of the wall. It looked deserted. Then she noticed the steel ladder against the wall, between the window and the door. It gave her an idea. She ran past the window, making no attempt to duck, and quickly climbed the first dozen steps of the ladder. Then she waited. Nothing happened. Then, just when she thought they hadn't fallen for her ploy, the barrel of a Colt .45 appeared hesitantly at the window. She had aroused their curiosity. The hand holding the revolver came into view and although she had a perfect shot she held back, willing him to lean further out of the window. Then, as suddenly as it had appeared, the revolver disappeared. She cursed softly to herself but at least she now knew there were two of them in the warehouse. The other man would be covering the trawler and jetty, probably with a high-powered rifle.

She tucked the Beretta into her hip holster and climbed to the top of the ladder where she hauled herself on to the roof, careful not to make any noise. Logic decreed that every warehouse had a skylight. This one was no different. The roof was firm under her weight and she moved cautiously up the forty-five-degree incline to the skylight. It, too, had no glass and, because of the bright sunlight, she had the perfect vantage point to survey the interior of the warehouse. Then she saw him—the gunman on the catwalk by the top window overlooking the jetty. He was no longer covering the jetty, his eyes now flickering between the two doors, waiting and watching. He saw her at the last moment but was blinded by the sunlight when he swung the Mauser SP66 sniper rifle towards the skylight. She shot him twice in the chest. One down, two to go.

From where she lay she couldn't see the second gunman, but she knew he was there. And he would have his gun trained on the skylight. Yet she had to chance it. She gripped her Beretta tightly in her hand and jumped nimbly through the skylight, hitting the catwalk with bended knees. A bullet ricocheted off the railing inches from where she was crouched. She managed to get off two shots at the retreating figure as he disappeared out on to the jetty. She knew she had missed him.

The two men would almost certainly be regrouping on the trawler for a last, determined stand. It made her think about cornered animals being the most dangerous. The stakes were now that bit higher but it only increased her determination to outwit them and recover the document case. She descended the stairs to the warehouse floor then crossed stealthily to the door and surveyed the trawler ten yards away. The gangplank was certainly out. A plan came to mind. She lined up several landmarks on the trawler's bow, then, with heart pounding, zigzagged her way towards the trawler. A movement on the bridge caught her eye and a moment later a bullet cracked inches from her ear. Then another. She launched herself over the side of the trawler, landing with bended knees, and didn't stop rolling until she had reached the safety of a pile of empty packing crates.

After catching her breath she made her way cautiously to the steps leading up to the bridge. She crept silently up the steps and kicked open the door, the Beretta gripped tightly in both hands. The bridge was deserted. There was also no sign of the document case. Where else could it be? The captain's cabin? She looked at a second, closed door to her right which she assumed led down to the crew quarters but made no move towards it—the gunman would be lying in wait for her. Instead she retraced her steps back on to the deck, her eyes continually scanning the surroundings for movement. Nothing stirred. She reached the hatchway and checked to see if it was booby-trapped. It was clean. After fanning the stairs with her Beretta she climbed through the hatchway and closed the door behind her. Now it would be impossible for them to steal up on her from the back without her knowing about it. The disadvantage was the semi-darkness and she had to be extra vigilant for any booby-traps. She came across a tripwire on the third stair. She stepped over it and used her Beretta as a wanding stick to check for any more tripwires on the remaining stairs. There were none.

She reached the bottom of the stairs and, with her back pressed against the wall, inched her way towards the captain's cabin at the end of the corridor. The door was partially open and she could see the document case lying on the desk in the corner of the cabin. It was too easy. As she crouched down to check the door for wires she noticed a movement at the other end of the corridor. The engine-room door was being opened. She kept up her pretence by continuing to feel around the edges of the door and it was only when the man had slipped out silently into the corridor that she pivoted on her toes and shot him twice in the chest. She kicked open the door and dived low into the cabin—there was no sign of the third man. A shadow fell across the porthole and she ducked down, Beretta at the ready. From where she was crouching she could see the shadow of a man heading away from the trawler towards her Mercedes at the end of the jetty.

She thought for a moment then, grabbing the document case, she squeezed through the porthole on to the deck.

The gangplank was useless as a means of escape. The only alternative was to manoeuvre underneath the jetty and come up behind the Mercedes. She tucked the document case into her baggy jeans then clambered over the side of the trawler and leapt the couple of feet on to a wooden strut running the length of the jetty. She grimaced as the murky water lapped around her ankles and her progress was slow as she negotiated her way from one slippery beam to the next like some nimble-footed acrobat. She reached the end of the jetty and silently climbed the wooden ladder to the top. The man was crouched behind the Mercedes, his eyes riveted on the trawler. Sensing someone behind him, he swung round to face her. She shot him twice. He slumped against the side of the car and looked down at the two yellow marks on his chest where the dye pellets had hit him.

"I'd say you were dead," Sabrina said with a wry grin.

Dave Swain, a former presidential bodyguard, pulled a pack of Marlboro from his pocket and extended it towards Sabrina.

"I don't, thanks," she said then ejected the clip from her Beretta.

He shrugged, lit one for himself, then pushed the pack back into his pocket.

Thirty of the two hundred and nine UNACO employees were field operatives who had been recruited from the police, military and intelligence services around the world. The ten teams were designated by the prefix "Strike Force" and, because of the perilous nature of their work, each operative had to undergo a stringent medical examination every four months. They had to spend five hours a week training in unarmed combat and another five hours firing an assortment

of weaponry at UNACO's advanced Test Center off the In-
terborough Parkway in Queens, which was situated entirely
underground to ensure maximum security. Outdoor activities
like hang-gliding, mountaineering and skiing were conducted at a secret camp in the backwoods of Pennsylvania.

Once a year each operative had to undergo the most rigorous test of all—to pit his or her wits against another Strike
Force team. The operative was given only an hour's notice
of the "assignment," whereas the Strike Force team was
given seventy-two hours to set up their defence. This was
then inspected by one of the Test Center's senior supervisors
who would note down the exact location of any "booby-
traps," "tripwires," etc. Should the operative trigger any of
these "devices" during the "assignment" it activated an
alarm and the test was over. It was a matter of pride more
than anything else to complete the "assignment," though
few operatives ever managed it. Not only had Sabrina out-
witted Strike Force Seven, she had done it in a record time
as well. She was smiling contentedly to herself when the jeep
pulled up behind her Mercedes.

Major Neville Smylie wasn't smiling when he climbed
from the passenger seat. Sabrina couldn't recall ever having
seen him smile. He was a dour, bald Englishman who had
distinguished himself with the SAS in Korea, Kenya, Malay-
sia, Oman and Northern Ireland before taking up the post as
head of the Test Center when UNACO was founded in 1980.
Nobody particularly liked him but they all respected him and
his criticisms were always taken seriously. They had saved
lives in the past.

Smylie had monitored Sabrina's progress on a closed-
circuit television in a van behind the warehouse and he
checked his notes and remarks on a clipboard before he ap-

proached her. "Give your magazines to Richards," he said, indicating his driver.

The magazines, which consisted of fluorescent yellow dye pellets, were produced especially for each operative's hand-gun or for whatever other weapons were used to make the "assignment" as realistic as possible. She handed her two magazines to Richards then looked around at the two men coming towards her. The marks from the dye pellets were clearly visible on their jackets. Richards relieved them of their magazines as well.

Smylie glanced up at a technician who was dismantling a video camera from its podium beside the warehouse door, then turned back to Sabrina. "If this were the Olympic pen-tathlon, Miss Carver, I'd be the first to congratulate you on breaking the record. But this isn't a race. I'd have much preferred it if you'd taken twice as long but been more me-thodical in your approach work. It's obvious you haven't learnt from last year's exercise. I quote: 'The operative shows signs of impulsiveness and overconfidence.' Those signs were still evident today."

"I'll bear your words in mind, sir."

"I hope so. They're for your benefit. We'll go through the video together within the next couple of days. And that in-cludes Strike Force Seven, Mr. Swain. You obviously need to tighten up in certain areas."

Sabrina unlocked the door of her Mercedes and climbed inside.

"I'd say you were dead," Swain said with evident satis-faction.

She noticed the strand of broken thread hanging from the bottom of the door and slumped back angrily in her seat, silently cursing both Swain and herself. But mainly herself.

Smylie made a note on his clipboard then squatted by the

Mercedes and fingered the thread. "It was theoretically wired to ten pounds of explosives. Why didn't you think to check? Impulsive? Overconfident?"

"Just stupid," she retorted.

"I don't think so," Smylie said then stood up. "By the way, I saw one of your colleagues on Range Four when I left the Test Center."

"Who? Mike or C. W.?"

"Whitlock." Smylie stared at the thread then shook his head and walked back to the jeep.

Sabrina slammed the door shut and started up the engine. She thought about C. W. Whitlock as she sped away from the jetty. He was one of her few true friends even though they only ever saw each other at work. And at that moment she couldn't think of anyone better to talk to about her obvious stupidity. Or was it overconfidence?

C. W. Whitlock lowered the Heckler & Koch PSG-I sniper rifle after the fourth shot and reached for the lukewarm coffee in the plastic cup on the bench in front of him. He didn't need to look through the telescope to know his grouping was non-existent. His shooting that day had been atrocious. He just wasn't concentrating on what he was doing. He picked up the Browning Mk2, his favourite handgun, and turned it over slowly in his hands.

He was a 44-year-old black with a light complexion and sharp features tempered by the neat moustache and the prescription glasses he wore because of his photosensitivity. He had spent much of his early life in England but after graduating from Oxford with a BA (Hons) he had returned to his native Kenya to join the Intelligence Corps, remaining there for ten years before taking up a new challenge at UNACO. Three years after arriving in New York he had married Carmen Rodriguez, a successful pediatrician who worked in Harlem. At first she had been supportive of his dangerous and secretive work but, as the years passed, she had become increasingly worried about his safety. Now, as far as he was concerned, she was being totally unreasonable, continually getting at him to leave UNACO and set up a small security firm with the money *she* had saved over the years. She had even gone as far as to find him a suitable site for his company. His cogent argument was that he had only another four years of field work left (all field operatives were "retired" at forty-eight) and then he would almost certainly be promoted to divisional head somewhere in the world. Not that it had made any impression on her. She told him she only had his interests at heart. He disagreed. If she did, then she would try to understand his loyalty to UNACO and to his Strike Force Three colleagues in particular. Neither of them was prepared to concede and it was putting an ever-increasing strain on the marriage.

He suddenly gripped the Browning in both hands and fired six shots in rapid succession at the cardboard silhouette fifty yards away.

"Not bad shooting for someone of your age." Martin Cohen looked up from the telescope and smiled. He was a forty-seven-year-old Israeli with wiry black hair and a thick moustache which he had a habit of stroking with his thumb and forefinger as he talked. A former Mossad agent and member of the controversial Mivtzam Elohim, the Israeli assassination squads, he and Whitlock had remained good friends ever since they joined UNACO as part of the original team in 1980.

"How long have you been standing there, Marty?"

"Not long. Is everything all right?"

"What do you mean?" Whitlock replied then looked through the telescope. Five of his bullets had hit the bull's-eye.

"You looked pretty upset just now."

"So would you if you'd been shooting as badly as I have this morning. That's the first decent grouping I've had."

Whitlock knew Cohen wasn't the kind of person he could talk to about his problems. He would sympathize but he wouldn't understand. Hannah Cohen, who had been a computer analyst with the Shin Beth and was now a senior programmer at UNACO headquarters, was totally supportive of her husband's work. Whitlock stared at the cardboard silhouette: who could he turn to for advice? He had always been regarded as the avuncular, imperturbable type to whom many an operative had come in times of personal distress. Now the boot was on the other foot and he was loath to admit that he couldn't bring himself to discuss his problems with anyone.

"C. W.?"

Whitlock looked around at Cohen and grinned. "Sorry, Marty. I was just wondering why it's taken me so long to get my grouping together."

"If something's bothering you, you know you can confide in me. How many times have I poured my heart out to you over a couple of beers at McFeely's?"

"Enough. Seriously though, nothing's bugging me. Honest. I'm just a bit tired, that's all."

"Carmen been keeping you up?" Cohen said with a knowing grin.

"You could say that."

"Hi, you guys," Sabrina called out from the foot of the stairs, then hurried over to them and hugged Whitlock tightly.

"You don't know how much I needed that," he said, then kissed her lightly on the cheek.

Cohen winked at her. "So how's the lovely Sabrina?"

"Dead," she replied then explained what had happened during the "assignment."

"I agree with you," Whitlock said once she had finished.

"It was stupid. A real dumb thing to do. What do you say, Marty?"

Cohen noticed the glint in Whitlock's eye. "Yeah, I'd have to go along with you. But then she is a blonde."

"Well that explains it," Whitlock rejoined.

Sabrina leaned back against the wall and folded her arms across her chest. "Ever thought of forming a double act?"

Whitlock grinned then handed her the Heckler & Koch sniper rifle as a peace offering. "I probably would go along with Smylie's assessment. You are brash and overconfident at times but you're also good. Damn good. And, in my opinion, that's all that matters."

Cohen nodded in agreement. "For all Smylie's attempts to inject some authenticity into his little games, it's still a world away from an actual assignment. We're dodging real bullets out there, not fluorescent yellow pellets. It's your neck on the block, not his. It's Mike and C. W. who depend on you to watch their backs, not him. Remember that."

She nodded.

"Talking of which, where is the third musketeer?" Cohen asked.

Whitlock and Sabrina exchanged glances and shrugged. Mike Graham was the UNACO enigma. A maverick with a non-conformist's attitude towards anything authoritarian or bureaucratic, especially if it involved his superiors.

"Agent Whitlock, Code Green call," a voice announced over the tannoy. "Please contact the switchboard immediately."

"Code Green? We're on standby," Whitlock said as the announcement was repeated.

Cohen put a restraining hand on Sabrina's arm as she was about to follow Whitlock to the telephone at the end of the range. "Something's bugging him."

She looked across to where Whitlock was standing. "What?"

"I wish I knew. Just watch him, Sabrina, for his own good."

Mike Graham couldn't believe his good fortune when he spotted the vacant parking space directly opposite the building he had come to New York to see. He drew abreast of the car in front of the space and was about to put his battered white '78 pick-up into reverse when he heard the sharp blast of a horn behind him. He glanced in the rearview mirror. A sleek black Isuzu Piazza was lined up behind the space, its cream-suited driver about to attempt a forward parking manoeuvre. Graham wiped the sweat from his forehead and screwed his eyes up in disbelief. Where the hell had it come from? It certainly hadn't been there when he checked his side mirror seconds earlier. He tapped his chest and jerked his thumb towards the parking space behind him.

The driver activated his electronic window and stuck out his head. "I saw it first," he shouted above the noise of his in-car stereo.

Graham shook his head. "Back off."

The driver touched his ear and shrugged.

Graham was fast losing his patience. He engaged the reverse gear but as he tried to swing back into the space the other driver edged his car forward, creating a stalemate. Graham put the pick-up in neutral and jumped out into the road, slamming the door behind him.

"Get that thing out of the way," the other driver shouted angrily at him.

Graham squatted down beside the driver's open window, careful not to touch the car which he scanned with obvious distaste. He waited until the driver had turned the music down before speaking. "I'll tell you what's going to happen, city boy. That 'thing,' as you call it, is going to park in that space in front of you."

"Like hell it is—"

"Shut up, I haven't finished talking. As you can see, that 'thing' has already been through the wars so another couple of dents won't make any difference. On the other hand, your piece of spray-painted tin won't look so good with a crumpled hood. Park there, and I'll bulldoze you out of the way." Graham leaned forward, his finger inches from the driver's face. "Make your choice, city boy."

"You're mad," the driver blurted out.

"Yeah?" Graham replied nonchalantly as he walked back to his pick-up.

The driver's nerve broke and he accelerated the Piazza away, disappearing around the nearest corner.

Graham allowed himself a faint smile of satisfaction. He was thirty-seven years old with a rich tan and a muscular physique which he kept in peak condition with a rigorous programme of running and weight training. His unkempt, tousled collar-length auburn hair framed a boyishly handsome face which drew its strength from the penetrating intensity of his pale-blue eyes.

He parked the pick-up then, pocketing the keys, slowly surveyed the apartment building on the other side of the street. Olmsted Heights, named after the man accredited with designing Central Park, had been a part of the Murray Hill district for as long as Graham could remember. It had been his home for five years, until the tragedy which had shattered his life so abruptly. He crossed the road, his hands tucked into the pockets of his faded jeans, then paused to stare at each of the ten concrete steps which led up to the two plate-glass doors. The initials OH, in red italics, were engraved across both doors, just as they had been when he had last seen them. Unable to see behind the doors because of the sun's blinding reflection, he sat down on the top step and allowed his mind to drift back in time as it had done so often since that fateful October day two years earlier.

Like so many of his contemporaries, he had been scarred at an early age by the horrors of Vietnam. He had received his draft papers barely a month after fulfilling a lifetime dream by signing as a rookie quarterback for the New York Giants, the team he had supported since childhood, but a shoulder injury in Vietnam quickly put paid to his promising career and he spent the next two years in Thailand helping the CIA train local tribesmen sympathetic to the South Vietnamese cause. He returned to the United States where, after extensive mental and physical tests, he was recruited by Colonel Charles Beckwith for the elite anti-terrorist squad, Delta. He served with distinction and his loyalty was rewarded eleven years later when he was promoted to head its B-squadron. Their first mission under his command took them to Libya but, as they were about to attack the terrorist base, news reached him that his wife and five-year-old son had been kidnapped outside their apartment by four Arab-speaking men. He was given the option to abort the mission but he refused to back down and although the base was destroyed the leaders managed to escape. His family were never found, despite one of the most intensive covert manhunts in FBI history.

"He used to sit there for hours with his football waiting for you to come home. He was a great kid, Mr. Graham."

Graham looked around at the grey-haired Negro standing in the doorway. Like Olmsted Heights, the concierge had also been a part of the Murray Hill district for as long as Graham could remember.

"Hello Ben," Graham said and shook the extended hand.

Ben grimaced as he struggled to ease himself on to the

step beside Graham. "I thought it was you in that junker but I wasn't sure until you told off that kid for trying to steal your old parking place. Then I knew it had to be you."

"Yeah?" Graham muttered absently as he stared at the pavement. "You saw it, didn't you?"

"Saw what?"

"Carrie and Mikey being kidnapped."

"Don't reopen old wounds, Mr. Graham."

"They've never healed, Ben." Graham gestured towards the pavement. "Where were they standing?"

"Don't—"

"Where?" Graham cut in sharply.

"Right in front of us. It all happened so quickly. Mrs. Graham was getting the groceries from the trunk of that little Ford of hers and Mike was bouncing his football against the wall at the bottom of the steps. I remember her scolding him: 'Ben will have to wipe down that wall if you leave any marks.' Then this black Mercedes drew up beside the Ford and two men grabbed her from behind and pushed her into the back seat. A third man made a grab for Mike. You'd have been proud of him, Mr. Graham. He dodged that son-of-a-bitch like a true quarterback. She shouted to him. . . ." Ben trailed off, shaking his head as he struggled to relive the incident again.

"Go on," Graham hissed under his breath.

"It's not doing—"

"Go on, Ben. Please."

"She shouted, 'Run, Mike, run.' I'd come out here by now but my damn arthritis wasn't doing me any favours. Then she saw me. 'Help Mike, Ben, please help him.' It's the last thing she ever said . . . to me. I was so helpless to do anything. Then they fired over my head and by the time I'd got to my feet the Mercedes had sped off. I'll never forget

Mrs. Graham's words as long as I live. I failed her when she needed me most.''

"You didn't fail her, Ben. I did.''

They lapsed into silence, each caught in his own private world of guilt.

"Are you still living in New York?'' Ben asked.

"Vermont. I've got a cabin on the edge of Lake Champlain, near Burlington.''

The beeper clipped to Graham's belt suddenly activated and he quickly silenced it.

"What's that?''

"Work,'' Graham replied. "Where's the nearest phone?''

"You can use the one in my office.''

"Thanks anyway, but I'd prefer to use a pay phone.''

"There's one at the end of the block.''

"Morning, Ben,'' an elderly woman called out from the foot of the steps.

"Morning, Mrs. Camilieri,'' Ben replied then got to his feet and took the packet of groceries from her.

She stared at Graham. "You used to live here, didn't you?''

"No,'' Graham replied with a quick smile. "I'm from out of town. I seemed to have got lost and I was asking the concierge here for directions.''

"You look so much like that nice Mr. Graham who used to live here. His wife and son were killed by terrorists. Such a lovely family. It was so tragic.''

"Come on, Mrs. Camilieri,'' Ben said taking her arm.

When he looked around Graham had gone.

"You remember the Grahams, Ben?''

"I'll never forget them,'' he muttered then slowly walked her up the steps and into the foyer.

FOUR

Sarah Thomas was nineteen when she entered the Miss Oregon beauty contest, more as a dare than anything else. Much to her astonishment, she won it. She was suddenly plagued by agents and talent scouts who saw her future on the silver screen but, having heard the stories about starlets who waited tables and washed up in seedy diners while their big break never came, she decided against gambling her future in Hollywood and went to secretarial school instead.

That had been twelve years ago. Although she had lost none of her beauty, her blonde hair was now cut short and her provocative tight-fitting jeans and T-shirts had long since given way to elegant Armani and Chanel suits and monogrammed Pucci blouses. For the past four years she had been working as a secretary in a sparsely furnished office on the twenty-second floor of the United Nations Building in New York. The notepaper she used for typing memos wasn't headed and the company, Llewelyn and Lee, whose name she always used when answering any of the four black telephones on her desk, was fictitious. In fact, only a handful of delegates at the United Nations really knew what lay behind that unmarked outer door.

Her office was an antechamber to UNACO headquarters. The wall opposite the door, constructed of rows of teak slats, contained two seamless sliding doors which could only be activated by miniature sonic transmitters. The door to the left led into the Director's private office. The door to the right led into the UNACO Command Center.

Malcolm Philpott had spent the morning in the Command Center where he was being updated on the progress of the three Strike Force teams currently on assignment. He was a tall, gaunt Scot in his mid-fifties with thinning red hair and a pronounced limp on his left leg, the result of an injury sustained during the Korean War. After a successful career as an MI5 handler he had gone on to head Scotland Yard's Special Branch for seven years before his appointment as UNACO Director in 1980. His was a thankless task and although his brash and stubborn attitude had brought him into conflict with the United Nations Secretary-General in the past he had the respect of almost every government and intelligence agency in the world.

There were exceptions. An unsuccessful hijack at Venice's Marco Polo Airport had resulted in the deaths of seven passengers and two members of the Carabinieri. The four hijackers, thought to be North Korean, had then escaped to Libya where, by all accounts, they were being treated as revolutionary heroes by the government. UNACO had been asked to send in a team to flush them out and Philpott had dispatched Strike Force Nine to Tripoli the previous day. Not only had the Libyan authorities refused to cooperate, they had also arrested the UNACO team less than an hour after their arrival. Philpott was faced with a double headache: to get his team out of the high-security jail and to apprehend, or eliminate, the hijackers. He would have to send in another Strike Force team.

He ignored the noise of the printers, telexes and telephones around him, his concentration centered solely on the analyst who was explaining to him, by means of one of the numerous charts which lined the walls of the spacious, soundproofed room, the type of terrain to be found around the high-security jail.

"I want a summary of that on my desk in half an hour," Philpott said the moment the analyst had finished speaking.

"I'll get on to it right away, sir."

Philpott then crossed to a VDU at the end of a bank of computer terminals where a serious-faced man was running his fingers deftly over the keyboard, his eyes only occasionally flickering up to the screen in front of him.

"I've managed to narrow the list down to twenty-three, sir," the man said as he continued to feed more information into the computer. "But the Italians have made life difficult by not being able to identify any of the terrorists."

"We only get the difficult ones, Jack. I'm briefing a team in an hour's time. Can you have a concise list of suspects by then?"

"I'll have it for you in thirty minutes, sir."

"Good man."

"Colonel Philpott? Telephone," a bespectacled man called out from behind the VDU. "It's Sarah."

Philpott grabbed the receiver. "Yes, Sarah?"

"Strike Force Three are here, sir."

"Good. Is Sergei there?"

"Mr. Kolchinsky's already in your office."

"Send them in. I'll be through in a minute."

"Yes, sir."

Philpott handed the receiver back to the bespectacled man

then looked around the room. He had a feeling it was going to be a very long day.

Sergei Kolchinsky replaced the receiver after speaking to Sarah and stood up from behind Philpott's desk.

He was fifty-two years old with thinning black hair and a doleful face which had earned him the nickname of ''Bloodhound'' amongst some of the operatives. It was also a term of respect. He had a nose for trouble and a brilliant tactical mind which he had used to help crack some of UNACO's toughest assignments in the past. He had served the KGB with distinction—first in Russia, then for sixteen years as a military attaché in the West—before his posting to UNACO as Philpott's deputy to replace another former KGB operative who had been caught spying for his Kremlin masters. Although pedantic at times, especially when it came to the expense accounts each operative had to submit after an assignment, he was one of the most popular characters at UNACO.

He activated the door with the miniature sonic transmitter on Philpott's desk and Graham, Whitlock and Sabrina entered, each shaking his hand in turn. After closing the door, he indicated the two black leather couches against the wall then pushed a cigarette between his lips and lit it.

''Anyone for coffee?'' Whitlock asked as he crossed to the dispenser.

''I could do with one after this morning,'' Sabrina replied as she settled herself on one of the couches.

Graham shook his head.

Kolchinsky pointed to his full cup then turned to Sabrina. ''How did it go?''

''Not too well but you'll read all about it in the report.''

''Who were you up against?'' Graham asked.

"Seven."

"Swain?" Graham retorted, his lips curled up at the edges.

"Do I detect a note of acrimony in your voice, Michael?" Kolchinsky cocked an eyebrow in Graham's direction.

"Damn right you do. For someone who spent five years running beside Reagan's limo, he's got a hell of an opinion of himself. I've got nothing but respect for Colonel Philpott, but I honestly can't understand why he brought Swain here. Christ, I wouldn't trust the bastard to be a pall-bearer at my funeral." Graham glanced at Sabrina. "I hope you got him."

"Twice, in the chest."

"Pity they weren't real bullets." Graham shrugged at Kolchinsky's furrowed expression. "I don't like the guy, okay?"

"I would never have guessed," Kolchinsky said facetiously then wagged a finger of warning at him. "One day you may need Swain to watch your back."

"I watch my own back. I don't need some two-bit presidential flunkey to do it for me."

Kolchinsky gave Whitlock and Sabrina a despairing look, then turned to the wall behind the desk as the built-in door panel slid open and Philpott entered from the Command Center. The door closed behind him. He greeted his operatives then sat down in his padded chair and leaned his cane against the desk. Kolchinsky handed him a file and the two men spoke together in whispers.

"What have you got against Swain?" Sabrina asked Graham.

"Swain was with a group put forward for Delta about six years ago. He doesn't know it, but I was watching when one of our corporals put them through their paces. I could see straight away that he wasn't Delta material. He was too gungho. He was turned down and I went on leave a couple of days later and thought no more of it. Then, when I got back, I

found that the corporal had been backtelled. Demoted, in
other words. Swain and a couple of his cronies had put in an
official complaint that he'd mistreated them during the pre-
lim. As I said, I'd seen it all and there was never any question
of them being mistreated. If there had, I'd have been the first
to sort the corporal out. Well, I tried to put my side of the
story across to my superior but by then it was too late. The
corporal had lost his stripes. The decision stood. He left
Delta soon afterwards, totally disillusioned with life. Last I
heard he was running a gasoline station in some jerkwater in
Nebraska. That's what I've got against Swain.''

"Mike, Sabrina? I hate to interrupt your intimate conversation but we do have an assignment to discuss,'' Philpott
said abruptly.

"Hardly intimate,'' Graham muttered and shifted further
away from Sabrina.

Philpott, satisfied he had their attention, opened the file
in front of him. "What do you know about the 'Night
Watch'?''

"It's a codeword for the converted Boeing 707 the Vice-
President would use in a time of war should the President be
killed,'' Graham replied.

"Not *that* 'Nightwatch'!'' Philpott said exasperatedly.
"I'm talking about the painting. It's been in every newspaper
and on every TV station for the past month. You couldn't
have missed it, not even in that backwater of yours.''

"I didn't miss it, sir, I just didn't take much notice.''

"Then I suggest you start taking some notice. It's your
next assignment. The 'Night Watch' which arrived at the Met
this morning has been verified as a fake.''

"A fake?'' Whitlock said in amazement.

Philpott nodded. "It's up to the three of you to find the
original.''

"Why us, sir? Surely the Feds can handle it?"

"They would, Mike, if we could be certain the switch took place on American soil. We can't. It could have taken place in any of the six countries, if we include Holland. There's more to it than that though. What isn't public knowledge is that the five countries involved in the tour each put up a bond of fifty million dollars to ensure the painting's safety while it was under their particular jurisdiction. Those were the only terms under which the Rijksmuseum would release the painting in the first place."

"And because nobody knows where the switch took place, none of the countries are prepared to admit responsibility so as to avoid paying out on the bond," Sabrina deduced.

"Precisely," Philpott said then tamped a wad of tobacco into his pipe. "And with that kind of attitude, the original may never be recovered."

"I still don't see why we can't work with the FBI. After all, the fake was discovered here in America."

"You're overlooking one point, C. W.," Philpott said, pausing to light his pipe. He blew the smoke upwards then pointed the pipe's stem at Whitlock. "White House logic. If the FBI are seen to be investigating the matter then it may seem to some that the Americans are accepting responsibility for the loss of the original."

"That's crazy," Whitlock rejoined.

"That's the White House for you," Graham said. "The last time the buck stopped there was on Truman's last day in office. It's been on the move ever since."

"What have we got to go on?" Sabrina asked.

"Very little," Kolchinsky said, entering the conversation for the first time. "A distraught assistant curator from the Rijksmuseum and a videotape of the loading procedure which is being kept under lock and key for us in Amsterdam. As the colonel said, the switch could have taken place in any of six countries. We have to find it.''

"It'll be like looking for a needle in a haystack,'' Sabrina said.

"And if you look long and hard enough, you'll find it,'' Kolchinsky replied. "It's a Code Green assignment, we do have time on our hands.''

"Whoever's behind the theft will certainly have the painting tucked away safely in their private gallery, well out of harm's way,'' Philpott added then sat forward, his face grim. "You'll be liaising with Sergei on this one. I've got a Code Red on my hands.'' He briefly explained the situation in Libya.

"Who are you sending in, sir?'' Sabrina asked.

"Strike Force Two.''

"Marty's team?''

Philpott nodded. "Along with you, C. W., Martin's the most experienced field operative we have at UNACO. I need experience on this one.''

"We've got the credentials to pull it off,'' Graham said looking from Sabrina to Whitlock.

"I don't doubt it, Mike, but I'm not sending them in with guns blazing. It's an extremely delicate situation and that's why I need a diplomat, not a battering ram. Martin and his team fit the bill.''

"And we don't?'' Graham responded.

"*You* don't,'' Philpott answered with a faint smile. "It is a nice try, Mike, but I'm afraid you're stuck with the painting.''

"Where do we start?'' Sabrina asked, getting to her feet.

"The Met. They're waiting for us there,'' Kolchinsky replied.

Philpott used his sonic transmitter to activate the sliding

door. "Good luck. Oh, C. W., may I have a word with you?"

Whitlock waited until the others had left the room before approaching Philpott's desk. "Is something wrong, sir?"

"You tell me. There are rumours that you haven't quite been yourself recently."

Whitlock was momentarily tempted to spill out his problems to Philpott. It wasn't as if they were strangers. They had known each other ever since Philpott had recruited him at Oxford for MI5. Then the moment passed. He just couldn't bring himself to discuss his private life with anyone. He would sort out his own problems, in time.

"Not myself? I'm fine, sir. I had a medical only last week. The doctor gave me a clean bill of health."

"I did get the report. You know what I mean."

"I *am* fine, sir. Honestly. I've been a bit tired recently, that's all."

"Well, you know my door's always open if you've got something on your mind."

"I appreciate that, sir."

Philpott watched Whitlock leave his office then closed the door after him. His uncertainty as to Whitlock's mental state was soon forgotten when he turned his attention back to the forthcoming Code Red operation in Libya.

Stanholme moved to the window and peered through the venetian blind at the street below. The queue gathering outside the museum was growing in size and part of it was already lost from view as it snaked down Fifth Avenue towards the Whitney Museum. Hundreds more were waiting behind the museum in Central Park. He had already been down twice to face the restless crowd to apologize for the late opening. The first time he had blamed the delay on the fact that the painting had to be officially authenticated by the appropriate art expert, in itself a rather sick joke under the circumstances. The second time he had blamed the press, explaining that some of the TV network presenters had requested more time to complete their reports. That had been half an hour ago and he didn't relish the idea of facing the crowd for a third time. Where were these people that he had been told were coming to investigate the matter? And who were they? None of his superiors would tell him. If, in fact, they even knew themselves. It all seemed so furtive.

The door opened and Van Dehn entered, ashen-faced, having spent the past twenty minutes on the telephone to the Rijksmuseum.

Armand pushed aside the cold coffee and placed his elbows on the table, his chin resting on his clenched fists. "Well?"

"Well what?" Van Dehn retorted, slumping into the nearest armchair.

"What did the museum have to say about your incompetence?"

"It's none of your damn business!" Van Dehn shot back then glared at Stanholme. "I've taken just about all I can from him. Get him off my back."

There was a knock at the door. Stanholme, grateful for the timely interruption, hurried over to open it.

"Dr. Stanholme?"

"Yes," came the cautious reply.

"My name's Kolchinsky. I believe you were told to expect me?"

"Thank God you're here. Please, come in."

Kolchinsky entered, followed by Graham, Sabrina and Whitlock. He introduced them to Stanholme who, in turn, introduced Armand and Van Dehn.

Armand sat back in his chair and studied them with both interest and suspicion. When Stanholme had told him that this Kolchinsky would be leading the investigation he had naturally assumed that he would be an American with Russian forebears. But an actual Russian? That meant they couldn't be from the NYPD, FBI or CIA. And two of them were dressed in jeans and sweatshirts. No insurance company investigator would dress like that. So what was left? Private detectives? He doubted it, not for a theft on that scale. Then who were they working for? His curiosity got the better of him and he voiced the question.

"We're not at liberty to say," Kolchinsky replied apologetically.

"Surely we hâve a right to know?" Armand retorted, mistaking Kolchinsky's tone of voice as a sign of weakness.

"We're here to investigate the disappearance of the original 'Night Watch.' That's all you need to know," Kolchinsky said firmly then turned to Stanholme. "Can we see the forgery? I believe it's already been hung in the gallery?"

"That's right. We didn't want to arouse any unnecessary suspicion, especially with the press hovering around here like a pack of vultures. If they suspected for one moment that something was amiss . . ." Stanholme trailed off and shook his head. "It would make headline news all over the world."

Leaving Van Dehn behind in the office, Stanholme led the way up a flight of stairs to the second floor where the museum's European art was housed. The forgery had been given a gallery to itself. It hung on the wall opposite the door and had been roped off at a distance of six feet. Stanholme explained that the back of the painting was wired to an ultra-sensitive alarm system which would be triggered should anyone attempt to touch either the frame or the canvas. In addition, armed guards would be on duty twenty-four hours a day while the painting was hanging in the museum. It was part of the strict security programme the Rijksmuseum had insisted be implemented at all five participating galleries before the painting even left Amsterdam.

Sabrina had seen the original in the Rijksmuseum and the forgery was just as she remembered it. It was truly the work of a genius. "How does the forger manage to crack the paint to make the painting look older without actually damaging the canvas as well?" she asked without looking at Armand who was standing beside her.

Armand answered after a moment's thought. "First he would size the canvas using some viscous agent like varnish or resin. This not only prevents the paint from being absorbed once the background's applied, it's also vital for craquelure to be successful."

"Craquelure?"

"The cracking of the paint. So once he's sized the canvas, he then has to prepare the paint. This he does by squeezing all the tubes of paint on to a large sheet of blotting paper and leaving it to stand overnight. The blotting paper will absorb all the oils and impurities in the paint. The next day he'll mix the paint with a solution of zinc white and egg tempera and use that on the canvas. A second layer of size would then be put on the painting once it's dry and the canvas placed in front of a fire. As the size dries and contracts, so the paint will crack. A hair-dryer could be used instead of a fire. Even an oven. The result would be the same. The picture would be finished with a coat of tone varnish, usually made up of copal and vibert brown. The brown can be diluted to date a painting to the forger's specifications. Another trick is to apply the varnish before the paint's dried so that they'll harden together and make it impossible to remove the varnish without damaging the painting as well. It means the age of the paint can never be tested.''

"What about X-rays and radiocarbon dating?'' Whitlock asked. "Surely the forger has ways of cheating them as well?''

"As I've said, one way to cheat radiocarbon dating is to let the paint and varnish dry together. Another is to use the mount from an old potboiler.'' Armand noticed the frown on Sabrina's face. "A potboiler's a term we use to describe an inferior work of art that's done purely for money.'' He gestured to the painting. "Take 'Night Watch,' for example. All the forger had to do was find a potboiler dating back to the seventeenth century.''

"Surely it would be difficult to find a painting that size?'' Sabrina asked.

"The original 'Night Watch' is fourteen feet by twelve. Granted, you don't come across paintings that size every day but the forger would have the right contacts who could get their hands on one without too much difficulty.

"Well, once he has the potboiler the forger would first steam the brown paper off the back of the mount. Then, once that's done, he has to remove any nails without scuffing or damaging the mount in any way. Remember, he's only interested in the mount. He then steams the old canvas off the mount and substitutes his own work in its place before sticking it back together with flour paste. A good forger will even sprinkle a little dust over the joins to add to its authenticity. Now he's got round the X-ray because it would only pick up an image if one painting had been done over another, a popular forgery technique before the advent of the X-ray machine.''

"Ingenious.''

"It has to be, Miss Carver. Art forgery is big business

these days. If the forger doesn't keep ahead of modern technology then he's going to be caught. It's as simple as that.''

Kolchinsky crossed to where Graham was standing. "What's wrong, Michael?''

"Nothing," Graham replied indifferently. "I just never was much into art. Take this painting. Fake or not, it does nothing for me.''

"I know what you mean," Kolchinsky agreed. "But our opinions aren't important. We're only here to find the original.''

Graham raked his fingers through his hair. "It makes you wonder, will people like Armand be drooling over Warhol's art in three hundred years' time?''

Kolchinsky smiled then put a hand lightly on Graham's shoulder. "I want you and Sabrina to get a statement from Van Dehn.''

"A confession would be more to the point.''

"You think he's involved?''

"It's a hunch, that's all.''

Kolchinsky beckoned Whitlock and Sabrina over. "C. W., talk to Armand, see what you can come up with in the way of forgers. We'll cross-check it with the list being drawn up at headquarters. Sabrina, I want you and Michael to see what you can get out of Van Dehn.''

Stanholme put his hand on Kolchinsky's arm. "Sorry to interrupt, but is it all right if we open the doors to the public? They're getting very restless out there.''

"Yes, we've finished in here, thank you." Kolchinsky waited until Stanholme was out of earshot before continuing. "I've got to get back to help the colonel. Call Sarah when you're through here, I'll tell her to have a car on standby. Oh, and Michael? Follow up on that hunch of yours. It's the best lead we've got so far.''

* * *

Sarah replaced the receiver and smiled at them. "Mr. Kolchinsky will see you now."

As if in response to her words, the sliding door opened and they entered Philpott's office. Kolchinsky, who was seated behind the desk, activated the transmitter and the door closed again.

He looked at each face in turn then leaned back in the padded chair and gave a resigned sigh. "No breakthrough then?"

"We grilled Van Dehn but he stuck to his story." Sabrina ejected a miniature cassette from the Sony micro-cassette player in her bag and placed it on the desk in front of Kolchinsky. "It's all there."

"He's good, I'll give him that," Graham said slumping on to one of the black couches.

"So your hunch is still there?"

"Yeah, only stronger. He's a worried man all right, but not because the switch was made while he was in charge of the painting. He's worried because the forgery's been discovered. If Armand hadn't been such an authority on the painting then the switch would never have been detected. It would have been returned to the Rijksmuseum and nobody would have been any the wiser. Who knows how long it would have hung there undetected? Perhaps forever. Certainly long enough to get Van Dehn off the hook. But now he knows that if we track the painting down the collector's hardly going to keep his mouth shut to save the others involved in the theft. Including Van Dehn."

Kolchinsky looked at Sabrina. "Well, what did you make of Van Dehn? Do you go along with Michael's hunch?"

"I agree that Van Dehn was worried but I don't feel as strongly as Mike does about his guilt. Having said that though, I've worked with Mike long enough to know never to dismiss his hunches out of hand. They've solved cases before.''

"If Michael is right then we could be faced with a new problem. What's to stop Van Dehn from contacting the person with the original 'Night Watch' and telling them what's happened? It could send the painting even further underground.''

"It's a valid point, in theory,'' Whitlock said. "But if he is behind the switch, then it's fair to assume that he's being well paid for his services. And it's also fair to assume that he won't have been paid up front for those services. It would have been a down payment with the balance to come once the forgery's safely back in the Rijksmuseum. So why spill the beans and risk forfeiting the money owing to him? It's not as if it's common knowledge that the painting hanging in the Met is a forgery. But then this is all just speculation.''

"I don't understand you guys. Especially you, Sergei.'' Graham tapped the folder on his knee. "What about this tour report you sent with the driver for us to read on the way back here? There's one aspect of this tour which sticks out like a sore thumb. Security. Each gallery—'' he paused to list them on his fingers, "the Kunsthistorisches Museum, Vienna; the Dahlem Gallery, Berlin; the Louvre, Paris; the National Gallery, London and now the Met—laid on the kind of security presence any head of state would have been proud of. Each country used its own security team, none of whom had ever met until they reported for duty. So there's no way they could have collaborated at such short notice. The painting wasn't even vulnerable while in transit between countries. Take the London–New York flight, for example. Two Feds and two senior officers from Scotland Yard watched the painting from the moment it left the National Gallery until it was loaded into the armoured van at JFK Airport. All four were given twenty-four hours' notice of their assignment. Hardly time to hatch a plan and have a forgery done, is it? The only person who had both the time and the opportunity to make the switch was Van Dehn. Can't you see that?"

"I agree with you, Michael, there is a strong case against Van Dehn but just remember, we're dealing in facts, not theories. At this present time there isn't a shred of evidence against him. If he *is* guilty, then it's up to us to prove it. A hunch isn't good enough."

The telephone rang.

"Excuse me," Kolchinsky said picking up the receiver. He listened attentively then spoke softly into the mouthpiece before hanging up. "That was Dr. Stanholme. The results of their radiocarbon dating tests have come through. The mount is mid-seventeenth century."

"That could be a clue in itself." Sabrina turned to Whitlock. "Remember what Armand said about using the mount from an old potboiler to fool the radiocarbon dating?"

Whitlock nodded. "I see what you're getting at. A dealer may well remember selling a canvas that size, especially if it was bought by, or on behalf of, a known forger."

"It could also have been stolen," Graham added.

"That's a possibility as well," Whitlock admitted.

"I hate to dampen your spirits but aren't you overlooking a couple of *minor* points?"

"The old potboiler could have been bought, or stolen, anywhere in the world at any time up to three, four years ago." Sabrina gave Kolchinsky a grim smile. "Sure it's a long shot, Sergei, but at least it's a clue and they're in short supply at the moment."

"It's worth a try," Kolchinsky said after some thought. "I'll get on to Jacques Rust in Zurich as soon as the Command Center lets me have the list of forgers they're drawing up. He can get his men to check the names out."

"I think our man will be on their list. The fake is a masterpiece in itself and as Armand said, there's only a handful of forgers who could have done it."

"I wouldn't bank on it, C. W. I'll ask Jacques to brief our Amsterdam contact so you should have all the information you need waiting for you at your hotel." Kolchinsky removed three envelopes from the drawer and tossed them on to the desk.

Each envelope contained a summary of the assignment, which had to be destroyed after reading; an airline ticket; a selection of maps of the city; written confirmation of their hotel reservations; a brief character sketch of their UNACO contact and a sum of money in guilders. There was no limit to the amount of money an operative could spend while on assignment (they all carried two credit cards for emergencies) but it all had to be accounted for to Kolchinsky with chits and receipts to back up the figure work.

Sabrina handed out the envelopes then looked at Kolchinsky. "What's the latest on Strike Force Nine in Libya?"

"No new developments. The Secretary-General's meeting the Libyan ambassador to the UN this afternoon. He means well but it's not going to work. That's why we've put Strike Force Two on a red alert standby."

"What are the chances of the press getting hold of the story?" Sabrina asked.

"They already have. The Libyan government issued a statement this morning. I've got a copy of it here." Kolchinsky tapped the folder on his desk. "None of the men were carrying any ID so there's no way the Libyans can find out who they really are. Our main worry is the Libyans' threat to put them on trial as soon as possible. If found guilty, and

I'd say that was a mere formality, they could be shot as mercenaries.'' He consulted his watch. "Anyway, that's not your problem. You've got a plane to catch in three hours."

"Three hours!" Graham exclaimed. "I've only brought enough clothes with me to last until after the marathon tomorrow. I can hardly travel to Amsterdam in a vest and running shorts."

"I'll lend you some clothes," Whitlock offered.

"No offence, C. W., but our tastes in clothes aren't too similar."

"What are you going to need, Michael?"

"A couple of T-shirts. A couple of sweatshirts. I guess I can get my jeans washed at the hotel."

"Use your UNACO credit cards to buy whatever you need. And get another pair of jeans, if that's what you *must* wear. I'd hate you to be caught with your pants down."

They laughed.

"I'll be joining you in Amsterdam as soon as I possibly can. It'll all depend on how quickly we can resolve the Libyan crisis." Kolchinsky activated the door for them.

Sabrina chuckled to herself once they were in the corridor. "I don't know how you do it, Mike. I wouldn't mind buying a few clothes on my UNACO credit card."

"I bet you wouldn't, as long as they were sporting designer labels and hanging in some trendy Fifth Avenue boutique."

"I was only kidding," she said softly as she stared after Graham's retreating figure.

"You know Mike," Whitlock said, then tried to put a reassuring arm around her shoulders.

"I'm okay," she retorted gruffly and headed for the lift.

He rubbed his hands over his face and sighed deeply. As if he didn't have enough to worry about with Carmen's

mounting resentment against his work, now Graham was
settling back into his old routine of getting at Sabrina whenever the opportunity presented itself. And, as always, he was
stuck in the middle. He glanced at his watch. Carmen would
be home from the surgery and that meant there would be
another confrontation when he returned to their Central Park
apartment to pack for the Amsterdam trip. It was inevitable.

The lift doors parted and he found himself facing a flus-
tered teacher surrounded by a group of ten-year-old school-
boys. He exchanged a quick smile with her then entered
the lift. The doors closed and he automatically reached for
the main lobby button. He needn't have bothered. One of the
brats had pushed every button from the twenty-second floor
to the main lobby.

As if he didn't have enough to worry about . . . .

FIVE

Tree-lined canals, hump-backed bridges, multicoloured fleets of houseboats and narrow cobbled streets packed with cyclists of all ages. Above all, though, Whitlock remembered Amsterdam for its *jenever*, a potent juniper-flavoured spirit which had once left him with the kind of hangover that would have converted an alcoholic to abstinence. Perhaps understandably, it was the only time in his life he had ever been drunk. It had happened twenty-five years earlier when he and a group of university friends had spent a week of their summer break in Holland. It was the era of enlightenment when hippies with flowers in their hair listened to the words of Timothy Leary and the music of Janis Joplin while passing around the communal hashpipe.

Whitlock, standing on the steps of the Rijksmuseum, looked out over the Singelgracht, the Ring Canal, and realized that little had changed since his last visit to the city. Only the hippies were gone, replaced by a new generation of teenagers who listened to the words and beat—he couldn't bring himself to call it music—of talentless bands on ghetto blasters perched on their shoulders, the noise blaring out for all to hear. It reminded him of his *jenever* hangover.

He climbed the remaining steps of the imposing red-brick building and entered the foyer where he asked an attendant to phone Professor Hendrik Broodendyk, the museum's Director-General, and inform him of his arrival.

When Broodendyk appeared, Whitlock was stunned by his uncanny resemblance to Sydney Greenstreet: the thinning black hair, greying at the temples; the heavy, fleshy jowls; the beady, penetrating eyes; and the corpulent twenty-stone bulk which had been the actor's trademark in the 1940s.

They shook hands then Broodendyk led Whitlock across the foyer to his office opposite the library and print room.

"Your Mr. Kolchinsky led me to believe there would be three of you," Broodendyk said after easing himself on to the armless chair behind the heavy teak desk.

"There are," Whitlock replied, seating himself in one of the burgundy-coloured armchairs. "My colleagues are following another line of investigation."

This seemed to satisfy Broodendyk who then reached for the telephone. "Can I get you some tea or coffee?"

"No, thank you. I've just had some coffee with my breakfast."

"Where are you staying?"

"The Park. You must know it, it's only a stone's throw away from here."

"I know it well. I always book the museum's guests in there." Broodendyk removed a videotape from the top drawer and placed it on the desk in front of Whitlock. "It was shot by one of our security team. I don't know what you hope to see but your Mr. Kolchinsky was quite adamant that I let you have it. I've had a VCR and a wide-screen television set put in a room down the corridor for you. The staff have been given strict instructions not to disturb you.''

"I'd like to ask you some questions before I look at the tape."

"Certainly." Broodendyk took a gold-plated cigarette case from the inside pocket of his alpaca jacket and extended it towards Whitlock who declined with a raised hand. "Do you mind if I smoke?"

"Not at all."

Broodendyk fitted a cigarette into an ivory holder and lit it with a Dunhill lighter. It reminded Whitlock of a scene out of some 1940s gangster film.

"I'd like a little background on Mils van Dehn."

Broodendyk shrugged his shoulders, only it looked more like a shudder. "I've known Mils for eight years, ever since I took up the post of Director-General here at the Rijksmuseum. He's one of the longest serving staff members but I couldn't tell you offhand how long he's been here. Sixteen, perhaps seventeen years. I can have it checked for you."

"That won't be necessary."

"Mils is one of those little grey men you find in every company. You know the kind I mean? Domineering wife, a house he'll never own, no ambition. He'd happily remain assistant curator until the day he retires. That's why I was pleasantly surprised when he suggested the idea of sending the 'Night Watch' on some kind of European tour. At least it showed initiative."

"It was his idea?" Whitlock asked, his interest aroused.

"*Ja*. He came to see me last year. I initially dismissed the idea out of hand but after some thought I came to realize that he actually might be on to something. You see, Mr. Whitlock, I've always harboured a dream to have the 'Mona Lisa' hang in the Rijksmuseum one day. So I thought if I let the

Louvre have the 'Night Watch' on loan, then it might bring my dream that bit closer to reality."

"So Van Dehn only suggested the idea to you once?"

Broodendyk bit on the holder as he pondered Whitlock's question. "He might have brought it up again, I can't remember, but he certainly didn't pester me about it. I'd have remembered that."

"And once you'd approved the tour itinerary, did Van Dehn put himself forward to accompany the painting?"

"No, I chose him because it was his idea in the first place." Broodendyk tapped the ash from his cigarette into a square ashtray at his elbow. "You seem very interested in Mils."

"I'm merely trying to get at the truth. That's what you want, isn't it?"

"Look, for all his blandness Mils is probably the most honest person I've ever known. His integrity has always been beyond reproach. That's why I had no hesitation in reassuring him that I had no intention of firing him over what's happened."

"When's he due back?"

Broodendyk glanced at his desk clock. "His flight should have landed at six o'clock this morning. I told him to take a few days off but he said he wanted to get back to work as soon as possible. I can understand that. Sitting at home would only have had him climbing the walls with worry and frustration."

"I'd like to see him when he gets here."

"I'll tell him."

Whitlock picked up the videotape and got to his feet. "Thanks for your time. Now, how do I get to this room you've set aside for me?"

"It's the second door down the corridor. It's unlocked."

Broodendyk stared at the door after Whitlock had left then

stubbed out his cigarette in the ashtray. Could Van Dehn be involved in the theft? He dismissed the idea as preposterous and turned his attention to the day's agenda in his private diary.

Amsterdam's main flea market on Valkenburgerstraat was bustling that humid, overcast Friday morning as the resident stallholders haggled over prices with locals and tourists alike in an attempt to clear as much of their wares as possible before the market closed for the weekend. Tourists continually made the mistake of walking away after being unable to agree on a price, fully expecting the stallholder to call them back. It never happened. A stallholder would rather forfeit the sale than lose face, especially to a foreigner. It was stubborn Dutch pride.

Graham still couldn't fathom why their contact had chosen to meet them at the flea market. Why not the hotel? Twice he and Sabrina had become separated in the jostling crowd and she had finally had to loop her hand through his arm as he shoved his way irritably through the mêlée of shoppers. The meeting was scheduled for eleven o'clock at the fabric stall at the far end of the market bordering on Rapenburgerstraat. That was something else Graham couldn't understand. Why there? Why not meet at the entrance? Why the damn flea market in the first place, he thought again to himself.

They reached the fabric stall ten minutes late for the meeting. It consisted of a dozen trestle tables seemingly layered with every fabric imaginable, from drill, gingham and calico to the more exotic chambray, crêpe-de-chine and tulle. The couple behind the trestle tables were being rushed off their feet—measuring, cutting, folding. Yet by the amount of money changing hands, and the constant clamour of would-be buyers, it certainly looked to be a lucrative business.

"Mike? Sabrina?"

They swung round. The man was in his late forties with silvery-grey hair and a strong, handsome face. He was carrying a black attaché case in his left hand, the initials PdJ inscribed on the lid.

"I'm Pieter de Jongh," the man said and extended a manicured hand in greeting. There were gold rings on three of his fingers.

"Why choose this place to meet?" Graham asked shaking De Jongh's hand.

"It'll become apparent in a minute." De Jongh stepped forward to allow a couple to pass behind him. "Let's walk. Friday's not the best day to be here unless you're after some bargains."

"Has Jacques come up with anything?" Graham asked as he fell in step beside De Jongh.

De Jongh shook his head. "All the names on the list have been eliminated from the enquiry. Jacques had his men check them out last night."

"So we're back to square one?" Sabrina muttered.

"Not necessarily. I had a long talk to Jacques on the telephone this morning and we're both of the opinion that the forgery almost certainly originated here in Amsterdam."

"Why?" Graham asked.

"Two-and-a-half years ago a very grand, but basically worthless, painting was stolen from a house here in Amsterdam. Nothing else was taken, even though there was a showcase of porcelain figurines dating back to William the Silent standing beside the painting. The painting, by an obscure seventeenth-century Dutch artist, measured fifteen feet by fifteen feet."

"The perfect size," Sabrina exclaimed. "The forger could then have taken into account the section that was cut off in 1715."

"Don't get your hopes up too much, it may well be a dead end."

"Have you followed it up?" Graham asked.

"I can hardly follow it up, Mike. I am, after all, a legitimate Amsterdam businessman. Asking those kind of questions could blow my cover." De Jongh stopped at the entrance to a narrow, cobbled side street. "There's a shop up there specializing in ceramics. It's owned by Frank Maartens, the city's leading fence. If anyone knows what happened to the painting, or who stole it, he will." He looked at Graham. "That's why I arranged to meet you at the market. Even with a map and directions I doubt you'd have found the shop by yourselves."

"I can believe it," Graham said looking around him.

De Jongh opened his attaché case and handed them each a cloth-wrapped Beretta which they slipped into their parka pockets without unwrapping.

"Is Maartens dangerous?" Sabrina asked.

"He's always shied away from violence," De Jongh replied, then took a sheet of paper from his jacket pocket and gave it to Graham. "It's a list of unsolved cases we know involve Maartens. We couldn't back any of them up with substantiated evidence but use it to call his bluff if the need arises. The threat of a third term in jail could well make him talk." He handed a key to Sabrina. "It opens a locker at the Central Station. Put your handguns in it once you've finished with them and leave the key at the hotel reception desk. I'll pick it up. You've got my number, call me if you need anything. Well, you'll have to excuse me, I've got a lunch appointment for twelve-thirty." He shook hands with them again then headed back towards the flea market and was quickly swallowed up in the crowd.

Graham read the list then gave it to Sabrina. It contained details of the stolen painting and, underneath, an outline of seven dated robberies from which goods had been passed on to Maartens to be fenced.

They made their way up the cobbled side street to a small shop sandwiched between a pancake bar and a laundrette. The name F. MAARTENS was painted above the small bay window displaying an assortment of ceramic wares in different shapes and sizes. The bell jangled above the door as they entered. It was a small, dingy shop with dozens of unpainted ceramic pots and figurines on dusty shelves which ran the perimeter of the room. Graham crossed to the counter and tapped the bell. A door behind the counter opened and a middle-aged woman appeared from a back room still straightening a scarf over her head. He could see the outline of the curlers underneath the flimsy material.

"Kan ik u helpen?" she asked indifferently.

"We're looking for Frank Maartens," Graham said.

"He's busy, upstairs," came the sharp response.

Graham leaned across the counter. "Then get him."

She looked away, unable to hold his withering stare.

"Get him!" Graham repeated.

She disappeared through the door and he could hear her heels on the uncarpeted stairs as she went in search of her husband.

Sabrina leaned back against the counter, her arms folded across her chest. "Talk about creepsville."

Graham followed her eyes. "You'll find dozens like it in New York. Samuel Johnson would probably have called it the last refuge of a failure."

They exchanged glances as a pungent smell of stale sweat

filled their nostrils and, turning around, found themselves facing a fat man in his mid-sixties with a week-old growth and unwashed brown hair which hung in strands down the side of his face.

"You want to see me?" the man said from the doorway.

"If you're Frank Maartens," Graham replied.

"*Ja*, I'm Maartens. What do you want?"

"Information."

Maartens grinned, his nicotine-stained teeth visible behind his cracked lips. "I'm not an informer."

"Pity," Graham said then unfolded the sheet of paper for Maartens to see. "The Van Hughen robbery, December '86. You fenced the goods and paid the team the equivalent of two thousand dollars. The police estimated the goods to be worth more in the region of twenty-five thousand dollars. Then there was the diamond heist outside the Gasson Diamond House in March '87—"

"Who are you?" Maartens blurted out.

"Who we are doesn't concern you. What does is that you double-crossed your colleagues and once they find out they're going to want revenge. The only problem is they're doing time, but if you just happened to land up in the same prison as them—"

"What do you want to know?" Maartens cut in anxiously and wiped the back of his hand nervously across his forehead.

"A painting was stolen two-and-a-half years ago from a house in," Graham paused to consult the list, "De Clerq Street. The robbery was unusual for two reasons. First, the size of the painting. Fifteen feet by fifteen. And second, nothing else was stolen. What I want to know is, who was behind the robbery?"

"I never handled that painting. I'd have remembered something that size."

"I never said you did. I want to know who pulled it off."

Maartens chuckled nervously. "*Mijnheer*, I'd tell you if I knew. Honestly I would."

Graham shrugged and folded the paper. "I guess we're wasting our time here. The police should be interested in the list though."

"Wait, please," Maartens pleaded as they turned to leave. "I can find out for you."

"You've got five minutes, then we're going to the police."

Maartens nodded apprehensively then reached for the telephone, his finger trembling as he started to dial. He replaced the receiver after the second call, the relief obvious on his face. "The man you want is Jan Lemmer."

"What do you know about him?" Sabrina asked entering the conversation for the first time.

"He used to be a boxer. He's now employed mainly for . . ." Maartens scratched his greasy hair as he struggled to find the word he wanted, "strong-arm business. You understand?"

"Yeah," Graham answered. "So where can we find him?"

"He lives on a houseboat near the Westermarkt in the Jordaan."

"Which canal?" Graham pressed.

"Prinsengracht. I don't know exactly where but he is well known in that area."

"And you're sure he was involved in the burglary?" Sabrina asked.

"*Ja*, I have good sources. You will tear up the paper now?"

"After we've seen Lemmer," Graham said.

"But I told you what you wanted to know."

"We're going to hold it as a safeguard," Sabrina told him.

"What does this 'safeguard' mean?" Maartens asked anxiously.

"It means if you tell Lemmer we're on our way to see him then this paper goes to the police," Graham said.

"I tell Lemmer!" Maartens snapped, his face flushed with anger. He spat on the floor. "I never talk to him. He's scum, filth!"

"We'll hold on to it anyway," Sabrina said.

"But how do I know you will tear it up after you've seen Lemmer?"

Graham opened the door for Sabrina then looked at Maartens. "You don't."

They flagged down a taxi on Valkenburgerstraat and Graham told the driver to take them to the Western Market, adding that there would be an extra ten guilders in it for him if he did it in under fifteen minutes. It was a challenge the driver readily accepted.

The videotape finished and Whitlock used the remote control to rewind it again. How many times had he watched it? Eight? Ten? He had already lost count. And each time he had come to the same conclusion. It would have been impossible for the paintings to have been switched at the Rijksmuseum. The video camera had recorded every detail on film: the painting had been carefully taken down from the wall of Room 224, wrapped and boxed, then carried down the stairs, across the foyer, and out into the Museumstraat where dozens of press photographers had been waiting to catch the moment for posterity. The cameraman had kept the video running while the painting was loaded into the back of the armoured van and rather dramatically used the moment when the doors were slammed shut to end the film. And, as the saying goes, the camera never lies. . . .

The videotape spooled back to the beginning but he made no attempt to activate the ''play'' button again. Instead he sat staring at the blank screen. His mind was wandering, just as it had been doing ever since their departure from New York the previous day. He had been lost in thought for most of the flight and Sabrina had even commented on his unusual taciturnity, saying how they normally never stopped talking when they flew together. Much as he cared for her, he found it impossible to confide in her. He found it impossible to confide in anybody. His problems with Carmen were personal and he and she had to find the solution alone. And those problems were fast coming to a head. He had tried, as always, to explain his position in his normal phlegmatic way but when Carmen had shouted at him, accusing him of caring more about his job than he did about her, his equanimity had finally snapped and for a brief, terrifying moment he had wanted to hit her. He stormed out of the apartment, slamming the door furiously behind him. That had been twenty hours ago. He wanted to call her but the anger and bitterness were still simmering inside him and one wrong word from either of them could start the recriminations all over again. He would call, in time.

There was a sharp rap on the door.

''Come in,'' Whitlock called out.

Van Dehn entered, his face pale and drawn. His suit was creased and rumpled as if he had slept in it the previous night. Whitlock commented on the fact.

''I wish it were true,'' Van Dehn replied rubbing his bloodshot eyes. ''I didn't get a wink of sleep on the aeroplane. I came here straight from the airport. I haven't even been home yet.''

''Have you told your wife you're back?''

''Fortunately she's not here. She didn't want to stay by

herself while I was away so she went to see her mother in Deventer. She's not due back until the end of the week. Professor Broodendyk said you wanted to see me?''

"I'd like to ask you some questions.''

"Would you mind if I ordered some coffee first?''

"Help yourself,'' Whitlock replied, indicating the telephone on the shelf against the wall.

Van Dehn placed the order then crossed to the table and sat down facing Whitlock. "Your colleague, Graham, thinks I'm guilty. I can see it by the way he looks at me.'' He shrugged dejectedly. "Not that I blame him. I am the one person who's been with the painting ever since it left here. I'd also be suspicious if I were in his shoes.''

Whitlock ignored Van Dehn's self-pity. "One of the conditions laid down by the Rijksmuseum was that each gallery or museum would videotape the arrival and departure of the painting from their premises. KLM, who've been transporting the painting between countries, videotaped the loading and off-loading at each of the international airports. All those tapes have been studied by representatives of our organization and, like myself, they've come up with nothing. That leaves one grey area—the time the painting was in the security vans.''

There was a knock at the door and a member of the canteen staff entered with a tray which she left in front of Van Dehn.

Van Dehn poured some coffee into the cup, added a dash of milk, then stirred it slowly. "You also think I'm guilty, don't you?''

"Look, a serious crime's been committed and it's up to my colleagues and me to find out who's behind it. I make no excuses for treading on toes if it gets me any nearer the truth.''

Van Dehn slumped back in his chair. "I'm sorry. I just

feel as if the odds are stacked up against me. What do you want to know about the security vans?''

"I understand from the reports that each country laid on a police escort for the security van from the airport to the gallery.''

"And vice versa," Van Dehn added. "And each country also had to provide two armed guards to sit with me in the back of the van for the duration of the journey.''

"Were these guards employed by the gallery or were they with a private firm hired by the gallery?''

"They were all from private firms.''

"Except for the Rijksmuseum.''

"No, we also used a private firm.''

"You only used their staff. The museum had its own security van built especially for the occasion," Whitlock said, consulting the dossier in front of him.

"That was Professor Broodendyk's idea. He wanted maximum publicity for the museum. He got it as well. Millions of people around the world saw the van on television. They would also have seen the logo advertising the museum on the side of the van.''

"And who chose the security firm?''

"Professor Broodendyk. He put it out to tender.''

"And how did he come to choose Keppler's?''

"They offered to do it for nothing.''

"So what did they get out of the deal? No publicity, no money.''

"On the contrary. They placed advertisements, all endorsed by Professor Broodendyk, in several of our national newspapers to say that they had handled the security arrangements for the painting's transportation to the airport. It was far better than having pictures of their van beamed around the world to television viewers who had no use for their services anyway. I believe they've doubled their turnover since those advertisements appeared in the press. So both the Rijksmuseum and Keppler's got the publicity they wanted.''

"And who chose the guards?''

"The security firm's MD, Horst Keppler." Van Dehn sipped his coffee then forced a weak smile. "I see what you're getting at, Mr. Whitlock. You think I could have been in collusion with the two guards. I hate to disillusion you, but for obvious security reasons Keppler kept all his men in suspense until that morning before announcing which two would be accompanying the painting to the airport. Nobody, not even the Chief of Police, knew their identities until Keppler made them public.''

"Keppler drove the van himself. I'd have thought that was a bit irregular.''

"He wasn't going to take any chances with such a priceless cargo." Van Dehn finished his coffee and replaced the cup carefully on the saucer. "And when you investigate Keppler, which I'm sure you will be doing, I think you'll find more than enough evidence to clear him of any involvement in the theft.''

"Evidence?'' Whitlock asked curiously.

"He's one of the most respected and sought-after security advisers in Amsterdam. I doubt he would have gained that kind of reputation if he weren't totally trustworthy.''

"Thank you, Mr. Van Dehn. I'll call you if I need to talk to you again.''

Van Dehn rose slowly to his feet. "I didn't steal the painting, Mr. Whitlock. I wouldn't do anything to discredit the museum. You must believe me.''

Whitlock said nothing.

Van Dehn swallowed nervously then left the room.

Whitlock was pleased with the way the questioning had

gone. The answers to most of his questions had been in the
dossier and the rest he could have got from Broodendyk. He
had purposely let Van Dehn take center stage—it had given
him a chance to watch Van Dehn on his own territory. Van
Dehn had started off nervously but when he assumed Whitlock was floundering he had gone on the offensive, almost to
the point of overconfidence, then, as he left, the self-pity had
suddenly emerged again. Whitlock had always believed
strongly in physiognomy and his conclusions were rarely
wrong. He was certain Van Dehn was involved in the switch
and, if it had happened in the back of the security van on the
way to Schiphol Airport, as he believed, then it would mean
tying in Keppler and the two guards as well. He already had
a file on Keppler and, as Van Dehn had rightly said, nobody
had anything but praise and admiration for him. Could Keppler be the brains behind it all? Or was there a draughtsman,
someone who had planned the crime without actually taking
part in it? And who now had the original painting? Keppler?
The draughtsman, if there was one? He knew he could go
on speculating for hours without achieving anything concrete. He had to prove Van Dehn's guilt. But how? The answer *had* to be on the videotape.

He picked up the remote control and pressed the "play"
button again.

Maartens had been right, Jan Lemmer was well known in
Jordaan. His twenty-five-foot houseboat was moored within
sight of the West Church, its green and yellow paint already
beginning to flake off in unsightly scabs from months of
neglect. It looked deserted.

Graham, his right hand curled around the Beretta in his
pocket, approached the houseboat cautiously and bent down
to peer through one of the windows facing out on to the

street. The sun's reflection off the glass made it impossible for him to see inside.

"What do you want?" a teenage girl demanded in a thick German accent as she emerged from the cabin onto the deck.

"I'm looking for Jan Lemmer," Graham said.

"Don't know him. Go away."

The man who emerged from the cabin was in his mid-thirties with a cruel face scarred from years of teenage acne. He was dressed in a pair of jeans and a white T-shirt. The tattoo on the side of his neck depicted two bloodstained knives crossing each other with the word *GEVAAR*, danger, underneath them in red lettering.

"You Lemmer?" Graham asked.

"*Ja*. What do you want?"

"To talk to you."

"Then talk."

"Not in front of your *daughter*," Graham retorted sharply.

"I'm not his daughter," the teenager snapped and grabbed Lemmer's arm.

Lemmer shrugged her off then grinned at Graham. "I like your humour, American."

"Wait until you hear the punchline. Either you talk to us or you talk to the police."

"You better come aboard." Lemmer turned to the teenager. "Take a walk."

"But Jan—"

"I said take a walk, Heidi. And I don't want to see you for half an hour. Understand?"

She nodded sullenly then jumped on to the pavement and headed up Bloemstraat in search of some company to while away the time.

"She's only a kid," Sabrina said in disgust.

"Eighteen," Lemmer countered with an indifferent shrug.

"She's sixteen, if that," Graham hissed.

"What about her parents? Do they know she's here?" Sabrina asked.

"She's a runaway. From Berlin. So, what do you want to talk to me about?"

"A robbery," Graham said.

Lemmer led them into the cabin. It was a shambles. The cushions from the benches on either side were strewn across the floor; empty bottles, dirty glasses and overflowing ashtrays littered the two cork tables and half-eaten takeaways were piled up beside the sliding door.

"I had some friends round last night," Lemmer said as if trying to justify the mess.

The both noticed the syringe and open sachet of heroin seconds before Lemmer covered them with a cushion.

Lemmer sat down, his hand resting lightly on the cushion. "What's this about a robbery, Mr. . . . I didn't get your name. Or the lady's."

"No, you didn't," Graham replied. "Two-and-a-half years ago a painting, measuring fifteen feet square, was stolen from a house in De Clerq Street. Remember it?"

"You think I had something to do with it?" Lemmer asked in a tone of amazement.

Graham, who had been pacing the floor, stopped in front of Lemmer. "We have a witness who would swear to it in a court of law. We also have an underage runaway living on this houseboat. And finally, we have a bag of heroin under the cushion beside you. You'll be lucky to get off with ten years."

Lemmer flung himself at Graham, activating the switchblade he had palmed from his back pocket moments earlier. The six-inch blade sliced across the front of Graham's parka as the two men crashed to the floor. Sabrina gripped the barrel of her Beretta tightly in her hand and aimed the butt down on to the bone behind Lemmer's left ear. Lemmer, sensing her behind him, looked round and the butt struck him in the face inches from his eye. He howled like a wounded animal as blood spurted from the gash but before he had time to react she hit him again, this time behind the ear. The switchblade dropped from his limp hand and he slumped, unconscious, over Graham.

Lemmer came round when the ice-cold water was splashed on to his face. He shook his head groggily but when he tried to move his hands he found them secured with a length of rope to the arms of a wooden chair which Graham had found in the bedroom below deck. His ankles were tied to the legs of the chair. He struggled furiously to free himself then sagged back in the chair, his head pounding. His spirits were soon raised when he noticed the crimson stain across the front of Graham's parka. The switchblade *had* cut him.

Graham read Lemmer's thoughts and squatted down in front of him. "It's your blood. Look at your vest."

"Bastard!" Lemmer snarled after looking down at his blood-spattered clothing.

"Who did you steal the painting for?" Sabrina asked.

"Go to hell, bitch!"

Sabrina shrugged. "At least I tried."

Graham pointed to Lemmer's arms. "No needle marks."

"I'm not on the needle."

"Dealers rarely are." Graham held up the syringe. "I'm sure you know what a 'hotshot' is."

The blood drained from Lemmer's face.

"I thought so. I'm sure you've used them before to get rid of troublesome customers. What did you substitute for the heroin? Strychnine? Battery acid?" Graham nodded at Lemmer's horrified expression. "I found some powdered battery acid in the engine-room. Enough to fill the syringe. I'm told the agony's unbearable before you do actually die. It's all a matter of finding the vein.''

Lemmer blinked as the sweat ran down his forehead into his eyes. ''You wouldn't do it.''

''One of the first lessons I learnt as a soldier was never to underestimate the enemy.'' Graham prodded the skin in and around the crook of Lemmer's right arm. ''It should only take me a couple of seconds to find the vein.''

''Who did you steal the painting for?'' Sabrina repeated.

''I've found it,'' Graham announced then pressed the tip of the needle against Lemmer's skin.

''Okay, I'll tell you,'' Lemmer shouted breathlessly, his eyes riveted on the needle. ''His name's Hamilton. Terence Hamilton.''

''And where can we find this Terence Hamilton?'' Sabrina asked.

''Kalverstraat. Near Madame Tussaud. He owns a gallery there.''

''Why did he want the painting?'' Sabrina pressed.

''He didn't say,'' Lemmer replied, struggling to speak as the saliva drained from his mouth.

Graham broke the skin with the tip of the needle.

''I don't know, I swear I don't know,'' Lemmer screamed, his face twisted in terror. ''All he said was that there was a thousand guilders in it for me. Five hundred for my two accomplices. We lifted the painting and took it to his gallery. He paid us and we left. I don't know what happened to it after that. You've got to believe me.''

Graham discarded the syringe then forced a handkerchief into Lemmer's mouth before crossing to where Sabrina was standing by the sliding door. He glanced back at Lemmer. ''Don't worry, your *daughter* will be back soon.''

There was only hatred in Lemmer's eyes.

"That was a neat trick pretending the talcum powder you found in the bedroom was residual battery acid," Sabrina said once they were clear of the houseboat. "Thank God he didn't call your bluff."

Graham shrugged. "He'd be dead if he had."

"But talc's harmless," Sabrina said with a puzzled frown.

"Yeah, *talc* is," Graham replied then turned his attention to finding a taxi.

Sabrina told the driver where to take them then slammed shut the perspex window and turned angrily to Graham. "You lied to me, Mike. It's the same old story over and over again. When are you going to start trusting me? Or is that expecting too much?"

Graham pondered her words as he stared at the meter through the perspex partition. "I do trust you, Sabrina. If I didn't, I would have put in for a transfer a long time ago."

His calmness surprised her and helped to take the sting out of her anger. "So why do you keep deceiving me if you trust me like you say?"

"You really don't understand, do you?"

Her emotions had ranged from anger to guilt in the space of a few seconds. "No," she said hesitantly.

"You know I underwent psychiatric therapy after Carrie and Mikey were kidnapped?"

She nodded, her eyes fixed on his face. He was giving her a rare, and probably brief, insight into the complexity of his embittered character.

"You also probably know I refused to cooperate with the staff. My attitude was one of total negativity towards any kind of breakthrough." He smiled to himself. "I believe I've even become a case study for psychiatry students at Princeton.''

''You had your reasons,'' she said softly.

''Yeah, and one of them had to do with trust. I was a Delta man for eleven years and I made a lot of friends in that time, especially in the latter years after I married Carrie. We'd spend Christmas with our families but New Year's was always a Delta affair. The party was held every year at the same farm in Kansas where we could make as much noise as we wanted until all hours of the morning. What I'm trying to say is that Delta was one big family. Then came the kidnapping. Someone, perhaps there were more, I don't know, let word slip of our mission in Libya. Whether it was intentional or unintentional is neither here nor there. What mattered was that all the deep-rooted trust I'd built up over those eleven years was lost in an instant. So when I joined UNACO I had to start from scratch again. As I said, I do trust you. But only up to a point. I feel the same way about C. W. It's going to be a long haul back to like it was at Delta.''

''But it can never be like Delta again, can't you see that?''

''Yeah, I know, but at the moment I need a yardstick and Delta's the only one I've got.'' He stared at the passing traffic then turned back to her. ''What would you have done if I'd told you back on the houseboat that it was battery acid, and not talcum powder, in the syringe?''

''I wouldn't have let it go as far as it did. You're so unpredictable, I couldn't have been sure that you wouldn't have injected Lemmer if he hadn't cooperated with us.''

''I'd have done it without batting an eyelid.''

''And killed him in cold blood?''

He shook his head sadly. ''We're so different. I've got no qualms about lowering myself to Lemmer's level to get the information I want. You, on the other hand, would rather treat him with kid gloves.''

"That's not true," she snapped back angrily. "I hate Lemmer and his kind just as much as you do but acting as judge, jury and executioner isn't the answer. They have to be brought to justice.''

"Justice? Ah yes, that's when drug pushers like Lemmer get ten years in jail for destroying countless innocent lives with their filthy trade but are back on the streets five years later to carry on where they left off. And justice is jailing a terrorist for life for murdering innocent people in the name of some cause the anarchistic bastard doesn't even understand, then letting him go when more anarchistic bastards hold more innocent people to ransom. Why don't you ask the victims' families what they think of this so-called justice?''

"I know what you're saying, Mike, but if you're prepared to kill the likes of Lemmer in cold blood then you've become an anarchist as well.''

"I don't agree. They're opposing the law, I'm upholding it. There is a difference.''

"It's a fine line, a very fine line.''

"And I'll continue to walk it until judicial systems around the world start to show more compassion towards the victims instead of trying to find irrelevant excuses for the defendants' behaviour.''

The taxi stopped and the driver rapped on the perspex partition to point out the gallery to them. It had once been the home of a wealthy Dutch nobleman and the date it was built, 1673, was visible on the ornately carved gablestone above one of the second floor windows. The words DE TERENCE HAMILTON GALERIJ, with the telephone number

underneath, were painted in black italics above the archi-
trave.

"I'll handle it," Sabrina said and opened the door.

"Worried what I might do to this Hamilton guy?"

"It had crossed my mind," she replied then indicated the
bloodstain on his parka. "That also might attract the wrong
kind of attention."

"Yeah, I guess so," he muttered then slumped back in the
seat.

She asked the driver to wait then crossed the street to the
gallery. Judging by the pictures adorning the walls she quickly
realized that the gallery specialized in prints of Dutch artists:
from the fifteenth-century biblical scenes of Bosch and
Geertgen through to the Modernist, Mondrian, and the Ex-
pressionist, Kruyder, of the twentieth century.

"Kan ik u helpen?" an assistant asked behind her.

"I hope so," Sabrina said giving the young woman a quick
smile. "I'd like to see Mr. Hamilton."

"Do you have an appointment?" the assistant asked in
impeccable English.

"I'm afraid not but I'm sure he'll want to see me anyway.
We have a mutual acquaintance. Jan Lemmer."

The assistant excused herself then returned a minute later.
"Mr. Hamilton has asked that you go straight up to his office.
It's at the top of those wooden stairs over there."

Sabrina climbed the stairs and found herself facing a ve-
neered door with the words: T. HAMILTON—DIRECTEUR
inscribed on it. She knocked.

"Come in."

Hamilton, a craggy-faced man in his late sixties, sat be-
hind a black desk surrounded by the cubist art of Braque and
Picasso. An enlarged print of Pyke Koch's disturbing
"Shooting Gallery" hung on the wall behind the desk.

"I believe you wanted to see me?" Hamilton said in a soft, effeminate voice then flicked a manicured hand in the direction of the leather chair in front of his desk. "Please, sit down, Miss . . . I don't believe my sales assistant gave me your name over the telephone."

"She didn't. I'm sure you're a busy man, Mr. Hamilton, so I'll come straight to the point. Two-and-a-half years ago a man called Jan Lemmer and two accomplices broke into a house on De Clerq Street and stole a worthless painting by a little-known seventeenth-century artist, Johan Seegers. They brought the painting to you. I want to know what happened to it after that."

He touched his cravat and smiled. "I'm afraid I don't know what you're talking about. And as you so rightly said, I am a busy man. So if you'd excuse me . . ." He indicated the door behind her.

She decided to play her hand Graham-style, and hope it wouldn't backfire on her. She grabbed the letter-opener from his desk and used it to tear a jagged scar across the nearest print, Picasso's "Acrobat and Young Harlequin."

"My God, what are you doing?" Hamilton shouted in horror, springing to his feet.

"Sit down," she replied stressing each word.

He did as he was told, his eyes flickering between the letter-opener in her hand and the damaged print on the wall behind her.

"You've got two options open to you," she told him. "The first is to call the police and have me arrested for vandalism. The second is to cooperate with me."

He stared at the telephone on his desk.

"Call them—but just remember, Lemmer's already confessed and his evidence would probably be enough to convict you as well. Even if you were acquitted, your career as an art dealer in Amsterdam would be over. That I *can* promise you.''

''Just who are you?''

She said nothing.

''All right,'' he said, unable to hold her withering stare any longer. ''I remember the Seegers painting.''

''Who wanted it?''

''A forger called Mikhailovich Toysgen.''

Toysgen? The name wasn't on the UNACO list.

''He isn't known here in the West,'' he said reading her puzzled expression. ''His paintings were, and still are by all accounts, immensely popular amongst the underground movements in Moscow. It's even rumoured that one of his Rembrandts is hanging somewhere in the Kremlin.''

''Go on,'' she prompted, careful to keep the excitement out of her voice.

''He specializes in seventeenth-century Dutch masters. I've only ever met him twice, once in Moscow, and the other time here in Amsterdam when he came to collect the Seegers painting.''

''Where can I find him?''

''I don't know. As I said, I've only met him once here in Amsterdam. An educated guess, and that's all it is, would be somewhere in the Jordaan. It's the nucleus of the city's art world. Try the Bohemer, a bar on Laurier Street. It's a regular haunt of young artists. Most of them don't have two pennies to rub together so a few guilders should be enough to loosen their tongues.''

''What does he look like?''

''Early fifties, short, balding.''

She left him staring at the damaged print and returned to the taxi.

"You took your time," Graham said after she had climbed in beside him.

"It was worth it." She told the driver where to take them, then, after closing the perspex partition, she recounted her conversation with Hamilton, this time making no effort to conceal the excitement in her voice.

Sabrina telephoned Whitlock from the callbox outside the Bohemer to update him on the latest developments, while inside the bar Graham had found out where Toysgen lived for the price of a round of drinks. His apartment was in Eiken-houtstraat, one of the numerous tributaries running off Roz-enstraat, less than half a mile away from the bar where Toysgen was a regular, but unsociable, drinker. The four young artists with Graham had never spoken to Toysgen (they only knew where he lived because one of them had once followed him there) and even the barman admitted he only knew him as "Mick." Toysgen, always dressed in the same unfashion-able black suit, would arrive every weekday at three-thirty in the afternoon, sit in the same corner of the bar, and drink a *borrel* of *jenever* with a pint of Lambek as a chaser. He always left at exactly three-forty-five. He had never deviated from the ritual in two years. By the time Sabrina had finished on the telephone Graham had built up a picture of Toysgen: an antisocial recluse who used his talent as an artist to prove to himself that he was better than those around him.

They walked the half mile to Eikenhoutstraat. Toysgen's apartment turned out to be on the top floor of a converted sixteenth-century red brick warehouse. The hoisting beam still jutted out from the roof but its wheel had long since rusted from years of disuse. The ground floor entrance led directly on to the cobbled sidestreet and consequently they were able to enter the building unchallenged.

The apartment door was open. Toysgen lay in the uncarpeted hallway, his sightless eyes staring up at them. His throat had been cut from ear to ear.

The fire escape door banged shut at the end of the corridor. Graham told Sabrina to check the apartment, then, unholstering his Beretta, sprinted the length of the corridor and flung open the door. He could hear the sound of footsteps pounding down the metal stairs. He gave chase. The door at the foot of the stairs was flung back against the wall, then silence. He reached the door seconds later, eased it open, and slipped out into the alley at the side of the building. He looked up and down the alley. It was deserted. To his left Eikenhoutstraat, to his right another alley. He chose to go left but had taken barely half a dozen steps when he heard a car's engine behind him. He swung round. A pale-blue Ford Granada had swung into the alley and was headed straight for him. Lemmer was behind the wheel. Graham glanced towards the fire escape door—he would never reach it before the car hit him. It was also too far to run to the safety of Eikenhoutstraat. And all the time the Granada was bearing down on him. He loosed off two shots at the oncoming car. Lemmer ducked as the bullets harmlessly pocked the windscreen. Graham dropped the Beretta and lunged at a windowsill on the side of the building, his muscles straining as he hoisted himself away from the road. He pulled his legs up sharply until his heels were touching his buttocks. Lemmer slewed the car against the side of the building and the passenger door buckled in a shower of sparks. The roof brushed Graham's knees but by the time he had dropped back on to the road and retrieved his Beretta the Granada had disappeared out into Eikenhoutstraat. He ran to the mouth of the alley but the Granada was gone. He cursed angrily, reholstered his Beretta, then returned to Toysgen's apartment where he told Sabrina what had happened.

"How could he have known we were on to Toysgen?" she asked once he had finished speaking.

He shrugged then gestured around him. "Find anything?"

"Not yet, but I still have to check the atelier."

They entered the atelier and looked around. The workbench, which ran the length of the wall opposite the door, was littered with brushes, palettes, bottles, jars and dozens of tubes of oil paints, many of which had fallen on to the floor where they had been trodden into the wooden boards. To their right were five paint-splattered easels. Four were empty. The fifth carried a canvas hidden underneath a paint-streaked white sheet. Sabrina removed the sheet and found herself looking at an unfinished reproduction of Vermeer's "The Lace Maker." A thought suddenly flashed through her mind. Would it have been used in a switch similar to the one involving the "Night Watch"?

"Sabrina, look at this."

She crossed to where Graham was crouched down in front of a batch of canvases. He pushed several of them to the side then pointed to the one now at the front. It was an eight foot by eight foot version of the "Night Watch," perfectly reproduced. She took a closer look at the dot in the center of the drum. It was crimson.

"I'd say we've found our forger," she said.

He nodded then moved to the door. "We're wasting our time here. UNACO can send round a couple of boffins to collect the paintings before they fall into the wrong hands."

"Where are we going?"

"Back to Lemmer's houseboat."

"If he's there," she said.

"There's only one way to find out. Come on, let's go."

* * *

A police cordon had been erected a hundred yards around Lemmer's houseboat. An ambulance and two police cars were parked beside the houseboat and a police launch, anchored in the canal, was being used as a base by a team of frogmen.

"What happened?" Sabrina asked the pipe-smoking man beside her.

"It's terrible, terrible," the man said shaking his head in disbelief. "I knew them both. Our houseboat isn't far from here."

"But what happened?"

"He killed her. She was only sixteen. He was never any good for her but she wouldn't listen to reason. She thought the world of him. I suppose she looked up to him as a kind of father figure. She was a runaway, you see."

"How did she die?" she asked knowing how morbid the question sounded.

"I overheard a policeman say that her throat had been cut. It's terrible, she was only a child."

"Have the police caught him?"

"No, he's on the run. He won't come back here. He wouldn't dare."

Graham nudged her and they left in search of a taxi to take them back to the Rijksmuseum.

Whitlock paused the videotape when Graham and Sabrina entered the room. "Well, what did you find out from Toysgen?"

"Not much, he's dead," Graham replied, crossing to the telephone. "All he said was that there's an inside man here at the museum. He died before he could tell us his name."

Sabrina turned to Graham in astonishment but he quickly

put his finger to his lips and beckoned them towards him. He held up the fountain pen lying beside the telephone. It contained a miniature transmitter in its cap.

"I'm meeting an informer tonight who knows the identity of this inside man." Graham replaced the pen in exactly the same position then moved to the door. "Come on, let's get something to eat."

Sabrina grabbed Graham's arm once they were in the foyer. "How did you know about the transmitter?"

"Call it a hunch. How else would Lemmer have got to Toysgen so quickly?" Graham gave Whitlock a reassuring pat on the back. "Stop looking so despondent. You didn't see it because you didn't know it was there."

"You bastard!" Sabrina snapped angrily at Graham. "No wonder you wanted me to call C. W. and tell him about Toysgen. You knew Van Dehn would bug the telephone and you wanted to see how he'd react to the news. I hope you're satisfied."

"I'm satisfied," Graham answered. "I bet Van Dehn's sweating it out in his office right now. I bet he also knows where Lemmer's hiding out. All he needs to do is make one call and I'm a marked man."

"You want Lemmer to come after you?"

"He's no good to us hiding in some backstreet hotel, C. W. Toysgen's dead and Hamilton's nothing more than a glorified fence. Lemmer's the only person who can finger Van Dehn. We have to draw him out into the open."

"And what makes you so sure he'll go along with your little scenario?" Sabrina asked sharply. "He's killed twice already, what's he got to lose?"

"It's not so much what he's got to lose, it's what he's got to gain. A deal with the Public Prosecutor's office for in-

stance. A reduction of sentence if he agrees to turn state's
evidence.''

"We don't have any clout with the Public Prosecutor,
Mike.''

"We know that, C. W., but Lemmer doesn't.''

Sabrina shook her head in frustration. ''You don't care that
Toysgen's dead because of your tricks and double dealings,
do you?''

"There's always going to be casualties in war.''

"But his death was so needless—''

"That's enough,'' Whitlock interceded, his hands raised.
"If you want to get at each other's throats then do it in private. Now come on, let's get some lunch.''

"I've suddenly lost my appetite,'' Graham muttered.
"Anyway, I want to take a closer look at the museum's security van. It might throw up a clue.''

Whitlock was glad of the respite. ''Okay, we'll see you
back here in thirty minutes.''

Graham collected the keys to the van and its lock-up garage from Broodendyk's secretary, then made his way round
to the back of the museum. A row of ten garages lined a
gravel road which, he discovered, joined up with Museumstraat at the back of the building. He unlocked the door numbered 10 and pulled it open. Switching on the neon strip light
he was surprised to find that the interior of the garage was
spacious enough for him to walk around the van. It was a
white Toyota van with a mesh grille over the windscreen and
four-inch-thick reinforced side panels. He unlocked the windowless back doors and opened them. The back of the van
was empty except for an assortment of ropes and fasteners
scattered across the reinforced steel floor. He climbed inside
and tapped the walls with his knuckles—they were solid.
After relocking the doors he lay flat on the ground and pulled

himself underneath the van. Again he found nothing amiss. He walked back to the museum, returned the keys to Brood-endyk's secretary, then went to the team's room where he sat down and rewound the videotape. With a sense of apprehension he reached for the remote control and pressed the "play" button.

He was watching it for a fourth time when Whitlock and Sabrina returned.

She put a packet on the table beside him. "I thought you might be hungry by now."

It had been Whitlock's idea of a peace offering.

"Yeah, thanks," Graham replied without taking his eyes off the screen.

"Seen anything?" Whitlock asked.

"No," Graham replied tersely. "I might though if you gave me some peace to watch it."

Whitlock was about to snap back when Graham grabbed his arm and pointed at the fountain pen. He led them to the other side of the room.

"I think I might have picked up on something," Graham said in a barely audible whisper. "But Van Dehn mustn't suspect a thing. He's got to believe that the only way I can nail him is by meeting this mysterious informer tonight."

They left the room, closing the door silently behind them.

"Well?" Whitlock demanded. "I've sat through that video a good fifteen times and I'd swear there was nothing on it to suggest that the switch was made here in Amsterdam."

"I'd have agreed with you had I not seen the van."

"You found something in the van?" Sabrina asked.

"Nothing so obvious," Graham replied then looked at Whitlock. "I was able to walk around freely in the back of the van. On the video, however, one of the men had to squeeze his way to the front to secure the fasteners. It could have been the camera angle. It could even have been the proximity of the painting to the wall. But I still say it's worth investigating further.''

"Meaning?'' Whitlock asked.

"We get the men back to re-enact the loading procedure. That way we can see whether false panels had been fitted against the walls.''

"What are you going to use instead of the painting?'' Sabrina asked.

Graham was baffled.

Whitlock held up a finger. ''As far as I know, the museum had a second box constructed, the same weight and size as the one used to carry the painting, which was used in a series of dummy runs. I can't see them having thrown it away.''

"Can you talk to Broodendyk about it, C. W.?'' Graham asked. ''See if you can't set it up for tomorrow morning.''

"Sure,'' Whitlock replied then hurried down the corridor towards Broodendyk's office.

"And what are we going to do?'' Sabrina asked.

"You're going to watch the video and familiarize yourself with it. I'm going to eat that food you brought for me. I'm starving.''

The sole topic of conversation at dinner was work. It ranged from what they thought would happen when the loading procedure was re-enacted the following day to how they felt Strike Force Two would fare in Libya.

Graham drank the last of his coffee then dabbed his mouth with a napkin. ''Okay, I'm ready.''

Whitlock signed the bill to his room number then delved into his pocket and placed a button-shaped transmitter on the table. ''It can only be tracked within a radius of five hundred yards. So stick to the plan.''

"Yeah, yeah," Graham muttered and pocketed the transmitter. "Give me a couple of minutes' head start. Lemmer mustn't have any inkling that I'm being followed."

"We agreed on that," Whitlock said.

"*If* Lemmer's outside waiting to follow you," Sabrina added.

"He'll be out there all right. It's too good an opportunity for Van Dehn to miss."

They left the dining-room and rode the lift to the third floor. Their rooms were adjoining.

Whitlock paused outside his door. "Okay, synchronize watches."

"I make it eight-twenty-four," Graham said.

Whitlock and Sabrina agreed.

"You've got three minutes," Whitlock said.

"Three minutes," Graham repeated then disappeared into his room.

He automatically reached for his parka, then remembered the bloodstain and opened the wardrobe where the jacket Whitlock had lent him was hanging. He unhooked it and pulled it on. It was a near perfect fit. He pushed a clip into his Beretta and pocketed it. Although he had adapted to the Beretta, which Sabrina had initially suggested he use, he still secretly hankered after the Colt .45 he had used first in Vietnam and later with Delta. It was the more powerful handgun but its weakness was its magazine capacity. Seven rounds. The Beretta's magazine held fifteen rounds. Those eight extra bullets had made all the difference in past assignments.

The lift reached the foyer and he handed in his key at the reception desk before hurrying out into the street. The brightly lit Rijksmuseum stood less than a hundred yards away. He checked his watch. Ninety seconds were already up. He took the transmitter from his pocket and, looking around slowly at the approaching pedestrians, chose a middle-aged businessman clutching a battered leather brief-case as his target. As he drew abreast of the man he pretended to stumble against him and deftly dropped the transmitter into the man's jacket pocket. He immediately apologized for his clumsiness but the man just smiled and continued walking. At least the man was heading in the direction Whitlock and Sabrina had thought *he* would take. He pushed his hands into his pockets and hurried up the Stadshouderskade—in the opposite direction to the man. He was damned if he would be tagged like some homing pigeon. He would get Lemmer his way.

He made a show of pausing to glance in shop windows to see if he was being followed—Lemmer would expect it of him. Although he never saw Lemmer he knew the Dutchman would be somewhere behind him. He left the Stadshouder-skade at its junction with Hoofstraat and continued in the direction of Vondelpark, a 120-acre spread of lakes and lawns. It was the same route he had taken before dinner on the pretext of wanting to build up an appetite. He had found the warehouse in Burchstraat, one of the many sidestreets leading off from P.C. Hooftstraat. The warehouse was sim-ilar to the one Toysgen had lived in, only it was deserted. It was also condemned. He turned into Burchstraat and looked up at the warehouse silhouetted eerily in the dim street-lighting. He pushed the door open with his fingertips and winced as the creaking hinges seemed to echo around the silence of his surroundings. The windows had long since been vandalized and the light fell through the apertures, cast-ing uneven shadows across the graffiti-scrawled walls. He pulled the Beretta from his pocket and made his way cau-tiously to the stairs against the far wall. Part of the banister had collapsed and those stairs illuminated by the light were cracked and rotting. He decided against chancing them.

A shadow fell over him but as he turned Lemmer lunged through the window, catching him on the side of the head with his elbow. The Beretta spun from Graham's hand as both men crashed against the staircase, which collapsed under their combined weight. Graham snatched up a banister strut but before he could aim a blow at Lemmer he was caught in the midriff with a well-timed punch. He stumbled back against the wall and was showered in dust and plaster as the ceiling shook above him. Lemmer, sensing that Graham was winded, followed up with two more body punches. The piece of wood fell from Graham's hand and another punch, this time to the back of the head, dropped him to his knees. Lemmer scooped up a length of rusted chain and looped it around Graham's throat, twisting it savagely at the back of his neck. Graham clawed at the chain as it dug into his neck but he could make no impression on Lemmer's stranglehold. He felt himself losing consciousness. Lemmer, now holding the chain in one hand, used his other hand to pull the switchblade from his pocket and flick it open inches from his leg. He yanked on the chain to jerk Graham's neck back but, as he reached down to draw the blade across the exposed throat, the door behind him was kicked open with such force that it splintered against the adjacent wall. Sabrina shot Lemmer twice in the back. Lemmer swayed for a moment then dropped to the ground, impaling himself on his switchblade. Whitlock pushed past her and, pressing his Browning into the nape of Lemmer's neck, felt for a pulse. There was none. Sabrina pocketed her Beretta and hurried across to where Graham lay, the chain still wrapped around his neck. She eased it off carefully, gritting her teeth as she felt it pulling at the flesh. Although the links had broken the skin there was very little blood. She sat him up against the wall and dabbed the blood away with her handkerchief, her eyes continually flickering towards his face as she waited for him to regain consciousness.

Whitlock crouched beside her, his hand resting lightly on her shoulder. "How is he?"

"He'll be okay," she replied grimly. "He'll have a bruise for the next couple of weeks though."

Graham began to cough violently. He reached for his throat but Sabrina pushed his hand down—he would only aggravate the injury by rubbing it. His breathing was ragged and, after shaking his head in an attempt to clear the dizziness, he opened his eyes and looked from Sabrina to Whitlock then finally to Lemmer sprawled face down on the ground behind them.

"Dead," Whitlock said then shook his head angrily. "That should have been you. You can thank your lucky stars that Sabrina knows you like she does. She predicted you'd pull a stunt like this. That's why we kept you in our sights right from the time you left the hotel. Christ, Mike, what gets into you to try these madcap schemes? We're your partners, dammit! Is it really too much to ask you to work *with* us, not against us?"

Sabrina put her hand on Whitlock's arm. "Give him a chance, C. W. There'll be time for recriminations later."

Whitlock got to his feet and held out a hand towards Graham. "Come on then, let's get you back to the hotel."

"I can manage . . . by myself," Graham whispered in a rasping voice.

"Ever the independent," Whitlock said then turned his attention to dragging Lemmer's body underneath the partially collapsed staircase.

"My gun," Graham whispered and pointed in the general direction he thought it had gone.

Whitlock scoured the area and found the Beretta near the door. He pocketed it then hurried down into Hoofstraat where he flagged down a taxi and had it return with him to the warehouse. Graham, although unsteady on his feet, refused any assistance and got into the taxi by himself. Whitlock and Sabrina exchanged knowing glances then climbed in after him. She closed the door and instructed the driver to take them back to the hotel.

Whitlock entered his room, kicked off his shoes, and switched on the television set. A pop music programme. He changed channels. A studio discussion. The card on top of the television set explained in both Dutch and English that the BBC could be obtained on the third channel. He pressed the button. A *Carry On* film. He grunted in disgust but left it on and after checking the room for listening devices, the standard procedure for any operative who had left his room unattended for any length of time, he crossed to the bed. He positioned a pillow against the headboard before lying down and reaching for the copy of the *Herald Tribune* on the table beside him. He turned to the crossword, folded the newspaper in half, then picked up his fountain pen and read the first clue. After going through the first five clues without success he tossed the newspaper onto the floor and rubbed his eyes wearily. It had been a long day. He knew that was just an excuse, his mind was too preoccupied with other things to be bothered with some trivial crossword puzzle.

He had spent twenty-five minutes driving around Amsterdam in search of an all-night chemist to buy some pain-killers, only to be told on his return that Graham was already asleep. It had been a wasted trip. Graham worried him, risking his life for the sake of his stubborn, maverick pride. If he told Kolchinsky what had happened it could have serious repercussions for Graham. Kolchinsky would be obliged to report the matter to Philpott who had already reprimanded Graham verbally about his anomalous behaviour while on assignment. Another reprimand could lead to a written warning which Philpott would then have to pass on to the Secretary-General. Although the Secretary-General rarely interfered with UNACO, having complete confidence in Philpott, he still had the power to have Graham suspended indefinitely while his position was reviewed.

The telephone rang.

He lifted the receiver. "Hello?"

"C. W.?"

"Yes."

"It's Sergei."

He swung his legs off the bed and related the day's events to Kolchinsky, culminating in the fight between Graham and Lemmer.

"How bad is Michael's injury?"

"His neck's badly bruised, that's all."

"But if he was bugged like you say, why did it take you and Sabrina so long to get to him?" Kolchinsky demanded.

It was the question Whitlock had been dreading. Should he tell the truth, for Graham's own good, before his independence led to a fatal mistake? Or should he stand by a colleague whom he admired and respected as one of the best in UNACO? Then a thought struck him. If he told the truth and Graham was suspended after the assignment, it would be on the whim of a politician five thousand miles away. And he was damned if he would let that happen.

"It was my fault," he said after a brief silence. "I thought

Sabrina and I should hold back in case Lemmer saw us. I misjudged the distance.''

"It's not like you to make that kind of mistake, C. W.''

"I'm only human, Sergei. The main thing is we got there in time.''

"Are you sure nothing's bothering you? The colonel was worried about you before you left New York.''

Whitlock silently cursed Graham for heaping more suspicion on him. "I'm fine, Sergei. As I said, I made a mistake. We all make them. Me, you, even the colonel.''

"I guess so,'' Kolchinsky muttered.

"What's the latest on the Libyan assignment?''

"The Secretary-General held a private meeting with their ambassador earlier today.''

"And?''

"No joy. The Libyans are refusing to enter into any kind of negotiations.''

"And the Libyans still don't know who they are, or for what organization they're working?''

"No.''

"So when are you sending in Strike Force Two?''

"We're waiting for the nod from the Secretary-General. He's determined to exhaust all diplomatic channels first.''

"Damn politicians, all they do is sit on their backsides making decisions—''

"That's enough, C. W.,'' Kolchinsky cut in sharply. "We're just as frustrated over here but our hands are tied on this one. The Secretary-General believes what he's doing is right.''

"So did Chamberlain in '38,'' Whitlock snapped.

"It's no use debating the issue over the telephone, C. W. We can't make a move without the Secretary-General's say-so.''

"Will you be flying to Amsterdam tomorrow?"

"I'm going to be deskbound until . . ." Kolchinsky sighed deeply, "who knows? At least until the Secretary-General's decided how he wants to tackle the Libyan problem."

"I'll give you a call tomorrow then."

"Fine. If something should crop up I'll have Jacques Rust fly down from Zurich to handle it."

The line went dead.

Whitlock replaced the receiver then lay back on the bed, his hands cupped behind his head, his eyes staring absently at the ceiling. He knew exactly what Martin Cohen and his Strike Force Two colleagues would be feeling at that moment. Anger, tempered by frustration and uncertainty. It was all very well for the Secretary-General to want to handle the situation diplomatically, they weren't his friends sweating it out in some godforsaken jail. Not that the situation was new to him. Two years earlier, when Jacques Rust had still been a part of the team, the three of them (it had been Sabrina's baptism of fire if he remembered correctly) had been kept on standby while the Secretary-General attempted to negotiate the release of a UNACO operative from a Moroccan jail where he was being held for the clumsy killing of a Chinese double agent. Seventy hours later, with the Secretary-General finally admitting defeat, Strike Force Three were dispatched to Morocco to break their colleague out of jail. The mission had been a complete success and on their return to New York the operative had been hastily assigned a post at the Test Center.

The thought of New York guiltily reminded him of Carmen. He had promised to call her that night. But what if she was still angry? What if they had another bitter argument like the one they had had at the apartment before he left for the airport? He knew the only way to answer those doubts was to phone her. He was about to ring the apartment when he remembered it was the night she worked late at the surgery.

"Good evening, Dr. Whitlock's consulting rooms," a female voice answered.

"Laura, it's C. W. Whitlock. Is my wife still there?"

Like Carmen, Laura Dos Santos was Puerto Rican. She had been Carmen's receptionist for the past seven years.

"Yes, she's still here, Mr. Whitlock. I'll put you through to the surgery."

A second receiver was picked up. "Hello, Dr. Carmen Whitlock speaking."

"Hi, it's me. Can you talk?"

"I don't have anyone in the surgery right now if that's what you mean." Her voice was cold and remote.

"How are you?"

"I'm surprised you still care after your performance at the apartment yesterday."

He bit back his rising temper. Why the hell had he bothered calling her? It was obvious they were going to pick up the quarrel where they had left off the previous day.

"Carmen, I don't want to argue with you over the phone."

"No, you'd rather do that in person. Don't call me again, C. W. We'll discuss it all when you get back to New York."

"Why can't we discuss it now?" he demanded.

"Take care of yourself," she said in an emotional voice. The line went dead.

"Carmen?" he shouted into the mouthpiece. "Carmen, are you there?"

He slammed the receiver back into the cradle then went to run himself a hot bath.

It was going to be a long, restless night.

SIX

It had rained throughout the night, letting up only at dawn. Three hours later the heavy rainclouds still threatened the city and most commuters had wisely brought a raincoat or an umbrella in anticipation of the inevitable downpour.

Van Dehn was no exception, though he was regretting not having taken off his gaberdine raincoat before leaving for work in his Ford Fiesta. He brought the car to a halt when the lights changed to red at the intersection of Helmersstaat and the Stadshouderskade and wiped the sweat from his face with the back of his hand. He was scared. Lemmer should have called by midnight to confirm that he had killed Graham's mysterious informer. But no call. What had happened? Was the informer dead? Was Lemmer dead, or had he made a break for the Belgian border as he had been threatening to do the previous evening? Had he been arrested? These were the questions which had kept him awake for most of the night. The most worrying question of all, however, was whether this informer had managed to pass on whatever incriminating evidence they had to Graham. If they had, he could expect to be arrested once he reached the museum. This thought had given rise to much deliberation during the night. At one point he had even started to pack a suitcase in readiness to flee the country but logic had finally prevailed and he had abandoned the idea. If Graham had some concrete evidence against him why not have him arrested straight away? Why wait until the morning when he might, or might not, arrive for work at the museum? This had given him some peace of mind—he had even managed a couple of hours' sleep after that.

As he turned the car into Museumstraat he saw the security van parked in front of the main steps, its back doors open, exactly as it had been that morning when the original was taken to the airport. His initial feeling of uncertainty quickly mellowed to one of confidence. Why would they be re-enacting the loading procedure, which had been captured on film, unless they were grabbing at straws? He parked his car, wiped his face again, then climbed out and locked the door behind him.

Graham, Whitlock, Sabrina and Broodendyk watched from a vantage point behind the van as the four original removal men loaded the dummy container for a third successive time.

One of the men glanced back at them. "You want us to do as before?"

"Exactly the same," Graham called back.

One side of the container was lowered to the floor then pushed up against the side of the van and manoeuvred into place. Two of the men held it upright while the other two set about securing it with the ropes and fasteners. When they finished the spokesman tugged at the container and, satisfied that it was firmly harnessed, gave them a thumbs-up sign.

Graham looked at Broodendyk. "Well, you said this is where the cameraman stood to take the video. I think what you've seen speaks for itself."

Broodendyk shook his head in disbelief then looked round at Van Dehn. "Why, Mils? Money?"

Van Dehn swallowed nervously. "Professor Broodendyk, you don't think—" He stopped mid-sentence when Graham swung round to face him. The discoloured bruise stood out vividly against the open collar of his white shirt.

"We don't *think*, we know." Graham noticed Van Dehn's eyes riveted on the bruise. "Pretty, isn't it?"

"How—"

"How?" Graham repeated sarcastically. "Lemmer, that's how."

Van Dehn looked to Broodendyk, his last hope of an ally. "Who is this Lemmer? What's this all about?"

"I'll tell you what it's all about," Graham said when Broodendyk was reluctant to venture an explanation. "Yesterday I examined the van and was able to move about freely inside. But when I watched the video I noticed that one of the men had to squeeze his way to the front to secure the painting to the side of the van. I wasn't sure whether there was any significance in this so I had the four men brought back to re-enact the loading procedure. The four of us studied that section of the video this morning before getting the men to load the dummy container into the van. It was done three times, and each time with the same result. The man who had originally fastened the front of the painting had as much freedom in the van as I did. So why was it different in the video? Because false panels had been fitted in the van which tapered from the front to the rear, creating a false perspective that the camera wouldn't have been able to detect. You were locked in the back of the van with the two security guards from the time it left here until it arrived at the airport. Seeing that you had a police escort, the only time you could have switched containers was en route to the airport. Sound familiar?''

Van Dehn made a break for his car only to find the driver's door locked. He was about to flee towards the Singelgracht when Graham caught up with him and punched him in the stomach. Van Dehn crumpled to the ground, his hands gripped tightly over his midriff.

''Mike, that's enough,'' Whitlock shouted and pulled Graham away. ''What's got into you?''

Graham shrugged Whitlock's hand off his arm. ''I don't like people sending hatchet men after me.''

Sabrina noticed the four removal men approaching, their eyes narrowed as they took in the scene before them. ''Get rid of them,'' she said to Broodendyk.

Broodendyk hesitated.

''Do you want them to know about the switch?'' she added.

Broodendyk held up his hands as he moved towards them and within seconds they were heading back to the van, which was then driven to the lock-up garage.

Whitlock helped Van Dehn into the foyer where Broodendyk announced that the interrogation could be conducted in his study.

''Where will you go?'' Graham asked.

Broodendyk looked baffled.

''You don't have the necessary clearance to sit in on the questioning,'' Graham said to clarify the point.

''But I'm responsible for the painting. I have a right to know what happened to it.'' Broodendyk turned to Whitlock and Sabrina for support. They both shook their heads. ''Who would I need to contact to get this clearance?''

Sabrina shrugged. ''You could try your Prime Minister.''

''The Prime Minister?'' Broodendyk replied in amazement then threw up his hands in defeat. "Okay, I get the picture. How long will you need my study for?"

Sabrina spoke softly to Graham then turned back to Broodendyk. "We appreciate the offer but we'd prefer to use the room you had set aside for us yesterday."

"Will I be told anything?"

Sabrina watched Graham and Whitlock lead Van Dehn down the corridor before answering Broodendyk. "We're not at liberty to tell you anything. A report of our findings will be sent to your Prime Minister. It's completely up to him whether he forwards you a copy of the report."

Van Dehn looked up when Sabrina entered the room. He sat on one of the wooden chairs, his hands clasped tightly together on the table in front of him. Whitlock was perched on the sill of the room's only window and Graham was turning the fountain pen around absently in his fingers as he stared at the back of Van Dehn's head, willing him to try and make a break for it again. He still had a lot of pent-up anger to release.

"Are you guys ready?" Sabrina asked.

Graham nodded and tossed the pen on to the table. "Yours, I believe?"

Van Dehn picked the pen up, looked at it, then shook his head. "I've never seen it before in my life."

Graham grabbed Van Dehn by the collar, hauled him to his feet, and slammed him up against the wall. "I've had about all I can take from you. You *will* cooperate with us, that I promise you."

Van Dehn stared back defiantly at Graham. "You've got nothing on me and you know it. Your theory would never stand up in a court of law."

"But Lemmer's confession would," Whitlock said, appearing behind Graham.

"He never knew me by name. . . ." Van Dehn blurted out then trailed off as he realized what he'd just said.

Whitlock smiled as he crossed to the second wooden chair, turned it around and sat astride it, his arms resting on its back.

Van Dehn sat down again and glanced across at the telephone. "I want my lawyer present before I say anything else."

"You can have your lawyer present when you talk to the police," Whitlock replied.

"It's my right to have my lawyer here now!" Van Dehn retorted.

Whitlock nodded in agreement. "Sure it is, but before you call him bear in mind that we have to give the police a transcript of what's said in here. It's up to us what we leave out. They don't know who killed Toysgen. We do. They don't have the murder weapon. We do. They don't have a link between you and Lemmer. We do. Dropping the accessory to murder charge could mean the difference between ten years and life."

"What about Lemmer's confession? The police are sure to link us when they compare notes."

"Lemmer never made a confession. He's dead." Whitlock held Van Dehn's stare. "So you see, it would be in your best interests to cooperate with us."

"And what's to stop you from going back on your word once I've told you what I know?"

"Nothing," Whitlock replied matter-of-factly. "But we're the only chance you've got."

"I'll cooperate," Van Dehn said finally in a barely audible voice.

Sabrina removed the Sony micro-cassette player from her bag and placed it on the table between Whitlock and Van Dehn.

Whitlock activated it. "Who hired you to steal the painting?"

"André Drago."

Whitlock glanced at Graham and Sabrina but, like him, they had never heard the name before. "What do you know about him?"

"Only that he's the personal secretary to a multimillionaire called Martin Schrader."

"Schrader?" Whitlock muttered thoughtfully. "The name rings a bell. . . ."

Sabrina closed her eyes and pinched the bridge of her nose with her thumb and forefinger as she too struggled to place the name.

"You guys have got real short memories," Graham said looking from Whitlock to Sabrina. "Remember the big scandal that hit the European business community within months of the Russian invasion of Afghanistan in '79? Hecht, the German arms firm, were exposed after an undercover operation by European customs officers proved they were selling chemical weapons to the Russians for use against the Mujahideen. The board was forced to resign and the firm's owner, Martin Schrader, had to sell the company well below its market value. The last I heard he'd fled the country." He glanced at Van Dehn. "Where's he living now?"

"Rio de Janeiro."

"Did you ever meet him?" Sabrina asked.

"No. Drago handled everything."

"Why were you chosen and not, say, Broodendyk, or the curator, Geyser?" Whitlock asked.

"Broodendyk was never considered. He was too honest. Geyser drinks with a group of friends every weekend and Drago thought he might have let something slip in a moment of weakness. I hardly ever drink and I don't have many friends. He said I was the ideal choice."

"And who chose Toysgen?" Whitlock continued.

"Schrader, even though he never actually met him. As I said, Drago handled everything. Toysgen was smuggled out of Russia for the sole purpose of painting the forgery. He was the best forger in Moscow and Rembrandt had always been his favourite artist."

"Did Drago hire Hamilton and Lemmer as well?" Whitlock asked.

"No, I did. Drago put me in charge of the entire Amsterdam operation. My first task was to find a suitable mount for Toysgen to use for the back of his forgery. I approached Hamilton and he came up with the Seegers painting. It was perfect."

"Did Hamilton know why you wanted it?" Sabrina asked.

"No, he only knew I wanted a painting of that particular size. Toysgen told me to get it for him but as I didn't know any criminals, Hamilton suggested I use Lemmer. He used to work for Hamilton. I never met Lemmer. . . ." Van Dehn paused to glare at Whitlock. "We only spoke on the telephone using codenames. It was Drago's idea—he wanted as few people as possible to know what was going on."

"Whose idea was it to kill Toysgen?" Graham queried.

Van Dehn raked his fingers through his damp hair. "I panicked when I realized you were on to him. I had to silence him, he would have talked if you'd got to him first. I didn't want to do it, I really didn't. You must believe me."

"So you told Lemmer to kill him?" Whitlock said.

Van Dehn nodded dejectedly then noticed Whitlock pointing at the micro-cassette player. "Yes," he muttered.

"How did you come to recruit Keppler?" Sabrina asked.

Van Dehn stared at the turning spools then looked up

sharply at Whitlock. "You will edit all references to my in-volvement in the murder? You promised."

"Just answer the question," Graham snapped, hovering menacingly over Van Dehn. "How did you come to recruit Keppler?"

"I didn't. Drago recruited him."

Whitlock nodded to himself, recalling the discussion he had had with Van Dehn the previous day. "And he made sure of getting the contract by offering to transport the paint-ing to the airport for nothing."

"So you and the two guards switched the paintings on the way to the airport. After the forgery had been unloaded, Keppler didn't need a police escort to drive a supposedly empty van back to the museum, so he had plenty of time to offload the original and remove the false panels before re-turning to the museum. Am I right?"

"Yes," Van Dehn replied without looking at Graham.

"How much were you to be paid to make the switch?" Sabrina asked.

"I was promised ten million dollars if it succeeded."

"And how much were you paid in advance?" she contin-ued.

"Drago put a million dollars in a Swiss account for me. He said I'd receive the balance once the forgery was returned to the museum."

"What were the others paid?" Whitlock asked.

"Toysgen was paid half a million dollars, but it was more of a token gesture than anything else. He wasn't interested in the money. I paid Lemmer and Hamilton from an expense account Drago opened for me here in Amsterdam. I don't know about Keppler or his guards, I assume Drago paid them."

Graham sat on the edge of the desk. "One and a half million dollars plus expenses for one of the world's most priceless paintings. I'd say Schrader's got himself a bargain."

"Ten and a half million plus expenses," Van Dehn corrected him.

Graham eyed Van Dehn contemptuously. "You really are naïve, aren't you? Drago only put that million in your account to whet your appetite. He'd no intention of paying you the balance. You knew too much."

Van Dehn looked to Whitlock who nodded his head in agreement. "I'd have to go along with that. If he was sincere he'd have put at least half the money in this Swiss account of yours."

Van Dehn stared at his trembling hands. "How could I have been so blind? He's been using me all along, hasn't he?"

"Does Drago know the forgery's been discovered?" Sabrina asked, breaking the sudden silence.

Van Dehn shook his head. "No. He said that if the switch was discovered it would make headline news on every television station and in every newspaper around the world. He didn't bargain on an undercover investigation."

Graham smiled. "I love overconfident opposition, they always make mistakes."

His words reminded Sabrina of Smylie at the Test Center. He had called her impulsive and overconfident. She wondered whether Graham's words were indirectly aimed at her. But she wasn't in opposition to him. Well, she knew that . . . but did he?

"And you never thought of calling Drago?" Whitlock asked.

"And risk losing ten million dollars?"

"Did you know about the flaw in the forgery?" Sabrina asked.

"*Ja*, I knew about it. It's actually called a 'signature.' A lot of forgers incorporate them into their paintings. It's done to add a touch of individualism to the work. Drago knew about it as well but neither of us could get Toysgen to correct it."

"Did your wife know about the switch?" Whitlock asked.

Van Dehn stared guiltily at the micro-cassette player. "No. I intended to leave her and use the money to start a new life for myself. Our marriage has been over for years. It wouldn't have mattered what I'd done, she wouldn't have cared."

"Describe Drago," Whitlock said gruffly as he pushed any thoughts of his own marriage from his mind, determined to concentrate on the interrogation.

"Early thirties. He wore a lot of white. It matched his hair. It was bleached and cropped close to his head. He had a very thin face and wore wire-rimmed glasses. He smiled a lot but it never showed in his eyes. They always remained expressionless, almost as if he was looking through me. It was . . . unnerving." Van Dehn gestured towards the telephone. "Well, I've told you everything I know. Aren't you going to call the police now?"

"They won't be involved at this stage," Whitlock explained. "You'll be kept under house arrest until the painting's been recovered. Only then will charges be brought against you."

"That's against the law!" Van Dehn snapped.

"In theory," Whitlock replied.

"My lawyer will blow this wide open. Holding me against my wishes in my own home is a crime in itself."

"You're not making this any easier on yourself," Whitlock said. "I thought we'd already come to an arrangement?"

"We did, only you're twisting it now to suit your own purposes."

Graham leaned across the table, his finger inches from Van Dehn's face. "You start playing games with us and we'll see to it that you're a marked man even before you reach the prison gates. That's a promise."

Van Dehn wiped his hand across his clammy forehead. "Okay, I'll do what you want."

Graham and Whitlock led him from the room. Sabrina telephoned Pieter de Jongh who promised to have a twenty-four-hour guard mounted on Van Dehn's house, starting immediately. She replaced the receiver, picked up the micro-cassette player, and hurried after them.

Jacques Rust touched down at Schiphol Airport on board a Cessna 340 which was registered to one of UNACO's shell companies in Zurich. A black Mercedes was waiting on the runway to take him straight to the Park Hotel.

Rust was a forty-two-year-old Frenchman with thinning black hair, which he insisted on keeping short, and pale-blue eyes set into a ruggedly handsome face. After a distinguished career with the French Service de Documentation Extérieure et de Contre-Espionage spanning fourteen years, he had resigned to join UNACO where he and Whitlock had worked together until Philpott's budget was increased to allow him another ten operatives to add to the twenty he already had. Philpott and Kolchinsky then restructured UNACO's entire field operation and from this the revolutionary Strike Force teams were born. Sabrina was put with Rust and Whitlock so that she could learn the ropes as quickly as possible and within six months Strike Force Three was widely regarded as the most professional of the ten teams. Rust still believed this to be true. Graham, despite his maverick tendencies, had been an inspired replacement.

A year after its implementation, Strike Force Three was

dispatched to Marseilles to bust an international drug ring operating between France and Algeria. Rust was on a routine stakeout with Sabrina at the docks when they had come under fire and he was hit in the spine as he tried to withdraw to safer ground. It left him paralysed from the waist down. After his release from hospital he was installed at the Command Center as a senior adviser but when the head of European operations was killed in a car crash he was appointed as the dead man's successor, much to the surprise of many insiders who had assumed that the post would go to Kolchinsky. None of them had Philpott's vision. One of the reasons why Kolchinsky had jumped at the chance to join UNACO was to get away from his desk job at the Lubianka. He was essentially a field man. Rust's field days were over and he had been more than willing to try his hand at management. With his intelligence, his acute perception of European affairs and his invaluable contacts across the continent, he had been tailor-made for the job. Now, after a year as head of European operations, he had won over his critics with his friendliness, dedication and professionalism.

The Mercedes drew up in front of the Park Hotel. The driver jumped out, opened the boot, and removed the portable wheelchair which had been designed especially for Rust. The driver assembled it quickly then pushed it round to the back door. The doorman, having watched this from a distance, hurried over and opened the back door.

"Let me help you, sir."

Rust recoiled, his hands held up defensively in front of him. "I'm not incapable!"

"I'm sorry, sir," the doorman said.

Rust smiled ruefully. "*Non*, I'm the one who should apologize. I know you mean well, but I can manage by myself. Thank you anyway."

Rust pressed his hands down on to the seat and, using them to stabilize himself, shifted his body towards the open door. He then reached out to grab the nearest arm but only managed to knock it with his hand. Although the brakes were locked, the wheelchair still moved sideways. He cursed under his breath. The doorman stepped forward to reposition the wheelchair but the driver grabbed his arm and warned him not to interfere; it wouldn't be appreciated. Rust gripped the edge of the seat and leaned precariously out of the car to pull the wheelchair back towards him. This time he gripped the arm firmly and, using his other hand as an anchor, hoisted himself off the seat and edged towards the wheelchair. He twisted his body then, gritting his teeth, pushed himself backwards into the wheelchair. His face was red from the exertion. He activated the engine underneath the seat by means of a remote control built into one of the arms then unlocked the brakes and turned the wheelchair round to face the hotel.

"It's actually a lot easier than it looks," he said to the doorman.

The doorman doubted it. He doffed his cap in admiration then hurried towards a taxi which had pulled up behind the Mercedes.

"I shouldn't be very long," Rust said taking his attaché case from the driver.

"Yes, sir," the driver replied then climbed back behind the wheel.

Rust steered his wheelchair up to the electronic doors which parted in front of him, then, once in the foyer, he scanned the reception area for the prettiest receptionist and asked her for Sabrina's room number. She told him then alerted a porter who crossed to the lift to push the button for Rust.

"*Non, non,*" Rust called out then reached down the side

of his chair and produced a plastic pointer which he used to press the button.

It was a short distance from the lift to Sabrina's room. He knocked once on the door.

Sabrina opened it.

"Bonjour, chérie, comment vas-tu?"

She kissed him lightly on both cheeks then stood aside to let him pass. *"Très bien, et toi?"*

"Ah, *bien, bien.* As always when I see you."

"Flatterer," she said giving him a mock reproving look. "So, how was your flight?"

"Uneventful, fortunately." He moved to the small fridge beside the television set and helped himself to a can of Pepsi. "So where are the intrepid duo?"

She chuckled. "I'll call them."

Graham was the first to arrive.

They shook hands then Rust reached up and pushed back Graham's collar to reveal the full extent of the bruising around his throat.

"It looks nasty, Mike."

Graham shrugged. "It's part and parcel of the risks we take in this business."

"Don't remind me," Rust muttered then looked round when another knock sounded at the door. "That has to be C. W. Always the gentleman."

"Come in, C. W.," Sabrina called out.

Whitlock entered the room and grinned at Rust. "Jacques, how are you?"

"As ever, C. W., as ever."

After shaking hands with Rust, Whitlock sat on the edge of one of two double beds. "Has Sergei filled you in on the case?"

"Has he indeed!" Rust retorted with a smile. "You should have seen the telex he had sent through to me this morning. It seemed to go on forever." He opened his attaché case, removed a folder, then closed it again and placed it on the floor beside the wheelchair. "We came across an interesting link while compiling the backgrounds on Schrader and Drago for you. Horst Keppler was Schrader's chief of security at Hecht. His security firm here in Amsterdam is owned by Schrader."

"You can't accuse Schrader of bad planning," Sabrina said.

"What about Keppler's two employees who were in on the switch?" Graham asked. "Anything on them?"

"Yes," Rust replied and opened the folder. "Ernest de Vere, thirty-two years old. One conviction for bank robbery. Served seven years of a twelve-year sentence. Employed by Keppler two years ago."

"A convicted bank robber working for a security firm?" Whitlock screwed up his face. "The mind boggles."

"It gets better, C. W.," Rust said and consulted his folder again. "The second man is Rudi Oosterhuis, thirty-five years old. One conviction for holding up a security van. Served nine years of an eighteen-year sentence. Employed by Keppler eleven months ago. Four days after his release."

"They must have known while they were inside that Keppler intended to employ them on their release."

"It certainly looks that way, *chérie*," Rust agreed. "By all accounts they started their prison terms as troublemakers then, quite suddenly, they became model prisoners. Oosterhuis even went as far as to become a snitch to get on the good side of the warders. Their parole hearings were mere formalities. The governor claimed that the penal system had reformed both men."

"Talk about pulling the wool over their eyes," Graham muttered contemptuously.

"We've taken care of Lemmer and Toysgen. Their bodies

will turn up again before the trial. Lemmer certainly won't be missed in that time—the police will just assume he's still in hiding. I can't see Toysgen being missed either. He was a virtual recluse with no known friends. One of our men will be keeping an eye on the flat for the next few days in case any milk or newspapers are delivered.''

"I know one person who will miss Toysgen," Graham said then went on to explain about the barman at the Bohemer.

Rust made a note of Graham's observation. "We'll play it by ear, Mike, but I can't see it affecting the case. Even if this barman was to report Toysgen missing there's no way Schrader could find out.''

The telephone rang.

Sabrina answered it.

There was a hesitant pause. "Sabrina?"

"Speaking."

"It's Pieter de Jongh, is Jacques there?"

"One moment.'' She put her hand over the mouthpiece and told Rust who it was.

Rust frowned then wheeled himself across to where she was standing and took the receiver from her. His expression became increasingly sombre and he finally thanked De Jongh for calling before replacing the receiver.

"Van Dehn's dead.''

"Dead?" Sabrina exclaimed. "How?"

"Suicide. He hanged himself in the shower. Naturally we'll be conducting an internal investigation into how he managed to smuggle a tie into the bathroom but he did say something to the guards that might provide a clue as to why he killed himself. He said he was petrified of going to jail in case he was already a marked man. Why would he have said that?"

"He wasn't too impressed at the idea of being under house arrest so I told him if he didn't cooperate we could make

sure he was a marked man by the time he went to prison."
Graham stood up and walked to the window. "It was said to
frighten him, that's all."

"It obviously worked," Rust replied tersely.

"It had to be said, Jacques," Whitlock snapped at his ex-
partner. "Section 4b of the Charter states that: 'Any Strike
Force operative may place a suspect under house arrest if he,
or she, feels that the suspect could, in some way, jeopardize
the success of any given mission.' Legally we don't have any
right to hold a suspect prisoner in their own home so we have
to use whatever methods, however underhand, to implement
it. Don't come down on us for that. The alternative's having
some gung-ho lawyer screaming about injustice and threatening to expose UNACO to the world press."

"I'm not coming down on you, C. W. I'm well aware of the
problems surrounding Section 4b. I was once in the field, remember? What worries me is how the colonel's going to react
to the report I'll have to send him. You know how touchy he
can get about the methods Mike uses to get results."

"Why does he need to know?" Sabrina asked looking at
Rust. "Van Dehn was suicidal, he wasn't thinking straight.
Who knows what he meant about being a 'marked man'?"

"I don't need to hide behind a cover-up," Graham snapped
angrily. "Just tell him the truth. I've got nothing to hide."

"Stop being so stubborn, Mike." Rust nodded to himself
as he contemplated Sabrina's idea. "I see your point, *chérie*.
I'll bear it in mind when I write up the report."

"What have you managed to dig up on Schrader and
Drago?" Whitlock asked, breaking the sudden silence.

Rust took a sip of Pepsi before answering. "I believe
Mike's filled you in on the events leading up to Schrader
having to sell Hecht. Well, I've had a more detailed character
sketch prepared for you to read on the aeroplane. We ran

Drago's name through our computers and came up with a big, round zero. It was almost as if he didn't exist. So we got on to Langley, hoping they might have something on him. Turns out he was a cipher clerk with Czech intelligence before his defection to the West five years ago. He went to Rio after the CIA had debriefed him and he's been working for Schrader for the last four years. Your contact in Rio will be able to tell you more. She's a personal friend of Schrader's.''

"She?'' Graham said suspiciously.

"Her name's Siobhan St. Jacques.''

"Sounds exotic,'' Whitlock said with a grin.

"She is by all accounts. There is a snag, though. She's on loan to us from the CIA.''

"That's brilliant!'' Graham exclaimed savagely. "Don't we have our own contact in Rio?''

"We did, but he was killed in a speedboat accident last year.''

"Ramirez. Yeah, I remember that. But why hasn't the colonel replaced him?''

"Because he couldn't find anyone suitable, Mike. He had to find someone who moved in the same circles as Ramirez. Someone with the same kind of friends. Nobody fitted the bill. Then he made some enquiries about Siobhan. Naturally the CIA weren't too impressed with his overtures. In fact, they refused even to discuss the matter, which was fairly understandable under the circumstances. She is, after all, probably their best agent in South America. Well as you can imagine, the colonel wasn't going to take it lying down so he went straight to the Secretary-General to plead his case. The Secretary-General contacted the President who, in turn, summoned the CIA Director to the White House. To cut a long story short, Siobhan is still primarily a CIA operative but she's at UNACO's disposal should we need her. It soured relations with Langley but then that's nothing new anyway. It didn't bother the colonel, he'd got what he wanted."

"Have you ever met her?"

"When do I get the time to go to Rio, Mike? No, I've never met her. She's good though, very much the professional."

"She'd have to be for the colonel to have gone to such lengths to recruit her," Sabrina said.

"But is she trustworthy?" Whitlock asked.

"She's been briefed on the case but that doesn't mean you have to discuss it with her. She's there to get you introduced to Schrader, that's all."

"What you're saying is she's CIA first and foremost, and needs to be handled with extreme caution."

Rust smiled at Graham's choice of words. "Caution, Mike, not antagonism. She's on our side."

"When do we leave?" Whitlock asked.

"Tonight, six o'clock." Rust opened his attaché case again and withdrew three sealed envelopes. "KLM flight 730 to Dakar and Rio. You'll get there in the early hours of tomorrow morning. Remember, Brazil's four hours behind European time. You'll be staying at the Meridien. Confirmed bookings. I don't know how the colonel managed it, what with it being Carnival time."

"Why such a lavish hotel?" Graham asked.

"Because you'll be posing as a wealthy New York businessman so it's imperative that you stay at one of the city's leading hotels." Rust took a deep breath, not looking forward to what he had to say next. "Sabrina will pose as your wife. You're supposedly on your honeymoon. I'm sorry, Mike, but it's the only way. It's a bastard of a thing to do to you after Carrie—"

"What the hell are you apologizing for, Jacques?" Graham

responded sharply when his wife's name was mentioned. He looked at Sabrina. "We'll do it. It's a job, nothing more."

Sabrina nodded.

"Siobhan will pretend to be a long-lost friend of yours," Rust said to Sabrina. "It should be enough to get both of you invited to the Riviera Club. Schrader owns it. Admittance is by invitation only. She also mentioned something to Sergei about a Carnival party Schrader holds ever year but she'll explain it all in more detail once you get to Rio."

"Where do I fit into this?" Whitlock asked.

"Back-up, *mon ami*." Rust's smile faltered when he saw the anger in Whitlock's eyes.

"It's always the same, isn't it? Good old C. W., he'll do the back-up. He doesn't mind. Well I do mind, Jacques. I mind being taken for granted." Whitlock got to his feet and left the room.

Rust stared at the door. "What was that about? He's always been a back-up man. It's what he does best."

"Perhaps that's the problem," Graham said. "He's got four years left before he's retired to some desk job at the Command Center. Has it crossed your mind that he might want to prove something to himself in the field before it's too late?"

"But C. W.'s never been ambitious."

"Not by your standards, Jacques, but everyone's ambitious in their own way."

Rust pondered Graham's words as he placed the three manila envelopes on the coffee table before delving into his briefcase and removing a small box which he handed to Sabrina.

She opened it. Inside, cushioned in cotton wool, was an eighteen-carat gold wedding ring. "It's beautiful," she said softy.

"I suppose it is for a prop," Rust retorted.

She could understand his antagonism. Like Graham, he

too had "lost" the only woman he had ever really loved. He had met Thérèse Mardin while he was with the SDECE. She had been a witness in a drugs case and he was given the task of protecting her for the duration of the trial. They had started dating almost immediately and within six months she had moved into his apartment. She had even given up her job at the Galeries Lafayette department store in Paris to move with him to New York when he was appointed to UNACO. Neither had wanted to get married so they lived together for the next eight years. Then, after the shooting, she became increasingly distant towards him, unable to accept that he would be crippled for the rest of his life. She returned to France while he was still in hospital and the last he heard she was living with a Swiss skier in Lucerne.

Sabrina suddenly noticed Rust staring at her. He smiled sadly. "You were thinking of Thérèse, *n'est-ce-pas*?"

"The ring made me think of her."

"Me too." Rust clapped his hands together. "Enough of that. You've got to prepare for your flight and I've got to get back to Zurich as soon as possible. Strike Force Two should be in Algeria by now—"

"So they've gone in after all?" Sabrina interrupted excitedly.

"I thought Sergei would have told you."

"When C. W. phoned New York the night officer was still on duty. We haven't had any contact with Sergei since yesterday."

"Well, they flew out last night. The plan is for them to cross into Libya tonight and spring the others either tomorrow or the day after." Rust activated his wheelchair. "I'll wish you good luck although I've never known any of you to need it before."

"We'll take it anyway," Sabrina said then kissed Rust on the cheek.

Rust shook Graham's hand. "I'm sorry about Sabrina having to play your wife, Mike."

"It's okay, Jacques. Honestly."

Sabrina opened the door and Rust paused beside her. "Say goodbye to C. W. for me. If he's got something on his mind he knows where to find me. If he wants to talk about it, that is." He shrugged, then disappeared down the corridor.

Sabrina turned back to the room and found Graham staring intently at her. She suddenly felt strangely self-conscious and took an involuntary step back, her flickering eyes trying to hold his mesmerizing stare. Her voice was hesitant when she spoke. "Mike, what's wrong?"

"I was wondering what Carrie would have made of all this."

"And?" she replied, the uncertainty still in her voice.

"She'd be jealous as hell." He walked out into the corridor then looked round at her. "But I reckon she'd have secretly approved."

Sabrina stood at the door for some time after Graham had returned to his room. Approved of what? Her? Or that she was impersonating his wife in the interests of the case?

She closed the door, undressed and took a long, hot shower. It was only when she wiped the steam from the wall mirror that she noticed she had been subconsciously smiling to herself.

SEVEN

They arrived at Rio de Janeiro's Galeão International Airport at two-thirty the following morning and took a taxi to the thirty-eight-floor Meridien hotel which stood at the foot of Sugar Loaf Mountain overlooking the Copacabana beach. Graham paid the taxi driver, who had helped to carry the suitcases into the foyer, then crossed to the reception desk to check in.

The receptionist tapped the name into the computer. "Mr. and Mrs. Graham. From New York?"

"Yeah, that's right."

"My congratulations, sir."

"Thanks," Graham muttered without much conviction.

The receptionist gave Graham a registration card to fill out. "Could I see your passports please?"

Graham took them from his pocket and placed them on the counter. He completed the card and pushed it across to the receptionist.

"We did have you and Mrs. Graham down originally for a cabana—it was all we had available yesterday when the booking came through. As luck would have it, though, one of our honeymoon suites became available this afternoon due to a late cancellation. We've put you in there at the same rate as you would have paid for the cabana.''

Graham rubbed his eyes wearily and shook his head in despair.

"Is something wrong, sir?"

"No, not at all." Graham forced a smile. "It's very kind of you to let us have the honeymoon suite at the same rate as the cabana.''

"Compliments of the General Manager, sir."

"Please thank him for me, will you?" Graham beckoned Sabrina over when the receptionist went to fetch the key. "We were originally down for a cabana. Now we've got the goddam honeymoon suite.''

Sabrina stifled a laugh then bit her lip as a smile crept across her face. "I'm sorry, Mike, but you've got to admit it is kind of funny.''

"I'm glad you think so."

The receptionist returned with the key and a sealed envelope. "This was dropped off earlier this evening for you, sir.''

Graham slit open the envelope and removed the card.

Mike, C. W., Sabrina
Hope you had a pleasant flight from Amsterdam. I'll be here at 10 o'clock tomorrow morning, looking forward to meeting you.
Siobhan

He handed it to Sabrina who, after reading it, gave it to Whitlock.

Graham put a hand lightly on Whitlock's shoulder. "See you in the morning. It's way past my bedtime.''

"Likewise. Sleep well, both of you."

The night porter picked up the two suitcases and led them to the lift. The honeymoon suite on the seventh floor was divided into two sections, a lounge and a bedroom.

Graham told the porter to leave the suitcases in the lounge and waited for him to go before turning to Sabrina. "You take the bed. I'll sleep on one of these couches in here."

She agreed and, picking up her Vuitton suitcase, disappeared into the bedroom. "Do you want to use the bathroom first?" she called out.

"Where is it?"

"Here, off the bedroom."

He entered the bedroom a moment later with his toilet bag. "Yeah, you'll take all night in there."

"Thanks." Her face suddenly became serious. "I'm worried about C. W. He's not himself. I thought he was quiet on the flight to Amsterdam but it was nothing compared to tonight. For all he said he might as well have been on another plane. He's always so chirpy and talkative when we fly together. And what about that incident in front of Jacques? I've never seen C. W. so angry. Why's he acting like this?"

"Carmen," came the immediate reply.

"Has he spoken to you about it?"

"No."

"So how can you tell?" she asked.

"I recognize the signs. I went through the same trouble with Carrie."

She sat down on the edge of the bed. "Then talk to him, Mike."

"No!" he shot back. "It's a private matter. They've got to sort it out themselves."

"But what if it's reached a stalemate?"

"God help him," he replied and closed the bathroom door behind him.

She shivered then suddenly remembered Martin Cohen's words. . . . "Something's bugging him. Just watch him, Sabrina, for his own good."

She promised herself she would, *for his own good*.

Graham was the first up in the morning and after a twenty-minute workout he draped a towel around his neck and went out on to the bedroom balcony. It was a near perfect day with only the occasional fluffy cloud drifting lazily across the azure sky and a cool refreshing breeze which made the heat pleasantly bearable. He wiped the sweat from his face and returned to the bedroom where, to keep up on the honeymoon façade, he ordered breakfast to the room for nine-thirty. He then shook Sabrina awake on his way to the bathroom and was surprised to find her up and dressed when he emerged a few minutes later.

Breakfast had arrived while he was in the bathroom and after buttering himself a warm roll he settled down to read the *Latin American Daily Post* which he had asked to be sent up with the order.

The telephone rang at ten o'clock but stopped after the third ring—Siobhan's signal to say she was waiting for them outside the hotel. Sabrina called Whitlock to say they were ready then left the room with Graham and rode the lift to the foyer. They met Whitlock at the reception desk and, after handing in their room keys, headed for the door.

"Sabrina?" a voice called out hesitantly behind them moments after they had emerged into the street. "Sabrina Carver?"

Sabrina spun round, a feigned look of surprise on her face.

Her frown was immediately replaced by a smile and she shook her head in amazement. "I don't believe it. Siobhan!"

They embraced then held each other at arm's length, both shaking their heads in disbelief.

Siobhan was a strikingly attractive thirty-year-old with a rich honey complexion that contrasted vividly with the white vest she was wearing tucked into a pair of skintight Levi jeans. Both garments served only to accentuate a figure that even Sabrina regarded with a little good-humoured envy. Her long black hair, plaited with rows of silver and gold beads, was combed back away from her face and fell halfway down her back. Her eyes flickered towards Graham and Whitlock and Sabrina introduced them to her.

"You, married?" Siobhan said aghast, her hand resting lightly on her chest.

"We're on our honeymoon," Sabrina replied with a grin and looped her hand under Graham's arm.

"That's fantastic. I'm so happy for you." Siobhan grinned back at her. "I still can't get over it, bumping into each other like this after all these years."

"We've got so much to talk about. Let's get a coffee somewhere."

"I know just the place. Come on, it's not far from here."

Graham grabbed Siobhan by the arm once they were out of sight of the hotel. "Okay, the acting's over. What's the plan?" he asked making no attempt to hide the antagonism in his voice.

Siobhan led them into a deserted sidestreet. "I can understand your animosity, Mike. I'm sure C. W. and Sabrina have similar doubts about me in the back of their minds, only they're not as direct as you are in airing them. I don't know what you've been told about my activities here in Rio but the bottom line is I work solely for the CIA. The understanding with Langley was that I'd help UNACO out in an emergency. My instructions are simple: to get you into the Schrader estate. And that's it. The rest is up to you. So let's at least *try* and get along, even if it is only an uneasy truce. How about it?''

Whitlock and Sabrina exchanged glances, shrugged, then nodded in agreement.

Graham was more reluctant to commit himself. "We'll see," was all he would say on the matter. "You never answered my question."

"I'll take you up Sugar Loaf this morning. You can see part of the Schrader estate from there. Then tonight I've managed to get you and Sabrina into the Riviera Club as personal guests of mine. Schrader will be there, he always is on the eve of the Carnival. We can catch a bus to Sugar Loaf not far from here. It's a lot cheaper than going by taxi.''

Siobhan let several buses pass the stop before flagging one down marked Urca which, she explained, would take them to within a couple of blocks of the cable car station. They boarded the bus through a squeaky turnstile and Siobhan led them up the aisle to the front where they sat down.

After paying the fares Siobhan twisted round in her seat until she could see Graham and Sabrina behind her. "What have you been told about me?"

"Nothing," Whitlock replied beside her. "You're supposed to fill us in.''

"Okay. Well, as you've probably guessed, Siobhan St. Jacques isn't my real name. It's Mary Smethurst. My mother's a Carioca and my father was a diplomat with the American consulate. He was killed in a plane crash when I was twelve.''

- "What's a Carioca?" Graham asked.

"Someone born and raised in Rio," Siobhan replied. "I

joined a modelling agency when I was eighteen and it was tactfully suggested that I change my name. Siobhan is my grandmother's name and Raymond St. Jacques is my favourite actor. A year later I was in Paris posing for the likes of *Vogue* and *Cosmopolitan* and although I was fairly successful over there I missed the sunshine and came back to Rio. I made a commercial for Varig, Brazil's national airline, and suddenly everybody knew my face. I've made several films since then but I'm still best remembered for that commercial. Most people don't know my name, to them I'll always be 'the Varig girl.' "

"How were you recruited into the CIA?" Graham asked.

"They initially approached me after the success of the commercial when I was being invited to all the big parties which, as you probably know, are meeting places for senior KGB officers from around the world. Well, once the CIA had proved to me that the KGB were instrumental in my father's death, I was more than willing to keep my ears open for any snippets of information the Russians might let slip after a few drinks. I did make one stipulation though. I wouldn't sleep with the bastards to get the information. They agreed. That was five years ago. Now I'm widely regarded as a staunch believer in the great socialist cause. It's the perfect cover." Siobhan got to her feet and rang the bell. "This is our stop."

They alighted through the door at the front of the bus and Siobhan stopped off at a curio shop to buy herself a straw hat and a pair of cheap sunglasses to spare the others any unnecessary attention once they reached the cable car station at the Estracao do Teleferico on Pasteur Avenue. In any event few people would have recognized her anyway. Most were tourists who had never seen the commercial.

The cable cars, which normally ran every twenty minutes, were now running at ten-minute intervals to accommodate the sheer volume of traffic. They joined the queue and it was another twenty-five minutes before they reached the turnstile where Whitlock already had his wallet out to pay the attendant. His one headache had always been foreign currency and a smiling Siobhan finally came to his aid by plucking the correct amount of money from the wallet and sliding it through the aperture in the glass partition to the attendant, who gave Whitlock a bored look as if she had seen it all before. She counted out the money then issued them with four tickets.

"There are two mountains," Siobhan explained as they boarded the cable car. "The first is Morro da Urca which is roughly half the size of Sugar Loaf, or Pão de Açúcar to give it its proper name. There's a restaurant on Morro da Urca where we can talk after you've seen the Schrader estate."

Sabrina's first thought on disembarking from the cable car and seeing Rio de Janeiro spread out before her was that the view had been well worth the visit. To her right was the city, laid out like an intricate papier-mâché model designed for some spoilt child on the whim of his opulent father. Yachts, accoutrements of the rich, peppered the tranquil waters of Botafogo Bay like miniature plastic toys fixed on to a sheet of flat ultramarine glass. To her left were the rugged mountains, carpeted in green velvet, stealing out into the Atlantic Ocean which was spread out as far as the eye could see. She could almost believe that it would crack into pieces were the smallest of pebbles to be dropped onto it. Her eyes finally took in the horizon where the wispy band of cloud kissing the distant mountain peaks looked as though it had been painted in to break the monotony of the ubiquitous cerulean sky. She sensed someone behind her and turned to find Graham standing there, his hands dug into the pockets of his baggy white trousers.

"It's beautiful, isn't it?" she said taking in the view again.

"Yeah," he muttered. "Come on, C. W.'s managed to hijack a telescope from a bunch of Germans. He reckons he can't keep them at bay much longer without reinforcements."

She chuckled then fell into step beside him and looped her hand under his arm. He glanced down at her hand but made no move to shrug it off.

Whitlock looked up from the eyepiece and beckoned Sabrina forward. "We're waiting for you, hurry up."

Sabrina smiled at the four middle-aged couples standing patiently behind Siobhan, apologized to them in German for the delay and promised to be quick so as not to inconvenience them any further. Their faces lit up on hearing their own language and one of the men told her to take as long as she wanted. She thanked him then leaned over the telescope, adjusted the sight to her specifications, and concentrated on the enlarged image in the eyepiece. All she saw was a mountain facing onto the Atlantic Ocean. Then she noticed something in the rock-face reflecting the sun's rays and, on closer inspection, realized it was actually a window. A massive window. It had to be a hundred feet wide. No, it was two windows with a twenty-foot gap between them. A movement caught her eye—a speedboat seemed to have emerged from the mountain! She blinked then peered through the eyepiece again. Suddenly it became obvious, an underground cavern. She couldn't see anything else so, after turning the sights until they were out of focus, she pretended to knock the telescope accidently with her arm so that the Germans had no way of knowing what she had been looking at.

She mentioned what she had seen as they walked back towards the queue waiting for the next cable car.

"I didn't see any cavern," Graham responded.

"Me neither," Whitlock agreed then turned to Siobhan. "Is there one?"

Siobhan nodded. "It's a natural formation in the mountain. Schrader's had a jetty built into it. He told me once that it's large enough to berth the *Golconda*, his private yacht. Not that I've ever seen it there, he usually keeps it moored in Botafogo Bay."

A cable car arrived before they could talk further, and on the way down Siobhan tried to spot the *Golconda* but, as luck would have it, it wasn't in Botafogo Bay. She thought no more of it and when the cable car stopped at the Morro da Urca station more than half the passengers alighted and headed for the restaurant.

"We might as well not bother," Whitlock said pointing to the queue. "We'll never get a table in there."

"Don't bet on it." Siobhan handed her straw hat and sunglasses to Whitlock then crossed to the restaurant and disappeared inside. Thirty seconds later she reappeared and beckoned them forward.

There were angry mutters from the other tourists.

"Seems all you need to get a table around here is a pretty face and a cute arse," one American said looking from Siobhan to Sabrina.

Graham stopped in front of the man and cast his eyes over the woman beside him. "If that's the case then I reckon you'll be out here all day."

Sabrina grabbed Graham's arm and pulled him into the restaurant before the man had time to react. "That wasn't called for, Mike."

Graham shrugged. "Perhaps not, but it might teach him to keep his mouth shut next time."

They were shown to a corner table.

Siobhan smiled triumphantly as she sat down. "Being a celebrity does have its advantages."

Graham levelled a finger at her. "Don't ever embarrass me like that again."

"Embarrass you?" Siobhan replied in amazement.

"You abused your status to get what you wanted. Has it ever occurred to you that the people you're upsetting are the same people who have made you into the celebrity you are today? You'd be *nothing* without them."

"I see what you're getting at but don't you think they would do exactly the same if they were in my shoes?"

"That's no excuse." Graham picked up the menu. "Just as long as we understand each other."

"Perfectly," she replied then held up her menu. "Who wants what?"

"What do you suggest?" Whitlock asked.

"Depends on how hungry you are?"

Sabrina glanced at her watch. "It's a bit early to eat."

"Yeah," Graham agreed. "I just want something to drink. Something cold."

"Then I'd suggest *chopinho* or *maté*, depending on your taste. *Chopinho*'s draught beer and *maté*'s a lemonade drink. Both are served chilled."

The general consensus was for the *maté* and Siobhan asked the waitress to bring a jug of it to the table.

"Can we get down to business now?" Graham asked once the waitress was out of earshot.

"How much do you know about Schrader and Drago?"

"We've all read a fairly comprehensive dossier on Schrader up until the time he left Germany," Sabrina replied. "But what we know about Drago could be written on the back of a postage stamp."

"Which is?"

"He was a low grade cipher clerk with Czech intelligence before his defection to the West," Sabrina answered.

"And we got that from your people in Langley," Whitlock added.

"It's the same story they fed me," Siobhan said grim-faced.

"Story?" Sabrina said, surprised. "Don't you believe it?"

"Personally, no." Siobhan smiled quickly. "Don't get me wrong, I'm not criticizing them for it. They must have their reasons."

"So you're saying there's more to Drago than meets the eye?" Whitlock queried.

"In my opinion, yes."

The waitress returned with a tray bearing the jug of *maté* and four glasses. She placed them on the table along with the bill and left.

Sabrina filled the glasses.

Siobhan took a sip before speaking. "Schrader arrived in Rio ten years ago with the fifty-five million dollars he'd got for selling the Hecht company. Well, being the shrewd businessman he is, he had an in-depth survey carried out of the real estate market in and around Rio before pouring all his money into Leblon, home of the rich. It was the kind of business venture that just couldn't fail. He's financed the building of apartment blocks, hotels, restaurants, amusement parks—you name it, he's had something to do with it. He owns a major part of Leblon and he's now widely regarded as one of the five leading businessmen in Brazil."

"What's his current worth?" Whitlock asked.

Siobhan threw up her hands in desperation. "It's impossible to say. It must certainly run into billions."

Whitlock whistled softly. "Not bad for the son of a Frankfurt cobbler."

"It's no secret that he's obsessed with money but there is another side to him. The philanthropist. He's started up several charities to help the *favelados*—"

"*Favelados?*" Graham interrupted.

"The slum dwellers. You couldn't have missed the slums if you were looking down on Rio as your plane came in to land. They've sprung up on every unclaimed hillside in Rio. Two million inhabitants, most of them from northern Brazil, who came here in the belief that the roads were paved with gold. It's especially tragic for the children. They're underfed, live in rags and many turn to crime to survive.

"Schrader was horrified when he saw the conditions the *favela* children have to live in and he promised to help them. He donates hundreds of thousands of dollars every year to ease their plight. His pleas for support from other millionaires have largely fallen on deaf ears—they just regard the slums as an eyesore in their beautiful city. So he throws lavish balls at his clubs, overcharges on everything, then gives all the money to his charities. He says it's one way of getting his peers to help the *favelados*."

"Is his halo tainted at all?"

"You're all heart, Mike. Sure his halo's tainted. His bribery payments to city officials far outweigh the money he donates to charity. That was the conclusion one of the city's leading journalists came to after a four-month investigation. He drowned under mysterious circumstances in Guanabara Bay a week before his allegations were due to go to press. The police investigation was a joke. A total cover-up. Then, the day before the report was to be printed, the newspaper's editor dropped it. He called it 'too speculative.' "

"So it was never published?" Whitlock asked.

"No, but I managed to get hold of a copy of it. It cost me a small fortune but it was worth every cent. It named names at the highest level of local government, all of them in Schrader's back pocket.''

"Where does Drago fit into the picture?'' Sabrina asked refilling her glass.

"His official title's Personal Security Executive. In other words, Schrader's personal bodyguard.''

"He was passing himself off as Schrader's personal secretary in Amsterdam,'' Sabrina said.

"He always does when he's negotiating business deals for Schrader. Schrader trusts him implicitly and, much as I dislike him, I've never known him to betray that trust in any way. He's the perfect foil for Schrader. A workaholic who shuns the limelight. Schrader, on the other hand, is the gregarious type who's never happier than when he's center-stage surrounded by his rich and influential friends.

"When Schrader hired Drago four years ago he gave him a priority objective—to bring the crime rate down in the *favelas*. Six months later he had a hundred and fifty of the *favelas*' most hardened criminals roaming the streets as self-styled vigilantes on the kind of salaries that ensured total loyalty. It's become street justice at its most primitive. Revolvers, knives, machetes, chains, lead pipes, baseball bats—one of them even carries a chainsaw around with him. They've become death squads who're above the law. The police don't interfere. They're thrilled that these vigilantes are taming a problem which, to them, had previously seemed out of control.

"He's managed to split public opinion right down the middle on this issue. Half call him a saviour, the other half call him a gangster enforcing his own laws in the *favelas*.'' ·

"And you think he's a gangster?'' Graham asked.

"I *know* he's a killer. I've prepared a list of fourteen people who were almost certainly murdered by Drago over the past four years. They were all shot once through the heart and in each case a CZ75 was used. It's the type of handgun Drago always carries with him. The list's in my car back at the hotel. I've also got the two Berettas and the Browning I was asked to get for you.''

Whitlock drained his glass. "Well, let's go.''

Graham got to his feet. "And will we have the pleasure of Drago's company at the Riviera Club tonight?''

Siobhan smiled. "You can count on it.''

Siobhan saw them back to their hotel then made her way to the nearest *orelhoe*, a public telephone in a large yellow protective dome, on the corner of the street. She rummaged through her handbag for a *ficha*, or token, to use for her call.

She fed a *ficha* into the slot then dialled the private line of the first secretary at the American consulate who had been her handler since she started to work for the CIA.

The receiver was lifted at the other end. "Casey Morgan, good afternoon.''

"Casey, it's Siobhan.''

"So how did it go?''

"As expected. I'll tell you more when I see you. Where do you want to meet?''

"The usual place. An hour's time.''

The usual place was a wooden bench beside the tranquil river in the Parque da Cidade, a quiet park nestled between the suburbs of São Conrado and Leblon.

Siobhan arrived first and crouched on the riverbank to feed the paddling Muscovy ducks from the bag of diced bread she had brought with her.

"They must be programmed like Pavlov's dogs by now,''

a voice said behind her. "I'd hate to think what would happen if you ever showed up here without any bread."

"I'm sure they'd survive the shock, Casey," she replied with a smile then crossed to the bench and sat down beside him.

Casey Morgan was a tall, angular man in his mid-fifties who had been in the diplomatic corps for thirty years, twenty-six of those as an operative with the CIA. He lit a cigarette then pushed the pack back into his jacket pocket. "Well, what did you get up to with our UNACO cousins?"

"Just what we agreed on last night," she replied then went on to describe the morning's events.

"So they didn't mention the envelope?"

She tossed a few cubes of bread to the four ducks which had ventured on to the riverbank. "Not a word. That doesn't mean they don't know about it, mind. We're dealing with professionals here, Casey."

"I don't doubt it for a minute," he muttered then took another drag on his cigarette. "I heard from Langley this morning."

"And?" she asked looking sharply at him.

"They're now certain the envelope came over with the painting. What's more, Drago intends to rendezvous with the KGB at Schrader's Carnival party tomorrow night to hand over the envelope. You'll have to lift it then. It's your only chance."

"Who are the KGB sending over to meet Drago?"

"They didn't say."

"You mean they *wouldn't* say!" she snapped. "Come off it, Casey, if Langley know the KGB are sending someone here then they also know his identity. Why are they playing this one so close to their chests?"

"Ours is not to reason why," he replied with a sigh.

"No, it's just to obey with blind devotion," she retorted irritably. "I'm the one who has to go out on a limb tomorrow night to get the envelope for them. If they can't trust me then why the hell did they recruit me in the first place?"

"I can understand your anger—"

"How can you? You've never been in the field before." She immediately regretted her outburst and squeezed his arm. "I'm sorry, Casey, I didn't mean to snap at you like that. It's just that Langley gets me so worked up at times."

"Only *at times*? Count yourself one of the lucky few."

She smiled faintly then flung a handful of bread cubes on to the water. "I can understand if they don't want to divulge the contents of the envelope but it gets a bit much when they won't even say who the KGB are sending out here. They'll be the first to jump down my throat if Drago hands over the envelope before I can get to him. If I am to get it, then I've got to know what his contact looks like. Can't you see that?"

Morgan nodded. "I hear what you're saying, Siobhan, but there's nothing I can do about it."

"Phone Langley, make them see some sense."

"It wouldn't help, nobody in the department knows who it is either."

She frowned, puzzled. "I don't understand."

"A decision was taken at the highest level to keep the name a secret."

"How high?" she asked.

"The President and the Agency's Director."

"It doesn't make any sense," she said in bewilderment. "Surely our people in the KGB know who it is?"

He shook his head. "The KGB's also closed ranks at the top."

"Casey, what the hell's in that envelope?"

Morgan dropped his cigarette and crushed it underfoot.

"I was told something in the strictest of confidence yesterday. I'd be finished if it ever leaked out, but we've always been honest with each other in the past and anyway, as you said, you're the one who has to go out on a limb tomorrow night to get the envelope back." He stared at his feet then slowly looked up at her. "Have you ever heard of the Alpha program?"

"Sure I've heard of it. Its contents are known only to a handful of people."

"Including the President and the Agency's Director."

"You mean . . ." she trailed off, her eyes wide in amazement.

"All I was told was that the contents of the envelope have come from the Alpha program."

"But how could someone like Drago get hold of that kind of classified information?"

"I don't know any more than that." Morgan stood up then looked down at her. "And it came from the highest level."

"How high?"

"Let me put it this way—I've never spoken to the President," he replied then walked across the lawn towards the road.

She smiled to herself then emptied the remnants of the bag into the midst of the gathering ducks.

EIGHT

Graham was sweating by the time the taxi drew up in front of the Riviera Club on the Avenida Vieira Souto overlooking the tranquil waters of Ipanema Beach. He glanced at his watch: eight-forty. Siobhan had told them to be there at eight-thirty. At least they were in keeping with local custom—Cariocas were never punctual. He paid the driver then climbed out of the taxi. He was wearing a black dinner suit, black bowtie and a white Cardin shirt which had taken him the best part of the afternoon to find. Sabrina, on the other hand, had found what she wanted straight away: a black strapless dress and a black bolero-styled jacket. She had decided on the minimum amount of jewellery—a pair of diamond earrings and a matching necklace—and, with her hair up, she looked the refinement of elegance and beauty.

"You look good," he said almost grudgingly after helping her from the taxi.

"Thanks," she replied with a smile, knowing it would be the only compliment he paid her that evening.

"Give me your hand."

"What?" she replied.

He held out his hand towards her. "We're supposed to be newlyweds, remember?"

A uniformed doorman, with the build and face of a boxer, opened one of the two plate-glass doors for them and touched his cap politely as they entered the plush foyer. Graham crossed to the marble desk where the receptionist greeted him warmly before asking his name. He told her and she fed it into a computer hidden from view under the counter.

"Would you care to take a seat while I call Miss St. Jacques to tell her you've arrived?"

"Thank you," Graham replied.

He rejoined Sabrina and they were about to sit down when André Drago emerged from the restaurant at the end of the corridor. As he approached them they both remembered Van Dehn's perfect description of him: a thin face, wire-rimmed glasses and bleached hair cropped close to his skull. And his preference for white. He was wearing a dinner suit and silk bowtie—but only the trousers were black.

Drago introduced himself, the smile never reaching his eyes. "Please, if you'd care to follow me, Miss St. Jacques is waiting for you in the casino." He led them to a flight of red-carpeted stairs. "Are you familiar with Brazilian art?"

They shook their heads.

Drago paused halfway up the stairs and gestured to a row of paintings on the wall to their left. "We have, amongst others, a Pancetti, a Djanira and a Di Cavalcanti." He smiled fleetingly. "All originals of course."

"Aren't you tempting fate by hanging originals in such an open place?" Sabrina asked.

"We did have an attempted burglary about eighteen months ago." Drago indicated the visitors' book on a table beside the red padded double doors. "Would you care to sign it, Mr. Graham?"

"Sure."

"Were the burglars caught?" Sabrina asked.

Drago removed a gold fountain pen from his jacket pocket, unscrewed the cap, then handed it to Graham. He turned back to Sabrina. "An over-zealous guard shot them both. Such a tragic waste of life."

Graham signed the book then handed the pen back to Drago who pulled open one of the doors and stood aside to let them pass. The room's predominant feature was wood: walls of Norwegian pine and a ceiling of Honduran mahogany. It was the ceiling which caught their attention with its intricately designed web of geometric forms and shapes illuminated by a magnificent three-tiered Czechoslovakian crystal chandelier.

Drago followed their eyes. "Rumour has it that the ceiling once adorned one of the ballrooms in King Pedro the Second's summer palace at Petropolis. I doubt we'll ever find out the truth, but at least it makes a good story."

They descended the steps into the main body of the casino. To their left were the craps tables and the roulette wheels, to their right the card tables. The bar was situated on another raised section of the floor on the opposite side of the room.

Siobhan kissed them lightly on both cheeks, a traditional Brazilian greeting, then turned to Drago. "Mr. Schrader asked to be informed of Mr. and Mrs. Graham's arrival."

Drago eyed her coldly then crossed to a table near the wall and whispered in the ear of a man seated with his back to the room. He waited for a reply then returned to the bar. "Mr. Schrader's apologies, he'll be with you as soon as he's finished his game. Would you care for a drink meantime?"

"A glass of dry white wine for me," Sabrina said to the hovering barman.

"The coldest bottle of Perrier water in the house," Graham added.

Schrader laughed loudly, patted his opponent's arm, then got to his feet and made his way towards the bar. He was a powerfully built fifty-three-year-old with a rich tan and fine brown hair which was beginning to grey at the temples. The aquiline nose strengthened, rather than marred, his rugged features and Sabrina could well understand why he was so popular amongst the women who moved in his affluent circles.

Siobhan waited until he had mounted the steps before making the introductions.

"I hope André's been looking after you in my absence," Schrader said in a deep voice as he shook Graham's hand.

"The perfect host," Graham replied glancing at Drago who had discreetly withdrawn to the railing where he stood with his hands behind his back.

"Good. Ah, your drinks." Schrader initialled the chit for the barman. "So when did you get married?"

"Yesterday," Graham replied.

"Yesterday?" Schrader clapped his hands together. "This calls for a celebration. Champagne."

Drago snapped his fingers at the nearest barman. "A bottle of Roederer Cristal for Mr. Schrader. Four glasses."

"I believe you and Siobhan are old friends?" Schrader said to Sabrina.

She caught Siobhan's eye and smiled at her. Nothing had been left to chance when they had fabricated their friendship over lunch that afternoon. Once the details had been thrashed out they had fired questions at each other to ensure that they knew their roles. They had to be believable, which meant the story had to be as realistic as possible.

"We met when we were working as models in Paris. It

seems like a lifetime ago now. How long was it, Siobhan? Ten years?''

Siobhan fiddled thoughtfully with one of the beads in her hair. "I was in Paris . . . nine years ago. It must be nine years ago."

"We shared a flat on the Left Bank for a year then I went to London and Siobhan went to Milan. We promised to keep in contact but we somehow lost touch. . . ."

"And now, nine years later, we bump into each other outside the Meridien," Siobhan continued then touched Sabrina on the arm as if to share the joke. "What's more, I find out she's gone and got herself married."

The barman opened the bottle of champagne and Graham put his hand over the mouth of the nearest glass. "Not for me, I'll stick with the Perrier."

Schrader handed a glass each to Siobhan and Sabrina then held up his own in a toast. "To the newlyweds. You're a very lucky man, Mr. Graham."

Graham smiled. "Mrs. Graham's a very special lady."

The ambiguity of the words wasn't lost on Sabrina. Even so, she still couldn't get over the way he was playing his part to perfection. It was as if he *were* a newlywed husband: the stolen glances, the fleeting smiles, the occasional touch—it was all so realistic.

"Siobhan tells me you're in the haulage business."

"Right, in New York." Graham took a business card from his wallet and handed it to Schrader.

"Mike Graham, Managing Director, Whitaker Haulage," Schrader read off the card.

"I bought out Joe Whitaker three years ago but with the reputation the company's got it would have been crazy to change the name."

"A shrewd move," Schrader said then handed the card to Drago.

It was just what Graham had wanted him to do. Drago would check out the company and, finding that all the facts tallied, it would add to their credibility. Whitaker Haulage was actually one of UNACO's duboks: a company fronting for an intelligence agency. Business cards had been printed for every field operative for each of the duboks, the majority of which were based in and around New York, and when needed half a dozen of them would be issued from stock and included in the assignment dossier. Only a handful of employees at each dubok were UNACO personnel, their jobs being to back up a field operative's cover story should the need arise. The rest of the workforce were oblivious to the deception, or to the fact that all profits from these duboks were discreetly channelled into a bank account to be used exclusively by UNICEF.

What Graham didn't know was that Drago had made those enquiries earlier when Siobhan had first called the club to say she would be inviting them as her personal guests. He had also found out from a contact on Wall Street that Whitaker Haulage was a solid, reputable firm worth in the region of five million dollars. Schrader insisted on knowing the financial position of every individual who came to his club— in the case of members it was to differentiate between friends and acquaintances, in the case of guests it was to decide whether their credit was good enough to invite them to gamble at his table.

Schrader drank down his champagne then placed the glass on the counter. "Are you a gambling man, Mr. Graham?"

Graham shrugged. "Depends on the stakes."

"The stakes can always be altered to suit a player's requirements. The reason I ask is that I left a game of blackjack to meet you and your lovely wife and I was wondering whether you would care to join us at the table?''

''Why not?''

''Good.'' Schrader turned to Sabrina and Siobhan. ''You're both more than welcome to come and watch.''

''Sure.'' Siobhan glanced at Sabrina. ''It should be fun.''

Fun? Sabrina thought to herself. It would be anything but fun. Graham would be gambling with UNACO money and that would have to be explained to Kolchinsky once they returned to New York. And, because she was with him, Kolchinsky would apportion the blame. But what could she do? Graham had never been one to listen to reason, especially if it came from her.

''Sabrina?''

She looked up at Siobhan. ''Sorry, I was miles away.''

''Thinking about all the money Mike could win?'' Siobhan said with a grin.

Sabrina forced a quick smile then tucked her hand into the crook of Graham's arm and they followed Schrader down the stairs on to the casino floor.

''No lecture?'' Graham whispered with a hint of sarcasm in his voice.

''Why bother? You wouldn't listen anyway.''

''We have to play up to Schrader if we're going to have any chance of getting invited to his party tomorrow night, you know that.''

''I also know Sergei will carpet us when we get back.''

''Only if I lose.''

The table had six betting spaces on the layout. Three of them were taken. Schrader introduced Graham to the players: Major Alonso of the Chilean consulate; Raoul Lajes, a local businessman; and a sweating Frenchman called Grenelle.

Drago leaned over Graham's shoulder. "The croupier will give you as many chips as you want and you can settle up with him once you leave the table."

"It's Las Vegas rules here in Rio, isn't it?" Graham said without looking round at Drago.

"Correct, but this is a private club," Drago replied with a smile. "Mr. Schrader is allowed to implement his own rules so long as they fall within the framework of the international blackjack rules."

"Are five-card tricks recognized in the club?"

"They are," Drago replied.

Graham waited until Drago had taken up a position behind Schrader before looking across at the croupier. "What's the bet limit?"

"A minimum of one thousand cruzeiros, a maximum of fifteen thousand."

Graham made a quick mental calculation. A maximum bet of just over two thousand dollars. Pin money. "Fifteen thousand cruzeiros," he said to the croupier.

Sabrina bit back her anger at Graham's irrationality. It was always the same, he just couldn't turn down a challenge, irrespective of the harm it could do to himself or to UNACO in general.

The croupier gave him two blue Cr$5,000 chips and five white Cr$1,000 chips.

Graham pushed the two Cr$5,000 chips into the betting space in front of him and when all the bets had been placed the croupier dealt each player a card, face down. He dealt his own face up—an ace. He then dealt a second card to each of the five players, again face down. His own card was also dealt face down but he immediately turned it over to see whether he had a natural. A king. He did—twenty-one. The game was now purely academic for the players unless any of them had a natural as well, in which case his bet would be returned to him. None did, so the croupier recovered their bets and cards.

Graham put the five remaining Cr$1,000 chips in the betting space for the next game. The croupier's first card was a five. Graham's cards were a queen and a four. Schrader, Alonso and Lajes all "bust" and Grenelle announced that he would "stay" after being dealt a third card.

"Monsieur?" the croupier addressed Graham.

"Hit me," Graham replied.

The croupier slid the card from the shoe and turned it face up. A ten.

"Bust," Graham announced gruffly and pushed the cards away from him.

The croupier "stayed" on nineteen. Grenelle turned his cards over. A king and two fives. He dabbed the sweat from his balding pate and raked his winnings towards him like some apprehensive miser.

Graham leaned forward to catch Schrader's eye. "Let's cut the crap and up the stakes."

"By all means. Shall we say fifty thousand cruzeiros?"

"Shall we say two hundred and fifty thousand American dollars?"

A gasp went up from the small group of onlookers. Sabrina shook her head in disbelief. It was just the kind of lunacy that would get him transferred to the Test Center. Her first thought was to try to reason with him, make him see sense before it was too late. Only she couldn't, not without jeopardizing the assignment. Then she caught sight of Siobhan's smile.

"You think it's funny?" she asked incredulously.

"It's exciting," Siobhan answered. "He's really put Martin on the spot."

"Well?" Graham broke the silence. "You know I can cover the bet otherwise you wouldn't have invited me to join the game."

Schrader tugged at his lower lip as he contemplated the bet. "One game?"

"A one-off. Me against the bank."

Schrader smiled. "You've got yourself a deal, Mr. Graham."

Word quickly spread through the casino and games were hastily concluded so that customers and staff alike could join the growing semi-circle of onlookers gathering around the table. Lajes and Alonso vacated their stools to join the crowd of onlookers. Grenelle stuffed his chips into his pocket then, much to Graham's surprise, wished him luck before withdrawing.

Drago had the croupier empty the shoe then offered it to Graham to inspect. Next he placed three new packs of cards on the table and Graham checked, then broke, the seals.

Schrader turned to the croupier. "Henri, deal for Mr. Graham."

"*Oui, monsieur,*" the croupier replied then took the cards from Drago.

Graham looked round as Sabrina approached him. "Save the lecture," he said softly.

"I'll leave that to the colonel," she whispered back. "You're crazy, Mike, you know he'll crucify you when he finds out what's happened."

"Only if I lose. You could wish me luck."

"You know I do." She squeezed his arm and then went back to where Siobhan was standing.

The croupier placed the three-pack deck in front of Graham and asked him to cut them. Graham did it and the croupier then placed the deck in the shoe, face down. Schrader and Drago flanked the croupier, their hands clasped behind their backs.

"The game is blackjack," Schrader announced for the benefit of the onlookers. "House rules. Mr. Graham's bet is two hundred and fifty thousand dollars." He lowered his voice when he spoke to Graham. "Henri will call out the denomination of each card so that the crowd will know what's happening. Any objections?"

"None at all." Graham looked up at Henri. "Let's play."

Henri dealt the first card. "Monsieur Graham—three." He dealt one for the bank. "The house—eight."

Graham sighed with relief. No natural.

Henri dealt the second card. "Monsieur Graham—three." He dealt the second house card face down.

"Hit me," Graham said.

"Monsieur Graham—two."

A buzz of excitement ran through the crowd. There was already talk of a five-card trick. But the next card would be the crucial one. Graham, only too well aware of this, wiped the sweat from his forehead with the tips of his fingers before it could escape down the side of his face. His throat was dry—he could do with a sip of that champagne after all. He pushed the thought from his mind then met Henri's eyes and nodded.

Henri slid the card from the shoe and deftly flicked it face up on to the table. "Monsieur Graham—seven."

There were stifled gasps from the crowd—fifteen in four cards. Although a five-card trick was still a possibility, the odds were greatly reduced. As the game stood, it now had to favour the house. Private bets began to change hands and as the speculation mounted around her, Sabrina could barely contain her excitement. All he needed was the turn of a friendly card. She chewed the inside of her mouth anxiously; he *had* to do it. Graham, unaffected by the growing impatience around him, tapped his finger on the table as he stared contemplatively at the cards in front of him. His eyes finally flickered up to Henri's face. He nodded. Neither Schrader nor Drago showed any emotion when the card was dealt and this only added to the suspense.

Henri placed it face up beside the other four cards then cleared his throat before speaking. "Monsieur Graham— one."

There was a spontaneous burst of applause from those who had won on their private bets. Sabrina and Siobhan hugged each other like excited schoolgirls then grinned sheepishly on realizing what they had done. Such was the noise that none of them heard Graham when he spoke again.

"Hit me."

Schrader, Drago and Henri exchanged glances. Had they heard him properly? He repeated himself.

"Ladies and gentlemen, please," Schrader pleaded, his hands raised. "The game isn't over yet. Mr. Graham has elected to take another card."

The stunned silence was followed by a chorus of arguments. There were those who felt he should have quit while he was ahead. Why was he tempting fate when the odds were now stacked even more against him? Others reasoned that, with the way the cards were turning, he had every right to believe he could pull off a six-card trick.

Sabrina refused to be drawn into the debate, preferring to keep her thoughts to herself. Although not fully understanding, or concurring with, his motives, she was the only person there who knew why he was taking the game to its very limit. It wasn't so much the challenge as the psychology which lay behind it. By taking on these challenges and overcoming the odds, he was proving to himself that he was psychologically stronger than his adversary. It had always baffled her but she knew how important it was to him. Yet the strangest twist of all was that he would invariably concede the challenge once he was satisfied in his own mind that he had won. According to him, it gave his adversary a false sense of superiority, a weakness he could exploit at a later stage. He was using this strategy against Schrader. He had beaten the house with his five-card trick and now he was prepared to throw the game.

~ Graham looked up at a waitress who had, on Schrader's orders, brought him a glass of Perrier water. He drank half of it in one gulp. "Let's play it this way. Henri deals me a sixth card, face down, and we leave it like that while the house plays out its hand. You've got no option but to go for a six-card trick. Should the house 'bust' and my card is six or over, I pay you two hundred and fifty thousand dollars. Should the house 'bust' and my card is five or less, you pay me out. It gives the game a bit of an edge."

Schrader agreed then explained the situation to the crowd and the bets began to change hands again.

"Hit me," Graham said softly and wiped the sweat from his forehead with the palm of his hand.

Henri fed the card from the shoe, face down. He then turned the second house card over. A four. He announced it to the crowd. Twelve from two cards, the worst possible blackjack hand. He dealt a third card—a queen. The house was 'bust.'

Graham picked up his five cards in one hand then slowly reached out his other hand for the sixth card. He slid it off the table without letting anyone see it and immediately slapped his forehead then, shaking his head, closed the six cards together and handed them to Henri. Drago smiled to himself. Sabrina closed her eyes and cursed Graham silently. This time he had gone too far.

Henri opened the six cards, fan-shaped, and counted them.

He then laid them out on the table. "The house 'bust.' Monsieur Graham has a six-card trick totalling twenty. In accordance with house rules Monsieur Graham must be paid out four times his original bet, which was two hundred and fifty thousand dollars. The house owes Monsieur Graham one million dollars."

Graham met Drago's withering stare then reached for his glass and drank the rest of the Perrier water.

Sabrina rolled her eyes when he looked up at her. "And here I thought you'd blown it."

"Yeah?" Graham replied nonchalantly.

"You're an intriguing man, Mr. Graham," Schrader said with a half-smile. "Why did you chance the sixth card?"

"Call it a hunch," Graham answered.

Schrader sat on the stool beside Graham and held out his hand towards Drago who offered him his leather-encased cheque book and the uncapped gold fountain pen. "Would you like me to make it out to you or to cash?"

"Take off the cost of the chips I bought earlier then make it out to a charity of your choice. I'm sure Miss St. Jacques will see that it reaches its destination."

Schrader's hand froze over the blank cheque and he cast a sidelong look at Graham. "You continue to amaze me, Mr. Graham."

"I don't see why. You've got some appalling slums in Rio where money like this could be well spent, especially if it's going to help the kids."

"I'm the chairman of a charity which deals solely with the *favela* children. It's called *Amanha*, which means 'tomorrow.' I think the name's self-explanatory."

"That's perfect," Graham said.

Schrader wrote out the cheque then tore it from the counterfoil and handed it to Siobhan. He climbed off his stool and shook Graham's hand. "Thank you, that was a wonderful gesture."

"As long as the kids benefit from it," Graham said.

"They will, I assure you." Schrader turned to the remainder of the crowd. "The show's over. Now get back to those tables, I need the revenue to make up for this."

There was a ripple of laughter as they trickled back towards the gaming tables to take up where they had left off.

"Allow me to buy you a drink at the bar," Schrader said to Graham and Sabrina.

"We'll get this round. You need the revenue, remember?" Sabrina replied with a cheeky grin.

Schrader laughed loudly. "I'll hold you to that," he said then walked with Siobhan to the bar.

"Mike—"

"Skip it," he cut in quickly. "The money would have gone to UNICEF anyway."

"It was your money and you know it."

"Look, that sort of money means nothing to me. I don't need it. Those kids do. They need every break they can get." Graham stood up. "Come on, we're expected at the bar."

They were shown to Schrader's personal table against the railing overlooking the casino floor and he waited until the waitress had left before speaking. "I'm having a party at my house tomorrow night. I have one every year to coincide with the start of the Carnival. Siobhan's come up with a great idea. Why not come along? Unless, of course, you've made previous arrangements."

Sabrina shook her head. "We've got nothing planned, have we, Mike?"

"No." Graham gave Schrader a quick smile. "We'd love to come, as long as it's not going to inconvenience you in any way."

"Of course not. It's settled then. I'll have the invitation delivered to your hotel in the morning. A car will be there at, let's say, eight-thirty tomorrow night to take you to my house. One thing though—please bring the invitation with you. It's for security reasons, you understand."

The waitress returned with the drinks and Graham paid for them.

"Well, I think I'll go and freshen up." Siobhan caught Sabrina's eye and indicated subtly for her to leave as well.

Sabrina took the hint and, after excusing herself, walked with Siobhan towards the ladies' room.

Siobhan put her hand lightly on Sabrina's arm as they reached the archway which branched off into the toilets and drew her to one side before taking an envelope from her bag and giving it to her. "I've been wanting to show this to you all night but I haven't had the chance. You do speak Portuguese, don't you?"

"I get by," Sabrina replied modestly and removed the single sheet of paper from the envelope. Three sentences had been scrawled across it with a blunt pencil. She translated them softly to herself. "Major drug shipment expected in Rio within the next few days. Mr. André Drago may be involved. Must meet with you urgently."

"I can't afford to get involved. It could blow my cover."

"Have you spoken to your informer yet?" Sabrina asked.

Siobhan shook her head. "I tried calling him when I got here but he wasn't at home. I'm going to try again now."

"I can ask C. W. to check it out. But will your informer talk to him?"

"I've got an idea," Siobhan said after a moment's thought. "I could tell Carlos that C. W. will have the letter with him as proof of his identity. He can choose his own rendezvous if he wants. You call C. W., explain the situation to him, and I'll get a taxi to take the letter to the hotel."

"It's worth a try, if you find your informer is home."

"He should be by now," Siobhan replied, glancing at her watch. "What about Mike?"

"I'll tell him later. Come on."

Drago stood motionless in the security room in the basement of the club, his eyes fixed on one of the ten closed-circuit television screens which lined the semi-circular wall in front of him. One of the cameras in the casino had been homed in on Sabrina and Siobhan and although there was no sound to accompany the picture he was still able to pick up snippets of conversation by reading their lips, a skill he had acquired while in Eastern Europe. He just wished he had completed the course because then he would have known everything they were saying, including the contents of the letter. He was certain the Graham woman had either read or translated it out loud but all he had understood was that something was expected in Rio and that he might be involved. But what was that "something"? The drugs? Or the envelope? And who were the Grahams? Were they also CIA, like Siobhan? He had discovered the truth about her only a year earlier, not that he had mentioned it to Schrader. It was his own ace to be used if and when he needed it.

His thoughts were interrupted when Sabrina and Siobhan headed for the exit. He grabbed the nearest telephone and snapped his fingers at one of the two guards. "Get Lavalle up here, now!" He rang the reception desk. "Marisa?" he cut in before the receptionist could speak.

"Yes."

"It's Drago. I'm in the security room. If Miss St. Jacques

or Mrs. Graham uses the reception phone I want to know who they're calling.''

''Yes, sir.''

He dropped the receiver back into its cradle just as Jean-Marie Lavalle entered the room. Lavalle, a gaunt-faced man in his mid-forties with a neatly trimmed black moustache and pockmarked cheeks, had been a senior officer with the Tonton Macoute before having to flee Haiti after the collapse of the Duvalier dynasty in 1987. This fact was known only to Drago. Officially, he was the head of security at the Riviera Club. Unofficially, he was Drago's most trusted lieutenant and his link to the controversial *favela* vigilantes.

Drago pointed to the screen monitoring the pictures from the foyer camera. Siobhan was standing by the reception desk, the telephone receiver held tightly against the side of her face as if she were talking softly into the mouthpiece. When she replaced the receiver she spoke briefly to Marisa who then reached under the counter and withdrew a leather-bound book, the club's directory of those telephone numbers most requested by staff and customers. Siobhan found the number she wanted, dialled out, then handed the receiver to Sabrina.

''Who's the blonde?'' Lavalle asked.

''That's what I'm hoping to find out.''

Sabrina hung up and Siobhan beckoned Marisa over to the counter again. Another brief conversation followed and Marisa gave her one of the club's official envelopes. Siobhan removed the opened envelope from her handbag, switched the sheet of paper to the second one and sealed it. She used Marisa's pen to write across the front of the envelope then headed towards the front doors.

Marisa called Drago and he listened in silence before hanging up. ''Know a man called Carlos Montero?''

"Yes, sir. Small-time crook, earns most of his cash as an informer."

"That figures. It seems this Montero sent Miss St. Jacques some letter and asked to meet with her to discuss its contents. Only she's not meeting him. A man called Whitlock is. The meeting's scheduled for the Café Cana in an hour's time. I want you to pick up this Montero *after* the meeting and find out what was in the letter. But wait until this Whitlock is out of the way. It's imperative that he doesn't know we're on to him."

"I understand, sir. Do you want me to have him tailed?"

"It's not necessary, I know where he's staying."

"What do you want us to do with Montero once he's talked?" Lavalle asked.

"The usual, then dump the body in Botafogo Bay. The sharks will do the rest."

Lavalle left the room.

Drago looked up at the monitors again and watched as Sabrina and Siobhan walked back across the casino floor to the bar. Top priority would be a thorough screening of the Grahams and this man Whitlock. Then, once he knew who he was dealing with, he would have them killed.

Whitlock had spent the evening pacing the floor of his hotel room, his mind in turmoil as he thought about Carmen back in New York. Part of him wanted to call her, to be reassured by the sound of her voice, but another part of him wisely argued that any selfish act like that could drive her even further away from him. She wanted time alone to think, that much had been evident when they had last spoken, but his impatience was slowly getting the better of him and twice he had had the receiver in his hand, ready to call her. It would be only a matter of time before he went through with it.

Then Sabrina had called.

He had jumped at the chance to meet Siobhan's informer—it would mean he would have something other than his marital problems to occupy his mind. Despite the heat he donned a lightweight jacket to conceal his holstered Browning Mk2, and, after picking up the envelope from the reception desk where it had been left for him, he went outside to hail himself a taxi.

Café Cana was a small diner on Avenida Presidente Vargas, the busiest street in the city. Whitlock paid the driver then entered the diner, pausing momentarily in the doorway to get his bearings. Sabrina had said Montero was a bespectacled, balding thirty-year-old and that he would be sitting at the table third from the door. He was there, a cup of coffee in one hand, a doughnut in the other. A newspaper was spread out across the table in front of him. Whitlock closed the door and crossed to the table where he sat down opposite Montero.

"That chair's already taken," Montero said without looking up. "I'm expecting someone."

"He's here."

Montero eyed him suspiciously. "Let's see some ID."

Whitlock tossed the envelope on the table.

Montero tore it open, glanced at the note, then handed it back to Whitlock. "Forgive me for staring, but when Miss St. Jacques said an Englishman would be meeting me I naturally assumed . . ." he trailed off with an awkward shrug.

"You naturally assumed I'd be white?"

Montero nodded guiltily. "I hope I haven't offended you."

"Not in the slightest." Whitlock glanced up at the waitress. "Coffee please."

"You should try the doughnuts," Montero said between mouthfuls. "They've got to be the best in town."

"No, just coffee," Whitlock said to the hovering waitress then turned to Montero. "Where did you pick up your English?"

"Night school. I used to be a guide for English-speaking tourists until I discovered the more lucrative aspects of crime. Well, let me tell you what I overheard last night." Montero took another bite from the doughnut and decided to speak and chew at the same time. "I was having a drink at a bar on Pasteur Avenue when five men came in and sat down at the table next to mine."

Whitlock grabbed Montero's wrist as he was about to push the last of the doughnut into his mouth. "Eat or talk, but not at the same time."

Montero dropped the doughnut on to his plate. The waitress returned with the coffee and dumped it in front of Whitlock before slapping the bill down on the edge of the table.

"Perhaps the doughnuts make up for the service," Whitlock muttered. "Go on with your story."

"These five men all work for André Drago's vigilante squad. You have heard about them?"

Whitlock nodded.

"They started to get a bit talkative after a few *cachacas*. *Cachaca*'s Brazil's answer to tequila. They weren't loud or rowdy, just talkative. I only heard snatches of the conversation but I got the gist of what they were talking about. I made a few notes on a paper napkin." Montero took the napkin from his pocket and unfolded it. "A Colombian freighter, the *Palmira*, will be passing Rio on its way to Montevideo within the next few days. Somewhere off the Rio coast a consignment of heroin will be transferred from the *Palmira* to the *Golconda*, Martin Schrader's yacht which Drago's allowed to use whenever he wants. The *Golconda* would never be challenged by the harbour police so, in theory, the drugs could be taken right into Schrader's private jetty and unloaded there. And that's it."

"A few questions. First, how come you knew them but

they didn't seem to know you? Surely your paths must have crossed before?''

"They know me all right, but not as I am now. I used to have a ragged beard and hair down to my shoulders. That was before I went to prison. I was released last week but now, as you can see, with short hair and no beard. Another reason why they spoke so openly was because I was with a date, a young lady from your part of the world. London. We spoke English the whole night. They must have thought that we didn't understand them.''

"You said in your note that Drago *may* be involved. Why the uncertainty?''

"I only heard them mention his name once but I didn't hear it properly in context.''

"Personally, what do you think?''

"If it were Schrader, I could put my hand on my heart and say with all honesty that he wouldn't be involved. Drago, I'm not so sure.''

"Why the certainty about Schrader?''

"Hasn't Miss St. Jacques told you about his son?''

"No.''

There was no mention of any children in the UNACO dossier.

"I'll tell you briefly what happened. Soon after Schrader arrived in Rio there was a story in one of the papers about a ten-year-old boy who had lost his family in a *favela* fire. Schrader was so taken by the story that he adopted the boy himself. The two of them were inseparable for the first couple of years but when the boy reached his teens he started to dabble in drugs. The first Schrader knew about it was when he identified the boy at the mortuary. He'd overdosed on heroin. From that day on Schrader's been waging his own private war against the Brazilian drug barons, especially those in Rio.''

"Why the uncertainty about Drago?"

"The way he's implemented Schrader's instructions in the *favelas* hasn't exactly endeared him to the country's drug barons so unless he's got his own distribution network set up somewhere I can't see any reason for him to be involved either."

"Who's to say he hasn't?"

"That's what makes it so uncertain. I wouldn't put it past him to double-cross Schrader, especially after the rumour I heard the other day. It seems one of Schrader's servants claims he overheard Drago on the phone saying he was going to give Rio an unforgettable farewell present before he left Brazil for good."

"And that farewell present could be the drugs," Whitlock replied.

"They could be but why would he leave Brazil for good? It would mean he'd lose everything he's built up for himself over the past four years. It doesn't make sense."

Whitlock took out his wallet. "How much do I owe you?"

"Nothing. Miss St. Jacques pays me. Thank you anyway."

Whitlock finished his coffee, picked up the bill, then got to his feet.

Montero looked up at him. "I may be a criminal but I still hate drugs as much as the next person. Stop them, mister, before it's too late."

Whitlock paid his bill and Montero watched him flag down a passing taxi then turned his attention back to the newspaper. He left the diner ten minutes later. Avenida Presidente Vargas was congested with traffic at that time of night and he decided to use the Metro to get home, which would be quicker than a taxi. He pushed his hands into his pockets and whistled softly to himself as he walked towards Central, the nearest of the subways. The passenger door of a black Mercedes in front of him was suddenly thrown open and Lavalle climbed out. Montero looked behind him. Two of Lavalle's men were closing in on him. He was unarmed, outnumbered and scared. There was only one means of escape—across the chaotic Avenida Presidente Vargas. He ran into the first lane where a silver BMW missed him by inches but as the driver slammed on the brakes a transit van ploughed into the back of the car. The two men looked to Lavalle for instruction. He shook his head. Montero, stranded between two lanes of traffic, darted in front of an oncoming bus. Its wing mirror clipped him on the back and he tumbled headlong into the path of an articulated lorry. He was already dead by the time his pulped body disappeared underneath the cab.

Lavalle lit a cigarette as the Mercedes drew abreast of the stationary lorry. He looked down at the body, cursed angrily, then ordered the driver to take him back to the Riviera Club.

"What do you make of it?" Sabrina asked Whitlock after he had recounted his conversation with Montero.

She and Graham had returned to the hotel an hour after Whitlock and gone straight to his room to discuss the evening's events.

"Well, remember what Siobhan said about the *Golconda*? It can only be moved with official permission from either Schrader or Drago. And after what Montero said about Schrader, I can't see him being involved. Which leaves Drago. The whys and wherefores may be unclear at the moment, but I'd say he's behind it."

"I agree," Graham replied. "And that means you can kiss your back-up duties goodbye. If that heroin shipment's due to be transferred to the *Golconda* some time tomorrow night then it's up to you to stop it."

"I'm not going to be able to pull it off by myself."

"Call Sergei, he'll jump at the chance to get out of the office," Sabrina said.

"Call him now." Graham pointed at the telephone. "He'll only be watching *Jeopardy* or one of those quiz shows he likes so much."

"I'll call him before I turn in. That way I can give him the day's report at the same time."

"I'm going to turn in myself." Graham stifled a yawn then looked at Sabrina. "Coming?"

She nodded. "That casino's tired me out."

"Before you two go, let me make sure I've got tomorrow's agenda straight. I'm to meet with this man Siobhan mentioned, Silva, the one who used to work for Schrader, to get the info on Schrader's private galleries."

"Yeah," Graham agreed. "Simply because you'll be able to slip in and out of the *favela* unnoticed. A white face is invariably given a pretty hostile reception. In return, I'll get a homing device on the *Golconda* for you by early afternoon."

They both looked at Sabrina.

She rolled her eyes. "Okay, so I've got to spend the day with Siobhan getting a costume ready for the party. It's not by choice, believe me."

"How come you don't have to get dressed up for this party as well, Mike?" Whitlock asked.

"The women's costumes are important. Fortunately it doesn't matter what the men wear."

"So much for equality," Sabrina muttered then followed Graham to the door.

They said goodnight to Whitlock and left.

Whitlock slumped on to the bed. *Jeopardy*, Carmen's favourite programme. Why had Graham mentioned it? It had brought all the pain back to the surface again. He rang the apartment in New York but slammed the receiver down after the first ring and rubbed his hands wearily over his face. Calling her wouldn't solve anything. He picked up the receiver again and rang UNACO headquarters.

"Llewelyn and Lee, good evening," Sarah's taped voice said on the answering machine. "Our office is closed right now but if you would care to leave your name and number after the tone one of our managers will be glad to get back to you in the morning."

"C. W. Whitlock, ID 1852963," he said after the tone.

There was a pause, then a click, then the receiver was picked up at the other end.

"Good evening, Mr. Whitlock," the duty officer said politely.

"Evening, Dave," Whitlock replied as he leafed through the standard UNACO code book. "I want a B3, a G5 and three fifteen-pound M8s loaded on to one of our planes within the hour."

A B3 was a swimmer delivery vehicle, a G5 a portable crane and an M8 a limpet mine.

"It's very short notice, Mr. Whitlock, all those items are packed away in the stores department."

"Then I suggest you tell 'stores' to pull their finger out and get it done. Now, patch me through to Mr. Kolchinsky."

Whitlock briefed Kolchinsky with the usual ambiguousness all UNACO operatives adopted over the telephone.

Kolchinsky, alerted by the reference to the drug shipment, hurriedly packed a suitcase and was on his way to John F. Kennedy Airport fifteen minutes after replacing the receiver in his bedroom.

NINE

Whitlock's first view of Rocinha, the largest of the *favelas*, was of layer upon layer of cardboard, plywood and tin shacks heaped together in a tangled maze of human misery and suffering. Yet, as the taxi driver had pointed out, the greatest irony of all was that these *favelados* had a better view of the city and surrounding bays than the multi-millionaires below them. The driver parked as close as he possibly could to the shanty Whitlock wanted and agreed to wait fifteen minutes for him. No more. He also warned Whitlock not to talk to any of the residents, as his accent would only draw an angry reaction. No tourist was welcome in Rocinha. Whitlock thanked him for the warning and made his way down a narrow alley, an uneven surface of rock-hard earth littered with rubbish and crawling with vermin. Children dressed in rags, their eyes wide at the sight of his new clothes, cowered back against a corrugated iron fence as he passed. He was about to stop and reassure them when he remembered the driver's cautionary warning. An obese woman in a sleeveless floral dress emerged from one of the shacks and he screwed up his face at the overpowering stench of stale sweat on her unwashed body. He quickened his pace until he reached the tin shack he wanted and knocked lightly on the open door, worried that if he knocked any harder the whole rickety contraption would collapse in front of him. A little girl appeared, her dress torn at the sleeve and her face smeared with mud and grime.

He tried his beleaguered Portuguese on her. *"Obrigada. Onde fica vossa pai?"*

She just stared at him.

He was about to call out when a grey-haired man emerged from a back room.

"Obrigado," the man said hesitantly.

"Obrigado. Are you Silva?"

The man's face broke into a wide grin. "Miss St. Jacques told me to expect you. Please, come in."

Whitlock was amazed by the man's crisp, accentless English. It seemed distinctly out of place in the squalor of their surroundings.

"I'm João Silva," the man said extending a hand.

Whitlock shook it firmly.

Silva put his hand on the little girl's shoulder. "My daughter, Louisa. She's deaf, that's why she didn't understand you at the door."

Whitlock squatted down in front of Louisa and tipped out the coins from his wallet into his hand. Her face lit up, her white teeth contrasting vividly with her dark skin. She looked to her father for guidance. He nodded and she carefully picked each coin from Whitlock's palm, then, clutching them to her midriff, hurried from the room.

"You're very kind," Silva said then gestured to one of the two armchairs in the room. Both were battered, but clean. "Your accent?" he asked sitting down opposite Whitlock. "Eton? Harrow?"

"Nothing so grand. Radley."

"I don't know it. You see, I was Mr. Schrader's personal valet for seven years and in that time I came into contact with many of his friends who came from all over the world."

"So what happened?" Whitlock asked looking around.

"You've no doubt heard of André Drago?"

"Frequently," Whitlock replied.

"Drago and I never got on from the day he arrived at Danaë—that's the name of Mr. Schrader's estate. He was jealous that I was closer to Mr. Schrader than he was. So he framed me. He had personal items belonging to Mr. Schrader planted in my room. Mr. Schrader refused to press charges against me but I was still fired. Drago then blacklisted me so that whenever I got a job he'd find out and call my superior to warn him of my past. I couldn't hold down a job and this eventually resulted in my wife walking out on me. All I have now is Louisa."

"And Drago did this just because he was jealous of you?"

"Yes. He saw me as a threat so he reduced me to this." Silva shook his head sadly. "The people here regard him as a saviour. But they only see the side of him he wants them to see."

Whitlock stared at the threadbare carpet. "Did Miss St. Jacques tell you what I wanted?"

"Yes, I've got it all here." Silva handed Whitlock a dozen sheets of paper. "It's the layout of the house as best I remember it. Naturally Mr. Schrader could have altered it since I left."

"And the galleries?"

"I've detailed 'The Sanctuary' as best I could—"

" 'The Sanctuary'?" Whitlock cut in.

"It's the gallery where Mr. Schrader would sit for hours on end, especially if something was troubling him. He maintained it had a great calming effect on him. A friend of his dubbed it 'The Sanctuary' and the name stuck. There's a second gallery somewhere behind 'The Sanctuary' but to the best of my knowledge, Mr. Schrader's never let anyone inside it.''

"Do you know what he keeps in there?"

"Original paintings. Well, that's what he once told me."

"I take it he has the only means of access?"

"Yes. All I know is that it's some kind of remote control device that he keeps in his bedroom safe. I've included the safe's exact location in one of the diagrams."

Whitlock had a quick look through the diagrams then withdrew an envelope from his pocket and handed it to Silva. "Fifty thousand cruzeiros, the fee you agreed on with Miss St. Jacques."

Silva took the money with a certain amount of reluctance. "I hate myself for selling out Mr. Schrader like this, he was always a good employer to me. I'm only doing it for Louisa. She deserves better than this."

"Where will you go?"

"Uruguay. My cousin's a foreman on a farm outside Tacuarembó. He's always said he could get me a job as a labourer, all I had to do was find the money to get down there. I know it's not much but at least Louisa will have the chance to grow up away from the misery of Rocinha. What future would she have here?"

Whitlock wished him luck then walked back to the waiting taxi.

The battered red Buick never merited a second glance as it drove through Rocinha. It was exactly what Drago wanted. Such was his desire for anonymity that he was wearing a pair of faded green overalls, a panama hat and dark sunglasses.

Lavalle, who sat up front beside Larrios, Drago's personal driver, wore similar green overalls and a sweat-stained baseball cap. All three men were armed.

Larrios brought the Buick to a stop then jumped out and opened the back door for Drago. Lavalle screwed a silencer on to the barrel of his Walther P5 then pushed it into his pocket and followed Drago down the narrow alleyway to the last in a row of tin shanties. Drago eased open the plywood door and entered. A scuffed leather suitcase stood in the center of the room. Drago was about to take a closer look at it when Silva appeared from the adjoining bedroom. He froze, his eyes darting between the two men, then looked behind him at Louisa who was sitting on the bedroom floor, her back to the door.

"What do you want here?" Silva asked bitterly. "You know you're not welcome."

"Since when does—"

"It's okay," Drago cut across Lavalle's outburst. "João's never forgiven me for proving him a thief in front of Mr. Schrader."

"A thief?" Silva snapped. "You framed me and you know it."

"Strange how nobody ever believed you." Drago tapped the suitcase with the side of his foot. "Going somewhere?"

"It's none of your business."

"I guess not," Drago replied with a shrug. "Tell me about this Englishman who came to see you earlier this morning. And before you deny it, one of the reports I received was from the taxi driver who brought him here."

"An Englishman did come here looking for information about Mr. Schrader. I told him I wouldn't help him so he left."

"Fifteen minutes later? Come, João, you can do better than that. What was his name?"

"I don't know," Silva replied truthfully.

Drago put an arm around Silva's shoulders and led him to the bedroom door. "She's a beautiful little girl. It would be tragic if something were to happen to her."

The anger drained from Silva's face. "Please, Mr. Drago, don't hurt her."

"I wouldn't, but Lavalle's done things to children that make even my stomach turn when I think about them. Don't force me to send him in there, João."

Silva shuddered. "I'll answer your questions, just don't let him hurt Louisa."

Drago sat on the arm of the nearest chair. "Who was this Englishman?"

"I don't know, he never told me his name. Please, Mr. Drago, you must believe me."

"I believe you, João," Drago replied with a placating smile. "Who arranged the meeting?"

"Miss St. Jacques."

"And what did he want?"

"He wanted plans of Danaë."

"Plans?" Drago frowned. "What sort of plans?"

"Plans of the house."

"Anywhere in particular?"

" 'The Sanctuary.' "

"Interesting." Drago stood up and pointed to the suitcase. "So you sold him these plans for enough money to get you out of Rocinha?"

"I did it for Louisa, she deserves better than this."

"How very touching," Drago sneered then looked at Lavalle. "Kill him."

Lavalle pulled the silenced Walther P5 from his pocket

and shot Silva through the heart. Silva stumbled backwards and fell heavily against the flimsy corrugated-iron wall. The vibration startled Louisa and she approached the door, her eyes wide with fear and uncertainty.

"What about her?" Lavalle asked without taking his eyes off Louisa.

"What do you think? She's a witness." Drago crossed to the front door then looked back at Lavalle. "I'll send you a couple of men to help dispose of the bodies."

He returned to the Buick and told Larrios to take him to the Riviera Club. Once they were clear of Rocinha he discarded the panama hat and sunglasses then unzipped the green overall to reveal a white shirt and a pair of black trousers. He took his tie from the glove compartment, put it on, then reached over and retrieved his jacket from the back seat. His wire-framed glasses were tucked into the breast pocket. Larrios dropped him off a block away from the Riviera Club and he walked the remaining distance, pausing once to adjust his tie in the reflection of a shop window.

"Afternoon, Mr. Drago," Marisa said when he entered the foyer.

He nodded in reply then helped himself to a copy of the *New York Times* from the pile of newspapers on the reception counter. "Ask the bar to send a beer to my office then get me the Metropolitan Museum of Art in New York." He went to his office on the second floor, hung his jacket behind the door, then sat down at his desk and checked the previous day's sales figures.

The telephone rang and he snatched up the receiver.

"The Metropolitan Museum on the line, Mr. Drago."

"Hello? Hello?" Drago shouted once Marisa had put him through.

"May I help you?" a cultured female voice asked quietly.

"Mils van Dehn, please."

"I'll put you through to Mr. Armand."

A second receiver was picked up. "Louis Armand, can I help you?"

"I'd like to speak to Mils van Dehn. Your switchboard operator put me through to you."

"I'm afraid Mr. Van Dehn isn't here. He returned to Amsterdam a couple of days ago. Try the Rijksmuseum. I'll give you their number—"

Drago cut him off then flipped through his personal book of telephone numbers, found Van Dehn's name and dialled the work number. "Mils van Dehn, please," he said when the Rijksmuseum answered.

"One moment, sir."

Drago pulled a pack of cigarettes towards him, took one out and lit it.

"*Goedemiddag*, Professor Hendrik Broodendyk."

"I'm trying to get hold of Mils van Dehn," Drago said struggling to control his rising temper.

"I'm afraid Mils won't be back at work for another few days."

"Is there any way I can get hold of him?"

"I'm afraid not. Perhaps I can take a message for you?"

"No, thank you." Drago hung up and inhaled deeply on the cigarette. Why had he been put through to Broodendyk?

The knock at the door interrupted his thoughts and a waiter entered with a tray bearing a glass and a bottle of Brahma. Drago signed the chit then dialled Van Dehn's home number. No reply. He still had one ace up his sleeve. Van Dehn had given him his mother-in-law's number in Deventer to be used only in an emergency.

A woman answered the phone.

"May I speak to Mils please?" Drago asked politely.

''Mils is not here. You wish to speak to his wife?'' Each word was carefully pronounced in a thick Dutch accent.

''That won't be necessary. Do you know where he is?''

''America, he has gone there with the painting—''

''Thank you, you've been most helpful,'' Drago cut in then replaced the receiver.

His instincts were right—the switch had been discovered.

He used the telephone again, this time to arrange for the bodies to be removed from Rocinha. He needed Lavalle back at the club so they could finalize the details of the *Golconda*'s movements that night. Not only would Lavalle be skipper of the *Golconda*, he would also be representing Drago in his dealings with the *Palmira*'s captain who, by all accounts, was quite capable of short-changing him on the deal he had made with the Colombian drug baron two months earlier. Four million dollars in cash (money he had skimmed off Schrader over a period of two years) in return for eighteen kilograms of heroin. And he was determined to get what he paid for, down to the last gram. Then, once the shipment was loaded on to the *Golconda*, it would be taken back to port where a van would be waiting to transport it to a secret laboratory in the city where it would be cut and adulterated, ready for use. But not in Brazil. It would once more be stored on board the *Golconda*, ready for Schrader's annual pilgrimage to Miami, a trip he always took as soon as the Carnival was over. What nobody knew was that he, Drago, would have vanished by the time the drugs reached the Miami streets. The envelope was his passport to a new life where he wouldn't have to look over his shoulder continually to see whether his former intelligence colleagues had finally managed to track him down, ready to fulfil the contract which had been hanging over his head ever since his defection to America five years earlier. A defection forced upon him by the CIA. Now he wanted

revenge against that system and what better way than to tempt
the teen-agers who flocked in their thousands to Florida every
summer with a lethal, habit-forming drug at the sort of un-
dercut price any high-school kid could afford? Then, once
his cut-price supply had run out, the new addicts would find
themselves having to pay the full price for their fix. Few
would have the money so they would turn to crime to get it.
The crime rate would rise and all the time the addicts would
be pushing themselves ever closer to the edge of destruction.

The greatest irony was Schrader's unwitting involvement
in the whole plan. His money had financed the drugs, his
jetty would be used to unload them and his yacht would be
used to transport them to Miami.

Were something to go wrong, Schrader had been set up to
take the fall.

The metallic silver 130-foot *Golconda*, with its steel hull,
aluminum superstructure and teak decks, had been Schrader's pride and joy ever since he had taken delivery of it from
the Italian Versilcraft Shipyards four years earlier. In addition
to the two staterooms, it contained another five double cab-
ins, a sun lounge, a saloon, a dining room and a galley
equipped to cater for up to five months at sea. It was powered
by two Caterpillar Marine diesel engines with a top speed of
fifteen knots and a cruising speed of twelve knots.

Graham parked the hired Audi Quattro beside the wire
fence and looked at the *Golconda* moored to a private jetty
twenty yards away. It looked deserted but he knew there were
at least two armed guards on board. Perhaps more. His original idea of attaching the homing device to the hull below
the waterline had been scuppered when Siobhan told him that
ever since a limpet mine had been found near the propeller
the *Golconda* never set sail without first having her hull

checked by a member of the crew. It had left him with one alternative—to board her and plant the homing device on the superstructure.

He climbed out of the Audi and slid a pair of sunglasses over his eyes. He was wearing a bright yellow T-shirt, a bandanna around his neck to hide his injury, a pair of plaid Bermuda shorts, sandals and a white stetson tilted down over his forehead. Duane Hitchins was a creation of his dating back to his Delta days: a loud, overbearing Texan with a lot of money and very few friends. The character, based on an officer he had come across in Vietnam, only ever surfaced when he needed a cover story to bluff his way out of a tricky situation. Trespassing on a private yacht was one such situation. Duane had yet to get into trouble—people were only too pleased to see the back of him as soon as possible.

The gates were locked. He took a nail-file from his pocket and quickly dispensed with the lock. The deck was still deserted by the time he reached the gangplank. After looking around he made his way on to the deck and crossed to the sliding door leading into the saloon. It was unlocked. He slid it open but as he stepped inside he broke the contact of an invisible infra-red beam, setting off a piercing alarm. He was still looking around for somewhere to conceal the homing device when a guard appeared, armed with a Star Z-84 sub-machine gun. Graham immediately became Duane Hitchins—thinking like him, reacting like him. He smiled nervously but made no move to raise his hands, which would only alert the guard to the device trapped between his thumb and palm. A second guard arrived, similarly armed.

"Can't you put that godawful noise off?" Graham asked in a Texan drawl.

The guards said nothing. A tall, blond man appeared and

snapped his fingers at one of the guards who hurried away to switch off the alarm.

"Hell, that's better," Graham said when the alarm stopped. "That's quite some siren you got there, boy. You the captain here?"

"*Ja*, Captain Horst Dietle," the man replied in a distinctive German accent. "Who are you?"

"Duane Hitchins at your service." Graham indicated the sub-machine gun aimed at his stomach. "That thing's making me kind of nervous."

Dietle motioned the guard to lower the sub-machine gun. "What are you doing here?"

Graham sat down on the nearest banquette, a puzzled look on his face. "Why, I've come to give you a damn good offer for your boat."

"Offer?"

"Yeah, I heard a rumour at the hotel that it was for sale. I'll better any price you've been offered for it up to now."

"This yacht is *not* for sale," Dietle replied indignantly.

"Hell, no. You're kiddin' me, right?"

"This yacht belongs to Martin Schrader and it is certainly not for sale."

"Call Marty, tell him to name his price. I'll get myself a bourbon at the bar while you're gone."

"Mr. Schrader is not selling the *Golconda*," Dietle snapped, his face flushed with anger. "Now either you leave or I will have you arrested for trespassing."

"Okay, I'm leaving." Graham pressed his hands into the soft, upholstered leather and slipped the homing device down the back of the seat before hauling himself to his feet. "Tell Marty I called, y'hear? He'll find me at the Palace Hotel if he changes his mind."

Dietle glared after Graham then turned on the guards, berating them for leaving the gates unlocked. They tried to protest their innocence but Dietle cut across their words and ordered them to secure the gates behind Graham.

Graham tossed the stetson on to the back seat the moment he was out of view of the *Golconda* then switched on the radio, found a music station, and hummed softly to himself for the rest of the drive back to the hotel.

A coachload of tourists were checking in at the reception desk and after getting his key he had to pick his way through the luggage to reach the lift. He pressed the button then stood back, the stetson gripped tightly in both hands behind his back.

"Enjoying Rio, Duane?"

Graham looked round and smiled at Kolchinsky. "Sergei? When did you get into town?"

"A couple of hours ago," Kolchinsky replied. "I'm staying at the Caesar Park."

They stepped into the lift and Graham pressed the button for the seventh floor.

"So what's your alter ego been up to this time?"

Graham explained briefly what had happened on board the *Golconda*.

Kolchinsky chuckled. "You've got Duane down to a T, haven't you?"

"I'm not sure whether to take that as a compliment or an insult," Graham replied then paused outside the room, the key poised over the lock. "Sabrina's not here. She'll only be back later this afternoon."

"Where's she gone?"

"I'll explain it all in a minute. Let me get out of these awful clothes first."

"Is C. W. here?"

Graham unlocked the door. "Yeah, he should be."

Kolchinsky looked around the room. "This is nice. Very nice."

"It should be, it's the goddam honeymoon suite," Graham growled.

Kolchinsky chuckled then sat down. "I'll call C. W., we'll meet him by the pool. It's too nice a day to be stuck indoors."

"Sabrina wrote down his extension number. It should be by the phone," Graham called out from the bedroom.

Kolchinsky found it and dialled the number. There was no reply. He then called the switchboard and asked them to page him.

When Whitlock rang the room it turned out he was already at the poolside. Kolchinsky told him they would meet him there in a couple of minutes. Graham, having changed into a pair of blue shorts and a white T-shirt, emerged from the bedroom and they rode the lift back to the foyer.

Whitlock, wearing a pair of swimming trunks and with a towel draped around his neck, waved at them to catch their attention and they crossed to the umbrella-shaded table and sat down. A waiter took their order then left.

"You look like you're having fun," Kolchinsky said dabbing the sweat from his neck with a handkerchief.

"I might as well while I can," Whitlock replied with a smile.

The waiter returned with their order and Graham signed the chit.

Kolchinsky dispensed with the glass and drank a mouthful of beer from the bottle. He wiped the froth from his mouth before speaking. "Who's going to update me on the latest developments?"

They took it in turns to relate the morning's events.

"So you won't have had a chance to look through those plans yet?" Kolchinsky asked Graham.

"Not yet."

"I brought them with me," Whitlock said, indicating Silva's plans on the table in front of him. They were rolled up together and secured with an elastic band. "The drawing isn't up to much but the detail's excellent."

Graham removed the elastic band then sat back to study the diagrams more closely.

"So what's this yacht like you hired?" Kolchinsky asked Whitlock.

"Pretty old, but the engine's in good condition. It's the first thing I checked." Whitlock took a sip of beer. "Was there any trouble getting the gear I asked for last night?"

"None at all. It was all loaded on to the plane by the time I got to JFK. It's at the airport, in two crates, so we'll be able to get them on to the yacht without arousing any suspicion."

"What's the latest on Strike Force Two?" Graham asked.

"They're due to hit the jail at midnight, Libyan time." Kolchinsky checked his watch. "That's in under six hours' time."

"What are their chances?" Whitlock asked.

"Good. They won't be as restricted as you were when you broke Masterson out of the Moroccan jail. Morocco's an original signatory of the UNACO Charter. Libya, on the other hand, has always refused to cooperate with us."

"So anything goes?" Graham looked up from the papers.

"They'll resort to firepower if there's no other way out. It doesn't mean they'll have carte blanche to re-enact a *Rambo* script."

Whitlock pushed his empty glass away from him and stood

up. "It's already three o'clock, Sergei. We've got a lot to do this afternoon."

Kolchinsky nodded then patted Graham lightly on the shoulder. "Good luck tonight, Michael."

"Yeah," Graham muttered absently without looking up.

"Enjoy the party, Mike," Whitlock said with a faint smile, knowing how much Graham hated social events of any kind.

"Yeah," Graham repeated as he continued to study the diagrams.

Whitlock and Kolchinsky exchanged amused glances then walked back to the foyer.

Graham poured over the diagrams for another fifteen minutes then, once he was satisfied with the plan he had in mind, he caught the waiter's attention and ordered another Perrier water.

TEN

<hr>

"Aren't you ready yet?" Graham shouted through the closed bathroom door.

"Another five minutes," Sabrina called back.

Graham shook his head in despair—she had been in the bathroom for the past hour.

"Are *you* ready?" she asked.

"Ages ago," he replied then slumped on to the bed and clasped his hands behind his head.

"Are you wearing that shirt I bought for you?"

"Yeah," he replied with a grimace.

It was a blue, red and yellow madras shirt, the kind of garment Duane would wear. He wore it with the bandanna tied loosely around his neck, a pair of jeans, canvas shoes and a kitsch white peak cap with RIO emblazoned across it. It had been a present from Siobhan and he felt obliged to wear it if only to enter into the spirit of Carnival.

"Siobhan's a really nice person once you get to know her," Sabrina suddenly called out. "It's just a matter of getting behind that showbiz facade of hers."

"A-ha," Graham muttered.

"She had a pretty tough childhood by all accounts. Her mother was an alcoholic and it was left to her father to raise her as best he could. When he died she ran away from home and joined a gang of pickpockets working out of the *favelas*. Then, when the pickpocket ring was busted, she was sent back home only to find that her mother had remarried. Her stepfather was also an alcoholic. He beat her so she ran away from home again. That's when she was discovered by the modelling agency. She got married when she was twenty. Her husband was a freelance photographer based in Paris. That's how she got the break to work over there."

"Are they still together?"

"I don't think so. She didn't seem to want to talk about it so I didn't push it."

He looked round when she emerged from the bathroom. She was wearing a figure-hugging white lacy leotard, a silver-sequinned bikini and a silver-and-gold lamé cape fastened loosely around her throat.

"Well, what do you think?"

"You'd get arrested if you walked down Fifth Avenue like that."

She chuckled. "I'll take that as a compliment. Actually, this is fairly conservative according to Siobhan. It seems the women at these parties all vie with each other to see who can produce the most daring costume of the evening. The more erotic and exotic the better."

"I'd say your costume was pretty daring." He shrugged. "Perhaps I've just led a really sheltered life."

"Sure, Mike," she said with a smile.

"Carrie would never have been seen in something like that. But then she always was a bit prudish."

It was the first time she had ever heard him say anything detrimental about Carrie. He had always spoken of her as if she were a deity on a hallowed pedestal. Was this some kind of catharsis?

"We had our differences like any other couple," he added as if in answer to her thoughts. "I guess you could say she was the typical daughter of a hard-line Republican senator."

"Her father was a senator?"

"Senator Howard D. Walsh of Delaware."

" 'Hawk' Walsh?"

"Yeah, so called because of his aggressive stance on foreign policy issues, especially in Central America."

"He was the scourge of the Democrats. I know my father never liked him."

"Neither did I but I used to keep the peace for Carrie's sake."

"Was she . . . as radical as him?" she asked hesitantly, knowing he might well change the subject as he had done before when he felt she was prying too deeply into his past.

"You think I'd have married her if she was?"

"Do you still visit her parents?"

"Her mother died before the wedding. The last time I saw 'Hawk' was the day after Carrie and Mikey disappeared." He began to pace the floor angrily, his hands clenched tightly at his sides. "I realized then just what a hypocrite he really was. One of his campaign promises was to pressurize the then Reagan administration into taking even tougher measures against terrorism than it already had. You know what he said to me after I got back from Libya? 'I would have made any deal with them to get my daughter and grandson back safely, irrespective of how many innocent American lives were lost in the process.' Those were his exact words. They'll haunt me for the rest of my life. The two-faced bastard!" He punched the wall angrily then spun round to face her. "Did he think I took the decision lightly to sacrifice my own family? But I knew that if I backed down, those terrorists would have carried out their bombing raids in several of our major cities, causing untold death and destruction. I did what I believed was right. Not that he cared. Not a damn.'' He walked out on to the balcony where he sucked in several mouthfuls of air before returning to the bedroom. "I'm sorry for shouting at you like that. It's just that 'Hawk' Walsh is a very touchy subject.''

"I can see why," she said softly. "And if anyone should be apologizing, it should be me for poking my nose in where it doesn't belong.''

"Forget it," he replied dismissively.

The telephone rang. It was the reception calling to say that their driver had arrived.

"So you still think I'd get arrested?" she asked as they left the room.

"*Molested*, more likely.''

Heads turned when they emerged from the lift and crossed the foyer to the middle-aged chauffeur standing at the reception desk.

"You Mr. Schrader's driver?" Graham asked after handing in the key.

"Yes, sir. My name's Felipe, I'm your personal driver for the evening. Would you care to follow me?" He led them out into the forecourt where a polished champagne-coloured Rolls-Royce Corniche was parked.

"Very nice," Graham said running his hand over the roof.

"Mr. Schrader has a fleet of them.''

"A fleet?" Graham rejoined. "How many in all?''

"Fifteen. Each has a different driver." Felipe opened the back door for them then closed it once they were inside and climbed behind the wheel. "You will find a television set, a telephone, a drinks cabinet and four music channels to choose from in the unit in front of you. Please feel free to use these facilities and should you need me you'll find a two-way radio in the panel on the right-hand side of the unit. I hope you'll enjoy the ride.'' He activated a button on the dashboard and a sheet of soundproof glass slid into place, dividing the front and back seats of the car.

"What do you fancy? Music or TV?" Sabrina asked once the car had joined the traffic on Avenida Atlantica.

"Music," came the quick reply.

The types of music were listed in both English and Portuguese on a brass plaque in front of her.

"Well, you can have either classical, country and western, jazz or MPB."

"What's MPB?"

"*Musica Popular Brasiliera*. The samba, bossa nova, ethnic music in other words."

"We'll be hearing enough of that at this party. Let's see what he calls jazz."

She flicked on the switch.

He listened for a few moments before identifying the musician. "Dizzy Gillespie. At least he's got good taste in jazz."

"I don't believe it. We've actually got something in common."

"You like jazz?" he asked, mildly surprised.

"I live for it," she replied with a grin.

"Yeah? I took you for one of those pop freaks."

She shrugged. "Sure I listen to pop but jazz has always been my first love. Especially live jazz. Ali's Alley, Village Vanguard, West Boondock. Those are my favourites."

"Those names bring back *some* memories." He leaned his head back on the seat and stared at the white padded roof. "Fat Tuesday's on Third Avenue was my favourite club but I haven't been back since I moved away from New York."

Jazz remained the sole topic of conversation for the rest of the journey.

Lavalle crushed his cigarette underfoot then looked at the *Golconda*, its superstructure streaked with the last rays of the setting sun, before unlocking the padlock on the gate with a key given to him by Drago and beckoning towards the nearest of the two black Mercedeses. Three men got out. Like him, they were dressed in black. They followed him across the jetty, up the gangplank and on to the *Golconda*'s deck. He cupped his hands around his mouth and called out for Dietle who emerged through a hatchway moments later with the two armed guards close behind him.

"Jean-Marie, what are you doing here?" Dietle asked curiously.

"It's a bit delicate, Horst." Lavalle shot a quick look at the guards. "Can we talk somewhere private?"

"*Ja*, of course. Come to my cabin."

"Horst, one thing." Lavalle put his hand lightly on Dietle's arm. "How many men have you got on board at the moment?"

"Just two guards. The crew are not due back until next week. Mr. Schrader always gives them shore leave over the Carnival period. Why do you ask?"

"I'll explain in your cabin."

Dietle led the way down a flight of stairs and along a teak-panelled corridor to his cabin. "So what is this all about?" he asked closing the door behind them.

"I'll be able to explain it better with a chart of the local area. Have you got one?"

"Of course I have," Dietle replied indignantly. "Which area in particular?"

"Leme Point," Lavalle said using the first name that came to mind.

Dietle crossed to the table to find the chart. Lavalle stole up behind him, the silk scarf already taut between his hands. When Drago had specifically stipulated that there was to be no blood shed during the killings, Lavalle had automatically thought of the scarf he had used to such deadly effect with the Tonton Macoute. It was similar to the weapon used by the Thugs in India, the only difference being that he knotted a pebble in the middle of the scarf as opposed to the Thugs' traditional rupee. He looped the scarf around Dietle's neck and tightened it savagely. Dietle's fingers raked at the pebble as it dug ever deeper into his windpipe but within seconds he had fallen to his knees, his movements becoming weaker until his body finally went limp. Lavalle kept up the pressure for another thirty seconds before unwinding the scarf and pushing it back into his pocket. He returned to the deck where his men were waiting for him. As he had instructed, the two guards had also been garrotted, their bodies lying inside the nearest of the hatchways. Lavalle signalled to the second Mercedes and two men jumped out and approached the yacht, each carrying a holdall. The two Mercedeses started up and drove off into the night. The holdalls were opened and the weapons distributed. Six Heckler & Koch MP5 sub-machine guns and five CZ75 automatics. Lavalle was already carrying his Walther P5.

After deactivating the alarm two of the men donned scuba gear and disappeared over the side of the yacht to check the hull. They surfaced five minutes later and gave Lavalle the thumbs-up sign. He handed the ignition key to one of the men then went back to the captain's cabin, this time to call Drago and tell him that the first phase of the operation had been carried out successfully.

* * *

Kolchinsky and Whitlock were standing on the deck of the sixty-five-foot *Copacabana Queen* when the *Golconda*'s engines revved into life. Kolchinsky picked up a pair of Baird night vision binoculars and watched as the two divers were helped off with their oxygen cylinders before handing the binoculars to Whitlock.

"What sort of head start are we going to give them?" Whitlock asked.

"A couple of miles. There's no need to advertise ourselves."

Whitlock trained the binoculars on the shimmering lights of the city behind them. "I wonder how Mike and Sabrina are getting on at Schrader's party?"

Kolchinsky held up a can of Coca-Cola in a facetious toast. "They can only be having more fun than us."

The Rolls-Royce Corniche came to a halt in front of a pair of ten-foot wrought-iron gates and Felipe contacted the control room, situated within the house itself, by means of a radio handset clipped to the dashboard. A closed-circuit television camera panned the car before the gates were electronically opened to admit them. The driveway snaked through an endless expanse of green lawns illuminated by powerful floodlights and patrolled by armed dog-handlers. It ended a mile further on at a second, smaller gate with the name "Danaë" arched over it in gold lettering. It, too, was activated electronically from the control room and as the car turned into a spacious, circular courtyard the mountain appeared in front of them like some giant monolithic sentinel. Felipe stopped the car in front of a glass-fronted reception area and a man in a gold diamanté suit and top hat hurried forward to open the back door.

Felipe opened his window. "Mr. Graham, just let any member of staff know when you're ready to leave and they'll have me paged. I hope you both enjoy the party." He put the Corniche into gear and drove back down the driveway.

"I see you're admiring Mr. Schrader's mountain," the man in the diamanté suit said in a distinctive Jamaican accent.

"It seemed to appear out of nowhere," Sabrina answered craning her neck to look up at its brightly lit rockface.

"It's the way Mr. Schrader designed the approach road. He's always full of surprises." The man indicated the black-and-white tiled reception area. "If you would care to follow me?"

The electronic doors parted in front of them and they crossed to a small semi-circular desk where a beautiful light-skinned Carioca gave them a friendly smile and asked for their invitation. Graham handed her the card and she fed the name into a computer. It appeared on the VDU with the letters VIP/AD in brackets after it. Drago had listed them as special guests. The arrival of VIPs had to be telephoned through to the house so that either Schrader or Drago could welcome them in person. She handed the invitation to the Jamaican then picked up the telephone as he led them to the lift. It transported them three hundred feet into the mountain before the door opened on to another reception area. The Jamaican handed the invitation to the receptionist, bowed curtly to Graham and Sabrina, then disappeared back into the lift.

A steel door slid open to the right of the reception desk and Drago appeared, a fixed smile on his face. The door closed behind him. He shook Graham's hand and gave Sabrina a quick nod of acknowledgement. "I'm so glad you could both make it. Mr. Schrader's apologies, he was wanting to meet you personally but he was waylaid by the mayor's wife before he could get here. She insisted he dance with her. What could he say?''

''The perils of being a host,'' Sabrina said with a wry smile.

Drago's mouth twitched in a half-smile. ''Quite so, Mrs. Graham. Well, I'm sure you both want to join the party so let me show you the way.'' He pushed his identity card into the slot by the steel door which opened into another lift.

''How tall is the mountain?'' Sabrina asked.

Drago pressed a button and the door closed. ''The mountain itself is nine hundred and seventeen feet above sea level. That's about two hundred and eighty metres. The reception area where you came in is three hundred feet above sea level.''

''And how high are we going?'' she asked.

''The garden is eight hundred feet above sea level. That's where the party's being held.''

The lift stopped and the door opened on to a mosaic-tiled patio. Drago gestured through the plate-glass doors to the dozens of colourfully dressed people mingling on the newly cut lawn and around the Olympic-sized swimming pool. He then pointed out the red-and-white striped marquee in the middle of the garden and explained that it contained a seventeen-piece percussion band, which specialized in *Carnaval* music, and a dance floor that could accommodate up to two hundred people at any given time. He opened one of the soundproof doors with his ID card and the noise of the party suddenly flooded into the patio. They descended the half dozen steps to the lawn where a white-jacketed waiter was waiting for them with two glasses on his tray.

''I took the liberty of ordering your drinks for you when I heard you'd arrived,'' Drago said indicating the tray. ''A dry white wine and Perrier water. It you'd prefer something else I'll gladly have it changed for you.''

''No, this is great,'' Graham replied taking the two glasses from the tray and handing one of them to Sabrina.

''Ah, here comes Mr. Schrader. If you'll excuse me, I have a lot to attend to. I'm sure we'll bump into each other again during the course of the evening when we can talk some more.'' Drago smiled at Schrader then crossed to where a group of businessmen were huddled in conversation beside the swimming pool.

Schrader was dressed in a pair of white shorts and a floral shirt. He shook their hands warmly. ''So glad you could come. I hope André extended my apologies when he met you?''

''Yeah, I believe the mayor's wife snared you for a dance?''

''A fate worse than death, Mr. Graham. Avoid her at all costs. She has a penchant for young millionaires.''

''How will I know her?''

''You'll hear her long before you see her.'' Schrader appraised Sabrina's costume. ''You look quite stunning tonight, Mrs. Graham.''

''Thank you,'' Sabrina replied with a smile.

''I hope you won't begrudge me a couple of dances with your lovely wife?'' Schrader said turning to Graham.

''Not at all. I'm sure she'll be glad to dance with someone who doesn't have two left feet. I'm afraid I'm no Fred Astaire.''

Schrader laughed then took two identical silver charms from his pocket and handed one to each of them. They were shaped in the form of a clenched fist with a raised thumb between the second and third finger. ''It's called a *figa*,'' he told them. ''It was originally worn by the slaves to bring them fertility and good luck. Now it's a tourist gimmick but there are those who say it does work if you believe strongly enough in its power. I've worn one ever since I got here and, as you can see, it hasn't done me any harm.''

"So you actually believe in its power?" Graham asked turning the amulet around in his fingers.

"Certainly. But then I was as skeptical as you are when I first heard about it. It's only because I've come to understand its significance that I believe so strongly in its power.''

Graham shrugged then eased the chain over his head and straightened the amulet until it was in the center of his chest. "At least it might keep the mayor's wife away from me.''

"Never make fun of voodoo, Mike, not in Brazil," Siobhan said behind him. Like most of the women there, she wore an outfit more erotic than exotic. It consisted of a black satin basque, black stockings and a black-and-white striped tanga.

Graham ran his eyes the length of her body before holding her stare. "You can believe in it if you want but it's all a sham as far as I'm concerned.''

"You would consider it a sham. You're a free-thinker. I've seen too many voodoo-related deaths for me not to believe.''

"You've convinced yourself they're related, it suits your belief. In reality there will be a perfectly logical explanation for all those deaths.''

Sabrina put her hand on his arm. "Come on, this is a party. Lighten up.''

"Okay, no more talk of voodoo," Graham agreed.

"Mrs. Graham—''

"Why the formality? It's Mike and Sabrina." Siobhan looked at them. "Right?''

"Right," Sabrina replied with a shrug.

"In that case, Sabrina, would you care to dance?" Schrader asked.

"I'd love to."

Siobhan watched Schrader and Sabrina walk toward the marquee. "She thinks the world of you."

"Sounds like the two of you had an interesting chat today," Graham retorted.

"We did, but not in the way you think. You're so lucky. Everybody thinks that because I'm a film star I must have loads of friends. The truth is I've never been so lonely in my life."

Graham stared at his glass. "Sabrina said you were married."

"Jeff's dead," she replied softly.

"I'm sorry."

"He was stabbed outside a nightclub in Paris six years ago by a drug dealer who had mistaken him for a rival dealer." She shrugged, smiled quickly, then handed him her glass. "I wouldn't say no to a refill."

"What are you drinking?"

"Same as you. The bar's down by the pool. I'll walk with you."

"I always thought the Carnival was about dressing up," he said as they crossed the lawn. "Most of the women here look like they've had a bad night playing strip poker."

She smiled. "The *bailes* are totally different to the *Passarela do Samba*—"

"You've lost me already," he interrupted.

She stopped and gestured around them. "This is a *baile*, a ball. They're always sexually active, especially those held at the more exclusive hotels and nightclubs. At those kind of places it's not uncommon to find three women to every man. Martin doesn't encourage that sort of obvious promiscuity and only a few of us are allowed to attend his *Carnaval baile* unescorted.

"The *Passarela do Samba*, or Samba Parade, on the other hand, is what you see on television. It's a tourist attraction, relying on floats and costumes to draw the crowds. So the more colourful and imaginative it is, the more successful it's going to be the next time round."

Graham recognized the man approaching as Raoul Lajes, one of those who had been at Schrader's blackjack table the previous night. Lajes was dressed in a bright floral shirt and a pair of plaid shorts with a paper lei draped around his sweaty neck. He asked Siobhan in Portuguese for a dance. She shook her head but when she tried to get past him he grabbed her arm, this time demanding that she dance with him.

Graham broke Lajes' grip on Siobhan's arm and pointed a finger of warning to him. "I don't speak Portuguese but it's obvious she doesn't want to go anywhere with you. Now leave her alone."

"The benevolent gambler," Lajes sneered at Graham. "What do you care about her anyway? She's not with you. Or is she? Perhaps I should have a word with your wife. If she's available—"

Graham's punch caught Lajes on the side of the head, rocking him backwards into the swimming pool. Drago broke away from the couple he was talking to and hurried to the poolside where he issued a series of curt orders in Portuguese to two of the waiters. They ran to the edge of the pool to help Lajes out of the water. A gash had opened up across the corner of Lajes' left eyebrow and the blood was running down the side of his face. His wife tilted his head to the side, inspected the wound, then snapped at the nearest waiter to bring her a cloth filled with ice cubes. Drago countermanded her instructions and beckoned them towards him. Schrader and Sabrina, who had heard the commotion as they emerged from the marquee, pushed through the crowd of onlookers and Siobhan told them what had happened.

Drago spoke to three eyewitnesses then turned back to Lajes. "If you're not off this estate in five minutes, I'll have you arrested."

"What about him—"

"Shut up, Maria!" Lajes snapped at his wife when she pointed at Graham. He looked at Schrader. "Don't put our friendship on the line like this, Martin."

"Don't talk to me about friendship, you're the one who abused my hospitality," Schrader shot back angrily. "You heard what André said. Now leave."

"You weren't even here, Martin," Maria snapped. "You'll believe anything Drago tells you."

"Maria, that's enough!" Lajes shouted.

"No, for once I'm going to speak my mind because nobody else around here has the guts to do it." Maria met Schrader's stare. "Drago's using you, Martin, can't you see that? You gave him a whiff of power and it's turned him into a corrupt megalomaniac. The sooner you get rid of him, the sooner you'll get back the respect you had before you let him take over. Get rid of him, or he'll destroy you." She grabbed her husband's arm and steered him towards the house.

Schrader shook his head sadly as he watched them disappear into the lift. "Maria's always had a big mouth. She'll be Raoul's downfall yet."

"And he's always a bit of a handful after a few drinks," Drago added.

"He didn't look drunk to me," Graham said.

"He was drunk all right," Schrader replied. "Raoul's one of those people who just never show it. The only telltale sign is his aggressiveness, especially in his attitude towards women."

"Maria's got him exactly where she wants him," Siobhan explained. "Drink's his only outlet. It gives him the courage to get out from under her thumb and prove his manhood to himself."

"Enough about Raoul and Maria," Schrader said then looked at Siobhan. "Dance?"

"Sure." She winked at Sabrina. "See you later."

Drago excused himself and headed for the bar.

"Did you have to hit him?" Sabrina demanded of Graham once they were alone. "Couldn't you have backed down just this one time?"

"I had my reasons for hitting him. Let's leave it at that. I'm going to get the transmitter from the safe. Keep Schrader occupied."

"You still haven't told me how you intend to get into his room. You can't get in through the door, it's operated by remote control."

"That's according to Silva's diagram. Not only that, all public areas in the house are monitored by closed-circuit television cameras. I couldn't have got in through the door anyway."

"You're evading the question."

"I'll tell you later," he countered.

She extended her hands in a pleading gesture. "I'm your partner, Mike. What more can I do to make you trust me?"

He contemplated her words before speaking. "Okay. My guess is that there are no cameras in either the bathrooms or in Schrader's suite. They have to draw the line somewhere. Silva's diagram shows a bathroom right beside Schrader's suite so, in theory, I should be able to get from the bathroom to the suite without being seen."

"I know this is probably a stupid question, but how? As far as I can see, the only way . . ." she trailed off and shook her head in disbelief when she realized what she was about to say.

"There is only one way. Through the bathroom window, across the rockface and onto the bedroom balcony."

"That's sheer madness!"

"Keep your voice down," he hissed angrily. "This is exactly the reason why I don't like discussing anything with you before I do it. You take on this role of the overprotective mother terrified that her little boy might graze his knee."

"I take on that role because I care about you." She sighed then continued in a soft, calm voice. "You've got no tackle to back you up. All it takes is one mistake for you to fall."

"The object of the exercise is not to make mistakes," he said with thinly veiled sarcasm. "I've done this kind of manoeuvre with Delta and I've never had to rely on my back-up ropes."

"But at least they were there in case you *did* need them."

"You're missing the point, Sabrina. I didn't need them, can't you see that? It's all psychological. You used the word 'mistake.' Mistakes are caused by hesitancy, uncertainty, even stupidity. In a word, *fear*. And as I've told you before, I don't believe in the concept of fear. It's a chimera which anyone can overcome with an absolute belief in themselves. I believe in myself. I also believe I can cross that rockface without falling. If I had the slightest doubt, I wouldn't even consider attempting it." He smiled at her. "I'll be okay, I promise you."

"Be careful," she said then kissed him lightly on the cheek.

"I intend to be. Now go on, keep an eye on Schrader."

"What about Drago?"

"He'll be keeping an eye on me, you can be sure of that."

No sooner had they split up than Drago, watching discreetly from the bar, unclipped the two-way radio from his belt and told the duty officer in the control room to monitor Graham's every move personally once he entered the house.

Graham reached the red-and-white tiled patio which, as in Silva's diagram, led into a poolroom. Although both tables were occupied, none of the players took any notice of him when he passed them and slipped through the sliding door into a cream-coloured hall, its walls lined with what looked like a collection of original Rembrandts and Vermeers but which were, in fact, perfect reproductions by some of the world's foremost forgers. He visualized Silva's diagram again—a spiral staircase leading down to a larger hall, at the end of which was Schrader's bedroom suite. He had to squeeze past a couple sitting hand-in-hand halfway down the stairs who, judging by their mischievous grins, were meeting secretly away from their respective spouses. His suspicions were confirmed when the man, who was a little drunk, made a "sshh" sound and pressed his finger against his lips. Graham played along. He glanced around furtively then pressed his finger to his lips and began to tiptoe down the stairs. They both started giggling. On reaching the foot of the stairs he thrust his hands into his pockets and pretended to be interested in the paintings on the walls on either side of him. It was imperative that he act as naturally as possible knowing that the discreet closed-circuit television cameras would be monitoring his every step. He moved slowly down the cavernous hallway, pausing every so often to take a closer look at a particular painting, desperately trying to simulate some kind of interest in its contents. It reminded him of those first few weeks when he had started to date Carrie. She loved ballet and opera, neither of which interested him in the slightest, but such was his determination to impress her that he had spent several tedious evenings both at the New York

State Theatre and the Metropolitan Opera House before it became too much for him and he had to admit defeat. It turned out she had known all along that he had been putting on a pretence but she had decided against saying anything, maintaining it was his fault for not having been honest with her in the first place. They reached an understanding after that—he would go to the ball games with his sporty friends and she would go to the ballet and the opera with her aesthetic friends. It had turned out to be the perfect solution.

He reached the end of the hall and found himself facing a pair of ornately carved tagua doors. To the right of them was a plain white door, seemingly out of place in such grand surroundings. He pushed open the door and locked it behind him. The room was small with a toilet and washbasin. He suddenly wondered why Schrader hadn't just knocked down the wall and incorporated the room into his suite. How many people would actually use it? He dismissed the thought and moved to the window. He tied the lace curtain to one side then eased open the window and, kneeling on the lowered toilet cover, peered down at the waves crashing against the foot of the mountain directly beneath him. The room had to be at least six hundred and fifty feet above sea level. He craned his neck further through the open window to assess the distance between it and Schrader's balcony—twenty feet at the most. Then, on closer inspection of the rockface, he saw that not only was its surface craggy and uneven, perfect for climbing, but the mountain itself actually sloped backwards the higher it went. The gradient couldn't have been more than twenty degrees, but it helped. The only disadvantage would be the lack of light. He would have to rely solely on the moon.

He stripped off his jeans to reveal a pair of tight-fitting wetsuit pants underneath them then, tossing his shirt and bandanna on to the floor, he climbed on to the ledge above the washbasin and swivelled round so that he was squatting with his back to the window. He eased himself backwards then lowered his legs until he felt he had a solid foothold on the rockface beneath him. The rock was cold and asperous to the touch as he inched himself away from the bathroom window, each step tentative as he probed and tapped with the soles of his shoes until he felt it safe enough to move his other foot into position. A cloud suddenly blocked out the moon, denying him his only source of light. He cursed angrily to himself, not daring to move, his body pressed tightly against the side of the mountain. A succession of explosions startled him and he inclined his head slightly to see a firework display briefly illuminate the sky over Ipanema Beach in a kaleidoscope of vivid colour before melting away into the darkness. The moon reappeared as suddenly as it had vanished and he was able to continue to edge his way slowly and methodically towards the balcony.

He was within a few feet of it when his foot slipped on a piece of loose rock. He grabbed at a protrusion of rock with his right hand but it crumbled in his grasp. His fingers raked at the rockface then locked into the aperture of a narrow crevice inches from his face. Then, as he struggled to get a better grip, his fingers brushed against the body of a two-lined bat roosting inside the crevice. It took flight, the tip of its wing brushing the side of his face. He instinctively jerked his head back and lost his grip in the crevice. He also lost his footing and for a terrifying moment all that prevented him from falling was the grip of his left hand on the rockface. His legs swayed precariously from side to side and he stifled a cry as his left knee slammed against the mountain. He dug his fingers into the crevice again and probed with his feet, despite the sharp pain in his left leg, to regain his footing on the rockface. Once he had done it he exhaled deeply and rested his forehead on the back of his hand. He was furious with himself. He had panicked. And panic was fear. So much for all his damn theories! He winced, his eyes stinging from the sweat running down his face on to his chest. He shook his head, splattering his shoulders with sweat, but within seconds the sweat was running down his face again. He covered the last few feet without further incident then clamped one hand, then the other, around the protective railing and hauled himself over it on to the balcony. He slumped down against the railing, and tilted his head back until it rested on one of the struts. He closed his eyes.

He remained motionless for almost a minute, the gentle breeze fanning his sweating body, before he opened his eyes and looked at his knee. The gash was superficial though blood was oozing down the wetsuit on to his canvas shoes. They were black and the discolouring was barely visible. He got to his feet then crossed to the open sliding door and was about to step inside when he remembered the infra-red beam protecting the sliding door on the *Golconda*. Would Schrader have installed one in his suite? He put himself in Schrader's position. The door faced out on to a balcony and a 650-foot drop. How could anybody get in? He smiled—apart from himself, that is. So why bother? He went inside. He scooped up a crumpled towel from the floor and, after wiping the blood from his wetsuit, tied it around the gash to prevent any blood from seeping on to the carpet. He went into the bathroom, closed the door behind him, then switched on the light. The room was dominated by a sunken bath set in marble with gold taps and handrails. It was extravagant, but effective. He found a roll of bandage in one of the wall cabinets and after unwinding the bloody towel from his knee he dabbed some disinfectant on to the gash then secured the bandage around it, knotting it tightly at the back of his leg. He buried the towel amongst the dirty linen in a washing basket in the corner of the room then switched off the light and returned to the bedroom, making straight for the Van Gogh forgery on the wall to the right of the sliding door.

The painting, which Silva maintained fronted Schrader's personal safe, was exactly where he had drawn it in one of the diagrams. Graham felt around the edges and found that the frame was hinged to the wall on one side. He opened it. The safe was there. Then joy turned to horror. Silva had described it as having a combination lock, the kind of safe Graham had learnt to crack while at Delta. The safe in front of him was key-operated! He punched the wall in anger then slumped down against it and ran his hands through his damp hair. Schrader had changed the safe since Silva's dismissal. He finally got to his feet, closed the painting, then walked out on to the balcony where he rested his arms on the railing and stared at the illuminated window silhouetted invitingly against the dark, unfriendly rockface. A prolonged absence from the party would alert Drago who might even go as far as to have the toilet door broken down on the pretext of being concerned for Graham's welfare if there was no reply to his knocking.

The sooner he got back, the better.

Schrader dabbed the sweat from his face with a mono-grammed handkerchief as he and Siobhan emerged from the marquee. He waved away a hovering waiter and smiled at Sabrina. "The two of you will be the death of me yet," he said breathlessly. "I'm shattered."

"And here I thought I could sweet-talk you into teaching me more about the samba," Sabrina said grinning at Siob-han.

"Later," Schrader replied pocketing the handkerchief. "Much later. Not that you need any tuition, you're a natural."

"I don't feel like one after watching Siobhan on the dance floor."

"Don't forget, I grew up with the samba. Martin's right though, you do have a natural rhythm when it comes to dancing. You'd pick up the movements in no time at all."

"So where's Mike?" Schrader asked looking around the garden.

"He's gone for a walk."

"Nothing wrong, I hope?"

Sabrina smiled. "No, nothing like that. He loves to go off on his own every now and then. He's very independent."

Siobhan excused herself and crossed to a group of friends who had just arrived at the party.

Sabrina stared after her. "Siobhan tells me you're something of an art connoisseur."

"She flatters me. I love collecting paintings but I'd hardly call myself a connoisseur. Are you interested in art?"

"Very much on an amateur basis. I'm afraid I don't get to as many exhibitions as I'd like to. That's what comes of dating a sports fanatic."

"I can believe that. Mike certainly looks the sporting type."

"Is there any one particular period which interests you?"

"The Renaissance," came the immediate reply. "The only problem is all the great works of that period are either owned by museums or private collectors who won't sell at any price. So I have to make do with second best but, as the saying goes, imitation is the sincerest form of flattery."

"You mean . . . forgeries?" she asked feigning surprise.

"It's all quite legal, I assure you," he replied hoping to

allay her concern. "I would only be breaking the law if I tried to pass any of them off as originals in public."

"So your whole collection consists of forgeries?"

"Part of it. Has Siobhan told you about 'The Sanctuary'?"

"She did mention something about it but I didn't really understand what she was on about."

"Would you like to see it?"

"Sure, why not?"

"I'll ask André to tell Mike where we are should he get back before us."

"No, don't." She gave him a scheming look. "He walked off and left me. I'll show him two can play that game."

"Good for you." He gestured towards the house. "Shall we go?"

She felt the relief flood through her—the last thing Mike needed was for her to give Drago an excuse to go and look for him.

"So where did you meet Mike?"

"At the United Nations," she replied truthfully. "I work there."

"Really? What do you do?"

"I'm a translator. French mainly."

"Sounds fascinating," he said taking an ID card from his shirt pocket to activate a metal door. It slid open to reveal a lift.

She entered the lift. "It can be, especially when the superpowers are at each other's throats."

He pressed a button then stood back, his hands clasped in front of him. "I met my wife at university."

"I didn't know you were married."

"Legally I am, but Katerina and I have been separated for the last ten years. She's a devout Roman Catholic so divorce is out of the question. Not that I'd ever want to remarry anyway. I'm enjoying my freedom too much.''

''I bet you've had your fair share of marriage proposals since you arrived here,'' she said with a grin.

A look of anger crossed his face. ''Of course, but then that's to be expected. Rio's plagued with gold-diggers but I always dismiss their intentions with the contempt they deserve.''

The lift stopped and they emerged into a short, red-carpeted corridor which led to a white padded door. He activated the door with the ID card then stood aside to let her pass. The white room contained seven paintings: three on the right, three on the left, and one in the center of the wall opposite the door. It was this one which caught her attention. A still life—an old table bearing two long-stemmed pipes; a glass lying on its side; a flute; a candle which had petered out; a stack of dog-eared history books; and in the center, dominant in its position on top of the books, a skull.

''It's mesmerizing, isn't it?'' he said quietly behind her. ''Harmen Steenwijck's 'Vanitas.' The original was painted around 1640. It's now hanging in the De Lakenhal Museum in Leiden.''

''It's an obsession with death,'' she said without taking her eyes off it.

''A perfect description.'' He put his hand lightly on her arm and she instinctively pulled away from him. ''Sorry, I didn't mean to startle you. Look at all the paintings in context. There is a theme, albeit a personal one. On the left are Rembrandt's 'The Syndics,' Ferdinand Bol's 'The Governors of the Leper Colony' and Mathieu Le Nain's 'Reunion of the Amateurs.' The three on the right are all Constables— 'Hampstead Heath,' 'West End Fields' and 'Salisbury Cathedral from the Meadows.' And then in the center, 'Vanitas.' ''

''And they're all forgeries?''

''Unfortunately, yes. Each has a brass plaque underneath it to say where the original's hanging.''

She folded her arms across her chest and studied the paintings. ''The three on the left are of groups of men in discussion. The syndicate, Hecht's board of directors; the leper colony—outcasts—a reference to the workers in your factories who produced the weapons; and the amateurs, the bureaucrats in power who forced you to resign and sell the company. Then, on the right, the landscapes. Nature. Man and nature, the two most powerful forces on earth. But even they have to succumb to the greatest force of all—death.'' She looked round at Schrader. ''A bit theatrical, I know, but how did I do?''

He was dumbfounded. ''Nobody has ever pieced it together so perfectly. It's as if you read my mind. But how did you know about my involvement in the Hecht scandal?''

''Mike told me. I hope I haven't upset you by dredging it up again?''

''Heavens, no. I'm just surprised he remembers back that long. It's been a good ten years now.''

''He has one of those retentive memories most people would kill for. And what does he fill it with? Sporting facts and figures. What a waste.''

''I still can't get over it. As I said, nobody's ever managed to piece it together before.''

''There has to be a first time for everything,'' she replied with a modest shrug. ''What I want to know is why you call the place 'The Sanctuary'?''

''I'll be able to demonstrate it better to you if you sit in that chair behind you.''

"Chair?" she said looking round in bewilderment.

The padded leather armchair and the wooden cabinet beside it were both white and had blended in so well with their surroundings that she hadn't noticed either of them when she entered the room.

She gathered up her cape and eased herself into the armchair. It was as if she were sitting on air. Schrader crouched beside the chair and opened the cabinet. Inside were an Accuphase Compact Disc player, an SRM-71 valve energizer and a pair of white Stax Gamma headphones. The top shelf was reserved for a large selection of classical compact discs. He asked her to choose one. She traced her fingernail along the cases, hoping to find her favourite piece of classical music. She did—Prokofiev's *Cinderella Suite*. She pulled it out and scanned the credits. The St. Louis Symphony Orchestra conducted by Leonard Slatkin. She had seen them both in concert, albeit on different occasions. Her parents were avid concert-goers so whenever they flew up from Miami to visit her she always made sure she had three tickets to either the Carnegie Hall or the Avery Fisher Hall. Although she invariably enjoyed the concerts, she never went by herself (or with an escort), preferring instead to spend her time with her friends at one of her favourite jazz clubs.

Schrader took the compact disc from her, nodded consentingly at her choice, then fed it into the player. He handed her the headphones and, after explaining what to do, retreated quietly to the corner of the room where he turned down the dimmer switch until they were shrouded in darkness. She slipped on the headphones then closed her eyes, attempting to drain her mind of all outside thoughts. Try as she might, she couldn't do it. A shadowy figure remained entrenched in the back of her mind, haunting her subconscious, its silhouette clinging precariously to a dark, forbidding structure. *Believe in him, like he believes in himself*, she said to herself and the vision began to fade like some celluloid illusion. She repeated the words in her mind until it had disappeared completely. She suddenly felt totally relaxed and reached out to start the compact disc player. Then, after letting the introduction play for a few seconds, she pressed a button built into the arm of the chair. It activated a dozen multicoloured laser lights fitted discreetly into the ceiling. Only then did she open her eyes. She allowed herself to be mesmerized by the lights as they filtered across the walls, creating a kaleidoscope of subtle illusions around her.

Then she remembered Schrader's words: "I find it very therapeutic. It's as if I've finally bridged the gap between the past and the present to be with the great masters that I've come to admire so much over the years. I guess you could call it a temporary sanctuary from the bitterness and animosity of the outside world. Everyone who sits in the chair will undergo a different experience. It all depends on your subconscious thoughts."

She found herself staring at "Vanitas." The skull. The lights scythed across each other, diffusing uneven beams across the painting, distorting the skull into hideous forms and shapes. But it was all in the mind. She felt herself tensing but, try as she might, she couldn't look away from "Vanitas." She was losing her grip on the situation. Then, without warning, the shadowy figure came back into her thoughts. Only now it was falling into a bottomless void. Falling, falling . . .

"No," she screamed and ripped the headphones from her ears.

Schrader turned the light back on and hurried over to her. "Sabrina, are you all right?"

She wiped her clammy forehead with the back of her hand. "I'm sorry, I don't know what came over me."

"I do. 'Vanitas.' It has that effect on some people. As I said to you, it depends solely on your subconscious. I'm sorry."

"Why? You can't be responsible for my thoughts." She picked up the headphones and turned them around in her hands. "I hope I haven't damaged them."

"They're not important," he said taking them from her and placing them on the cabinet. "You look like you could do with a brandy."

She pulled a face and shook her head. "I hate the stuff. I wouldn't mind a bit of fresh air, it suddenly feels like an oven in here."

"I won't be a moment. I've just got to switch everything off."

She crossed to "Vanitas." It was so different in the full light. So very different.

"Are you ready?"

"Sure."

"Mike will probably be back by now," he said as they entered the lift.

"I certainly hope so," she answered softly.

Graham climbed back into the toilet, jumped nimbly to the floor, then closed the window behind him. He splashed cold water over his face and chest then sat on the edge of the toilet seat and towelled himself down. His knee was throbbing but he was more concerned about the blood than the pain. The blood hadn't, as yet, seeped through the bandage and he was hopeful that the bleeding had stopped altogether. He zipped up his jeans then pulled on his shirt and knotted the bandanna around his neck before reaching for the towel again to wipe it across his sweating face.

There was a sharp knock at the door.

"Mr. Graham?" It was Drago.

"I won't be a minute," Graham called back as he wiped the scuff marks from the window sill.

"Are you all right in there?"

"Yeah, I've just got a bit of a stomach upset." Graham checked the room then crossed to the door and opened it.

"My God, you look awful," Drago explained. "We have several doctors here tonight. I'll get one of them to take a look at you."

"I'm okay. Really. I feel a bit weak, that's all." Graham paused at the foot of the stairs. "How did you know I was in there?"

"All public areas in the house are monitored by closed-circuit television cameras. For security reasons, you understand. The duty officer saw you heading towards Mr. Schrader's suite, those doors to the left of the toilet, so he naturally kept his eye on you. When you hadn't come out of the toilet after ten minutes he thought something might be wrong and contacted me. It's that simple."

"But how did he know my name?"

"Like myself, the duty officer knows the name of every guest here tonight."

"I'm impressed," Graham said.

"It's not as impressive as it sounds, I assure you. Ninety-nine per cent of those here tonight are invited to all of Mr. Schrader's parties. And as you may have gathered from Miss St. Jacques, Mr. Schrader throws a lot of parties. There's a closed-circuit television camera in the reception area downstairs, so whenever anyone arrives the receptionist feeds their name into the computer, which is linked to a terminal in the control room, and the name appears on both screens. It's then just a case of matching the face to the name. That accounts for the other one per cent.''

''I can see why Schrader holds you in such high esteem. You obviously know your business.''

''I have to, Mr. Graham. Like anyone in his position, Mr. Schrader has his fair share of enemies. If they saw a weakness in his security system, they would exploit it. That weakness could cost him his life.''

''Fair comment,'' Graham agreed. ''By the way, you said something a moment ago which got me thinking. You say those doors next to the toilet lead into Schrader's suite?''

''That's right,'' Drago replied hesitantly.

''So why doesn't he just knock the wall down and incorporate the toilet into the suite? Surely it can't be used that often?''

''It isn't. Has Miss St. Jacques told you about Roberto?''

''No, not that I recall.''

''Mr. Schrader adopted a boy—''

''She did tell me,'' Graham said remembering what Whitlock had told him. ''The kid who OD'd on heroin.''

''He overdosed in that toilet. Mr. Schrader doted on the boy more than most parents do on their *own* children. He vowed after the funeral never to demolish it as long as he lived here.'' Drago led them through the poolroom and out on to the patio where he looked across the garden. He pointed towards the marquee. ''Your wife's over there. Can you see her?''

''Yeah, I see her.''

''Please don't hesitate to tell either Mr. Schrader or my-

self should you feel ill again. You'll receive the best possible treatment. If you'll excuse me.'' Drago headed for
the bar.

Graham was sure Drago had already seen through their
cover story which meant it would be only a matter of time
before he came after them. And they were no closer to
getting the painting back than when they had first arrived
in Rio de Janeiro. It didn't augur well for their chances of
ever getting it back. He took Sabrina to one side and told
her about the safe.

"So we're back to square one," she said grimly.

"It sure looks that way. We're going to have to sit
around the table with Sergei and C. W. tonight and hopefully come up with an alternative plan we can use within
the next twenty-four hours.''

"What now?''

"There's not much point staying—'' He stopped
abruptly when he caught sight of the man talking to Drago
at the bar.

"Mike, what's wrong?'' she asked following the direction of his gaze.

"It can't be,'' he said without taking his eyes off the
man's face.

The man looked towards the marquee. Graham put his
hand to his mouth and pretended to cough, effectively
shielding part of his face. Drago held out his hand in front
of him and the two men began to walk towards the marquee, both deep in conversation. Graham looked around
for a means of escape. He knew he couldn't get into the
marquee without being noticed but if he stayed where he
was there was a good chance the man would see him. He
had only one option open to him.

"Kiss me,'' he said to Sabrina.

"What?" she replied an amazement.

"Kiss me, and make it realistic."

He pulled her towards him and kissed her, one hand placed firmly in the small of her back, the other stroking across her bare neck. She pushed herself against him, running her fingers through his damp, tousled hair.

"They would be arrested for that in Russia," the man said in a rich Ukrainian accent as they passed them.

"American newlyweds," Drago said with the hint of a smile.

"Typical," the man grunted.

Graham began to kiss her neck. "Have they gone?" he whispered in her ear.

She opened her eyes guiltily. "They're standing at the entrance to the marquee."

"Facing us?"

"No."

He pushed her away from him. "Get Siobhan."

"Mike, what's—"

"Do it, Sabrina!" he snapped.

She glared at him then stormed off towards the bar. He ducked around the side of the marquee to wait for them.

"Mike, what's this all about?" Sabrina demanded on her return.

"Why don't you ask her?" Graham replied staring icily at Siobhan.

"Ask me what?" Siobhan asked in bewilderment.

"Why didn't you warn us about Drago's *friend*?"

"Friend? What friend?"

"How about a description to jog your memory. Mid-fifties, short black hair, grey moustache, distinctive *Russian* accent. Need I go on?"

"I know who you mean. He arrived while you were in

the house. I don't know who he is if that's what you're on about."

"And here I thought you were the local expert on the KGB hierarchy," Graham said sarcastically.

"I only know the ones who visit Rio regularly. I've never seen him before in my life."

"So who is he, Mike? You've obviously got us both at a disadvantage," Sabrina said coming to Siobhan's rescue.

"Does the name Yuri Leonov mean anything to either of you?"

They both nodded.

"That's Leonov?" Siobhan asked hesitantly.

"Yuri Leonov, head of Directorate K, the department responsible for the penetration of foreign intelligence services. Certainly one of the most powerful men in the KGB."

"I've always been led to believe that he's a hardliner who's never set foot outside Russia," Siobhan said holding Graham's stare. "Are you sure it's him?"

"Of course I'm sure. I met him face to face at the Finnish-Soviet border when I was with Delta." Graham touched Sabrina lightly on the arm. "That's why I staged the kissing scene. If he'd seen me our cover would have been blown."

Sabrina nodded understandingly. "So what's he doing here?"

"Sergei might be able to dig something up there." Graham turned to Siobhan. "I need to get out of here as quickly as possible. Can you have our driver . . ."

"Felipe," Sabrina prompted.

"Yeah, Felipe. Can you have him wait for us at reception. You'll have to make our excuses to Schrader. Tell him I wasn't feeling well. Drago can vouch for that."

"Leave everything to me. You two just get out of here."

"We intend to," Graham replied. "And thanks."

"Sure. I'll call you guys tomorrow. Noon-ish. I don't know about you, but I'll be dead to the world until then."

Graham and Sabrina cut round the back of the marquee only to find Drago and Leonov directly in front of them.

Drago looked up at them. "How's the stomach, Mr. Graham?"

"Still a bit tender," Graham replied forcing a smile.

"Americans," Leonov muttered contemptuously then continued his conversation with Drago.

"Are you sure it was him?" Sabrina asked once they had distanced themselves from the marquee.

"Positive. It's Leonov all right."

"But then why didn't he say anything? It was the perfect opportunity, especially in front of someone like Drago."

"It doesn't make any sense," he muttered as they climbed the steps. "It just doesn't make any sense."

Siobhan watched them disappear into the lift then turned to look at Leonov. So he was Drago's contact. It meant Drago *was* going to make the exchange at the party. And that meant he had to have the envelope with him. But which pocket? She would get only one chance to lift it so there was no room for error. Logically, it should be in his shirt pocket. But was it? *It had to be*, she said to herself. She took a sip of Perrier water to moisten her dry throat then walked over to the two men.

"Come on, André, you haven't danced all night."

"You know I never dance," Drago replied irritably.

"Well it's time you learnt."

She held out her hand then, pretending to catch her heel on a divot, stumbled heavily against him. The glass spun from his hand. The perfect distraction. She had already palmed the envelope from his shirt pocket and slipped it into her tanga pocket by the time he grabbed her to stop her from falling.

"André, I'm sorry," she apologized then picked up his glass. "Let me get you another drink."

"It's okay." Drago took the glass from her. "Are you all right?"

"Sure. I just feel so embarrassed." She looked down at the ladder in her stocking. "I'd better go and change. Please excuse me."

"And you in the West find her kind attractive?" Leonov asked watching her cross the lawn to the steps.

"I doubt whether there's a man here tonight who wouldn't willingly jeopardize his marriage just to spend one night with her." Drago snapped his fingers at a passing waiter. "Soda water, no ice."

"Does that include you?" Leonov glanced disdainfully towards the marquee entrance as the seventeen-piece band inside, back after a ten minute break, started the spot with a noisy samba which had the guests hurrying on to the dance floor in their dozens.

"I'm not married, Comrade Leonov," Drago replied then led Leonov away from the marquee towards a more secluded part of the garden.

"An evasive answer if ever I heard one."

"But truthful," Drago countered. "I'm neither married nor am I a Westerner."

"But you're content to stay in the West?"

"What alternative do I have? I can either take my chances out here or return home and face a firing squad." Drago took the glass from the waiter's tray, looked around, then turned back to Leonov. "I take it you do have the merchandise with you?"

"Naturally. And you have the envelope?"

Drago reached into his shirt pocket. It was empty. He patted his other pockets in desperation then stared in horror at Leonov. "It's gone. I had it—" He threw the glass down furiously. "Bitch!"

Leonov grabbed Drago's arm. "What's happened?"

"That bitch lifted the envelope when she fell against me." Drago unclipped the radio from his belt and pressed it to his lips. "Has the St. Jacques woman left yet?"

"Yes, sir, about a minute ago."

"Have Larrios bring a car round to the reception. I also want two guards, both armed."

"Yes, sir—"

Drago turned the radio off and looked at Leonov. "I'll be back within the hour. With the envelope."

"I'm not waiting while you sort out your problems. I should never have agreed to come here in the first place. I'll meet you, as planned, at the original rendezvous tomorrow night. If you don't show then I'll assume the deal's off and take the first available flight back to Moscow. I don't need to remind you what will happen if I do return empty-handed."

"Please, Comrade Leonov, just give me one hour," Drago pleaded.

"I won't give you one minute! Tomorrow night's your last chance to produce the envelope." Leonov signalled to a waiter and asked that his car be sent round to reception for him.

Drago hurried up the steps, across the mosaic foyer, and into the lift. A black Mercedes was waiting for him in the courtyard and no sooner had he climbed into the passenger seat than Larrios accelerated it away in a shriek of screeching tires towards the first of the two gates, both having been opened to prevent any further delay. Drago opening the glove compartment, removed the CZ75 he always kept there and screwed a silencer on to the end of the barrel. Only then did he look at the guards behind him: Santin, a burly ex-policeman who had been thrown off the force for taking bribes, mainly from Drago; and Canete, a former member of the Uruguayan Ejército Revolucionario del Pueblo, a left-wing guerilla movement, who had been forced to flee the country after being fingered as a police informer. They were perfect for what he had in mind.

Drago explained the situation briefly to them then unclipped the radio handset from the dashboard and asked the duty officer to find out the number of Siobhan's metallic gold Porsche Cabrio, one of the many stored in the control room computer. He repeated it for the others in the car then replaced the handset and sat back, a contented smile on his face. She had a headstart and a faster car but Larrios knew the road better than anyone. He anticipated catching up with her near the beachfront where the *Carnaval bandas*, the street parties, always brought the traffic to a virtual standstill at that time of year. Then he would kill her.

Siobhan was also thinking about the *bandas* as she neared the beachfront. She had participated in enough of them to know just how disruptive they could be to motorists in a hurry. The biter's about to be bitten, she thought angrily to herself on noticing the tailback in front of her. She brought the Cabrio to a stop then stuck her head out of the window to get a better look at the *banda* a hundred yards in front of her. It was big, about two hundred strong, which meant she could be there for some time. Drago

would have realized what had happened within minutes of
her leaving the party and set out in pursuit of her, not only
to retrieve the envelope, but also to teach her a lesson for
showing him up in front of Leonov. She looked in the
rearview mirror but the only car behind her was a battered
Volkswagon Beetle with an old Carioca behind the wheel.
Dare she risk staying where she was? Would Drago catch
up with her before the *banda* moved on? She had arranged
to meet her handler, Casey Morgan, in a side street off
Niemeyer Avenue at ten-thirty to hand over the envelope.
She glanced at her nine-carat Tissot bracelet watch, the
last present her husband had ever given to her: 10:24. If
the *banda* moved on within the next couple of minutes she
would make the rendezvous on time. If not, she would
have to abandon her beloved Cabrio and walk the rest of
the way. She drummed her fingers nervously on the steer-
ing wheel. Come on, come on, she said to herself and
peered out the window again. The *banda* showed no signs
of moving.

Then she saw the black Mercedes in her side mirror. It
was coming to a stop four cars back, and Larrios was
behind the wheel. It meant Drago was with him. Larrios
never drove for anyone else. She slumped back in her
seat—it would be only a matter of time before they spotted
her car. She had to move quickly. First she slipped off her
high heels, which would only slow her down. She would
run in her stockinged feet. Her sneakers? She had gone to
her aerobics class that morning, so the sneakers had to be
somewhere in the car. After a frantic search she found
them wrapped in her leotard behind the passenger seat.
She put them on then noticed the back door of the Mercedes open. Canete climbed out then bent down to peer
through the driver's window, presumably to get last minute

instructions from Drago. Not that she could see Drago; the passenger side was blocked from view by the cars behind her. She thought about trying to make a break for it, but quickly dismissed the idea. One thing the ERP had taught Canete was how to shoot straight. Her best bet was to let him come to her. He saw her when he stepped away from the Mercedes and he gave a thumbs-up sign to Drago. What worried her most of all was not being able to see Drago, who could easily get out of the car without her knowing. It was a chance she had to take. Canete started to walk towards the Cabrio. She switched off the ignition and curled her fingers around the door handle. At least she had the element of surprise on her side. It was all she had. Canete slipped his hand into his pocket on reaching the Cabrio and told her to get out of the car. She nodded, feigning uncertainty, her eyes flickering between him and the ignition key. He played straight into her hands and as he reached through the window to get the key she shoved the door open as hard as she could, catching him squarely in the stomach. He staggered back, winded, his face twisted in pain. She leapt from the car and sprinted towards the *banda*. It would provide a temporary sanctuary.

Drago and Santin sprang from the Mercedes and raced after her. She reached the *banda* twenty yards ahead of Drago and used the flamboyant costumes to hide herself from her pursuers. Santin was caught in a wave of female dancers but as he forced his way out he was immediately caught in another wave behind it. Drago was able to follow Siobhan with relative ease—her laddered stocking stood out amongst the sea of legs around her. When Canete arrived, limping, Drago told him to get round to the front of the parade to hem her in. Santin, having forced his way to the fringe of the *banda*, was closing in on her from the other side.

She reached the sidestreet where Morgan was waiting. He started up his white Audi. Santin pushed his way through the *banda* and made a grab for her but she sidestepped him and kicked him as hard as she could in the groin. He cried out and fell to the ground in agony. She turned back to the Audi. At that instant a single bullet hole dimpled the windscreen and a trickle of blood ran down the bridge of Morgan's nose from the wound in the center of his forehead. She spun round again, her eyes now wide with fear. Drago stood by the wall at the entrance to the sidestreet, the silenced CZ75 hanging loosely in his hand. His smile was chilling. As he stepped forward a group of laughing women grabbed him from behind and pulled him into the *banda*. She saw the fury in his eyes before he disappeared from view behind the building. She sprinted out of the side street, shoving aside a couple of drunken tourists who tried to make a grab for her. They laughed then stumbled forward to rejoin the *banda*. Her first thought was to get to a telephone. But she had no *fichas*. And she had no money to buy any. She ran to a newsstand then looked back over her shoulder to see if she was being followed. It was impossible to know, there were so many people in the street.

"Do you want something or not?" the stallholder asked her in Portuguese.

"I need a *ficha*, but I don't have any money." She removed her watch and placed it on the counter. "I'll pay for it with that. Please, you've got it let me have one. Just one."

He picked it up and turned it around in his fingers. "Are you in trouble?"

"Please, just give me the *ficha*," she pleaded then looked over the shoulder again. Still no sign of her pursuers.

"One *ficha* for this watch. What's the catch?"

A tear ran from the corner of her eye and she brushed it away with the back of her hand. "There's no catch. God, why won't you help me?"

He turned the watch around in his fingers again then reached under the counter and handed her a pack of *fichas*. She snatched them from him and ran to the row of public telephones on the opposite side of the street. She found the number for the Meridien in the directory and ripped open the packet, spilling a couple of *fichas* on to the pavement, then, after pushing one into the slot, she dialled the number with a trembling finger.

"Mike Graham, please." she blurted out the moment her call was answered.

The switchboard operator connected her to the room.

"Hello?"

"Mike, it's Siobhan. You've got to help me. Casey's dead, and now they're coming after me—"

"Siobhan!" Graham cut in. "Just calm down and tell me what's happened."

"Drago killed Casey, my handler at the consulate. He just shot him in cold blood. Now he's coming after me. I've got the envelope."

"Envelope? Forget it. Where are you?"

"I'm on Niemeyer Avenue. I can't stay here, Drago's right on my tail."

"Okay, where can we meet you?"

She looked around. "There's a hotel not far from here called the Valencia. I'll meet you there. And Mike, please hurry. I'm scared. They never said it was going to be like this.''

"We're on our way."

She replaced the receiver and mingled with another *banda* heading in the general direction of the Valencia.

Larrios, who had heard the entire conversation from the adjacent booth, smiled to himself then ran back to where he had parked the Mercedes a few minutes earlier. He told Drago what he had heard.

"It's nice to know I can rely on someone to do what I ask," Drago said with a contemptuous look at Santin and Canete.

"She caught us by surprise," Canete muttered defensively.

"Is that what you call it?" Drago retorted sarcastically then pointed a finger of warning at them. "One more mistake from either of you and you'll both find yourselves back on dog patrol for the next six months. Do I make myself clear?"

They nodded, unable to hold his penetrating stare.

"How long will it take for them to get from the Meridien to the Valencia?" Drago asked Larrios.

Larrios calculated the distance in his mind. "At least twenty minutes, and that's assuming they go by taxi. If they were able to drive there themselves it could take them anything up to thirty, thirty-five minutes. The Valencia's not the easiest of places to find if you don't know this area."

"What kind of hotel is that then?"

"I'd hardly call it a hotel, Mr. Drago. It's used mainly by prostitutes."

"And how far is it from here?"

"A couple of minutes by car," Larrios replied.

Drago checked the time. "Let's assume they got a taxi within two or three minutes of the call. How long ago was that? Five minutes? That means eight minutes have already elapsed. Start her up, Larrios. It's time we settled this business once and for all."

Sabrina had been in the bathroom, changing, when Siobhan rang. She pulled on a pair of jeans and a white T-shirt then hurried down to the foyer where Graham was waiting for her. They were both armed, their holstered Berettas tucked out of sight at the back of their jeans. He flagged down the first available taxi and although glancing suspiciously at them, the driver had merely nodded when Sabrina told him where they wanted to go. It took half an hour to reach the Valenica. Sabrina paid the driver then followed Graham into the gaudy reception area. It stank of cigarettes, joss sticks and cheap perfume. The acne-scarred youth behind the reception desk pushed a stick of gum into his mouth and began to chew it noisily, his eyes riveted on Sabrina.

Graham snapped his fingers inches from the youth's face to get his attention. "Miss St. Jacques, which room?"

The youth reluctantly tore his eyes away from Sabrina and prodded an envelope in front of him. "You Gray-ham?"

Graham picked up the envelope and slit it open with his finger. The sheet of paper inside read:

Mike, Sabrina
I'm in Room 8, at the end of the first floor. Knock twice, pause, then knock another three times. That way I'll know it's you.
Siobhan.

Graham handed the note to Sabrina then showed her the envelope which had his name written on it.

"The writing's different," she said.

"Yeah. Why write a note then get someone else to address the envelope?"

"Unless it's already been opened and resealed in a different envelope," she concluded.

"Exactly. There's a fire escape in the alley next to the hotel. You take that. I'll go in through the bedroom door." He grabbed her arm when she turned to the door. "Not that way. The kid over there will almost certainly have instructions to call the room the moment we're out of sight. We've got to make whoever's up there think we don't suspect anything. That means acting normally. You'll be able to get out on to the fire escape from the first floor."

She nodded, furious with herself for such a blatant lapse in judgement. It was imperative that she didn't allow her emotions to get the better of her.

They climbed the garish purple-carpeted stairs then unholstered the Berettas and continued to the end of the corridor, where Sabrina gingerly opened the fire exit and peered out at the metal staircase against the side of the hotel. It would be a simple task to get into position outside the open bedroom window. She told him to give her twenty seconds then disappeared out onto the landing, closing the door silently behind her. He pressed himself against the wall beside the door, the Beretta gripped tightly in his right hand, and counted to twenty before knocking twice, pausing, then knocking another three times. The door opposite him opened fractionally and the tip of Santin's silenced UZI came into view. Graham flung himself at the door, hitting it with his shoulder. Santin cried out in pain as the edge of the door struck him in the face, knocking him backwards into the room, the UZI spinning from his hands. Graham eased the door open and entered the room cautiously. He saw Santin at the last possible moment and had no chance to defend himself against the blow that struck him on the shoulder. Santin dropped the lampstand and ran to the balcony, scrambled over the railing, and climbed down the trellis against the side of the hotel. Graham got to the balcony just in time to see Santin reach the street and disappear into the midst of a passing *banda*.

"Mike, are you okay?" Sabrina asked from the doorway.

"Yeah," Graham replied rubbing his shoulder gingerly. "What happened?"

"He got away. How about you?"

She held up the UZI in her hand and indicated the room behind her. "The other one's in there. I managed to sneak up on him when you knocked on the door. He's out cold."

Graham found Santin's UZI partially hidden under the bed and took it through to the other room with him. He dragged Canete away from the door and closed it behind him.

"Mike?" Sabrina called out from the bathroom.

Graham hurried through to the bathroom. Siobhan had been shot through the heart and her body dumped in the empty bath. He got a sheet from the bedroom and covered her body with it. Only then did he look at Sabrina but when he tried to put a consoling hand on her arm she shrugged it off and sat on the edge of the bath, the Beretta gripped tightly in both hands. She suddenly got up and made for the door.

He blocked her path. "Killing him isn't the answer, Sabrina. You know that. And anyway, he didn't do it. Remember what Siobhan said about Drago's method of execution. A single bullet through the heart."

She stared at the unconscious figure of Canete then let her gun hand fall to her side. "We were the first people she'd felt at ease with since she lost her father. She told me that this afternoon. I reckon she and I could have become good friends over the years. Now—'' She stopped abruptly and turned to Graham. ''We've got a prisoner to interrogate.''

''Yeah. You bring some water, I'll prop him up against the wall.''

When she returned to the bedroom with a glass of water she found Canete sitting up against the built-in cupboard, his head lolling on his chest, a trickle of blood running down the back of his neck from the cut behind his ear where she had hit him. She threw the water into Canete's face. Canete's head jerked up and when he opened his eyes he found himself staring down the barrel of Graham's Beretta. A sharp pain speared through his head but he remained motionless, fearful that any sudden movement might provoke Graham into pulling the trigger. Graham asked him his name. Canete told him.

''Who do you work for?'' Graham's voice was acidic.

Canete said nothing.

Graham slammed his palm against Canete's forehead, cracking his head back painfully against the cupboard. Canete cried out and clamped his hands on either side of his head. Graham did it again, only harder. Canete wrapped his arms over his head, his face creased with pain.

''I can understand you not wanting to say anything without a lawyer present. Let's face it, a triple murder rap can be pretty serious. Unless, of course, you think Drago can get you off. I don't think he'll bother, you're the perfect scapegoat.''

''Mr. Drago will help me''

''So you admit that you work for Drago?'' Sabrina asked.

Canete's mouth twisted in a contemptuous sneer.

Graham struck him across the face with the barrel of his

Beretta, tearing open a gash in his cheek. Canete screamed and clutched his cheek. Blood seeped through his fingers.

"Answer the question otherwise I'll start to break your fingers, one by one."

"I work for Drago," Canete shouted then turned to Sabrina, his face racked with pain. "I need towel. Much blood."

"You'll get a towel when you've answered the questions," Graham snapped. "Tell us about the envelope."

Canete was about to deny any knowledge of it until he noticed Graham tapping the butt of the Beretta rhythmically in the palm of his hand. The beat got harder with every stroke. "Envelope, it belong to Mr. Drago. I not know what inside." He met Graham's eyes and shook his head fearfully. "I not know."

"How did he know Miss St. Jacques was here?"

"Larrios, he hear—"

"Who's Larrios?" Graham demanded.

Canete flinched. "He drive for Mr. Drago."

"Go on," Sabrina said.

"Larrios, he hear her talk on phone. Tell Mr. Drago. We come here. Larrios, he know boy at *recepcão*, I not know in *inglês*."

"Reception."

Canete glanced up at Sabrina. *"Fala português?"*

"Stick to English!" Graham snapped.

"Sim, I speak *inglês,"* Canete replied eagerly. "Mr. Drago give boy money to show him letter. We come to room. Mr. Drago ask for envelope. She say she not have it. He say he kill her if she not give it him. She give it him."

"Then what?" Sabrina prompted.

"She shot."

"Who shot her?" Graham asked.

Canete wiped the sweat from his forehead, leaving behind a smear of blood from his hand. "Mr. Drago shoot her. He tell me and Santin to put body in bath and wait for you."

"Did he tell you to kill us?" Sabrina asked.

"Sim."

Graham stood up and took Sabrina to one side. "He's no good to us. It's Drago we want."

"Mike, he's our one chance of nailing Drago. His testimony could put Drago away for life."

"And just how long do you think he'd last in police custody knowing what he does? Drago would have him killed before he'd even had a chance to put pen to paper."

Canete launched himself at them, knocking Sabrina to the ground, before grabbing one of the UZIs from the chair against the far wall. He was still turning when they shot him. Both bullets took him in the chest and the UZI spun from his hands as he fell through the open window. They crossed to the window. He was lying face down on the fire escape, his right arm twisted and broken from the fall. Graham went out onto the landing and, pressing the Beretta into Canetes neck, felt for a pulse. He shook his head then clambered back into the room.

"Let's get the hell out of here," he said reholstering his Beretta. "Drago's sure to send some of his men round when he finds out what's happened. I, for one, don't want to be here when they arrive. Especially if they're cops."

They closed the door behind them then walked the length of the deserted corridor, down the narrow stairs and into the foyer.

"I've got something for you from the lady in Room 8," Graham said beckoning the youth towards him.

The youth stood up and crossed to the desk, still chewing noisily on the gum. Graham pulled the Beretta from the holster and brought the butt down savagely on to the youth's nose. The youth screamed in agony and stumbled back against the wall, his hands covering his shattered nose. Graham pushed the Beretta back into its holster and led Sabrina out into the street.

"What's in that envelope and why is it so damn important to Drago?" Graham snapped as they walked towards Niemeyer Avenue.

"Whatever it is, it's obviously as important to the CIA as it is to Drago."

"And the KGB," he added.

"We still don't know that for sure."

"So why is Leonov here? I hardly think it's for the Carnival."

He flagged down a passing taxi and they returned to the hotel.

ELEVEN

Kolchinsky flicked the cigarette butt over the side of the *Copacabana Queen* then glanced at his luminous watch: 11:07. And still no sign of the *Palmira*. He helped himself to another cigarette from the pack on the bench beside him, lit it, then looked across at Whitlock who was leaning on the railing, lost in thought. Something was certainly bothering him, but Kolchinsky had never been the kind of person who would try to pressure someone into talking about their problems. He was there if Whitlock needed a sympathetic ear. There was nothing more irksome than a meddling, amateur psychiatrist who probed and pried into someone's personal problems in the blinkered belief that they alone could sort those problems out.

"You're pretty quiet over there," Whitlock called out.

"I could say the same about you," Kolchinsky replied then got to his feet and crossed to where Whitlock was standing.

"I guess I was," Whitlock said staring out to sea. "Sergei, how supportive was Vasilisa of your work?"

Kolchinsky leaned his arms on the railing as he pondered

the question. "Let me put it this way, she hated the West."
He noticed the look of uncertainty on Whitlock's face. "She
was very much a homebody and hated to be parted from her
family for any length of time. So you can imagine what sixteen years in the West must have done to her."

"Didn't you ever talk about it?"

"Vasilisa came from a military family. She was brought
up to believe that a wife's place was at her husband's side,
irrespective of where he went or what he did. Of course I
tried to talk to her about it but every time she would either
change the subject or say how proud she was that the KGB
had chosen me to represent them in the West. The only hint
I ever got of her feelings was her refusal to have any children
while I was stationed outside Russia. She was determined
that our children should be raised properly, in Russia, surrounded by their relatives. We had always planned a family
but within a month of our return a doctor told her she had
cancer of the stomach. She was dead a year later."

"Life can be a real bastard at times."

"It all depends on how you look at it. Vasilisa was a wonderful wife, I certainly don't have any regrets."

"I could say the same about Carmen," Whitlock said at
length. "I just wish I could understand her."

"Want to talk about it?"

"There really isn't much to talk about, Sergei. She wants
me to leave UNACO. I want to stay. That's it in a nutshell."

Kolchinsky remained silent, sensing that Whitlock was
struggling to marshal his thoughts and put them into words.

"I've got four years left in the field. I want to stay with
UNACO after I'm retired. Only she can't see that. She wants
me to resign now and take up a post as a security consultant.
I don't want to be installing security systems in Fifth Avenue
boutiques for the rest of my life. Can you understand that?"

"What if something were to happen to you in the next four years? Do you think she wants to be left a widow?"

"So you think she's right?" Whitlock snapped defensively. "And here I thought you'd be the one person who would understand my situation."

"I'm playing the devil's advocate, C. W.," Kolchinsky replied softly then threw the cigarette into the water. "I'm merely trying to make you see it from her perspective. It's not for me to pass judgement, it's a personal matter between the two of you. The only way you're going to resolve it is by sitting down together and talking it out."

Whitlock turned around and leaned against the railing, his arms folded across his chest. "What is better than wisdom? Woman. And what is better than a good woman? Nothing."

Kolchinsky gave him a puzzled look.

"Chaucer, a fourteenth-century writer."

"I know who Chaucer is. I can see his point."

"So can I, at times." Whitlock shook his head slowly to himself. "She can't lose, Sergei, that's what really gets to me."

"It works both ways, C. W., remember that."

"Meaning?"

"Meaning she'll be thinking along the same lines as you are. And from what you've told me about her, I see her as the kind of woman who's at her most vulnerable when it comes to matters of the heart."

"So what you're saying is that you think she'll be the first to back down?"

"That's your interpretation. I told you, I'm not taking sides." Kolchinsky looked up as a burst of fireworks lit up the sky over Leblon. "Just don't make a decision that you'll regret for the rest of your life. It could force the two of you even further apart."

"I hear what you're saying, Sergei. And thanks."

Kolchinsky returned to the bench and picked up the night vision binoculars. He focused them on the *Golconda* and immediately noticed the activity on board. Two of the crewmen were crouched by the railing, ready to unfurl a rope ladder down the side of the hull. He looked beyond the *Golconda*. The *Palmira* was anchored about five hundred yards to starboard and a lifeboat was being lowered into the water. He called Whitlock over, handed him the binoculars, then started up the portable crane's silent engine. Whitlock joined him and between them they swung the swimmer delivery vehicle over the side of the yacht and eased it down gently until its hull was touching the water. Kolchinsky locked the crane's brakes and they turned their attention to the scuba gear. It was the re-breather, or closed-circuit, type which worked on the principle of re-using the expelled breath and converting it back into oxygen. There would be no air bubbles to give them away. They each strapped a breathing bag to their chests then pulled the two-litre high-pressure oxygen bottles on to their backs and, after slipping on rubber gloves, descended the side of the yacht into the water. They spat into their face masks and rinsed them in the sea to prevent them from misting then secured them over their faces and swam the short distance to the swimmer delivery vehicle. Kolchinsky climbed into the front compartment and Whitlock got in behind him, careful not to touch the three fifteen-pound limpet mines at his feet. Whitlock pushed the mouthpiece between his lips and opened the valve on the oxygen bottle. He sucked in several times before he tasted the pure oxygen. Then, leaning forward, he tapped Kolchinsky on the shoulder and gave him a thumbs-up sign. Kolchinsky pressed a button on the panel in front of him, releasing the swimmer delivery vehicle from the crane. He started up the engine, dived it gently below the waves, then switched on the lights.

Lavalle emerged from the bridge and descended the stairs to the deck and lit himself a cigarette while he waited for the *Palmira*'s lifeboat to dock alongside the *Golconda*. A length of rope was tossed up from the lifeboat and caught by one of the men on deck who secured it firmly to the railing. The lifeboat's three occupants scrambled up the rope ladder on-to the deck. The one carrying the grey holdall was a short, wiry-haired man with a leathery skin bronzed from years in the sun.

"The name's Lee O'Brien, captain of the *Palmira*," he announced in a strong Australian accent. "You Drago?"

Lavalle realized the psychological advantage in assuming Drago's identity and nodded. He ignored O'Brien's extended hand, indicating instead the holdall. "Are those the goods?"

O'Brien tossed it on to the deck at Lavalle's feet.

"Check it," Lavalle said to the crewman who picked it up. "Eighteen kilos of smack. I want to know if it's so much as a gram out."

The crewman disappeared through one of the hatchways behind them.

"I don't know anything about it if it's short," O'Brien said sharply.

"Then you've got nothing to worry about. The Colombians wouldn't short-change us on this kind of deal." Lavalle gestured towards the saloon. "Let's have a drink while we wait to see if it's all there."

O'Brien followed Lavalle into the saloon and looked around in awe. "Jeez, this is sure some place you got here."

"What are you drinking?" Lavalle asked from behind the bar.

"Beer." O'Brien sat on a bar stool and leaned his elbows on the counter. "I never carried drugs before. Only contraband. And I smuggled illegals into America when I was doing the Havana-Miami run a couple of years back."

"The stakes get that much higher when drugs are involved."

"I can believe that. You're not from round here, are you?"

"No."

O'Brien shrugged at Lavalle's curt riposte and took a mouthful of the ice cold beer. "So what's this Carnival really like? I hear it's unbelievable."

"It's good for business."

"I bet," O'Brien said with a grin.

A crewman hurried into the saloon and spoke to Lavalle in Portuguese.

"Put two men on standby. And have my equipment made ready," Lavalle replied in English then unholstered his Walther and pointed it at O'Brien. "What are you trying to pull?"

"I don't know what you're talking about," O'Brien replied, his eyes wide with fear. "I told you, I didn't tamper with the stuff—"

"I'm not talking about that! A light's been seen under the water near the *Golconda*'s hull. What's the game?"

"I don't know anything about a light. Honest I don't."

Lavalle pressed the barrel between O'Brien's eyes. "I won't ask you again."

"God Almighty, Mr. Drago, I swear I don't know anything about it. Please believe me."

"I'll deal with you later," Lavalle snarled then ducked out from behind the counter and made his way to the deck where he immediately pointed at the two men who had accompanied O'Brien from the *Palmira*. "Take them into the saloon. And watch them."

The nearest crewman nodded and shoved them roughly in the back. Both spun round to face Lavalle, protesting at the way they were being treated.

"Shoot the next one who opens his mouth," Lavalle snapped.

Neither spoke again as they were led away.

Lavalle looked up at the crewman on the bridge then indicated the two men standing by the railing, both wearing standard scuba gear and armed with spearguns. "I want the hull lights switched on the moment they go over the side."

"Yes, sir."

"Ready?" Lavalle asked the divers.

They gave him a thumbs-up sign.

"Go!"

Whitlock, working by Halolight, a disc-shaped light secured to a strip of rubber and worn as a headband, was attaching the last of the three mines to the *Golconda*'s hull when the two powerful underwater spotlights were activated from the bridge. He hardly had time to react to them before the divers hit the water and made their way towards him. He was still priming the timing device and the slightest error could detonate the mine prematurely. It meant he was the perfect target for the approaching divers. Where was Kolchinsky? One of the divers noticed the mine beside the propeller shaft and indicated that he was going to take a closer look at it. The second diver continued towards Whitlock, the speargun now clenched tightly in his hands.

Kolchinsky was caught in a dilemma as he unclipped the speargun from the side of the swimmer delivery vehicle— which of the divers to shoot? The first diver, who would trigger off the detonator if he tampered with the suction pads holding the mine against the hull, or the second diver who was closing in on the helpless Whitlock? His dilemma was quickly resolved when the first diver reached the mine and attacked the suction pad with his knife. Kolchinsky fired at him but the bolt went wide. The second diver swivelled round to face Kolchinsky who was desperately trying to reload his speargun. Kolchinsky knew he couldn't do it in time.

The yacht's engines suddenly came to life, sucking the first diver into the spinning propeller blades. Whitlock looked away sharply, fighting to swallow the rising bile in his throat as the illuminated water around him darkened with blood. The second diver was transfixed with horror, giving Kolchinsky those precious few seconds to rearm himself. He squeezed the trigger. The bolt took the diver in the chest and the speargun fell from his hand as his hunched, lifeless body sank slowly out of sight.

Whitlock locked the timer—seven minutes to detonation. All three mines were timed to detonate simultaneously. The engines were abruptly switched off and seconds later Lavalle dived into the water, a rubber-handled survival knife in his right hand. Kolchinsky used his last bolt but Lavalle evaded it and closed in on Whitlock. He lashed out with the knife but although Whitlock was able to parry the blow, he lost his own knife in the process. Now he was unarmed. Kolchinsky was about to go to Whitlock's aid when he noticed a movement out of the corner of his eye. A twelve-foot great white shark loomed out of the darkness, attracted by the profusion of blood in the water. And it was heading straight for him! He slammed the perspex canopy over his head. The shark brushed the canopy and he was able to see the intricate network of scars on its greyish underbelly. He shivered, unable to take his eyes off it. It disappeared into the darkness but he knew it would be back. Had Whitlock seen it?

The shark reappeared and homed in like a bullet on the two men. Only then did Whitlock see it, its jaws open to reveal the row of serrated teeth which could tear a man in half. With a strength born out of sheer terror he ripped off Lavalle's face mask and propelled himself sideways, knowing the shark couldn't match his sudden change in direction. Làvalle, unaware of the shark, was still struggling without his face mask when it took him from behind. Whitlock swam back to the swimmer delivery vehicle and climbed inside, securing the canopy after him. A second great white appeared and attacked the remains of Lavalle's mutilated body.

Kolchinsky was both mesmerized and revolted by what he saw. Mesmerized by the sharks' sleek, streamlined bodies as they thrashed wildly from side to side, their clamp-like jaws locked on to the flesh, neither prepared to concede to the other; and revolted not only by the manic ferocity of the attack but also by the idea that he himself could have been the shark's target. Whitlock jabbed him painfully in the back. He looked around and Whitlock held up four fingers. Four minutes to detonation. Kolchinsky turned on the headlight then manoeuvred the swimmer delivery vehicle around until it was facing south-west on the compass dial in front of him. Their progress seemed painfully slow but they were well clear of the *Golconda* when the mines detonated. The swimmer delivery vehicle was buffeted gently by the vibration from the resulting explosion and Kolchinsky nosed it up to the surface where they pulled back the canopy, spat out their mouthpieces and removed their face masks.

The *Golconda* was listing heavily to starboard and although the stern was ablaze the *Palmira*'s crew were making no attempt to tackle the fire. It would be pointless. The *Golconda* was beyond help.

"What I'd give to be a fly on the wall when Drago finds out what's happened to his precious cargo. Not to mention Schrader's reaction when he discovers his beloved yacht's at the bottom of the sea. It should certainly liven up the party a bit."

"Sure," Kolchinsky muttered, still reliving the shark attack in his mind. He would never forget it as long as he lived.

"Sergei, are you okay?"

"I'm fine," Kolchinsky replied quickly. "Let's get back to the yacht. We've done what we came here to do."

"What's happened?" Schrader asked anxiously as he entered Drago's office. "You sounded agitated over the phone."

Drago picked up his half-smoked cigarette from the edge of the ashtray, took a long drag, then stubbed it out. "I received a call from the coastguard."

"And?"

Drago stared at his feet. "The *Golconda* was taken out to sea this evening."

"On whose authority? I gave strict instructions that it remain moored in Botafogo Bay until we leave for Florida."

"I know that, sir."

"Dammit, André, what's happened?" Schrader snapped, his patience at an end.

"There was an explosion aboard her. She sank."

Schrader moved to the window and stared out over the sea. "You're telling me that the *Golconda*'s sunk?"

"Yes, sir," Drago replied softly. "I haven't got the full story yet—"

Schrader grabbed Drago and slammed him up against the wall. "Then I suggest you get it. Fast!"

"Yes, sir," Drago mumbled.

"What kind of security operation are you running here, André? Where were your bloody guards when these people decided to take my yacht for a spin? Where were they?"

"I'm having it checked out right now, sir. If any of them were guilty of negligence—"

"What do you mean 'if'?" Schrader turned back to the window. "*If* they weren't negligent then my yacht would still be moored in Botafogo Bay. Not so?"

"Yes, sir."

"Yes, sir," Schrader repeated then banged his fist down on the desk. "I want answers, and I want them quickly."

"You'll get them, sir, I promise you."

Schrader walked to the door, activated it, then pointed a finger at Drago. "If you don't get to the bottom of this, you're out. Finished. That *I* promise you."

Drago sank into his chair behind the desk after Schrader had gone and tossed his wire-framed glasses on the blotter in front of him. He wiped his hands over his face then reached for another cigarette. Just what the hell had happened? The initial reports had been vague but he knew it had to be sabotage. It couldn't have been Graham or the woman. Which left Whitlock. Not that he cared. So he had lost the shipment—Schrader had financed it. He still had the envelope, his passport to freedom, and he would be meeting Leonov the following night to conclude the deal. Then he would get as far away from Rio de Janeiro as possible. No more Schrader, no more *favela* vigilantes, but most of all, no more looking over his shoulder to sée if some shadowy gunman was about to put a bullet in his back.

No, he didn't care any more.

* * *

"It's impossible," Kolchinsky said after Graham and Sabrina had recounted the events at Schrader's party. "You must be mistaken, Michael. Yuri Leonov has never left Russia in his life. And even if he did, Rio's the last place he would visit."

"It was him, Sergei. I'd swear to it."

Kolchinsky remained unconvinced. "I don't believe it. Not Yuri."

Sabrina took the telephone from the coffee table and put it on the couch beside Kolchinsky. "Mike saw him, you didn't. I think you at least owe him the benefit of the doubt."

"Okay, I'll make a couple of calls if it'll make you happy. At least it'll prove I'm right."

Graham put his hand on the receiver before Kolchinsky could pick it up. "If you are right and it's not Leonov, I'll pay for those calls out of my own pocket."

"It's your money," Kolchinsky said lifting the receiver.

There was a knock at the door.

"Food!" Whitlock exclaimed on opening it.

The waiter placed the tray on the coffee table. Sabrina signed the chit and he left.

"Drinks, anyone?" Graham asked opening the fridge.

"What have you got?"

"Quit messing about, C. W. What do you want? I'll tell you if it's here."

Whitlock helped himself to a toasted steak sandwich. "I'll take a beer, if it's there."

"It's here. Sabrina?"

"The usual, thanks."

"What about Thomas?" Graham asked referring to Kolchinsky.

The telephone was answered at the other end before Kolchinsky could counter Graham's sarcasm.

Whitlock took the beer from Graham and joined Sabrina on the balcony. "You've got a great view from here."

"It's the honeymoon suite, remember?" she replied as fireworks lit up the sky over Ipanema Beach.

"What does your average honeymoon couple care about the view?"

"He says speaking from experience," she said with a cheeky smile.

He finished the sandwich then wiped his fingers on a paper napkin. "I'm sorry about Siobhan. I know the two of you got on pretty well."

"We did," she replied softly. "I just hope the colonel can get Langley to tell him about this envelope Drago cherishes so much. We've got a right to know, it's part of the case now."

"Sergei seemed confident that the colonel would get to the bottom of it after he spoke to him on the phone. And let's face it, if anyone can squeeze the truth out of the Langley boys, it's the colonel."

"That's true."

Graham appeared behind them and handed Sabrina the glass of Diet Pepsi he had poured for her. "You guys don't have to stop talking just because I'm here."

Sabrina shrugged. "We were talking about Drago's envelope, that's all."

Graham took a bite of his sandwich then leaned on the railing and watched a colourful *banda* passing beneath them. "Drago. Who is he? Or should I say, who was he? Siobhan was right, he was certainly no cipher clerk. And what's so important about this damn envelope which has got the CIA and the KGB both trying to get their hands on it?"

"*If* the KGB are after it," Whitlock corrected him.

"Then what's Leonov doing in Rio?" Graham retorted.

"If it's Leonov," Whitlock replied cautiously.

"It's Leonov," Kolchinsky said from the doorway. "Michael, I owe you an apology."

"Forget it. So what did you find out?"

"Only that he's in Rio on official business. I'll make some more calls later tonight and see what else I can find out. I still can't believe it. Yuri, here in Rio."

"It's getting pretty crowded out here," Graham said. "Let's go inside."

"So we're no closer to getting the painting back," Whitlock muttered as he sat down on the couch beside Kolchinsky.

"We did our best!" Graham snapped. "How the hell was I supposed to know the safe had been changed?"

"Ease up, Mike," Whitlock said calmly. "I know you guys did your best. I was making an observation, that's all."

"Yeah?" Graham replied, the hostility still in his voice.

"Mike, you never told me the rest of your plan," Sabrina said trying to defuse the tension.

"It doesn't matter now, we couldn't have used it without the transmitter to get into Schrader's private gallery."

"Come on, Mike, you went through enough trying to get it."

Graham shrugged. "Ever heard of the *motodeltoplan*?"

"Sure, it's a motorized hang-glider developed by spetsnaz in the last couple of years."

"Well, true to form, the Test Center ripped off the blueprint and developed their own version of it."

"They have?" Whitlock said. "So how come I don't know anything about it? Sergei?"

Kolchinsky shifted uncomfortably in his seat. "We only took delivery of it a fortnight ago. It's still supposed to be under wraps but when Michael outlined his plan to me this afternoon I suggested he use it. I've had three of them sent out. They should arrive early tomorrow morning. Who knows, we might still need them.''

"So the plan was to use the hang-gliders to get past security and then use the transmitter to recover the painting?'' Sabrina frowned. "But how would we have got into the house? We'd have needed . . .'' she trailed off when Graham produced a pass from his pocket and tossed it onto the table.

"I lifted it off one of the guards.''

Whitlock picked it up and turned it around in his hands. It was a basic magnetic strip card with the guard's name and photograph on its face side. "It's nothing special. I'd have expected a more elaborate security system.''

"You'd have to get into the house first before you could use it,'' Sabrina replied. "And that, for your average intruder, would be an impossibility in itself.''

"Well, who's got any suggestions for a new plan?'' Graham asked, looking at each face in turn.

"Wouldn't it be great if we could just walk in and take it,'' Sabrina said glumly.

Kolchinsky drank a mouthful of beer then replaced the bottle on the table. "That's exactly what we are going to do. Well, at least I am.''

"Come on, Sergei, be serious.''

"I am, C. W.'' Kolchinsky turned to Graham. "I had reservations about your plan when you first outlined it to me. It was too . . . gung-ho, but I went along with it because it was the only one we had at the time. I then devised my own back-up plan. It's actually quite simple. I arrive, unannounced, at Schrader's house claiming to be Toysgen. He doesn't know Toysgen's dead—''

"There's a flaw in it already, Sergei.''

"Let me run through it first, Michael, then you can pick

at it as much as you want. Having convinced Schrader that
I'm Toysgen I then give him a spiel about how Van Dehn and
Keppler have double-crossed me and that I'm almost certain
they've forwarded the forgery on to him and kept the original
for themselves to resell at a later date. I then conduct a fake
chemical test to prove to him that he is in possession of the
forgery and suggest I return to Amsterdam with the painting
and switch it for the original. I would send the original to
him and sell the forgery to Van Dehn and Keppler for the
money they supposedly owe me. If he agrees to let me take
the original then we're home and dry. It can be hanging in
the Met the day after tomorrow.''

"Drago knows Toysgen, he met him in Amsterdam. How
are you going to get round that?''

"Drago won't be there, Michael. I was originally going
to have him called away from the house on some pretext or
other, but with Yuri here it makes the whole thing that much
easier. I'll call, pretending to be Yuri, and ask to meet him
within the hour, preferably somewhere in town. Then, with
Drago out of the way, C. W. and I will drive to the main
gate and ask to see Schrader.''

"Where do I fit into this?'' Whitlock asked.

"You're my driver.''

"What if he calls the Met to check on Van Dehn?'' Sabrina asked.

"I've had Pieter de Jongh flown out from Amsterdam.
He'll be at the Met tomorrow for just such an eventuality.''

"I think you might have something here, Sergei,'' Whitlock said after a thoughtful pause. "It all depends on whether
Schrader's prepared to let you take the painting.''

"Put yourself in his shoes,'' Kolchinsky replied. "He's
gone to a great deal of trouble to get the original 'Night
Watch' for his private collection. Then he's told that the

painting he's been sent is the forgery, by the person he believes painted it. I can't see that he's got any alternative other than to go along with the suggestion. What good is the forgery to him?''

"If he believes you."

"He'll believe me, C. W. I can be very persuasive when I want to be. You know that."

"It's worth a try," Graham conceded. "What do you want Sabrina and me to do?"

"Nothing. Schrader knows you."

"What time are we out in the morning?" Whitlock asked.

"I'll meet you in the foyer at eight-thirty."

"It's gone two already." Whitlock got to his feet and stifled a yawn. "I hate to break up the party but I'm off to bed."

"And I'd better get back to my hotel if I'm going to make some more phone calls before I turn in."

Sabrina closed the door after them then turned to Graham and pointed at his leg. "I noticed you limping. What's wrong?"

"I took a knock on the mountain. It's nothing."

"I've heard that before. Let me take a look at it for you."

"I'm okay," he retorted irritably. "I'll see to it in the shower. Now stop mothering me."

"I was only trying to help," she snapped back. "But then I should have known better, shouldn't I?"

"Yeah, you should. I can take care of my own injuries." He stormed off to the bathroom and slammed the door behind him.

She threw up her hands in despair but no sooner had she slumped on to the nearest couch than a deep, anguished yell had her running for the bathroom door. She flung it open. Graham was seated on a stool with his jeans round his ankles, his hands clamped around his leg inches above the blood-stained bandage covering his injured knee.

"What happened?" she asked anxiously.

"I caught my jeans on the bandage as I was taking them off. Je-sus, it's sore."

"You'll have to cut the wetsuit off then soak the bandage off in the shower." She picked up a pair of scissors from the windowsill. "Use these. I'll put a fresh dressing on it when you come out. Unless, of course, you don't want to be mothered."

He smiled faintly but said nothing. She closed the door behind her and switched on the radio. Once she had found the Voice of America she lay down on the bed and closed her eyes.

Graham emerged from the bathroom a few minutes later, wearing a white vest and a pair of blue shorts, and looked down at her as he towelled his wet hair, uncertain as to whether she was asleep or not.

"Did you get the bandage off?" she asked without opening her eyes.

"Yeah," he replied sitting on the bed.

She swung her legs off the bed and took a blue canvas bag from her suitcase. It was a standard UNACO first-aid kit which every field operative had to draw from the stores before an assignment. She knelt in front of him and turned his leg slightly to get a better look at the injury. A gash, roughly two inches long, running diagonally across his knee.

"Well, will I live?" he asked draping the towel around his neck.

"With a bit of luck." She opened the canvas bag and removed a bottle of disinfectant, a cotton swab and a length of bandage. "Brace yourself for the sting," she warned after sprinkling the cotton swab with disinfectant.

"O-kay," he replied and winced as she dabbed the cotton swab over the gash.

"It's going to leave a scar, you realize that?"

"Some people collect snapshots to remind them of the countries they've visited. I collect scars."

She doubted whether she had ever seen him so relaxed, a total contrast to his mood before he went into the shower. The UNACO enigma. She smiled to herself as she wound the bandage around his knee then, after securing it with a safety pin, she returned the canvas bag to her suitcase. She was surprised to find him staring at his own reflection in the wall mirror when she turned away from the cupboard. He hated mirrors, calling them props to encourage vanity. So what was he doing?

He caught sight of her watching him. "All that talk about scars brought back some memories. Vietnam in particular."

She felt a surge of excitement run through her. He had *never* spoken to anyone at UNACO about his time in Vietnam. It was his "taboo subject," as Whitlock had once put it.

"This is the baby that put an end to my football career," he said tracing his finger along a faint scar on his right shoulder.

"What happened?" she asked.

He sat on the bed and clenched his hands together. "Fragmentation grenade. I couldn't move my arm for three months. It was the most humiliating time of my life. I had to be dressed every day, I had to have my food cut up for me. Christ, I even had to have an orderly help me when I wanted to piss. Then, one day, a fresh-faced kid just out of medical school told me I'd never be able to move my arm again. It was the perfect incentive. The hell I was going to give him the satisfaction of being right. Smug little bastard. So I turned to physiotherapy. Eight months later I was posted to Thailand as an instructor to help train the Meo mercenaries. I still can't move my arm further back than this.'' He held his right arm out in front of him then eased it back until it was in line with the side of his body. ''It's got something to do with the socket joint. I never understood the technical jargon. So my hopes of becoming a Dan Marino or a Jim McMahon were dashed at the age of nineteen.''

''They're football players, aren't they?'' she asked hesitantly.

''They're two of the best quarterbacks in the game.''

''I don't follow football,'' she said with an apologetic smile. ''I've never been to a game in my life.''

''Never?'' he asked in astonishment.

She shook her head. ''The nearest I came was when I was dating a guy who was as fanatical about the game as you are. He was always trying to persuade me to go to the Meadowlands with him, but I was just never interested enough.''

''I don't blame you, not if he wanted you to go to the Meadowlands. You don't want to be seen supporting the Jets.''

She laughed. ''You guys and your football. He used to say the same kind of things about the Giants.''

''Sounds like you're well rid of him,'' he said with a smile then stood up and stifled a yawn. ''It's been quite a day and I, for one, am ready for bed.''

She yawned as well. ''Me too. Just think, we should be home this time tomorrow.''

''I'd say that all depends on Sergei, wouldn't you?''

''I guess so.''

''See you in the morning.'' He crossed to the nearest couch to prepare his bed.

''I guess so,'' she muttered again then disappeared into the bathroom.

TWELVE

"Is this the best you could do, Sergei?" Whitlock asked disdainfully as he slowly circled the battered white Isuzu van parked outside the hotel. "You'd get arrested if you tried to drive this junker in New York. Why this?"

"Because you're a poor *favelado* who I've hired to take me to see Schrader. We can hardly arrive there in a polished Hertz van, can we? This is perfect. I bought it for a hundred dollars last night. It's just what we need."

"You never said anything about me being a *favelado*. I'm not dressed for the part."

"You'll find some clothes in the back of the van. I'm pretty sure they'll fit you."

Whitlock opened the back doors and climbed inside. He leapt out a moment later, a look of horror and revulsion on his face. "Those clothes stink, Sergei."

"They would do, I bought them from a hobo near my hotel this morning. You have to be convincing, C. W., it's the only way we can fool Schrader."

"Fine, I'll get some clothes from a second-hand shop and wear those."

Kolchinsky shook his head.

"Sergei, I am not wearing those clothes. They're probably infested with lice and fleas and God knows what other parasites. And as for the smell . . ."

"I can't force you. We'll have to abort the plan and go back to the drawing board. Come on, we'd better go and wake Michael and Sabrina and see if we can't come up with something else."

"You'd abort the plan for something as trivial as this?"

"It's not trivial, C. W. Toysgen was the kind of person who would have hired a *favelado* rather than some smooth-talking taxi driver. If you arrive there smelling of Paco Rabanne those guards are going to notice it pretty quickly and pass the information on to Schrader."

"Okay, I'll wear the clothes," Whitlock said grudgingly and disappeared into the back of the van again.

Kolchinsky smiled to himself and slid into the passenger seat.

Whitlock changed into the sweat-stained shirt, threadbare flannels and scuffed brown shoes then slammed the back doors and climbed in beside Kolchinsky. "Now I understand what's meant by method acting," he muttered facetiously, his face a grimace of disgust.

Kolchinsky wound down his window but decided against making light of the situation. He doubted whether it would be appreciated.

"I hope you know the way," Whitlock said starting the van.

"I drove up there earlier this morning." Kolchinsky took a map from the dashboard and opened it out on his knees. "The turn-off is on Niemeyer Avenue."

"That means a lot to me, Sergei."

"You drive. I'll navigate."

They reached the turn-off twenty minutes later.

"There's a deserted cafeteria about a mile up the road," Kolchinsky said breaking the lingering silence. "I'll use the public phone there to call Drago."

Whitlock changed down a gear as the gradient of the road became steeper and waved on the cars behind him. On reaching the cafeteria Kolchinsky got out of the van and walked to the yellow domed telephone. He pushed a *ficha* into the slot and dialled the number.

"Danaë. *Bom dia*, good morning," a friendly female voice answered.

"Could I speak to André Drago."

"May I ask who's calling?"

"Leonov."

"One moment, sir. I'll see if Mr. Drago's available."

There was a pause then: "Drago speaking."

"It's Leonov, I have to see you immediately."

"What's wrong? I thought you said we'd meet at the beach house tonight?"

"Why don't you announce the rendezvous to the whole world?" Kolchinsky snapped in typical Leonov fashion.

Drago sighed down the line. "I'm sorry, I've just got a lot on my mind at the moment."

"I'll meet you outside the Carmen Miranda Museum in thirty minutes."

"Do you want me to bring the envelope?" Drago asked hesitantly.

"Of course." Kolchinsky hung up and returned to the van.

"Did he buy it?" Whitlock asked.

"He thinks he's meeting Leonov in thirty minutes on the other side of town. That should give us ample time to get in and out of Danaë."

"But how will we know when Drago's left the estate?"

Kolchinsky took a pair of binoculars from the glove compartment. "With these. Come on, I'll show you."

Whitlock followed Kolchinsky to the protective railing around the perimeter of the parking bay. The view was spectacular—Ipanema and Leblon spread out below them like a photograph in a glossy travel brochure.

Kolchinsky handed the binoculars to Whitlock then pointed to the nearest of the mountains beyond São Conrado Beach. "Look about a third of the way up. See anything?"

"Trees," Whitlock replied. "And more trees."

"That's the road. It's lined with them. Look higher."

"I don't know what I'm—hang on, I can see a gate. It must be all of ten feet high." Whitlock lowered the binoculars. "Is that the entrance?"

Kolchinsky took the binoculars from Whitlock and put them to his eyes. "It's the only way in or out of Danaë. Drago will have to use it."

"But how did you know where to look?"

"I didn't. It was luck. I'd seen the gate when I'd driven up there but it was only when I stopped here on the way back that I saw them through the binoculars."

A movement caught Whitlock's eye and he tapped Kolchinsky on the arm. "Forget the gates. Check out twelve o'clock."

Kolchinsky swung the binoculars upwards. A white Gazelle helicopter rose from the top of the mountain then banked away sharply and levelled out over São Conrado Beach. He focused the binoculars on the cockpit. There was no mistaking the white-haired figure of Drago strapped in beside the helmeted pilot.

"You still want to go through with it?" Whitlock asked.

"Of course. We've still got a good thirty minutes on him. That's enough."

They rejoined the motorway and took the signposted turn-off to Danaë a mile further on. The road twisted its way up the mountain then straightened out for the last two hundred yards before they reached the imposing wrought-iron gates at the entrance to the estate.

Kolchinsky climbed from the van, glanced up at the closed-circuit television camera, then approached the intercom system beside the gate and pressed the button. "I'd like to see Martin Schrader."

"Do you have an appointment?" a male voice replied.

"No, but it's imperative that I see him."

"Mr. Schrader won't see anybody without an appointment."

"I don't have an appointment because I haven't had a chance to make one. I flew in from Amsterdam this morning."

"I've told you—"

"I know, Mr. Schrader won't see anybody without an appointment. Let me put it this way. I'm flying back to Amsterdam at one o'clock this afternoon and if I don't see Mr. Schrader before then he's going to lose on a business deal worth millions of dollars. And it will be your fault."

There was a lengthy pause. "Very well, I'll contact Mr. Schrader and ask him if he'll see you. What is the name?"

"Toysgen."

"Spell it," came the curt reply.

Kolchinsky did. "Tell him it's about the painting. He'll know what I mean."

A minute later there was a metallic click and the gates swung open. Kolchinsky climbed back into the van and Whitlock drove it into the grounds. The gates closed behind them. An armed guard signalled for them to stop in front of the second gate. He eyed the van with obvious distaste then moved to the driver's window and looked inside.

"Is something wrong?" Kolchinsky asked.

The guard walked round to the passenger window, glad to get away from the stench of Whitlock's clothing. "I look in back," he said tapping the side of the van.

"It's open," Kolchinsky said.

The guard opened the back doors. It was empty. He closed the doors again and waved them through. Whitlock drove the van into the spacious courtyard and pulled up in front of the reception. Kolchinsky reached under his seat for a black attaché case.

"What's in there?"

"Hopefully enough to convince Schrader to part with the painting." Kolchinsky got out and crossed to the plate-glass doors which parted in front of him.

The receptionist smiled at him. "Good morning, Mr. Toysgen. Mr. Schrader has asked that you go straight up. The lift is over there."

"Which floor?"

"There is only one button," she replied.

Unknown to Kolchinsky, the contents of his attaché case were analysed in the control room by an X-ray camera mounted discreetly into the wall as he waited for the lift to arrive. A green light flashed on the receptionist's desk and she activated a switch to open the lift door. Kolchinsky clenched the case in front of him and stared at his shoes as the lift ascended the three hundred feet to the second reception area, where another receptionist led him to the steel door and opened it with her magnetic strip ID card. She selected a button and they were transported to the next level. The door opened on to a sun lounge. Schrader was standing at the window, his hands clasped behind his back.

"Mr. Toysgen's here, sir," the receptionist announced.

Schrader turned away from the window. "Thank you, Carla."

She disappeared back into the lift.

Schrader shook Kolchinsky's hand then gestured to one of the rattan chairs. "Please, sit down. Can I get you anything? Tea? Coffee? A little breakfast?"

"Thank you, no. I only have a few hours in Rio so I'd like to come straight to the point, if I may?"

"Please do."

Kolchinsky pretended to fidget nervously with the handle of his attaché case. "I really don't know how to put this, Mr. Schrader. I mean, you've been so good to me in the past."

"Put it as bluntly as possible. That way there can be no misunderstandings."

"Very well." Kolchinsky wet his lips. "I have reason to believe that the 'Night Watch' Van Dehn gave you is a forgery."

Schrader stared at the carpet then crossed to the window. "Tell me more."

"He's working in conjunction with a man called Horst Keppler—"

"Keppler?" Schrader snapped then gave Kolchinsky an apologetic smile. "Please continue."

"I assume you are familiar with the original plan to switch the paintings?"

"I'm the one who devised it in the first place."

"I had no idea," Kolchinsky replied truthfully. "The first part of the switch went according to plan. Van Dehn switched the forgery for the original in the back of the van then took it on to Vienna with him. Keppler, however, returned to his office and switched the original for the second forgery which was then forwarded on to you.''

"There was a second forgery?'' Schrader asked in astonishment.

"I did them both, but I'd never have agreed if I'd known that Van Dehn was going to cheat you, Mr. Schrader. You must believe that.''

"So where's the original now?''

"In Keppler's warehouse. If, in fact, it is the original. That's why I came here to make sure.''

Schrader stroked his nose thoughtfully. "How did you come by this information?''

"Through De Vere and Oosterhuis, Keppler's two employees who were in on the switch as well. I should say ex-employees. Keppler fired them without paying them for the job. They couldn't go to the police, not with their records, so they came to see me instead. We discussed the possibilities and decided that I should come out here to see if you do have the original or not.''

Schrader poured himself a Scotch. "Do you know what they intend to do with the original? If it is the original.''

"Oosterhuis said he overheard Keppler on the telephone talking to someone who had agreed to double your original offer to Van Dehn. He thought the name sounded like Averheart.''

Schrader's jaw hardened and his hand whitened around the glass. "Eberhart. Ralph Eberhart. It's exactly the kind of underhand stunt he'd pull, especially if he knew he was screwing me out of a deal. What can we do?''

"We first have to conduct a chemical test to see if you do have the forgery.'' Kolchinsky patted his attaché case. "I've brought the necessary items with me for the test. What I need are two samples to test in the solution. Both, say, an inch in diameter. One from the 'Night Watch' and the other from a painting you *know* definitely dates back to the sixteenth or seventeenth century. Can that be arranged?''

''Certainly.''

Kolchinsky moved to the window after Schrader had left the room. He glanced at his watch. Drago had already been gone eighteen minutes.

When Schrader returned he had the samples in two envelopes, marked A and B. Kolchinsky opened his attaché case and removed a wooden rack containing two test-tubes. He placed it on the table then took out a bottle of colourless liquid sealed with a cork stopper and held it up to the light. The performance had to be good.

''What is that exactly?'' Schrader asked.

''Diluted hydrochloric acid.'' Kolchinsky uncorked the stopper and poured two equal measures into the test-tubes then glanced up at Schrader and noticed the frown on his face. ''Don't you know this test?''

''I can't say I do.''

''Oh, I just assumed you did. It's really quite simple. It works on the principle that the older the paint, the slower it will take to separate from the canvas. So if the 'Night Watch' Keppler forwarded on to you is a forgery, then the paint's going to dissolve that much quicker in the acid solution than the paint from the other sample. You are certain the other painting is an original from the sixteenth or seventeenth century?''

''I had it authenticated—1641.'' Schrader took a sip of Scotch then pointed at the test-tubes. ''Won't the canvases be dissolved as well?''

''Good point. They would in a stronger solution. This solution has a pH of five. It's fairly weak, but still strong enough to dissolve the paint. Especially fresh paint.''

"It's ingenious."

"It is, to a point," Kolchinsky removed two strips of lit-mus paper from his case and dipped them into the test-tubes. They both turned red. "Acid, right?"

Schrader nodded.

"Could I have something to drink, my throat's really dry?"

"What would you like?" Schrader asked.

"A small Scotch please." Kolchinsky took a pack of cig-arettes from his pocket and opened it when Schrader turned his back on him. Inside were half a dozen cigarettes and a corked test-tube filled with water. He uncorked the test-tube, swopped it with one of the test-tubes in the rack, then pushed a cigarette between his lips before putting the pack back into his pocket.

"Your drink," Schrader said handing the glass to him.

Kolchinsky lit the cigarette then, using a pair of tweezers, took the 'Night Watch' sample from the envelope and put it in the diluted acid solution. He put the other sample in the water. Schrader crouched in front of the test-tubes, his eyes darting from one to the other. The paint in the acid solution began to dissolve. He slammed his fist angrily on the table then crossed to the window, his hands thrust into his pockets.

"How can I get the original?" he asked softly.

"I've got an idea but I don't know whether you'll go along with it."

"I'm listening."

Kolchinsky removed the pieces of canvas from the test-tubes, put them in one of the envelopes and dropped it into his attaché case. "I'll take the forgery back to Amsterdam with me. De Vere and Oosterhuis will steal the original from Keppler's warehouse and we'll then offer to sell the forgery back to him, *as the original*. He'll have no choice but to pay us with this Eberhart deal just around the corner."

"And the original?"

"I'll bring it to Rio then do some more tests for you to prove its authenticity."

"How do I know I can trust you?"

"We could have stolen the original from the warehouse without you being any the wiser and sold it on the black market at the kind of price Van Dehn and Keppler are asking. We didn't. We chose to level with you instead."

Schrader massaged his forehead thoughtfully then reached for the telephone. "Carla, tell Ramon I want the painting he helped me carry into 'The Sanctuary' a few minutes ago repacked in its original box and taken down to the main reception. And tell him I want it done now!" He replaced the receiver then walked Kolchinsky to the lift, inserted his ID card into the slot to open the door, then reached inside and pressed one of the buttons. "Don't try and double-cross me, Toysgen, because I'll kill you."

The door closed.

Kolchinsky's triumph was overshadowed by an uneasy sense of foreboding: twenty-eight minutes had already elapsed since the call to lure Drago away from the estate. It would be only a matter of time before Drago realized he had been set up. But how would he react? Kolchinsky knew what he would do if he were in Drago's shoes—radio ahead to the estate to check that nothing untoward had happened in his absence then, on hearing about Toysgen and his driver, have them detained so he could deal personally with the situation on his return. He only hoped he was wrong. . . .

When he emerged into the foyer the receptionist told him it would take another couple of minutes for the painting to arrive from "The Sanctuary." He walked out to the van and explained to Whitlock what had happened but before Whitlock could say anything four men appeared in the foyer carrying the crated "Night Watch" between them. Kolchinsky handed his attaché case to Whitlock then walked round to the back of the van and opened the doors. The crate was pushed up firmly against the inside wall and Kolchinsky used a set of fasteners to secure it in place. He locked the doors and got in beside Whitlock.

They drove through the first gate, following the gentle contours of the driveway, and Whitlock gave a whoop of delight when the road eventually levelled out a hundred yards from the main gates which had been opened in advance of their arrival.

Then, suddenly, the gates started to close.

"We'll make it," Whitlock hissed between clenched teeth.

Kolchinsky's eyes widened in horror. "We won't make it. Brake, C. W., brake!"

"Like hell I will," Whitlock retorted and pressed the accelerator pedal to the floor.

The wing mirrors were sheared off and the paint raked from the side of the van as it squeezed between the closing gates and Whitlock had to swing the wheel violently to avoid hitting a tree on the opposite side of the road.

"If we'd hit those gates—"

"Spare the lecture, Sergei. Bandits at three o'clock."

The white Gazelle helicopter buzzed them once then disappeared from view behind a cluster of tall mahogany trees.

"I'll try and outrun them. We'll be safe once we reach the main road."

"*If* we reach the main road," Kolchinsky corrected him. "Who knows what sort of arsenal Drago's got up there?"

"But what use would it be to him? If he shoots up the van he risks damaging the painting as well. Schrader would crucify him if that happened."

The helicopter took up a position above the van and Drago

hailed them through a megaphone. "Pull over to the side of the road and neither of you will be harmed. I repeat, pull over to the side of the road."

Whitlock swung the van into the first bend in the road and the temporary sanctuary of an avenue of mahogany trees. The pilot decided it would be too dangerous to go in after them and Drago told him to take the helicopter over the trees where they could follow the van by catching glimpses of its roof through the canopy of branches.

Kolchinsky shaded his eyes from the flickering rays of sunlight as he peered up through the windscreen but although he could hear the rotors above them, he couldn't see the helicopter itself. He slumped back in the seat and dabbed the sweat from his forehead with an already damp handkerchief then, taking the four *fichas* from the glove compartment, stuffed them into Whitlocks's shirt pocket. "You'll have to make a run for it if Drago does manage to stop the van. Call Michael and tell him what's happened."

"What about you?"

"I'd only slow you down."

The helicopter tucked in behind the van the moment it emerged from the trees and Drago squeezed off four shots in rapid succession at the rear tyres. One bullet found its mark and Whitlock had to use all his driving skills to prevent the van from slewing off the road. He managed to regain control of the wheel and brought the van to a halt.

"Go!" Kolchinsky snapped, noticing the hesitation in Whitlock's eyes.

Whitlock flung open the door and dived to the ground but didn't stop rolling until he reached the safety of the dense undergrowth. Drago jumped from the helicopter as its skids touched the road and ran to the spot where Whitlock had disappeared into the thicket. Nothing moved. A black Mercedes screeched to a halt beside the helicopter and four men leapt out and ran to where Drago was standing. They were each armed with a Heckler & Koch MP5 machine-pistol. He sent three of them in after Whitlock then turned his attention to the van. The cab section was deserted but, on closer inspection, he noticed a sliding panel between it and the back of the van. He told the fourth guard to watch the sliding panel then moved to the back doors and tugged at the bulky padlock. He took a step back and shot it off then, discarding the twisted remains, yanked open the doors. Kolchinsky stared at the CZ75 and slowly raised his hands. Drago ordered him out then pushed him up against the side of the van and frisked him. He was clean. The guards produced a pair of handcuffs and Kolchinsky's wrists were manacled behind his back.

"I'll send someone down to change the tyre," Drago told the guard. "But God help you if anything should happen to the painting before they arrive."

The guard swallowed nervously. "What if the driver returns?"

"Kill him!" Drago snapped then grabbed Kolchinsky's arm and led him to the waiting helicopter.

Whitlock crouched ever lower behind the bush when one of the guards paused only yards away from him to wipe his forearm across his sweating face. He would normally have jumped the guard but the stench of his clothes was so nauseating that any sudden movement would almost certainly give him away. When the guard finally moved in, Whitlock crept forward until he could see the Mercedes parked at the side of the road. It was his only chance. The helicopter had already taken off which meant it would be only a matter of time before Drago set about trying to extract whatever information he wanted from Kolchinsky. And Kolchinsky would be able to hold out only for so long. . . .

Whitlock looked around and, deciding it was all clear, darted from his hiding place and sprinted towards the Mercedes. He had almost reached the clearing when he caught sight of the guard out of the corner of his eye, and he flung himself to the ground a split second before a burst of gunfire chewed into the fir trees behind him. The guard approached Whitlock cautiously and kicked him in the ribs. Whitlock didn't move. The guard rolled him on to his back. Whitlock grabbed the MP5 with both hands, twisted the barrel away from his body, then lashed out with his foot, catching the guard squarely in the stomach. He wrenched the machine-pistol from the guard's hands and ran the short distance to the Mercedes. A second guard emerged from the bushes and Whitlock shot him before climbing behind the wheel and hot-wiring the ignition system. The guard Drago had detailed to stay with the van fired at the Mercedes as it passed but the bullets merely pocked its reinforced bodywork. Whitlock negotiated the last couple of bends in the road then rejoined the motorway in search of the nearest public telephone.

Schrader turned away from the window when the lift door opened and Drago led Kolchinsky into the sun lounge. "Take the handcuffs off, André."

Drago knew better than to argue and did as he was told.

"Sit down," Schrader said indicating the rattan chair Kolchinsky had sat in earlier that morning.

Kolchinsky sat down and folded his arms across his chest.

"I must compliment you on a good scam. A very good scam. And you so nearly pulled it off. Fortunately André had the good sense to call me once he realized you'd sent him on a wild-goose chase. He was able to verify that you weren't

Toysgen from the description I gave him. He also told me about the red dot in the forgery, something I hadn't known about up until then.'' Schrader sat down in the chair opposite Kolchinsky. ''How long have you known about the switch?''

Kolchinsky stared at the carpet.

''You will talk, one way or the other. I can assure you you'll save yourself a great deal of trouble by talking to me.''

Kolchinsky continued to stare at the carpet.

Schrader leaned forward, his forearms resting on his knees. ''Don't force me to hand you over to André. He's broken stronger men than you in the past. I don't know how he does it, nor do I ever want to know. I hate violence, but there are times when I have to safeguard my own interests. This is one of them. For your own sake, answer my questions. Now how long have you known about the switch?''

Kolchinsky remained silent.

Schrader slumped back in his chair. ''I've done my best. I honestly thought you'd have had more sense than this. André, take him away.''

Kolchinsky had to stall for time but he knew what he had in mind could easily backfire on him. It was a risk he had to take. He shrugged off Drago's hand. ''I sunk the *Golconda*.''

''*You?*'' Schrader said in amazement. ''But why?''

''Ask Drago.''

''Ask me what?'' Drago replied sharply then hauled Kolchinsky to his feet. ''Come on, you've wasted enough of Mr. Schrader's time as it is.''

''Wait, André, let him talk.''

''He's playing for time, sir, can't you see that? I'll get the truth out of him.''

''Then what?'' Kolchinsky challenged. ''You'd have to kill me, wouldn't you? You couldn't risk the chance of your boss finding out what you've been doing behind his back.''

"I've had enough of this—"

"Shut up, André!" Schrader approached Kolchinsky. "Who are you?"

"My name wouldn't mean anything to you." Kolchinsky looked at Drago. "Tell him why you had the *Golconda* hijacked last night."

"You obviously know more about it than I do," Drago replied contemptuously. "Why don't you tell us?"

"Well?" Schrader prompted.

"Drago made a deal with a Colombian drug baron two months ago to supply him with eighteen kilograms of heroin," Kolchinsky said recalling what Philpott had told him over the telephone earlier that morning. "The *Golconda* was used to pick it up from a passing freighter. Who knows how many lives would have been destroyed had the heroin reached the streets."

"He's fabricated the whole thing to draw the pressure away from himself. You know I hate drugs as much as you do, Mr. Schrader."

"There's a lot more I can tell you about Drago but you've got enough to think about for the moment. It's up to you whether you want to investigate it further."

"You've spun enough lies about me," Drago snarled then snatched the handcuffs off the table. "Now it's time for us to talk. Alone."

"He'll kill me," Kolchinsky said to Schrader in a calm voice. "Oh, he'll call it an accident but it's the only way he can silence me. At least then you'll know I was telling the truth. He'll have proved his guilt."

The telephone rang.

Schrader answered it then handed the receiver to Drago and turned back to Kolchinsky. "If I find out you've been lying to me I'll gladly hand you over to André and he can do what he likes with you.''

"And if you find out I've been telling the truth?''

Schrader crossed to the window and slowly rubbed his hands over his face.

"Excuse me, sir?'' Drago said after replacing the receiver.

"What is it?'' Schrader retorted.

"The painting's downstairs in the foyer.''

"Have it put in 'The Sanctuary,' I'll see to it later. What about the driver? Has he been caught?''

Drago looked down at his feet. "No, sir, he managed to escape.''

Schrader shook his head in disgust. "First the *Golconda*, and now this. What the hell's happening, André?''

"He caught the men by surprise,'' Drago muttered.

"I don't want excuses. I want results. Now get out there and find him!''

Drago glared at Kolchinsky then headed towards the lift.

Schrader had Kolchinsky removed to one of the bedrooms then settled down to make the telephone calls he was dreading so much.

THIRTEEN

Graham reacted immediately to Whitlock's call by hiring a Ford van and driving out to the airport with Sabrina to collect the three UNACO crates before continuing on to the derelict cafeteria where Whitlock had arranged to meet them.

Sabrina jumped nimbly from the van, frowned, then sniffed the air suspiciously. "What's that awful smell?"

"Me," Whitlock retorted then looked past her as Graham got out from behind the wheel. "Mike, did you bring the clothes?"

"Yeah, they're in here," Graham threw the plastic bag to Whitlock. "You still haven't said what it's all about."

"I'll explain later. Get the crates out, I won't be a minute."

Graham and Sabrina shrugged at each other when Whitlock disappeared behind the Mercedes to change, then turned their attention to unloading the crates from the back of the van. Whitlock reappeared in a pair of jeans and a white shirt and they set about assembling the three eighteen-foot Super Scorpion hang-gliders, each powered by a thirty-kilowatt engine and capable of taking off in a distance of eight feet or

271

less. Each crate also contained an Armourshield CPV/25 bulletproof vest, an UZI with three forty-round magazines, a stun grenade, an L2 fragmentation grenade and a helmet with an in-built headset and integrated sight system for use with the six serrated bolts attached to the cross tube.

Graham, the most experienced pilot amongst them, elected to take off first. He strapped himself into the swing harness then switched on the engine. He pulled on the control frame until the wing was horizontal then, clamping his hands either side of the control frame to obtain pitch and roll control on the ground, he made a determined run across the carpark while at the same time pivoting the control frame to increase his angle of attack. He was airborne within seconds and immediately pulled himself towards the control frame to regain his flying speed. Sabrina and Whitlock followed him into the air, both executing the same copybook take-off he had done. They purposely headed inland to avoid the plethora of hanggliders over São Conrado Beach and switched off their engines on reaching the desired thousand feet. The view was even more spectacular than it had been from Sugar Loaf but they barely noticed it as the hang-gliders pitched down towards the mountain fortress of Danaë.

Graham was the first to spot the two guards on the helipad and he rolled his hang-glider to the left to deal with them. Whitlock and Sabrina dived their hang-gliders after him. Graham lined up one of the guards in the cross-hairs of the sight over his right eye and gently squeezed the trigger on the control frame. The bolt took the guard in the chest, spinning him round grotesquely before he collapsed to the ground. The second guard fired a burst from his Heckler & Koch machine-pistol at Graham's hang-glider as it passed above him. The bullets ripped into the wing and Graham struggled desperately to level out the hang-glider in preparation for an emergency landing. The guard raised the machine-pistol to fire again. Whitlock, knowing he didn't have time to get in an aimed shot, pitched his hang-glider down sharply, catching the guard on the shoulder with his foot. The guard stumbled against the railing, overbalanced, and fell screaming to his death. Graham managed to bring his hang-glider back across the helipad but as he made for the garden it yawed to the left and he found himself heading straight for the red and white marquee. He fought to come out of the roll by shifting his weight to the right of the hang-glider and the left side of the wing brushed the top of the marquee before he finally touched down safely on the grass. He unharnessed himself then ran to the entrance of the marquee to cover Whitlock and Sabrina when they came in to land. The garden was deserted. Surely the control room would have a camera mounted on the helipad? Were the other guards waiting for them in the house? Whitlock and Sabrina sprinted across to where he was crouched and surveyed their surroundings with equal suspicion.

"What's their game?" Sabrina asked. "They must know we're here."

"They know all right," Graham replied wiping the sweat from his eyes. "You can bet there's a camera focused on us right now."

"Come out with your hands in the air and none of you will be harmed," an amplified voice boomed across the deserted garden.

"Drago," Whitlock whispered as his eyes flickered around in search of the tannoy system. "He used a similar ploy to try and stop Sergei and me when we were in the van."

"You have exactly one minute to throw down your weapons and come out, otherwise we will open fire on the marquee. One minute."

Graham drew them away from the entrance. "C. W., you and Sabrina concentrate on finding Sergei. I'm going after the envelope."

"Forget the envelope," Whitlock retorted. "We're here to find Sergei and recover the painting."

"You remember the dossier on Schrader? He hates violence, especially involving guns. It's a throwback to his years in the arms trade. So you can bet he's already retreated to his private gallery, with the painting. And there's nothing we can do to get in there without the access transmitter. If I can get hold of the envelope we might be able to use it as a means of bargaining. It's our only chance."

"How are we going to get into the house?" Sabrina asked. "Drago's sure to have the garden covered."

"You can bet on it," Graham agreed then took two smoke canisters from the pouch around his waist.

"Where did you get those from?" Whitlock asked in amazement.

"I asked the Test Center to include them in the consignment. They're mighty handy at times like this."

"You have ten seconds left to throw down your weapons and come out."

Graham checked his watch. "I'll meet you in the main foyer in twenty minutes."

"Twenty minutes," Whitlock agreed.

Graham activated both canisters and flung them as close as he could to the house. Whitlock and Sabrina ducked out of the marquee, their bodies bent double as they hurried towards the smokescreen. Graham flung himself into the garden seconds before a fusillade of bullets raked the side of the marquee. He didn't stop rolling until he had reached a rockery where he waited until the billowing black smoke engulfed him before crawling the short distance across the lawn to the red and white patio, the UZI clenched tightly against his stomach. From the edge of the patio he could hear agitated voices coming from inside the poolroom. Another burst of gunfire. He smiled to himself. They were disoriented by the smoke and were firing blindly into it, hoping against the odds to score a lucky hit. More gunfire, but this time a lot closer to where he was crouched behind a stone fountain. He unclipped the stun grenade from his belt and crept stealthily across the patio until he reached the side of the house. The smoke was beginning to disperse and, using this to his advantage he pressed his back against the wall and made his way to the sliding door where he pulled out the pin and threw the grenade into the room. A shouted warning was abruptly cut short by a blinding explosion.

Graham waited for a few seconds then pivoted round to face the room, the UZI at the ready. One of the guards was unconscious, having struck his head on the pooltable when the grenade detonated. The second guard was kneeling on the floor, his hands clasped over his eyes, temporarily blinded by the explosion. Graham hit him behind the ear then retrieved the two Heckler & Koch MP5s, ejected the clips and tossed them out into the garden. He dropped the clips into a vase on the sideboard then moved to the sliding door leading into the hall. He stood to the side of the door and pulled it open, fully expecting to be pinned down by a concentrated bout of gunfire. Silence. Was there someone out there waiting to pick him off the moment he emerged through the doorway? If there was, where would they have positioned themselves? He visualized the hall in his mind—it had to be at the top of the stairs. And they were at least fifty feet away from the poolroom. He dived low through the doorway and rolled to the temporary sanctuary of the wall. Still silence. He noticed the closed-circuit television camera on the opposite wall and after shooting it out he started to leopard-crawl towards the stairs, pausing every few seconds to look over his shoulder to make sure that nobody was coming up behind him. He reached the end of the wall and swivelled round to fan the stairs with his UZI. They were deserted. It had to be a trap.

He moved to the lift and inserted the ID card into the slot to open the door. Only then did it dawn on him—the *lift* was the trap! He would be the perfect target in such a confined space. An idea came to him: take the stairs and use the lift as a decoy. It was simple. *Too* simple. Drago would be expecting him to think like that. He cursed himself angrily for his oversight then got into the lift and pushed the button for the second floor. The lift began to descend into the mountain. He pressed himself up against the control panel making it impossible for him to be seen from the corridor once the lift reached its destination. The lift came to a gradual stop and as the door opened a volley of bullets ripped into the facing wall. A voice shouted in Portuguese then the barrel of a Heckler & Koch came into view. Graham grabbed it with his left hand, jerking the startled guard into the lift, and struck him across the temple with the butt of his UZI. The guard crumpled to the floor. Graham dived into the corridor and shot a second guard, who had been covering the stairs, as he was turning to see what had happened to his colleague. He picked up the two Heckler & Kochs, tossed them through an open window into the sea below, then moved cautiously towards the steel door at the end of the corridor. It slid back. He flung himself to the floor, the UZI trained on the doorway. All he could see was a mahogany desk and, behind it, a high-backed chair turned towards the window making it impossible for him to know whether anybody was sitting in it. He got to his feet and eyed the doorway suspiciously, sensing a trap.

"Come in, Mr. Graham," Drago called out from the chair. "I've been expecting you."

Graham's finger tightened on the trigger but he stopped short of firing at the back of the chair. He needed Drago alive. He stepped into the room and a handgun was immediately pressed against the side of his head. Not that it surprised him. Nor was he surprised that Drago was holding the gun.

"Drop the UZI and kick it away from you," Drago ordered.

Graham did as he was told. Drago pushed him up against the wall and frisked him. He unclipped the fragmentation grenade from Graham's belt then picked up the UZI, ejected the magazine, and put them on the filing cabinet behind his desk.

Graham looked from Drago to the chair. "Tape recorder?"

Drago flicked a switch on the door panel to close the door then swivelled the chair and indicated the tape recorder. "As I said, I've been expecting you. I had a feeling you'd be the one to come looking for me after that dramatic entrance in the garden. Very impressive." He lit a cigarette and perched on the corner of the desk, the CZ75 pointing at Graham's chest. "Unfortunately your colleagues have already freed the Russian and look as if they're heading for the main reception area. I presume that's where you agreed to meet them?" He smiled at Graham's silence. "I thought so. Don't worry, you'll still keep your rendezvous. Only I'll be with you, with some of my men."

"Then what? You don't honestly expect them just to throw down their weapons when I appear with a gun pointing at my head, do you? They're professionals, Drago, they don't give in to intimidation and blackmail."

"I'd say that all depends on the type of intimidation and blackmail used," Drago replied then took a long drag on his cigarette. "That 'marriage' of yours was very convincing. It even had me fooled for a while but once I'd seen through it I began to watch you both more closely. Glances, looks, gestures—little things like that. It was actually quite fascinating. If your partner isn't in love with you, then she's certainly very fond of you. Professional or not, she still has feelings and emotions like any other woman. And you, Graham, are her Achilles' heel."

"That's crap and you know it," Graham said defensively.

"We'll see." The telephone rang and Drago answered it without taking his eyes off Graham. He listened in silence then hung up. "You'll be glad to hear that your colleagues have reached the foyer safely. I'm sure you'd like to join them."

Graham flung himself at Drago, deflecting the gun with his left arm. Drago's instinctive shot fired harmlessly into the wall. They grappled for possession of the gun as they rolled across the desk before falling heavily on to the floor. The gun spun from Drago's hand. Graham tried to reach it but Drago grabbed his wrist and jerked him sideways against the wall then clawed for the holstered Bernadelli he kept strapped to the undersurface of the desk. He managed to draw it from the holster before Graham locked his arm around his throat and yanked him away from the desk. Graham saw the Bernadelli at the last moment possible and, grabbing Drago's arm, slammed the back of his hand against the edge of the desk. Drago cried out in pain but held on to the gun. Graham did it again, harder. The Bernadelli slipped from Drago's hand and came to rest underneath the desk, out of reach for either of them. Graham made a grab for the CZ75 behind him but Drago landed heavily on his back, sending him sprawling, knocking the gun from his hand. Drago kicked Graham in the ribs then hauled him to his feet and hit him twice in the stomach before delivering a jarring punch to the side of his face. Graham stumbled backwards and fell against the filing cabinet. Drago scooped up the CZ75 and spun round, the gun held at arm's length. He froze. Graham was kneeling beside the filing cabinet, the fragmentation grenade in one hand, the pin in the other hand.

"Go on, shoot," Graham challenged, the grenade held out threateningly in front of him.

"Are you mad, Graham? If that goes off we'll both be killed."

"Only if I take my thumb off the lever." Graham got to his feet and tossed the pin on to the table. "I'm going to count to five. If you haven't dropped the gun by then I'll release the grenade."

Drago swallowed nervously. "You've got to have some kind of death wish, Graham."

"One . . . two . . . three . . ."

Drago dropped the gun.

"Kick it over here."

Drago did as he was told.

Graham picked it up. "I'm already running behind schedule so I'm going to make this as simple as possible. Either you give me the envelope or I shoot you."

"Shoot me and you'll never get it."

"No, it'll just take me longer if I have to crack the safe myself."

"That's assuming it's in the safe," Drago replied but the arrogance had gone from his voice.

Graham aimed the automatic at an imaginary spot between Drago's eyes. "What's it going to be?"

Drago struggled to hold Graham's stare. There was no

mercy or compassion in his eyes, only hatred. A fierce, burning hatred. He knew calling Graham's bluff would be the last thing he ever did. He gestured with his head towards the safe. "It's in there."

"Use your left hand to open it. Put your right hand on top of your head and keep it there."

Drago clamped his gun hand on his head then crouched in front of the safe and turned the dial with his left hand. He opened the door and reached inside for the envelope lying on top of a pile of fawn-coloured folders at the back of the safe.

"Nice try, Drago. Now get the proper envelope."

Drago looked round in bewilderment. "This *is* the envelope I was going to give to Leonov. It's the one you wanted, isn't it?"

Graham knew he was taking a big risk but a hunch told him Drago was lying—and his hunches were seldom wrong. He looked inside the safe and noticed a section cut away at the back to make room for a small door which was built into the rock. He told Drago to open it.

"It's empty."

"Open it!"

Drago unscrambled the combination lock, opened the door, and removed the envelope.

"Put it in my shirt pocket," Graham ordered.

Drago did it. "What happens now?"

"We go down to the foyer. You're our safe passage out of here." Graham backed up to the filing cabinet, ejected the clip from the CZ75 and tossed the empty gun on to the desk. He pushed the magazine into the UZI and locked it into place by pressing it against his stomach. "Now, call off your guards. And speak English."

Drago glared at Graham as he passed the instructions on

to the control room. "We'll have a free passage down to the foyer," he said after replacing the receiver.

"I hope so for your sake." Graham gestured to Drago's ID card. "Put it in my trouser pocket."

Drago unclipped it and slipped it into Graham's pocket.

Graham activated the door from the desk panel then prodded Drago in the back with the UZI. "Put your hands on your head!"

Drago did as he was told then walked towards the open door. "How are we getting down there? Stairs or lift?"

"Lift, because if anything happens to me, it's going to happen to you as well. You'll have nowhere to run."

Drago eyed the door leading on to the stairs. It was his only chance. If Graham managed to get him to the foyer they would use him as a hostage to get out of Danaë. Then what would happen to him? He was only too aware of the primed grenade, and of Graham's threat to use it, but he would still have a few valuable seconds to get to safety before it detonated. The UZI was his immediate concern. He waited until they were level with the door before he pivoted around sharply and, knocking the UZI aside, punched Graham hard on the side of the head. The grenade fell to the floor. Drago flung open the door and sprinted up the stairs to safety. Graham tossed the grenade through the window behind him. It exploded in mid-air, blowing out the window and showering him with glass as he lay face down on the floor. He got to his feet and cursed himself furiously for being caught out so easily. What the hell was wrong with him? Whatever it was, it had nearly cost him his life. He dabbed his eyebrow with the back of his hand. Drago's punch had cut him, drawing blood. It infuriated him further. He opened the door and fanned the landing with the UZI. It was deserted. But for how much longer? He had to get to the foyer as quickly as possible to rendezvous with the others. There was no time to lose. He covered the two flights of stairs without encountering any guards then called through the door before pushing it open and entering the foyer.

Whitlock, who had been covering the door in case of a trap, lowered the UZI. "What the hell kept you?"

"It's a long story," Graham replied then managed a twisted grin on seeing Kolchinsky. "You okay, *tavarishch*?"

"Better than you by the looks of it," Kolchinsky replied.

"Where's Sabrina?" Graham asked looking around.

"She's crouched on the other side of the reception desk, watching the lift," Kolchinsky said then glanced out into the courtyard. "How are we going to get out of here? The gates are controlled from inside the house."

"From the control room." Graham pointed at the black Mercedes parked in the courtyard beside the van Kolchinsky and Whitlock had arrived in earlier. "You guys take that. I'll get the gates."

"How?" Kolchinsky asked.

"There isn't time to explain. Give me five minutes then get the hell out of here. The gates *will* be open."

"I'm coming with you," Sabrina said backing away from the desk, her UZI still trained on the lift door.

"I can handle it myself," Graham answered.

"You're going to need back-up," she said glancing over her shoulder at him.

"Let me do it my way, okay?" Graham turned to Whitlock. "I'm going to need the fragmentation grenade of yours."

Whitlock handed it to Graham.

"I'll meet you at that café in, say, thirty minutes," Graham said to no one in particular.

Kolchinsky looked at his watch. "Michael, I think what Sabrina—"

Graham didn't hear the rest as he closed the door silently behind him and descended the stairs to the basement where the control room was situated. At the bottom of the stairs he found himself faced with a steel door and, above it, a closed-circuit television camera encased in a glass box. His suspicions were confirmed when he struck the box with the butt of his UZI—it was reinforced glass. He stood to the side of the door and inserted Drago's card into the slot. The door opened and a burst of gunfire from inside the corridor peppered the wall opposite him. Then silence. He fired into the corridor as he dived low through the doorway but landed awkwardly on the concrete floor, the machine-pistol spinning from his hand. One of the guards had been killed outright but the second had only taken a bullet in his left shoulder and was still holding the Heckler & Koch in his right hand. He aimed it at Graham but before he could squeeze the trigger Sabrina appeared in the doorway and cut him down in a hail of bullets.

She picked up Graham's UZI and handed it to him. "I told you you'd need back-up."

"Yeah, you did. Thanks." He retrieved the ID card from the slot and the door automatically closed behind him.

"What now?" she asked looking at a second steel door at the end of the corridor.

"We take over the control room," he replied then took up a position at the side of the door and indicated for her to do the same on the other side.

"Mike, tell me what you're going to do!" she hissed.

He held up the ID card. "Open the door with this then throw in the grenade."

"But you'll destroy the equipment."

"I'm not taking out the pin." He grinned like a schoolboy. "But whoever's in there doesn't know that."

He fed the ID card into the slot then rolled the grenade into the room the moment the door started to open. A guard ran out into the corridor. Graham grabbed him by the arm and shoved him up against the wall, frisked him quickly, and took possession of a Walther P5 which he tucked into his own webbing belt.

"It's empty," Sabrina called out after retrieving the grenade.

Graham pushed the man back into the room and Sabrina closed the door behind them. The room was compact with a row of television screens covering one wall and, underneath them, a panel of buttons and switches resembling a sophisticated mixing desk. All buttons and switches were clearly numbered to correspond to the chart on the wall to their right.

"Fala inglês?" Sabrina asked.

"Sim," came the muttered reply.

"He speaks English," she said to Graham.

"I gathered that." Graham look at the man's name-tag. "Saltezar. You in charge here?"

"Yes," Saltezar retorted, his eyes riveted on the grenade in Sabrina's hand.

She held it up and tapped the pin with her finger. He inhaled sharply, furious with himself for being duped so easily.

"It's time," Graham said then turned to Saltezar. "Which of these switches operate the gates?"

"Work it out yourself," Saltezar snapped.

Graham hit him across the face with the UZI then pushed him against the wall and forced the Walther's barrel between his bleeding lips. "You were saying?"

"Eight and fifteen," Saltezar blurted out.

Sabrina sat down on one of the three swivel chairs in front

of the panel and checked the numbers against the wallchart. "Eight's the inner gate, fifteen's the main gate."

Graham hit Saltezar behind the ear with the Walther then propped him against the wall and sat down beside Sabrina.

She pointed at one of the screens. "They've taken the van! Why didn't they take the Merc? They can't hope to outrun Drago's men in that junker."

"You can bet your bottom dollar Sergei's behind it," he said angrily. "At least C. W.'s driving. If anyone can get them out safely, he can."

"They're through the first gate," she announced then flicked the corresponding switch down. The gate closed behind the van.

"Bandit at three o'clock," he said pointing to the black Mercedes cutting across the lawn towards the van.

"And at nine o'clock," she added grimly as a second black Mercedes came into view.

He looked more closely at the second Mercedes and banged his fist angrily on the desk. "It's Drago, in the passenger seat."

Both Mercedes began to gain on the van. The lead Mercedes cut out from behind the van on to the grass but Kolchinsky fired at it with Whitlock's UZI and Larrios had to take evasive action to avoid being hit. The Mercedes fell back and Drago tried to shoot out the van's tyres as he had done earlier from the helicopter. Whitlock responded by veering the van from side to side, making it that much harder for Drago to hit. Kolchinsky fired blindly behind him and again Larrios had to swing the wheel violently. The van reached the last bend in the driveway and as Whitlock straightened the wheel he could see the open gates a hundred yards ahead of him.

"Saltezar, close the gates! Close the gates!" Drago's voice

boomed out from the speaker on the wall. "Saltezar? Salte-zar?"

Graham waited until the van was ten yards away from the gates before activating the switch to close them.

"Saltezar, it's too late! Open them!" Drago screamed.

The van shot through the gates with inches to spare on either side and disappeared from the screen. Larrios braked violently and the Mercedes slewed sideways against the gates. The driver of the second Mercedes braked but the wheels locked and it smashed into the side of the first Mercedes.

"We did it," Sabrina said punching the air triumphantly.

Graham grinned. "Yeah. But Drago's going to be back and I for one don't want to be around when he gets here. I've got this sneaking feeling he's going to be really pissed off with us."

"Whatever gives you that idea?" she replied straight-faced.

"Alpha-Bravo-Zulu 643 to Saltezar, do you read me? Over."

They looked from the speaker to the screens, desperately trying to locate the source of the voice.

"Alpha-Bravo-Zulu 643 to Saltezar, do you read me? Over," the voice repeated.

"Answer it," Sabrina said indicating the handset. "And don't forget the accent."

"Saltezar speaking. Over."

"What's happening down there? Drago's going to have your arse, you know that?"

"We were temporarily overrun," Graham replied breath-lessly to help conceal his voice. "A man and a woman man-aged to get in here. We've only just overpowered them."

"Take me up, I've got to get after the van."

Sabrina grabbed Graham's arm and pointed at one of the

screens. Two men were sitting in the white Gazelle helicopter: the pilot, who was making some last minute checks on the instrument panel and, beside him, a guard armed with a Russian-made RPG-7 rocket launcher. Drago had ordered them in for the kill.

"Take me up!" the pilot snapped. "Saltezar, are you still there?"

Saltezar, who had regained consciousness when the pilot first came on the air, flung himself at Graham and shoved him against Sabrina, spilling them both on to the floor. He pressed two buttons on the control panel then made a grab for one of the fallen UZIs. Graham yanked the Walther from his belt and shot Saltezar twice in the chest, killing him instantly. Sabrina retrieved her UZI from Saltezar's hand then turned back to the screen.

The helipad doors had parted and the section of flooring underneath, containing the helicopter, was being raised slowly into place by a hydraulic press.

"It's like the one at Zurich HQ," Sabrina exclaimed.

"My thoughts exactly. And it had a systems fault which was only rectified after a near miss." Graham looked at the two flashing buttons on the control panel. "I need to know which is which. The numbers are seven and twenty-three."

She consulted the wallchart. "Seven's for the doors, twenty-three operates the hydraulic press. What are you going to do?"

"That all depends on whether the fault's been incorporated into this system as well."

"What fault?" she demanded. "I've never heard about it."

"It was hushed up." He met her questioning eyes. "The doors should have been fitted with a failsafe mechanism to ensure that they couldn't close while the hydraulic press was in operation. There wasn't one, so when the button was accidentally touched the doors started to close while the floor section was still rising. A quick-thinking technician hit the button to lower the hydraulic press and the doors missed the helicopter's rotors by inches.''

"You're going to crush the helicopter, aren't you?'' she said in horror.

"If I can. Sure it's barbaric, but so is that RPG-7. I don't have to tell you what a PG-7 grenade would do to the hang-gliders. They're our only means of escape now.''

She nodded reluctantly—he was right.

He pressed the button to stop the hydraulic press as the helicopter came level with the doors. He then pressed the button to activate the doors.

They hydraulic press stopped but the doors didn't move.

"Saltezar, what are you doing?'' the pilot yelled over the speaker.

Graham jabbed the button again. The doors began to close.

"Saltezar, the doors! Open them, for God's sake, open them!'' the pilot screamed.

The guard discarded the rocket launcher and jumped out of the helicopter, desperately looking around for a means of escape. The drop was a good forty feet. He was trapped. The pilot tried frantically to start the engine but the rotors had managed only one gyration before the doors impacted with the helicopter. Sabrina turned away as the helicopter buckled inwards like a plastic toy being crushed in a vice. Then it exploded. The damaged doors shuddered to a halt and a pieces of the burning wreckage tumbled into the machinery beneath the raised floor. The button shorted and within seconds the control panel was on fire.

Sabrina followed Graham into the corridor where he activated the door and, keeping to the stairs, they reached the garden unchallenged. Their initial fears that the hang-gliders might have been damaged, either by Drago's men or by debris from the explosion on the helipad above them, were unfounded and they took off, leaving behind Graham's original hang-glider with its perforated wing.

Kolchinsky and Whitlock were waiting for them when they came in to land beside the cafeteria.

"Are you guys okay?" Whitlock shouted.

Sabrina pulled off her helmet and shook her hair on to her shoulders. Her grin said it all.

Graham tossed his helmet aside and glared at Kolchinsky. "What the hell were you playing at back there? Why didn't you take the Merc? Worried you wouldn't be able to recoup your expenses? You can be really petty at times, Sergei."

"Have you quite finished?" Kolchinsky replied icily. "Because if you have I'd like to show you something. Or is that asking too much?"

Graham shook his head.

Kolchinsky walked round to the back of the van and beckoned Graham forward.

"Go with Mike," Whitlock said to Sabrina.

Kolchinsky waited until she had joined them before opening the doors and climbing into the back of the empty van. He unscrewed a false panel from the side of the van and pulled it away to reveal a packing crate identical to the one they had seen in Amsterdam. Graham pointed at it, incredulity on his face.

Kolchinsky nodded. "It's the original."

"You've lost me, Sergei," Sabrina said running her fingers through her hair.

"Likewise," Graham added.

"I installed the panel last night on the other side of the van to hide the forgery."

"Hang on," Graham pleaded. "How did you get hold of the forgery?"

"The Met sent it to me," Kolchinsky replied.

"So what's hanging in the Met?" Sabrina asked.

"Nothing. Today's Monday. The museum's closed. A UNACO Dornier is waiting at the airport to take the painting back to New York so that it can be back on display at the Met tomorrow morning."

"But what was the significance of putting the panel on the other side of the van?" Sabrina queried.

"I anticipated something going wrong. A hunch, that's all. And I knew that if my hunch was right, I wouldn't have very much time to swop the paintings. It proved to be the case. I climbed in here as soon as C. W. had gone and switched the panel to this side of the van so that the forgery was exposed. That's when Drago showed. It was close, believe me. Five seconds earlier and he would have caught me out."

Graham stared at his feet. "I guess an apology's in order."

"I'll settle for the envelope," Kolchinsky replied pointing to its outline in Graham's shirt pocket.

Graham gave it to him.

Whitlock clapped his hands together. "Well, the party's over. And the sooner we repack the hang-gliders, the sooner we can get back to the hotel."

"And the sooner you can take a bath," Sabrina added with a grin.

"That goes without saying," Whitlock replied giving Kolchinsky a dirty look.

"As you say in English, the end justified the means," Kolchinsky replied.

"What's going to happen to Schrader and Drago?" Sabrina asked.

"A warrant's already been issued for Drago's arrest for

attempting to smuggle narcotics into Brazil," Kolchinsky replied. "That alone should get him ten years. Schrader's situation's more tricky. We could have him arrested for stealing the 'Night Watch' but that would make headline news around the world. The Rijksmuseum, for one, doesn't want that kind of adverse publicity. The colonel's already been in contact with representatives of the five countries unwittingly involved in the duplicity, as well as representatives from Holland and Brazil, to try and resolve the matter one way or the other. I'll phone him as soon as we get back to the hotel to find out if they've reached a decision."

Whitlock looked up towards Danaë. "I'd hate to be in Schrader's shoes right now, I really would."

Sabrina followed Whitlock's gaze. "I'd hate to be in Drago's shoes once Schrader catches up with him."

"Yeah," Graham muttered then smiled to himself. "Perhaps Schrader will be arrested—for Drago's murder."

"I wouldn't be in the least bit surprised," Sabrina replied then followed the others to dismantle the hang-gliders.

Drago had to use the spare ID card he kept in the wallsafe in the main lounge to get back into his office. Ignoring the disarray around him, he retrieved the Bernadelli from the floor underneath the desk and reholstered it. He then slumped on to the high-back swivel chair and unholstered his CZ75, placing it on the desk in front of him. He patted his pockets in vain for his cigarettes and was about to rifle his drawers in search of a pack when the door slid open and Schrader entered the room. Drago sat back, knowing that no amount of words could compensate Schrader for what had happened.

"Fourteen men are dead. Fire's gutted the hangar and the control room, the helicopter's been destroyed, the helipad's irreparably damaged and the walls of the house wouldn't look out of place behind a firing range. Not that these statistics seem to be bothering you much.''

Drago leaned forward, his elbows resting on the desk. ''My resignation's immediate if that's what you want to hear. You can have it in writing if you want.''

Schrader moved to the window. ''Tell me, how long have you know that the 'Grahams' were a bogus couple? Or that they were in collusion with the Russian?''

''I suspected the 'Grahams' weren't who they claimed to be ever since I first met them at the Riviera Club but I haven't been able to come up with anything concrete to back up my suspicions. Their cover stories were impenetrable. As for the Russian, I didn't know he was part of their team until they came to rescue him.''

''Which they did, together with recovering the original 'Night Watch.' ''

''But that's impossible! You had it in the gallery with you, didn't you?''

''I thought so, until I unpacked it. The colour of the dot in the centre of the drum is red, not black. They must have made the switch in the van.''

''They couldn't . . .'' Drago trailed off and nodded his head slowly. ''Of course, false panels.''

Schrader sat down in the armchair in front of Drago's desk. ''That's not the main reason why I'm here. I made several phone calls while I was holed up in my gallery. One was to a senior police officer. The body of Siobhan St. Jacques was washed up on Botafogo Beach this morning.''

''Siobhan's dead?'' Drago said feigning a look of horror.

''She was shot once through the heart. The bullet's already been identified as a 9mm-Parabellum, the same kind of round you use in the CZ75.''

Drago's eyes flickered towards the pistol. "You don't think I had anything to do with it, Mr. Schrader?"

"I also made a call to Colombia. The Russian was right, wasn't he?"

"Right about what?"

"The drugs." Schrader pulled a Walther P5 from his jacket pocket then reached over to retrieve the CZ75. "I may not have handled a gun in years but even I couldn't miss from this distance. I'm going to hand your automatic over to the police so that they can match it up to the bullet taken from Siobhan's body. They'll be here in a few minutes."

Drago's mouth twitched in a nervous smile as he slowly reached for the holstered Bernadelli strapped to the under-surface of the desk. He had to keep Schrader talking. "I don't know anything about any drugs, I swear it."

"Renaldo Garcia flew to Rio two months ago and stayed at the Palace Hotel as your guest. He remembers you well because, as he so rightly pointed out, you're the kind of person who stands out in a crowd. My first reaction was to kill you. Then I had a better idea. Prison. I wonder how long you'd last amongst all those criminals you've helped to put behind bars?"

Drago eased the Bernadelli from the holster and shot Schrader from under the desk. The bullet took Schrader in the stomach. He slumped forward on to the carpet. He didn't move. Drago rang Larrios and told him to have a car waiting in the courtyard then, pocketing the two incriminating hand-guns, ran to the lift.

He was finished in Rio de Janeiro, but he still had some unfinished business to attend to before he left. And that meant recovering the envelope—at any cost.

FOURTEEN

Sabrina unlocked the door to the honeymoon suite but as she stepped inside a hard, cylindrical object was pressed into the small of her back. She immediately raised her hands to alert Kolchinsky and Graham behind her.

"Major Smylie was right. You are impulsive and overconfident."

Sabrina swung round. "Colonel Philpott!"

Philpott held up his walking cane. "Had I been Drago, and this a gun, I could have killed you."

"But Drago's in custody," she said purposely evading the point he was trying to make.

"He escaped before the police arrived at Danaë. I'm not saying he'll come after the three of you but he is desperate and that alone makes him so unpredictable. Just be careful."

"He'll be back, for this." Kolchinsky held up the envelope then handed it to Philpott.

Philpott crossed to the nearest couch and sat down. "Where's C. W.?"

"He's gone to take a shower," Sabrina replied.

"A shower?"

"Yes, sir. He'll be here as soon as he's finished."

"Get him up here, now!" Philpott snapped at her. "I've got to get back to New York to prepare for a meeting with the Secretary-General tomorrow morning. I don't have much time."

"I'll call him, sir."

"Oh, and Sabrina?" Philpott called after her. "Order me a pot of tea, I'm dying of thirst."

"When did you get in to Rio?" Kolchinsky asked sitting down beside Philpott.

"A couple of hours ago. I came straight here but was told at reception that Mike and Sabrina were out. So I decided to wait for them in here."

"How did you get in?" Graham asked opening the bottle of Perrier water he had taken from the fridge.

"I do have credit cards," Philpott answered with a smile. "I haven't always been deskbound, Mike."

Graham returned the smile then held up a can of Diet Pepsi towards Sabrina who was on the telephone to Whitlock. She nodded.

"Sergei, what do you want?"

"Coke, Pepsi, it doesn't matter."

Graham took the drinks to the coffee table then sat down.

"What's happened since I last spoke to you on the phone?" Philpott asked Kolchinsky. "I've only heard bits and pieces from the local police."

Kolchinsky outlined the events briefly from when he and Whitlock reached Danaë up until the time they met up again with Graham and Sabrina at the derelict cafeteria. Graham filled him in on how he came by the envelope.

"So the original painting's already on its way back to New York?"

"We loaded it on to the Dornier at Galeão Airport before coming here," Kolchinsky replied.

There was a knock at the door and Graham opened it to admit Whitlock.

"I hope I didn't get you out of your shower," Philpott said with thinly veiled sarcasm.

"No, sir, I didn't even get the chance to turn the water on before Sabrina called."

"I'm sure you'll survive another few minutes." Philpott removed a folder from his attaché case and placed it on the table. "I've got quite a bit to tell you, that's why I decided to come down in person instead of trying to relate it all to Sergei over the telephone. Let's deal with Schrader first." He looked at each face in turn. "You say none of you came into contact with him this morning?"

They shook their heads.

"But that was to be expected, sir. As it said in his dossier, his loathing of violence goes back to his time with Hecht. Only he was too shrewd a businessman ever to admit it."

"I have read the dossier, Sabrina. The reason I ask is because he was found shot in Drago's office."

Whitlock looked at Graham.

"I didn't do it," Graham said glaring at Whitlock.

"Nobody said you did," Philpott interceded to defuse the tension.

"Is he dead?" Kolchinsky asked.

"No, but he's in a serious condition at the Miguel Couto Hospital. The police are working on the assumption that Drago shot him but they won't know for sure until he's regained consciousness."

"*If* he regains consciousness," Sabrina said.

"The doctors are confident he'll make a full recovery. It's just a question of time."

There was another knock at the door and Sabrina made a show of peeping through the spyhole for Philpott's benefit before opening the door and taking the tray from the room service waiter. Graham signed the chit and the waiter left.

"Will Schrader be prosecuted?" Whitlock asked once Graham and Sabrina had resumed their seats.

Philpott poured himself a cup of tea, added a dash of milk, then stirred it. "It's been decided by the seven countries involved that *nobody* is to be prosecuted. They all want to keep the incident under wraps. Having said that though, other steps will be taken to punish those involved. Schrader has been made persona non grata here in Brazil and will be issued with a deportation order the moment he's sufficiently recovered. It gives him twenty-eight days to pack his things and get out. He'll lose millions in the process and that's what's sure to hurt him the most. Drago will be indicted for the murders of Siobhan St. Jacques and Casey Morgan, for attempting to smuggle heroin into the country as well as for countless charges of bribery and corruption involving some of the city's leading public officials. The President's assured me that heads are going to roll in a major clean-up campaign. He's personally taking charge of it. As for the Amsterdam connection, the Fraud Squad seized Horst Keppler's books yesterday and their findings have already led to his arrest."

"Was he genuinely fiddling the books or has he been framed to get a conviction against him?"

"You can be very cynical at times, Mike. He's genuinely been fiddling the books. If the Fraud Squad hadn't found anything, we'd have had to dig up something else to use against him. His two accomplices, De Vere and Oosterhuis, have also been arrested. Seems they were in on the fraud as well. No action is to be taken against the art dealer, Terence

Hamilton.'' Philpott opened the file and tossed a colour pass-port photograph on to the table. "Recognize him?"

It was of a man in his late twenties with thick red hair and a neatly trimmed red beard. He wore the rank of major on his tunic.

"Obviously not," Philpott said after they had studied the photograph. "Let me give you a clue. Shave off the beard, crop the hair and bleach it white and add a pair of wire-rimmed glasses."

Sabrina snatched up the photograph and used her hand first to block out the beard, then the hair. She shook her head in disbelief and handed the photograph to Graham.

"It looks nothing like Drago," Graham muttered and let Whitlock take the photograph from his fingers.

"It's not Drago," Philpott replied. "It's Andrzej Wund-zik, who, with a little help from the CIA, became André Drago."

"The CIA?" Kolchinsky said scratching his head. "You're losing me, Malcolm."

"You've lost us already, sir," Whitlock added, speaking for the others.

Philpott rifled through the sheets of paper in the folder until he found the one he wanted. "It took a lot of persuasion to get the CIA to part with this information. You'll under-stand why when I'm finished. First, a little background on Wundzik. He was born in Gdansk to military parents but was never an exceptional scholar, preferring instead to channel his energies into sport. He was an excellent track athlete but his first love was boxing and by the age of sixteen he was the junior lightweight champion of Poland."

"I can believe that," Graham muttered gingerly touching the cut above his left eye.

Philpott glanced at him, irritated by the interruption. "He

retired, undefeated, when he joined the SB, the Security Service, at the age of nineteen. He was trained at Bielany Academy then posted to the Bureau I-S, the most hated and feared of all SB departments. I'm sure you've come across it before, Sergei.''

Kolchinsky nodded grimly. ''It's run on similar lines to the SB's Tenth Department of the 1950s. In other words, unlimited powers and inhuman forms of interrogation.''

''He was sent to Gdansk to help deal with the growing Solidarity movement and was so successful in his purges that he had achieved the rank of major by twenty-eight. He was even being tipped in some circles as a future SB director. But he did have one weakness—money. And the CIA used it to turn him.'' Philpott picked up another sheet of paper. ''His recruitment meant the CIA had achieved their objective—to turn four senior members of the Eastern Bloc Intelligence Services. One each from Bulgaria and Poland, and two from the Soviet Union. They became known as the 'Quaternary.'

''Wundzik was the weak link right from the start. He spent his money carelessly and the CIA were worried that his detection could lead to a full scale inquisition within the rest of the Eastern Bloc Intelligence Services, especially the KGB where they had such a highly placed double agent. So, in a move to save the other three, they issued a 'burn notice' on Wundzik, knowing it would get back to the SB. They gave him an hour's notice before blowing his cover. He was smuggled across the Baltic to Sweden then flown on to the United States for a lengthy debriefing. The three remaining members of the 'Quaternary' were closely monitored by Langley but nothing happened. Wundzik's so-called 'defection' had worked, but with an SB death warrant already issued on him the CIA had to give him a new identity. He became a

Czechoslovakian as that was the only other Eastern European language he could speak. He changed his own appearance and was given a thorough background on the fictitious André Drago before being offered a free airline ticket to any part of the world. He chose Rio.''

"So the envelope contains the names of the other three double agents,'' Sabrina concluded.

"It contains the code names of all four agents. It seems Drago blackmailed a CIA computer analyst called Holden to hack into Langley's top secret Alpha program and find the code names of the three remaining members of the 'Quaternary.' Holden took the code names to Amsterdam, left them in a locker at the Central Station, and was then killed by a booby-trapped attaché case which he presumably thought contained the pay-off.''

"But why didn't the CIA stop Holden if they knew what he was doing?'' Graham asked.

"They only realized what had happened after Holden's body was identified. By then Drago had the envelope.''

"Why's Drago gone to these lengths to get the code names?'' Whitlock asked.

"Revenge, or that's how the Director of the CIA put it,'' Philpott replied. "Drago's never forgiven the CIA for blowing his cover and making him a wanted man for the rest of his life. The SB will only lift the contract on him once he's dead and, as you know, the Eastern Bloc countries specialize in tracking down their traitors. It seems as if he's trying to kill two birds with one stone by both 'burning' the 'Quaternary' and by making enough money out of it to start a new life in another country.''

Kolchinsky sat forward and rubbed the bridge of his nose thoughtfully. "Do the KGB know Wundzik and Drago are one and the same?''

"That's the same question I asked Langley. They say no. I'm not so sure."

"Sir, how much did Siobhan know?" Sabrina asked softly.

"Basically nothing. She was told that Drago would have the envelope with him at Schrader's party. She was to lift it and take it straight to her handler."

"But how did the CIA know he would have the envelope with him?" she pressed.

"Leonov told him to have it with him when they met."

"I still don't get it," she said screwing up her face. "How could they possibly know the KGB were sending Leonov at such short notice?"

"Because he told them."

"You're saying Leonov's working for the CIA? That's preposterous, Malcolm."

Philpott pushed the envelope across the table to Kolchinsky. "Open it. Two of the code names will be Phoenix and Jackdaw. Drago was Phoenix, Leonov *is* Jackdaw."

Kolchinsky tore open the envelope, removed the sheet of computer paper and unfolded it. It read:

1 Jackdaw
2 Sapphire
3 Hurricane
4 Phoenix

"I don't believe it," Kolchinsky said and dropped the paper on to the table. "How long has he been a double agent?"

"Six years according to Langley. He was the first one they recruited."

"Who's the other Russian?" Kolchinsky asked.

"All they said was that he's with the GRU."

Kolchinsky slumped back and clasped his hands over his

face. He finally let them drop and stared at Philpott. "If you'd asked me to list the five most dedicated KGB officers I've ever known, Yuri's name would have been in there somewhere. But if you'd asked me to list five KGB officers who hated the West, Yuri's name would have been top of the list. In capital letters. I just can't believe it. Yuri, a double agent."

"That's the beauty of it," Philpott replied. "Who would ever suspect him?"

"If the CIA knew Leonov was going to get the envelope back for them, why use Siobhan at all?" Sabrina asked.

"When Drago made it known to the KGB that he had the code names for sale they had to find someone they could trust implicitly to negotiate for it on their behalf. The CIA told Leonov to make sure he got the job. Not that he needed much persuasion—it was his neck on the block, after all. He put his name forward, knowing it was sure to arouse a certain amount of suspicion, especially amongst his critics." Philpott paused to take a sip of tea. "The CIA had to allay those suspicions by putting forward one of their own operatives to give the impression that they too were after the envelope."

"Siobhan," Sabrina said.

Philpott nodded. "The only problem was that Siobhan's CIA connection was one of Langley's best kept secrets. So they *accidentally* blew her cover to give Leonov the credibility he needed. It worked."

"Was she told that they'd blown her cover?" Whitlock asked.

"No."

"The bastards!" Sabrina hissed angrily.

"What about the list?" Whitlock asked prodding the paper with his finger.

"Officially, it's got nothing to do with us. Unofficially, I'm leaving it in Sergei's hands." Philpott cast a sidelong glance at Kolchinsky. "It's not as if the CIA even know we've got the envelope. Do what you think's best under the circumstances."

Kolchinsky folded the sheet of paper and slipped it into his pocket.

"There is something else." Philpott pushed the teacup away from him. "Martin Cohen was killed last night."

Whitlock got to his feet and left the room, closing the door silently behind him.

"What happened?" Sabrina asked.

"He was killed in the shootout with the hijackers at a farmhouse on the outskirts of Tripoli."

"And the hijackers?" Graham asked.

"Dead."

"How's Hannah taken it?" Kolchinsky asked.

"She's bearing up well. I've had her parents flown out from Israel to be with her." Philpott replaced the folder in his attaché case and stood up. "You'll have to excuse me. I've got a plane to catch."

"I'll give you a lift to the airport," Kolchinsky said.

"Good. I've got a few things I want to discuss with you anyway."

"Michael, have you got the van keys?"

Graham took the keys from his pocket and handed them to Kolchinsky.

"I'll see the two of you back at the UN," Philpott said to Graham and Sabrina. "What time's your flight?"

"Some time tomorrow morning," Sabrina replied. "Sergei made the arrangements."

"The ten o'clock flight to JFK," Kolchinsky said.

Philpott was about to say something about Whitlock, thought better of it, and left the room. Kolchinsky followed him.

"I never knew Marty that well," Sabrina said breaking the sudden silence. "He was always friendly to me but I got the feeling he resented me being a field operative as opposed to, say, a technician or a computer analyst like Hannah."

"He did."

"He told you?"

"He told C. W. Like you, I didn't know Marty that well."

"What did he say to C. W.?" she asked.

"He thought the field operation should be a male-orientated area and that you should have been assigned as a firearms instructor at the Test Center. It's just the kind of guy he was. A man's man, to use the old cliché."

There was a knock at the door.

Sabrina answered it.

The porter smiled politely at her. "Is Mr. Graham in?"

"Mike, it's for you," she called over her shoulder.

"I have message for you from Mr. Whitlock," the porter said to Graham. "He wants to see you in the foyer."

"Tell him I'll be down in a moment," Graham replied.

"Why didn't he just ring you from the foyer?" Sabrina asked after the porter had gone.

"He's got a lot on his mind. Look, I'll give you a ring if he wants me to go somewhere with him, otherwise I'll be in the hotel if anything should crop up." Graham hurried after the porter, shouting for him to hold the lift.

Sabrina closed the door then walked out on to the balcony.

There was another knock at the door.

She threw her hands up in despair and crossed the lounge to open it. Larrios stood in front of her, a dart gun in his right hand. He shot her in the neck. She staggered back into the room, her surroundings hazing over in a kaleidoscope of blurred colours. She made a grab for the couch, missed it, and fell to her knees. She suddenly remembered Philpott's warning about her being impulsive and overconfident. Then she pitched forward, unconscious.

Drago, wearing a blue trilby and dark sunglasses, pushed a laundry trolley into the room. He took the wedding ring off her finger then helped Larrios lift her into the trolley and cover her with the assortment of towels and sheets already in it. Larrios wheeled the trolley down the corridor and disappeared with it into the service lift.

Drago made his way to the foyer and walked towards Graham who was talking animatedly with the porter who had brought him the message. "I believe you're looking for me?" he said to Graham and dismissed the porter with a curt flick of the hand.

"Where's Whitlock?" Graham demanded.

"The last I saw of him he was heading down Atlantica Avenue towards Copacabana Beach. That's when I got the idea to use his name to lure you down here."

"You've got some nerve coming here, Drago. One phone call and half the city's police force will be around to arrest you."

"But then you'd never see the lovely Sabrina again," Drago replied handing the wedding ring to Graham.

Graham slammed Drago against the wall. "Where is she?"

"You're causing a scene, Graham, and that's not going to get us anywhere."

Graham reluctantly let him go.

Drago smiled at the approaching duty manager. "Sorry about that. It's my fault completely. My brother-in-law here lent me some money and I went and blew the lot at the Jockey Club. You know how addictive racing can be?"

"If you're going to fight, do it outside. Not in the hotel."

"It's okay now," Drago said reassuringly.

The duty manager eyed them suspiciously then walked back to his office.

"What's the deal? Her safe release for the envelope?"

"We understand each other. Let's say the Riviera Club in two hours' time." Drago noticed the uncertainty in Graham's eyes. "It's not open for business on Mondays. The front door will be unlocked. I'll be in the casino. Come unarmed and alone. I do have ways of verifying both in case you're thinking of trying to outwit me."

"That doesn't seem to be very difficult, does it?" Graham retorted caustically.

Drago's eyes narrowed angrily. "Not this time."

Graham pointed a finger of warning at Drago. "You harm her and I'll tear you apart with my bare hands."

"I got the impression the feelings between the two of you were very one-sided. Seems I was wrong." Drago glanced at his watch. "It's now one-twenty. Three-twenty in the Riviera Club."

Graham watched Drago leave the hotel then looked down at the wedding ring in his hand. He turned it around thoughtfully in his fingers then walked back to the lift.

"I still say I should be there as back-up."

"We've been through this before, Sergei. No firearms, no back-up. We've got to play it Drago's way, if only for Sabrina's sake."

Kolchinsky gave a resigned shrug. "First C. W. walks out and then Sabrina gets abducted. These things are supposed to happen in threes, aren't they? Be careful, Michael."

"Stop being so superstitious." Graham patted Kolchinsky on the shoulder. "And don't worry about C. W., he'll be back."

"But will he stay?"

"We'll only know that when we see him." Graham pocketed the envelope. "I want your word, Sergei. No back-up."

"No back-up," Kolchinsky muttered.

"I'll stick to the plan we agreed earlier. I promise."

Graham left the room, took the lift to the foyer, and flagged
down a passing taxi outside the hotel. Larrios, sitting in a
hired Ford Escort, started up the engine and cut out into the
traffic to tail the taxi at a safe distance.

The taxi pulled up in front of the Riviera Club and Graham
climbed out, paid the driver, then crossed to the entrance and
pushed on the two glass doors. One was unlocked. He slipped
inside and looked around the foyer, his eyes finally coming
to rest on the closed-circuit television camera above the reception cubicle. It was pointed at him. He crossed to the
stairs then glanced up at the camera again. It had tracked his
movements. He climbed the stairs and entered the casino.
Sabrina was sitting on the stairs on the other side of the room,
her hands manacled to the outside railing. A strip of adhesive
tape was secured over her mouth. Her eyes widened on seeing him and she shook her head, desperately trying to warn
him not to come any further. He ignored her and descended
the stairs on to the casino floor.

"That's far enough, Graham," Drago said from a doorway which had been out of sight of the casino entrance. He
held the CZ75 in his right hand. "No hardware, I'm impressed. I really thought you'd come in here with guns blazing."

"I would have, believe me, if I'd thought I could have got
them past the metal detector at the front doors."

"That's why I chose the club in the first place."

Graham looked across at Sabrina. "You okay?"

She nodded.

"Now that the pleasantries are over, have you got the envelope?"

'It's not quite that simple, Drago.''

"Meaning?" Drago asked stepping away from the doorway.

"You didn't honestly expect me just to walk in here, unarmed, and hand over the envelope without some kind of insurance to back me up, did you?"

"Go on."

"I've got a photocopy of the list in my pocket. Whitlock has the original." Graham checked his watch. "It's now three-twenty-two. In exactly eight minutes' time he'll ring the public phone across the street and if it isn't answered after the fifth ring, or if it is answered but only one of us can speak to him, he'll take the list, and a copy of your CIA file, to the Polish consulate and deliver it personally to the ambassador. I can guarantee you that within an hour the SB will have a team of specialists on a plane bound for Rio.''

Drago was visibly shaken by Graham's words. "Who *are* you?"

"It's not important. Let's just say we have friends in high places."

"How do I know Whitlock won't hand them over even if I do keep my side of the bargain?''

"You don't, just as we don't know that you won't shoot us once you've got the list." Graham glanced at his watch again. "Well, what's it going to be?"

"Let me see the list."

Graham dropped the envelope on to the roulette table beside him then stepped back when Drago waved him away. Drago approached the table and as his eyes flickered towards the envelope Graham took his chance and felled him with a low, bruising football tackle. The automatic spun from Drago's hand. Drago blocked Graham's initial punch then hit him in the face with a jarring right-left combination. Graham stumbled backwards and Drago followed through with two vicious kidney punches, dropping Graham to his knees. Drago picked up the automatic and aimed it at Graham's bowed head.

"Wundzik!"

Drago froze. It was the first he had heard the name spoken in five years. The SB had finally tracked him down. He always knew they would, in time. He turned slowly, expecting to find himself facing one, or more, of his ex-colleagues. Whitlock stood at the top of the stairs, the Browning gripped in both hands at arm's length. Drago laughed and raised the automatic to fire. Whitlock shot him through the heart. The automatic slipped from Drago's numb fingers and he felt unsteady on his leaden feet as a sudden dizziness overpowered him. He was dead by the time his body hit the carpet.

Larrios, who had been monitoring the situation from the control room in the basement, unholstered his Walther P5 and sprinted up the stairs leading to the casino. He darted through the doorway Drago had used moments earlier, ducked behind the nearest roulette table, and shot Whitlock in the chest. Whitlock fell back against the railing then slumped to the floor at the top of the stairs. Graham rolled across the carpet, grabbed Drago's CZ75, and shot Larrios under the table. Larrios dropped his gun as he stumbled backwards, his hands clutched tightly over his stomach wound. Graham pumped four more bullets into him, slamming him back against the wall. A trickle of blood seeped from the corner of Larrios' mouth as he slid lifelessly to the floor. Graham discarded the CZ75 and ran across to where Whitlock lay face down and turned him over gently on to his back.

Whitlock opened his eyes then took his hand away from his chest. His shirt was torn, but there was no blood. "Thank God I didn't take that shower after all. If I had I wouldn't still be wearing the Armourshield vest."

"I thought he'd killed you," Graham said indignantly then let Whitlock's head fall back against the railing.

"Sorry to disappoint you," Whitlock muttered then sat up and gingerly massaged the bruise on his chest.

Graham pulled the adhesive tape from Sabrina's mouth. "You okay?"

"I will be when you get these cuffs off me. The key's in Drago's pocket."

Graham found the key but as he turned back to Sabrina he caught sight of something on the floor. It was the *figa* amulet Schrader had given to him. The chain had snapped during the fight. He picked it up and tossed it on to Drago's body. "You'll need this where you're going."

Sabrina massaged her wrists after Graham unlocked the handcuffs then looked up at Whitlock as he approached them. "You couldn't have timed your entrance scene better."

Whitlock helped her to her feet and they sat at the bar. "I must have missed Mike by seconds at the hotel. Well, when Sergei told me what was going down I came round here as fast as I could. I know you said no back-up, Mike, but I reckon you needed it after all."

"Whatever gave you that impression?" Graham replied with a half-smile.

"Mike, what was in that envelope?" Sabrina asked.

"Nothing. Sergei and I made up the spiel about the Polish consulate knowing it would rattle Drago. That's when I was supposed to apprehend him. So much for that." Graham went behind the bar and searched half a dozen fridges before he found the Perrier water.

"I'll have one of those as well," Whitlock said.

Graham opened a second bottle of Perrier and gave it to Whitlock then scoured the rest of the fridges to find a can of Diet Pepsi for Sabrina. He poured it into a glass.

"Don't give up your day job, Mike," Whitlock quipped.

"I don't intend to," Graham replied then leaned his forearms on the counter. "How about you?"

"It's been preying on my mind a lot lately, as I'm sure you've both noticed. Carmen wants me to leave UNACO and set up my own security firm. I want to stay. That's the crux of the matter." Whitlock drank from the bottle then stared at his own reflection in the wall mirror behind Graham. "I had a long talk to her on the phone after I walked out on you guys. We're determined to save our marriage. At least we agree on that. It's about all we agree on at the moment. But I guess it's a start." He pushed the Perrier away from him. "Well, I'd say we've overstayed our welcome here."

Graham came round from behind the bar counter and stopped in front of Sabrina. "We've been in Rio for three days and in that time we haven't been near a beach. How about spending the rest of the afternoon in Ipanema?"

"Or Copacabana," she suggested.

"Or Copacabana," he agreed then turned to Whitlock. "Joining us?"

"Sure, why not. I could do with the company right now. But there is something I've got to do first."

"What?" Sabrina asked.

"Shower."

Graham and Sabrina smiled at each other then followed Whitlock to the door.

"You reckon he'll show?" Graham asked looking out of the van window.

"I'm sure of it," Kolchinsky replied then lit another cigarette.

"What did you say to him on the phone?"

Kolchinsky shrugged. "I told him I had the list and to meet me, as planned, at Drago's beach house at eight o'clock."

Graham stared out across Leme Beach. "An anonymous call?"

"Yes. That's why I'm sure he'll show up. He'll be intrigued."

"It's a neat place Drago had, isn't it?"

Kolchinsky craned his neck to look at the deserted beach house on the small ridge overlooking the beach. "It must have a great view but it's hardly very private, is it? The beach can only be fifty yards away."

"A voyeur's paradise," Graham said with a grin.

"How ironic then that it should have been owned by a misogynist," Kolchinsky replied tapping the ash from the end of his cigarette.

"Looks like we've got company," Graham announced as a pair of headlights pierced the darkness on the approach road.

Kolchinsky glanced at the dashboard clock. "Eight o'clock exactly. Yuri hasn't changed."

The black BMW 732i stopped twenty yards in front of the van. The driver opened the back door and Leonov got out, smoothed down his lightweight jacket, then walked to a spot halfway between the two vehicles. He shaded his eyes from the van's headlights to observe the approaching figure. "Sergei?" he gasped in astonishment. "What are you doing here? Where's Drago?"

"Drago's dead. I'm here to conclude his unfinished business. By the way, what should I call you? Yuri or *Jackdaw*?"

Leonov, having got over the initial shock of seeing Kolchinsky, smiled coldly. "Where does UNACO fit into this? I assume you are still with them?"

"What was the deal with Drago?" Kolchinsky asked ignoring Leonov's questions.

"Half a million dollars in uncut diamonds."

"Cheap at the price," Kolchinsky replied disdainfully. "One thing puzzles me. If the list was to be returned to the CIA, what would you have given to the KGB?"

"Another list with the codenames of four double agents, all expendable. Two Russian, one Bulgarian and one Pole. Just like the original 'Quaternary.' "

"Why, Yuri? Why the deceit?"

"You of all people should understand, Sergei. You hated the dictatorial, repressive methods of previous governments just as much as I did. It's only now, through the efforts of people like us, that things are changing for the better."

"The difference is I voiced my opinions, I didn't resort to treason and sell out my colleagues to the CIA."

"And look what good that openness did for you. Banished to the West as a military attaché never to be trusted again by the KGB hierarchy."

"At least my conscience lets me sleep at night. Does yours?"

"I didn't come here to swop ideologies, Sergei. I came for the list."

"It's not for sale."

"I want that list, Sergei, and I'll use force if necessary to get it." Leonov gestured to his driver behind him. "Major Nikolai Zlotin, one of the most decorated officers in spetsnaz history. I chose him personally to accompany me here."

"I've heard of Zlotin. I believe he's one of the best. So is my driver. You know him, I believe? Michael Graham."

Leonov's eyes flickered past Kolchinsky but all he could see was Graham's silhouette beside the van. "Now it all makes sense. I thought he'd joined the CIA after he left Delta, that's why I pretended I didn't know him at Schrader's party. But then that's CIA disinformation for you."

"UNACO disinformation," Kolchinsky corrected him.

"I can raise the price to one million dollars," Leonov said bluntly. "The stones are in the car. Take them, Sergei, and let me have the list."

"Why are the CIA prepared to pay one million dollars for four code names they already know? There's more to it than that, isn't there?"

Leonov sighed deeply then nodded. "Brad Holden managed to break through three security codes to get to the dossiers in the Alpha program. Apart from the four agents, only five other people, all of them in the CIA, knew these dossiers existed. That's how covert the 'Quaternary' has been over the past six years."

"So how did Holden manage to get past these security codes?"

"He helped set up the Alpha program. It was just a matter of finding the right security combination to break it. Well, once he had the four code names he transferred the dossiers from the Alpha program to another section of the computer. Nobody knows where. He invalidated the three existing security codes and introduced one of his own to hide the dossiers. Drago told Holden to write the new security code on the list and he was going to give it to the KGB to verify the authenticity of the dossiers. As you know, the KGB have professionals hacking into the Langley computer twenty-four hours a day so it can only be a matter of time before they break that single security code and find the dossiers. The CIA must get the code so that they can put the dossiers back behind the safety of their own security codes. Sergei, you've got to give me the list.''

Kolchinsky took the sheet of computer paper from his pocket and gave it to Leonov.

Leonov looked on both sides of the paper then stared at Kolchinsky in horror. ''The code's not here.''

''Either Holden didn't print it, hoping to make more money out of Drago, or Drago removed it hoping to make more money out of the CIA. We'll never know, will we?'' Kolchinsky returned to the van.

''What happened?'' Graham asked.

''We'll never know, Michael, we'll never know,'' Kolchinsky muttered as he watched the pathetic, hunched figure of Leonov walk slowly back to the BMW.

Graham decided against probing further and as he started up the van the first spots of rain splashed against the windscreen. He looked up at the sky—it was going to be a wet night. Then again, it was only a hunch.

About the Author

Alistair MacLean was the bestselling author of thirty books including world famous novels such as THE GUNS OF NAVARONE, WHERE EAGLES DARE and SANTORINI. When he died in 1987 he left behind several outlines for novels. The first of these was used as the basis for DEATH TRAIN by Alastair MacNeill.